T0355023

NEPHI'S WIFE

MADELYN S. PALMER

Order this book online at www.trafford.com
or email orders@trafford.com

Most Trafford titles are also available at major online book retailers.

Print information available on the last page.

ISBN: 978-1-6987-1781-4 (sc)
ISBN: 978-1-6987-1783-8 (hc)
ISBN: 978-1-6987-1782-1 (e)

Library of Congress Control Number: 2024920683

Trafford rev. 10/30/2024

www.trafford.com

North America & international
toll-free: 844-688-6899 (USA & Canada)
fax: 812 355 4082

CONTENTS

Chapter 1 Out of Jerusalem..1

Chapter 2 The Valley of Lemuel...25

Chapter 3 Place of the Broken Bow..57

Chapter 4 Nahom...89

Chapter 5 The Great Desert..142

Chapter 6 Bountiful..153

Chapter 7 The Sea...176

Chapter 8 The Promised Land...206

Bibliography of References Used..281

CHAPTER 1

OUT OF JERUSALEM

"Didi! Didi, where are you?" The echoes of my next older sister's voice reached me from the courtyard outside. I went to the window of the upper room I was sweeping and opened the shutters.

"Naola! I'm in here!" I called back. She picked up her skirts and ran to the window where I stood.

"Didi," she gasped. "You'd never believe who is here talking to Papa! And when we least expected it! He wants us all to come right away, so hurry!"

Before I had a chance to say a word, she turned, rushed back across the courtyard to one of the doors of the house, and disappeared inside. I couldn't help smiling as I closed the shutters. How characteristic of Naola to forget to tell me who the visitors were! I coaxed my stubborn dark hair back into place under my head shawl, and headed toward the large common room where Papa liked to receive visitors.

The first person I saw when I entered the room was indeed someone I was not expecting to see. It was my old playmate of years ago, now grown tall, muscular and strong, but unexpectedly handsome and . . . mature. This Nephi, fourth son of Lehi, had a look in his eye that spoke of the same idealism and energy I had seen before, but with something different. I suddenly noticed he was watching me. With heart pounding furiously, I lowered my eyes and quickly found a place to sit down. Oh, why did Naola have to choose this of all times to forget to tell me who the visitors were? Then I would have known to put on a fresh dress or at least my second-best head shawl!

"We welcome you, four sons of the house of Lehi," my father's deep, resonant voice carried across the room. A hush fell, except for the babbling of a small child. It was then I realized my older brothers, Mori and Gid, were also here with their families. This visit from the sons of Lehi must be no small matter, not just a visit to their sisters. I noticed that even Eli and Elizabeth, our house help, had joined us.

Papa continued, "You have come and desired that I gather my entire household together so that you might speak with us." Papa looked proudly around the room. "We are all gathered. I invite you now to speak."

The sons of Lehi all looked at each other, eyes conveying messages we could not understand, until finally Laman, the oldest of the four, stood forward.

"O Ishmael, and house of Ishmael, behold the gifts we bring you, complements of our father, Lehi, from our most recent journeying beyond Jerusalem." Laman indicated with his arm a polished wooden chest standing open by my father's chair, containing various cloths, spices, and fruits not easily available in the city nor the land near Jerusalem. I wondered if they were from one of Lehi's merchant trips to Egypt, or an exchange for his olive oil trade goods.

"Friends and family," Laman continued, "it is our will and pleasure to invite you on the journey of a lifetime with us!" His voice trailed off, and he stood gazing at my sister Riddah.

My family looked around at each other, confused. Nephi stood up and laid his hand on his brother's arm. Laman sat down.

Nephi continued, in the formality of guest speaking to host, "Ishmael and house of Ishmael, hearken to the words which I, we, now speak, for they are words given in truth and soberness. Our father, Lehi, in the name of the Lord God, sends us to you with an important message and a request. But first there is something I must tell you of our family's recent journeying."

He cleared his throat. "You are aware, I am sure, of the recent uprising of the people of this city against the preaching of my father and others like him. Most recently this took the form of threats against his very life." Nephi paused to search the eyes of his audience. "I believe you are also aware, house of Ishmael, that these threats came as a result of his urging them to repent of their evil ways or the Lord would destroy them and the city of Jerusalem."

Papa nodded his head slowly. I had not heard Lehi preach directly, but Papa had, and he had several times returned home and related to us the words of this "great teacher," who was also his lifelong friend and business trading associate.

Nephi continued as if driven, "Naturally Father was also concerned for the welfare of his family in this uncertain situation. Some time ago, he envisioned in a dream that his work in this city was finished, and that it was time to take himself and his family from this land, far away from the destruction that is now inevitable. The Lord would lead us to a Land of Promise, he has blessed us already in obtaining a record of the genealogy of our fathers and the teachings of the great prophets." Nephi paused, the shadow of a painful memory briefly crossing his face.

"Now we have been instructed, O Ishmael, to come before you, that you may accompany us to this chosen land with all your household, that you may escape the destructions that are imminent and partake of the blessings of the Lord, and that we might raise up a righteous posterity to his name." Nephi paused and glanced in my direction before continuing. "It is not merely a frivolous wish that you and your household accompany us on this journey, O Ishmael, it is the Lord's commandment if ye desire to obey." Nephi paused once more as he looked around the room. "This is the message we bring you from our father, Lehi. I am finished."

"Where is this Promised Land?" my oldest brother, Mori, asked. "The lands of Ephraim and Manasseh to the north?"

Nephi shook his head. "Even that land will not be safe. We are asked to go far into the wilderness to find the land that the Lord has prepared for us."

Everyone in the room remained in stunned silence as Nephi sat down. I couldn't help but ponder the meaning of one thing he had said. When he had mentioned posterity and glanced in my direction, I had dropped my gaze. Now my curiosity got the better of me and I looked up at him again. I had been right; he was still watching me. My heart started pounding all over again, but I kept my gaze steady.

This time it was his eyes that shifted, but only when Papa's voice cut through the silence.

"Nephi, son of Lehi, I am honored that I and my household have been chosen to come with you to this Land of Promise. I, too, have been concerned about what the destruction of Jerusalem would mean to my family. My heart is led to believe that you truly speak God's will, and my desire is to do as your father and the Lord bid, to come with you into the wilderness to this Promised Land." A murmur of voices began to rise, but Papa's raised hand stilled them. "How soon must we leave?"

"As soon as you can gather together the necessary provisions," Nephi answered. "My brothers and I will help you in your preparations."

The room erupted into conversation and commotion around me. Naola jumped up beside me, pulled me to my feet, and whirled me around. I caught glimpses of Mori and Gid talking angrily to each other and gesturing toward Papa.

"Isn't this exciting?" Naola giggled. "We'll get to experience the kind of adventures we only hear about in tales!" She skipped off to join her next older sisters, Riddah and Bekka, oohing and aahing over the gifts the sons of Lehi had brought.

I suddenly found myself face to face with Nephi. "Hello, Nephi," I said, nearly speechless for one of the first times of my life.

"Greetings, Devorah, daughter of Ishmael," he answered with the trace of a smile.

I pointed to his muscular arm. "You have grown strong since I saw you last."

He nodded. "Father has me doing most of the heavy lifting and smithing work for him now. My brothers seem to have a better knack at selling and trading than I do."

"Didi!" Papa's voice cut through the din. Didi wasn't my real name but was an endearment of Devorah. Papa had called me Didi ever since I was a toddler, and the name had stuck. Even my sisters and friends used it now.

"I'm sorry, Nephi. Papa is calling," I said, half with relief and half with regret, and turned away to look for Papa. I found him standing by the door, his mouth in a grim line.

"Didi," he said, his mouth relaxing a bit. "Mary is upset again, she just ran out of the room with that look on her face. Would you go talk to her?" Papa sighed. "I'm afraid she considers me the antagonist this time."

I nodded and left the room. Considering that we had guests and remembering what drastic things they had proposed, I guessed that Mary had gone to our bedroom. Sure enough, I found her there, quickly rolling some of her clothes and some food items into her apron. When I walked in, she jumped and clutched her apron to her.

"Don't say a word, Didi," she warned. "My mind is made up. I can't take this anymore, and I'm leaving. You know how long Papa has tried to find a husband for me: ten grueling years! I know Laman won't have me, and the others are too young, after all, I am twenty-five! Besides, Laman has his eye on Riddah. I'm preventing all of you from getting husbands, just because of this!" she pointed angrily to her lazy left eye. "No, it will be better for everyone if I leave now, and let all of you, my younger sisters, go with Lehi's sons and marry them."

I looked down at my feet for a moment praying I would say the right thing, and when I looked up at Mary again, I saw a tear slide down her cheek and splash onto her apron. I went over to her, put my arm around her, and dried her cheek with my hand.

"Mary," I said firmly, "we all love you and want you very much to stay with us. Riddah and Bekka may say some hard things that hurt you, but I know they feel the same way about wanting you with us. I think it is their way of letting out some of their frustrations in general, if they weren't complaining about the necessary marriage order, they would probably find something else to complain about."

Mary laughed shakily. "Yes, they probably would."

"Mary, we're not the only ones that want you along. Don't you remember what Nephi told us a few minutes ago? They want all of us to go with them, 'all of the house of Ishmael.' I didn't hear them say, 'all of the house of Ishmael except Mary because she's ineligible,' did you?"

"No," Mary faltered.

"Well then!" I continued, though Mary looked about ready to interrupt. "And I don't think they were just being polite either," I said hurriedly to prevent her from protesting. "Papa wouldn't have agreed so quickly to go with them if he wasn't fairly sure there was some way you could find a husband soon. And I don't think Lehi's sons would ask us to come join with them in marriage if there was no way we could marry them. Something tells me the Lord will provide a way."

Mary played with the bundle in her hands then looked up. "Thank you, Didi," she said, suddenly hugging me. "You have a way of comforting me I can't understand in one so young."

"Here, dry your eyes," I told her, emptying her apron and handing her a corner of it. "When you're ready, let's go back before they notice we're missing and think anything is wrong."

We spent the evening listening to Papa, my brothers, and the sons of Lehi discuss plans for the journey. We would be allowed to take very few personal belongings with us; most of each load had to consist of food, seed, tools, blankets, and other travel supplies. Throughout all our preparations, Papa warned us, we must let no one know of our plans to leave for good; with people seeking Lehi's life, any word leaking out about our leaving to join him might put us all in danger. If anyone asked about our activities, we were accompanying Papa on one of his merchant business trips and then to visit family.

The next two days, my sisters and I spent washing and packing garments and blankets, gathering sewing and cooking supplies, and airing out Papa's old tents. Mary went with Mama to purchase seeds, herbs, food supplies, and other small necessities, getting small amounts of items here and there so no one would suspect the large quantities we were actually accumulating. Lehi's sons cleaned and repaired tools and packed gear, keeping a low profile. Papa, Mori, and Gid "temporarily arranged" their business affairs. Eli and Elizabeth with their small baby boy also packed their things to come with us.

The third day, we finished packing our supplies and took care of last-minute details, filling the waterskins and larger barrels from the well, and checking that no necessity was forgotten. Long before dawn the next morning, Papa's donkeys were led into the courtyard, and quietly loaded up. Mary and I met each other roaming through the dark house for the last time, and we completed the tour together, arm in arm, carrying one candle between us. When everyone had gathered in the courtyard for the final time, Mama motioned us to silence and Papa spoke.

"Thank you for your great help and efforts, all of you," he said quietly then paused. "Before we go, I would like to leave a blessing on our group for our journey." He turned his back on the house, raised his arms, closed his eyes, and began. "O God our Father, we ask thee to bless us on this great journey that we undertake. We pray for strength, safety, and health . . ."

Unable to stop myself, my mind wandered to my life as it had been at Jerusalem. I felt sad at the thought of leaving my friends without being able to say farewell, but I also felt a Naola-like excitement at the thought of the adventures we would be experiencing. I shivered as I remembered one of my girlhood visions—inspired perhaps by Naola's idealism, perhaps by my frequent association in earlier years with Lehi's sons—of someday standing side by side with some man like Nephi for real, fighting against incredible odds, enemies both spiritual and earthly, and winning. Was this journey beginning the fulfillment of just such a dream?

I was pulled back to reality by the "Amen" of Papa's blessing. Lehi's sons went up to consult with him while the rest of us rechecked the packs on the animals, secured my brothers' little children atop bundles, and talked in whispers. Then suddenly we were on our way, pushing and prodding the laden beasts out of the courtyard and away from the house that was our home. On a quick impulse, I reached down and plucked a small white stone from the path.

Nephi appeared without warning at my side, and slipped a stick into my hand. "For the animals, so you don't have to yell at them," he said in a low voice. "Of course, this works on stubborn brothers and sisters too, so don't be afraid to use it. And don't lose it." I looked at him in pretended shock, and his serious expression turned into a grin. We followed the donkey ahead of us as it turned onto a side road, and suddenly Nephi was sober again. "My brothers and I will meet you again further on. It's safer if you are not seen with us until we're well away from Jerusalem." Nephi looked over his shoulder then back at me. "I think I've stayed with you too long already." He raised his hand as though to touch my shoulder but dropped it again and whispered, "Farewell, Didi," and was gone.

The stick Nephi gave me wasn't really needed, for the two donkeys I was escorting willingly followed the animals ahead of them. I was thankful for this, as we were taking roads leading away from Jerusalem that I was less familiar with and I did not want to lose the others in the darkness.

The animals in front of me suddenly stopped amidst some commotion from up front. The first donkey I was leading brayed at the animal ahead of him, and got kicked for his troubles. He reared back, knocking my other donkey, which stumbled sideways and fell into a gulley at the side of the road. The fallen animal's pack slipped, and he could not get up again. Their lead cords were hopelessly tangled. I tugged at the cord of the first donkey, trying to get him to follow me toward his fallen companion to loosen them, but he wouldn't budge. I finally remembered Nephi's stick, and whacked him just as Mori appeared behind him. The donkey jumped toward the ditch dragging me with him.

"There's a road patrol around the bend," Mori whispered hoarsely as he helped me get the standing donkey to calm down and untangle the cords in the darkness. "Remember we're going with Papa on a business trip and then to visit family. Just stay calm and everything will go all right." Then he was gone, and I began struggling madly to loosen the cords of the fallen animal's pack before the animals ahead should move again. The knot would not come, and I envisioned myself abandoned by my family and hauled before the soldiers of the patrol to explain what we were really doing with all these supplies. Then I drew a deep breath to calm myself, and shortly I managed to loosen the first knot. As I tackled the third, Mori returned to my side and, with his strong arms, helped me lift the load back onto the animal's back and tie it down again. "Sorry I took so long, Sis!" he said and was gone again.

I retrieved the stick Nephi had given me, just as the line ahead started moving forward again. The occasional clicking of a hoof hitting a stone made me a bit nervous now that I knew of the patrol ahead. After several agonizing minutes, once again the company halted, and the unintelligible calls of men's voices filtered back to us in the rear. Then the line moved slowly forward again, approaching a small campfire surrounded by half a dozen soldiers. I gripped my stick tightly to stop my trembling and concentrated on passing the fire without looking at the men. I thought of my girlhood dream and almost laughed at the impossible difference between my fears now and my courage in the dream. How could any girl in her right mind expect to become that kind of warrior?

Suddenly arms around my throat and waist jerked me from the line of animals, and I was half carried, half dragged toward the campfire up to face the chief of the patrol. Although startled half out of my wits, some part of my mind remained clear, and I figured that if I had something to hide, they would expect me to struggle. I let the soldier take me where he would, and when he released me, I gazed at the chief without wavering.

"So, Miss. It looks like your family is going on a long journey, eh?" I volunteered nothing. "Where might you be slipping off to in the dark of the night?"

"We're accompanying Papa on a business trip," I answered steadily and readjusted my shawl around my shoulders. "Is there any law against leaving this early in the morning?"

"No-o," the chief drawled and eyed me a moment in silence. Then he laughed. "Perhaps if it's only a business trip, they won't mind our keeping one of you here until they get back—for example, you." One of the soldiers next to him leered at me hungrily.

A chill went through me, and I could see Gid standing by his animals at the end of the line with a strange expression on his face, a mixture of indecision, anger, and disgust. I wanted to ask why anyone should be so angry about a family leaving Jerusalem but caught myself in time. In light of recent threats of war and political instability, there were many at Jerusalem who would do anything to destroy those who believed in the prophecies of Jerusalem's destruction, and that included us now for sure.

"They wouldn't be very pleased, sir," I chose my words carefully, saying a little prayer in my heart that I could say and do the right thing. "We were planning to visit family on the way, and well, a wedding is a big family celebration. But I suppose if my family had to leave me, they could, if it would put your mind more at ease." I smiled as sweetly as I could. "Would I be allowed to go back to our house while they're gone, or would I have to be watched here?"

Gid could stand it no longer. "Please, sir, you've got to let my sister go with us. We'll pay you handsomely—"

Two of the soldiers looked hopeful, but the chief's face hardened. "We no longer accept bribes!" he said. At a signal from him, the soldier beside me grasped my arms and pulled me to the far side of the fire. "We shall keep her here until you return."

Gid looked about ready to lose control of himself, and I shot him a look that I hoped would tell him to think before acting. For once he did not disappoint me. "Promise me you'll not hurt her. Or better yet, let me stay in her place."

"No, Gid," I found myself saying. "I'll be safe enough with the neighbors. Kora will feel better if you go with her and the children. You'll just have to give Aunt Hannah greetings from me, and try to convince Mary to help out at the wedding in my place. And perhaps I'll be able to join you in Hebron in the next few days after all. You never know."

We looked at each other for a moment, and then Gid spoke, "No, Sis. I'll stay. You need to be at the wedding. I'll see if I can talk Kora into staying with me—"

"It is enough," interrupted the chief. "We'll let you both go." The soldier holding me released me and pushed me toward Gid. "Have a pleasant journey to Hebron."

Gid grasped my arm and we led the last of the donkeys away from the patrol. In a few moments we had regained our family amidst silent hugs and tears. Kora looked pale, and though she didn't say a word, she refused to let go of Gid's arm until she was forced to sit astride her own animal again with her baby on her lap.

"I was so afraid I'd lost a daughter, Devorah," Mama commented in a low voice beside me just before we started off again.

Her words surprised me. I could not remember Mama expressing out loud such concern for me before. For Mary or Naola maybe. Apparently she had never felt the need to overprotect me, though her youngest. "I'm all right, Mama." I touched her hand and spoke words she herself had told us many times. "God protects those who put their trust in Him and do not fear."

It was evening before the sons of Lehi rejoined us. They had taken another route with their camels, faces half hidden by their head coverings, looking very much like a set of native desert travelers. It certainly brightened our spirits to have them with us again. We set up light camp a mile from the main road of travel and behind some hills, and cooked some supper. The little children were exhausted from their day of adventures and were the first ones to drop into sleep. I was still feeling some of Naola's excitement, and after the others had retired to their bedrolls, I stayed sitting up by the fire as it burned down, poking at it with my stick.

"A farthing for your thoughts," came a low masculine voice from behind me.

I jumped and turned toward the voice. It was Nephi. Once again it surprised me how much he had matured since we had last been together.

"I didn't mean to startle you, Didi," he said sitting down beside me. "Well, at least not that much!" He smiled. "You looked at me like I was a highway robber or something."

I laughed. "It's true I didn't recognize your voice at first!" I looked at him a moment. "Aren't you going to bed yet?"

Now it was his turn to laugh. "Much as I'd like to, no. My joking about highway robbers is not all untruth." He looked out into the darkness. "I'm taking the first shift of night watch."

I shivered and looked out over the dry land where it met the night sky. The sky was full of stars, more than I'd ever seen over Jerusalem. Then I looked back at Nephi and studied him a little more in the firelight. "You've changed a lot since we were together last. How long has it been, Nephi?"

He shrugged, his eyes still heavenward. "Three or four years at least. Since I started working with my father at his trade." Then his eyes returned to studying my face. "I was serious about wanting to know your thoughts. Why did you agree to come on this journey with us, Didi?"

"You mean I had a choice?" I joked. Nephi's expression didn't change from its seriousness. "I . . . I'm not absolutely sure, Nephi. Part of it may have had to do with it being your family we were joining, being friends for years and family by marriage through our older siblings, part of it is because I trust Papa to make correct decisions. But there is something more." I thought a minute, and Nephi did not interrupt. "There was a clear feeling that touched my heart and mind when you spoke, that made me feel that of all the things I believed in in this world, the most true at this moment were the prophecies of Lehi and other prophets of the destruction of Jerusalem, and that God wanted my family to join yours on this quest you spoke of. Your words have never affected me like that before, Nephi. Remember how I used to argue with you about everything you said?"

Nephi nodded slowly. "Do you think that's why the rest of your family came too? Did they feel that same way?"

I remembered how Gid and Mori had been arguing just after Nephi's announcement. They, second only to Papa, had the most to lose by leaving Jerusalem, and little to gain. And although they were religious, they had never admitted that they were believers in the recent prophecies about Jerusalem; certainly they weren't as staunch as Papa. It suddenly struck me as surprising that they had left Jerusalem at all, let alone so willingly.

Nephi must have sensed my surprise through the darkness. "Yes," he said slowly. "The spirit of the Lord was there to touch every person's heart in their own way. How else would they have come? It was the same for my own brothers . . . initially."

"Initially?" I queried. Nephi did not answer my question.

"Where is that stick I gave you?" he asked suddenly.

I held up the one I had been poking the fire with. "I'm lucky I even found it again." I laughed. "I guess I dropped it in the scuffle just outside the city. Anyway, someone picked it up and handed it to one of my nephews. He was the one that noticed and asked me about the 'pretty pictures' on my stick. It's Egyptian writing, isn't it, Nephi?"

He took the stick and examined it momentarily. "You dropped it in a scuffle? Just outside Jerusalem? I didn't hear about this." He looked concerned.

I laughed lightly. "Maybe the patrol soldiers were a little suspicious. They wanted to keep one of the daughters there with them while the family was 'on the business trip.' But they finally let us all go."

"Those filthy-minded dogs!" Nephi saw the surprise on my face. "It was you they took, wasn't it? Yet you had no idea of their intent . . . Never mind, Didi. Just be grateful they let you go." He took a slow deep breath in and out. I watched him roll the stick in his hands. "I knew when I wrote this, it was probably foolish."

"What does it say?"

He laughed, embarrassed. "It's nothing. It's probably just as well you can't read it."

"No, Nephi! Please tell me. I'd really like to know."

"'Didi, daughter of Ishmael. When you read these words, think of me. Nephi.'" He shook his head. "Really, it was an idiotic thing—"

"No, it was sweet. I wish I could have read it for myself."

Nephi was silent. "It could have cost you your life had it been found by those guards and traced you to our family," he murmured. He threw the stick down and stared at it. Then he picked it up and examined it again. He seemed to shake himself mentally, and he looked over at me. "You wish you could have read it yourself? Did you mean that?"

I thought a moment. "Yes, I did, and I do." It was rash, but I was going to say it anyway. "Nephi, would you teach me some of those characters? Well, unless it bothers you teaching them to a girl."

"No, it doesn't bother me a bit." He smiled. "I would love to do it. In fact, I promise you I will!"

The next day I found myself traveling next to Elizabeth and Eli, the couple that had been our house help in Jerusalem. I thought about Nephi's question to me, asking me what made me come out into the wilderness with the sons of Lehi, leaving our home and worldly possessions behind. Now I wondered why Elizabeth and Eli had come with us also.

"Elizabeth," I asked, "why did you leave Jerusalem with our family? Surely you could have found work with another family after we had gone?"

She smiled at me shyly. "Yes, I suppose we could have. Eli is such a good worker, and had dreams of becoming a butler for a rich family. But your family has been so good to us, we couldn't leave you without our assistance on this journey."

I think my mouth fell open at that reply. "But we are never coming back to Jerusalem! At least that is what Papa says."

Eli nodded. "We know. But we are also believers in the words of Jeremiah that if our people do not repent, Jerusalem will be destroyed. And now I believe the words of Lehi that the destruction is imminent."

He gazed at his infant son in Elizabeth's arms. "I do not want to raise my son in a city of wickedness or to have our family slaughtered or taken into captivity. I would much rather live in the desert if it meant the physical and spiritual safety of my family."

Elizabeth nodded. "Eli and I talked about it and both agreed that this was the best for us. We would rather have God and family in our lives than a stone house."

I thought about that the rest of that day. I had only considered what leaving Jerusalem would mean to me. This was the first time I thought about what it might mean to my siblings and future children. I decided that like Elizabeth, family and God meant more to me than the comforts of city life.

The next few days of travel were much the same as the first, except perhaps hotter. By the sixth day, we were all dusty, cranky, and sore from riding. The children were restless. The road had spread out into a dry plain covered with weedy grass and brush that Nephi explained was a river bed at certain days of the year. More of the travelers we passed had camels in their caravans, at which Gid and Mori's children pointed and waved. They were loaded with strange items for trade, and were dressed in costumes rarely seen at Jerusalem. Nephi pointed out to me which traveling groups were better equipped for desert travel, and I began to get a sense of some of the difficulties we might be facing ourselves in the journey ahead.

Initially in the journey, jokes and stories had been passed around the group for entertainment, especially by Lemuel, but soon conversation faded to a minimum. Now I could hear Bekka and Riddah exchanging ideas on what life would be like in our new homeland.

"I think I'd like a house with an enclosed courtyard," said Bekka, "where I can keep chickens and let my children play freely. You know, like Papa's."

"Ah, but think," returned Riddah, "how much prettier the courtyard would be with flowers and trees growing in the middle of it. And who knows? Perhaps this new land will be rich enough that you could even have a fountain in the garden!"

"How can you women talk on like this?" cut in Laman suddenly, who was traveling alongside them. "Why do you think we'll find even a fraction of the wealth and bounty we've had in whatever new land we settle in? How can we even be sure we'll all survive the journey there? You're all too happy leaving everything you've ever known behind in Jerusalem."

No one had an answer to his outburst. The whole company was shrouded in silence. I thought once again of my friends and the games we used to play, Sabbath days in the synagogue, feast days in the great temple on the hill, holidays when extended family came to visit, running on the hills outside the city with Naola and her pet sheep, Dan, sitting in the cool shade of the house during the heat of the day, the comfort of my own pillowed bed. I could just imagine what my sisters and brothers were thinking of, and perhaps regretting, having left behind.

"The turnoff's just ahead," Nephi's voice called out over the silence of the group. "We'll be skirting around the port city of—"

"No, it's not," Laman suddenly cut in, and urged his camel forward to the front of the line where Nephi was. "We should be hours away yet from that turnoff."

"No, it's there, by the three boulders on the crest of the next hill." Nephi raised his arm to point. "It is off in the distance, I admit, but I can see—"

"That's just the problem!" Laman burst out. "You're always asking us to see things that aren't there, just like Father. Like this destruction of Jerusalem. For all we know, you've collaborated with him so you can lead us out into the desert and tell us what to do. And we, your elder brothers, we only came out to make sure Mother and Father were protected and taken care of." He snorted. "Now get this straight, Nephi. I am in charge of this little expedition, and when it's time for the turnoff, I'll let you know."

"Beware, Laman," Nephi began quietly.

"Enough!" Laman made a slashing motion with his hand. "I have half a mind to turn around right now and take this group back to Jerusalem."

"Why don't you, Laman?" Lemuel spoke quietly at his side. "Why do we even need to leave Jerusalem now? Men have spoken of the destruction of our great city for a long time now, it could be years, perhaps generations away yet. And despite the change of kings, we have survived and resisted all our enemies so far! Besides, the destruction depends on the people becoming fully ripe in iniquity. Look how many believers are yet in the city, and with us there too, perhaps our presence would stay the destructions even longer."

"And look how peaceful our lives have been in that city!" Riddah's voice entering in to the discussion surprised me, although thinking about it now it was almost predictable. "It would be a shame to throw away our homes, our comforts, our friends sooner than we had to. I would come back with you, Laman." She smiled sweetly at him.

"Stop this!" Nephi's voice rang out clear over the others. "You do not know into what dangerous sands you are treading. If the Lord commands us to leave Jerusalem now, he means *now*."

"Little brother." It was now Lemuel's turn to face Nephi. "Look at the circumstances: the city gets too hot for Father, and it's time to leave with the family. And we've been in that valley in the desert how long now? A year! And sent back to Jerusalem how many times? And the city's still been there, no sign of disintegration or change. Where does that leave your 'now' now, Nephi?"

I could see that we were getting nowhere in discussion, and that the day was not getting any longer. "Come on, men." I said, prodding my donkey forward. "I think it's time we be heading onward."

"Ah, but which direction?" Lemuel asked. "It seems to me we have several differing opinions." He grinned lazily.

"To the Valley of Lemuel—" Nephi began.

"I say back to Jerusalem!" said Laman. "We can rest for a while, perhaps in some future time to leave before the destructions befall the city, but at least free from the rantings of a preaching visionary man and his puppet child."

"Sisters," said Riddah, "look at Mama and Papa. A week of journeying only and they are exhausted. Surely it can't be wrong for them to spend the remainder of their lives in peace in their own homes, with their children around them? We can leave the city to pursue this Promised Land when we need not worry about their welfare anymore."

"Riddah, we're fine," Mama began, but Riddah turned away.

"Riddah! Don't you see?" I exclaimed. "You are going on the assumption that Jerusalem will be there for quite a while! We can't afford to second guess the time period of the Lord. Do not do this foolish thing!"

"No, Didi." Mori and Gid now joined the group. "Laman and Lemuel speak wisdom. It is better that we return home until our families are old enough to withstand a desert journey. We will return with them." Abisha and Kora looked at each other then at their husbands and said nothing.

"Riddah," said Bekka, but her eyes were on Laman and Lemuel. "I'm with you."

"I . . . I don't know," faltered Naola. "A desert journey sounded so exciting."

"Remember the teachings of the prophets?" I asked her. "Not always is the right way easy to see, and not always are prophets accepted as such by their own people. Remember how you felt when you were first told of the pending destruction of Jerusalem, and again when invited to leave the city to join a family being guided by the Lord away from that destruction to a Land of Promise?" Her head was bowed and a tear dropped off her cheek. I took a deep breath. "Naola, is the way clear now?"

"I will go to the Valley of Lemuel with Nephi," she said, raising her head.

"As will I," smiled Sam, looking at Naola. He blushed. "I mean, I was going to all along."

"Mary?" Nephi looked at her earnestly.

"I will go where Mama and Papa go."

All eyes turned toward Ishmael and Leah.

"I will stay with you, dear, as always." Mama smiled at Papa. "I know you will make the right choice." I couldn't help but wonder to myself at Mama's wisdom, which never failed her, even in the tightest of situations. Papa couldn't help but choose the right thing when Mama looked to him like that.

"It is true we are aging," Papa began. "And that a desert trip would be difficult. But I also believe that when the Lord commands one to do something, one must do it when he asks it or forever regret it. We will join Lehi in the desert."

Eli and Elizabeth, standing behind Ishmael, smiled at each other and nodded.

"Oh, you fools, fools!" Laman said to himself. Then he turned to the rest of the group. "I was hoping more of you would think before blindly following the commands of a dreamer and his puppet son. But don't say I didn't warn you. The rest of us will return to Jerusalem."

"Laman!" The firmness of Nephi's voice startled me. Then it grew softer. "Laman, Lemuel. Must I always be an example to you? Throw off this hardness of your hearts, this blindness that covers your own souls. Do you realize what you are doing? You are turning your backs on the very word of the Lord!" Nephi drew a deep breath. "You cannot deny you know of his power, not after seeing the angel. You cannot deny that he has helped us in obtaining the plates of Laban, no other power on earth could have done it."

Most of our group gaped at Nephi in silence, but Riddah gasped out loud. Nephi glanced at Riddah then back at Laman and Lemuel. "You cannot deny that God has the power to deliver us from any danger, to give us the strength if need be, to cross a hundred deserts like this one, if we just have the faith in him. And if he has said it, we shall reach the Land of Promise. And if he has said it, Jerusalem will be destroyed. How can you close your eyes to the wickedness therein, with the many prophets they have slain or imprisoned, like Jeremiah in our very day, including attempting the life of our own father?"

Nephi looked at all of us and drew himself up tall. "I say this only once more, so remember it well. If you go up to Jerusalem again, you go at the peril of your own lives. If that is your wish, then go. But you will be destroyed with them! And, brothers, I say this not of my own will but because God urges me to say it."

Before any of us could move a muscle, Laman and Lemuel had pulled Nephi down from his animal.

"We need to have a talk, young man," said Laman. "You do not command God nor are you his special emissary." He looked over his shoulder at the rest of the group. "We'll be right back."

Nephi was walked by his brothers out of sight over the next roll of wilderness land. Each of us was lost in our own thoughts. I began to wonder what had ever brought me to side with Nephi to continue on this journey to who-knows-where. And Nephi had changed! I had not expected to see this almost fanatical sureness that what he knew and spoke was God's will. I could begin to understand his brothers' anger with him. And what had I told Naola in my own zeal? "Prophets are seldom accepted as such by their own people" or something like that. Was that true or was I only blinding myself too, trying to convince myself that all I've believed and felt up to now was correct? Or was I still hoping in my idealistic world that Nephi, my hero and friend from childhood, was still right?

Laman and Lemuel returned to our view but without Nephi.

"He wanted some time alone to think things through," Lemuel explained in answer to our queries. "He felt maybe it would be better after all if we all went back to Jerusalem for now, and when he rejoins us, you who want to go back into the desert can return with him."

"But didn't Nephi say we were nearing the turnoff to where Lehi is camped?" Papa asked. "Wouldn't it be just as easy to keep going there and let the rest of you return as you will later?"

"That would mean twice as much travel for those returning to Jerusalem, and it would never work anyway," Laman burst out. "Father would never let us return once we were with him again."

"Why do all of us have to go back to Jerusalem just because some of you want to stay there?" Naola asked. "Why can't those who want to, go back, and the rest of us go on to meet Lehi?"

"And split up the family?" Riddah gasped.

"It seems as though Laman's plan would do that anyway, don't you think?" Bekka answered. "It would split up his family." She turned to

Laman and Lemuel. "I don't suppose your father could be persuaded to return to Jerusalem with us, could he?"

Lemuel shook his head. "I very much doubt it."

Laman, at almost the same moment, added, "Never."

Bekka seemed to be thinking out loud. "If we return to Jerusalem, it looks as though Mama and Papa with three of our sisters will join Lehi, breaking up our family." She looked up at Riddah. "It seems that the only way to keep both families intact is to continue our journey and join Lehi."

Riddah grabbed Bekka by the shoulders. "Bekka! What are you saying? You are giving up your past and your future without a fight? Think, girl, think!"

"Didi," Naola spoke at my side. "Something's wrong, I know it. Look at Sam." I had not noticed before, but Sam was frowning, and as we watched, turned to look over his shoulder in the direction Nephi had been taken. "I was wondering. You know Nephi best in our family. Is it like him to change his mind suddenly like that?"

I wasn't sure I knew Nephi that well any more. "I . . . I don't know, Naola."

Naola dropped back to the edge of the group where Sam was and spoke softly. "Sam, something's on your mind. What is it?"

"Uh, nothing." He looked back over his shoulder again. "Well, at least not something you can do anything about. Or I for that matter."

"But the two of us?" Naola was concerned, but constantly optimistic. "Tell me."

"I . . . I just worry about Nephi. Someday they'll go too far."

"You don't think they've hurt him!" Naola's voice carried over the whole group of travelers. Everyone stopped talking and turned in our direction.

"What is this?" Papa was the first to recover. "Of what kind of wickedness are you accusing the sons of Lehi?"

Naola was instantly contrite. "Oh, Papa. I didn't mean . . ."

Sam drew a sudden breath. "He returns," he said quietly.

From the direction Nephi had been taken by his brothers, a lone figure came jogging into view. It was Nephi. He strode up to his brothers and faced them, panting slightly.

"How can you do this?" he asked, bewildered. "You not only do me a great wrong, you are turning your backs on the Lord. Brothers! Turn back before it is too late, before you destroy innocent people with you." Nephi was rubbing his wrists. They were red and swollen, something I had not noticed the last time we had seen him.

"Stop this speech, Nephi, I command you!" Laman reached out as though to grasp Nephi as he had earlier. But Nephi was quick and backed out of reach. Lemuel stepped forward to aid Laman, but Nephi found immediate asylum amongst the rest of our group.

It suddenly became clear to me what was going on. "Stop this instant!" I cried, hauling my donkey, who responded for once, to block Laman. "I don't know what is going on here exactly, but I don't like the looks of it. I see anger in you, Laman. And a man with anger cannot think straight." I grasped Laman's wrist. "Those marks on Nephi's wrists give you away, Laman and Lemuel. He was going to join us again later in Jerusalem? Not if you could help it, it seems. Oh, your father was right when he spoke of the wickedness of the people of Jerusalem. To think there are those among even the believers who would harm their own brother!"

"She's right, Laman. Listen to her." I could not believe my ears. It was Mori. "You are being a little harsh with your brother. If he's getting out of line, let Lehi deal with it. There is no justification for you if your brother is harmed while under your care and especially if you are the cause of it, in God's eyes or anybody else's."

No one in our whole group moved or spoke. Even the little children were quiet. Laman stood with bowed head. Lemuel fiddled with a stray cord on his pack animal and then lifted his head to watch Laman.

"Boys." It was Mama. "There have been some strong feelings expressed here today. I will not say who should take the blame, for that will solve nothing. But I do hope there will be more tolerance in the future." Mama looked around at us. She was never more stately and beautiful than when teaching her children. "As for today's destination, let me say this and you may each decide for yourselves. As a mother, if I were in Sariah's position, I would want all of my family together as long as possible, preferring that to even the luxuries of a home. And if that were not possible, I would want to at least say goodbye a last time to my children and give them my blessing. It would be ungrateful not to allow your mother and father that privilege."

Laman's head was in his hands. Lemuel was picking at his cord again. Suddenly Laman lifted his face, and his expression showed misery.

"Nephi, my brother," he said, his voice just audible. "I owe you an apology."

Nephi appeared from his place of protection, still a careful distance away, and looked at him.

Laman's gaze fell to the ground. "I deserve to be destroyed in Jerusalem. It was abominable of me to lose my temper at you for nought . . . I don't know what got into me . . . and then nearly destroying you. For a moment I really wanted . . ." He buried his face in his hands again.

"Nephi." Lemuel looked up at Nephi. "I also am at fault, brother"—his voice broke, then he continued—"For the same ill will and deeds. Can you . . . forgive me also?"

"Brothers," Nephi's voice trembled and he bit his lip. "I . . ." Then he squared his shoulders and his voice became firm. "Yes, Laman and Lemuel, my brothers, I forgive you from the bottom of my soul." Nephi stepped near to them and placed a hand on each of their shoulders. "But there is one other of whom you must ask forgiveness, for only he knows the true intent of your hearts and only he can grant the final pardon."

"It's the Lord, isn't it?" Lemuel asked, closing his eyes tightly.

"Oh, God!" Laman cried out and hid his face once more in his hands.

Nephi seemed satisfied and went over to mount his camel. Laman watched Nephi from between his fingers. When Nephi glanced back at him, Laman closed his eyes and moved his lips like he was praying. I wasn't so sure he really was.

When Laman and Lemuel finally looked up at the rest of us, and all had mounted their animals, Nephi directed his camel toward Lehi's camp. With no argument, the rest of us followed.

After a while in silence, Naola began to softly sing a story song. No one joined her on the first verse, and it began to look like the second was doomed to die when Sam's sure voice joined in. Soon Mori's and Gid's little ones were laughing and singing along, the dark mood of the recent scene forgotten.

During our next rest period, I maneuvered my donkey up near where Nephi was resting against his seated camel. I gently grasped his arm and held it out to inspect it. Not only was the wrist red and swollen, but in several areas, the skin was broken and raw.

"I don't think your mother would be pleased to see you this way," I said. "I think I have something here somewhere that would do just the trick."

Mary was really the one who understood herbs the best, but she had taught me some useful tricks. I found in my personal pack some powder of the kind I wanted, spat into a pinch of it to make a paste, and spread it onto his wrists. Then taking some strips of cloth from the same bag, I wrapped them around and tied them on snugly.

"It may look a little funny right now, but in the morning, you can take the cloth off and the redness should be gone." I paused and looked down at his ankles. "I think your ankles need some too."

Nephi nodded and stretched them out toward me. I made more of the herb paste, spread it over the sores on his ankles, and added strips of cloth as before.

I looked up at him and he smiled back. "Thanks, Didi," he said softly. "I appreciate it."

CHAPTER 2

The Valley of Lemuel

In what they called the Valley of Lemuel, an old dry river bed where Lehi and his family had set up their tents and planted crops, the soil was relatively rich compared to the surrounding desert land. A small stream, which ran dry surprisingly infrequently during the year, ran past the encampment on its way to the nearby sea, and the family had named it the River Laman. Lying in the midst of fairly mountainous country, the valley was at least a day's journey from any frequented roads. Only rarely had any of the desert inhabitants come upon the encampment.

We were met by a strong, fair-skinned man who looked too young to be Lehi. He had been sitting on a slight rise on the bank of the stream, rubbing something on what looked like an animal hide. When he saw us, he threw down his work and came running toward us.

Nephi jumped off his mount and was the first to meet him. "Zoram!" he cried and embraced him. Then he stood back and looked at him. "You look well."

Sam, Laman, and Lemuel took their turns embracing or greeting him. Then Nephi brought him over to the group.

"House of Ishmael, this is Zoram, the servant of Laban who helped us obtain the record of our fathers from Jerusalem. He also is responsible for recording the prophecies of Jeremiah on the brass plates. He has since joined our group and will accompany us to the Land of Promise. Please consider him family."

Nephi turned to Zoram and began listing to him our names. As I glanced over our group during introductions, I took special notice of Mary. She was sitting up straight in her saddle, a look of wonder in her eyes and a smile on her lips. She didn't take her eyes off Zoram, except when her name was given and he looked right at her, at which she blushed slightly and glanced down. I was more than grateful that she was having at last the opportunity to experience the "in like" flutters that every young woman should experience in her lifetime. I wondered if Zoram was the answer to Mary's predicament, and hoped that he would be a man deserving of Mary's goodness and understanding of her sensitivity.

With all the commotion, Lehi and Sariah were soon out of their tent and greeting us. I was surprised how healthy the two looked after many months of living in the desert. I hoped my own parents would be able to tolerate such rough living as gracefully. It was a joyful reunion, particularly for Sariah, who welcomed Mama warmly, then fussed at her sons and over Mori and Gid's children, hugging them like she didn't want to ever let them go. Then Lehi and Sariah greeted us each individually, after which Lehi and Papa separated themselves from the group, talking intently.

"Devorah," Sariah gave me a hug. "It is so good to see you again. Let me look at you." She stepped back and nodded approvingly. Her abdomen bulged slightly under her dress, and I wondered if she were with child. "My, how you and your sisters have grown." She laughed. "Don't I sound just like an old mother hen? When I told Lehi we needed wives for our sons, and Ishmael's family would be perfect, it didn't take him long to see what a good idea it was. I must tell you, Nephi never looked happier than when getting ready to fetch your family out of Jerusalem."

"Oh, Mother Sariah, you tease me," I said, but I shook my head mentally. Was it assumed without thought, Nephi and Didi, Didi and Nephi, or did we get any choice in the matter? And why should it bother me in the first place? It was the custom for marriages to be arranged. Hadn't I been doing the same thing, placing Mary and Zoram together in my mind just now? Three weeks ago I would have chosen Nephi first anyway, given a whole Jerusalem of handsome men.

Mori and Gid began setting up the tents we had brought, with the help of the sons of Lehi. Or perhaps I should say it was my brothers who helped the sons of Lehi put up the tents; with my brothers' recent years of working only in the city, it had been a long time since they had occasion to set up tents. The children ran down to the stream with Naola in tow while the rest of us began unloading the animals.

"Mommy! Mommy!" Mori's second oldest boy, Matthew, toddled up to his mother, Abisha. "More camels! See, see?" He pulled on her sleeve until she followed him around Lehi's tent. Soon she was back.

"Sariah," she said, a little confused. "You have only camels behind your tent. Where are your donkeys?"

Sariah laughed. "Camels will be the only animals used on the next leg of our journey. They really do much better on the softer sands of this part of the country than do donkeys. I suspect you'll soon be trading in all your animals for camels soon too."

"Oh, no!" Abisha said, looking horrified. "You're not going to get me on one of those smelly, spitting, mean-tempered things! I'd rather walk."

"Then I suspect you'll be doing just that," said Sariah mildly and, with the corners of her mouth turned upward slightly, returned to her work.

It was nearly dusk before things were set up and stowed away enough for us to rest our weary bones. It was about time for supper too. But Lehi gathered us together first.

"On the eve of our first day together, the house of Ishmael and the house of Lehi, and in remembrance of the multitude of blessings which the Lord has given us, in safely leaving Jerusalem and in protecting us in the wilderness, I think it is appropriate and important that we give the Lord thanks. I and my sons have built an altar just east of here, where we would like to offer sacrifice tonight in thanksgiving. Sam, would you fetch the lamb?"

I had only seen sacrifices offered in the temple in Jerusalem and that only from a distance amidst crowds and confusion. This night was distinctly different. A peace and comradeship reigned over our small group of two families. There was a dignity and sense of reverence shown in the motions of this man, Lehi, that I had not detected in others in the city. It did not occur to me until later to wonder how a non-Levite could offer sacrifice. During the service, I resolved I would do my best to remember the Lord, show more patience to those around me, and not complain should our future journeying become difficult.

The next several weeks were spent making preparations for the desert living ahead of us. Trips were made to the nearest seaside town to trade for more grain seeds and fruit, and our donkeys were traded in for the promised camels. The small crops Lehi's family had planted contributed to our daily sustenance, and the hills offered a variety of game which the men hunted as the need arose. It was a relatively peaceful time for our group as we adjusted to wilderness living, with little verbal reference to the homes we had left and no hint of the family feud we had witnessed on our journey here. None, that is, until Lehi gathered us together in front of the door of his tent one morning to speak to us.

"Sit down," he said. "I have something to say to all of you." We obeyed. When we were settled, he spoke again, "I have had a dream. A dream that is a vision." Laman and Lemuel looked at each other with exasperated expressions I only partly understood. "Because of this dream, I have reason to rejoice because of my two sons Sam and Nephi and their posterity." His glance moved to Naola, Mary, and me. "But I have reason to be sorrowful because of my sons Laman and Lemuel and their posterity." Lehi gazed at his two oldest sons and they looked away.

Lehi bowed his head and was silent a moment. Zoram looked at Laman and Lemuel, glanced at Nephi and Sam, and then began studying Mary. The rest of us watched Lehi.

Lehi looked up. "In my dream, I found myself in a vast and dark wilderness, more barren than this desert you see around you. As I was looking at it, a man dressed in white appeared and bade me follow him. I started after him, but in the darkness, he was soon lost to sight. The land became more barren, and as I continued on hour after hour, I began to fear I'd never see greenery and light again." Lehi paused. I remembered how desperately Riddah loved green trees and flowering courtyards, and it was a stark contrast to the wasteland Lehi was painting.

"At this point, I began praying unto the Lord, with increasing fervor, that I would be rescued from this dark wasteland. I was about ready to sink into despair when I found myself in a gigantic field larger than all the farming fields outside of Jerusalem put together. The darkness was gone, and I could see that some distance away was the most beautiful, lush fruit tree I had ever seen." I heard Riddah catch her breath. "I walked toward it, knowing somehow that this tree's fruit would satisfy all my hunger and thirst to the depths of my soul, that it was the source of that illusive happiness that all men seek." Laman and Lemuel exchanged looks again, and Lehi watched them as he continued.

"The fruit was sweet, more refreshing than any I've ever tasted. And it was white, so pure that the sun shining on it almost blinded me. I wanted to share the experience and the joy of it with you, my family," Lemuel rolled his eyes. "Yes, you Laman and Lemuel, the same as Sam and Nephi, and my daughters," Lehi nodded to all of his children then smiled at Sariah. "And my dear bride, Sariah." Sariah, at his side, reached out and laid her hand on his arm.

"As I looked about to find you, I saw a river running through the field, and it came near and passed the tree where I stood. And there at the head of it, I saw Sariah, Sam, and Nephi, looking as lost as I had felt while in the dark wasteland. I called and beckoned to catch their attention, and to my great joy they heard my voice, came unto the tree, and partook of the fruit also."

Lehi turned toward Laman and Lemuel. I was surprised to see a tear glistening on his cheek. "I carefully scanned the field and alongside the river to its head again, searching for my two other sons. With all my heart I wanted you to taste of the fruit that I had found and that had brought me such joy. I found you at last, my sons. I called and beckoned and pleaded that you would come unto the tree. Your mother and your younger brothers joined me also in trying to persuade you. But you would not." Lehi suddenly seemed to me older, more tired.

"Why? Why did you not come?" Lehi searched the faces of his two older sons as if the answer would be written there. "I've tried to be a good father and honest, teaching you of the ways of the Lord and setting a good example before you. I want to share with you the joy I feel. Why do you not partake?" The tears were rolling unashamedly down his cheeks. Laman and Lemuel were looking at the ground.

Sariah pulled at Lehi's sleeve. "Come, my husband. Come inside the tent and rest awhile—"

"No," said Lehi. He looked at her a moment as though he didn't recognize her. Then he shook his head, wiped his face with his sleeve, and looked around at the silent group. "No. The dream is not ended. There is more."

He took a deep breath. "There was a straight, narrow path leading through the field toward the tree, with a rod of iron alongside it. There were also other people in the dream, all of whom seemed to be searching for something intently. They seemed to be searching for fulfillment, for the joy I felt, for the way to the tree where I stood. But behold, a dark mist appeared, blinding their way and preventing them from finding the tree. Some found the path to the tree but lost it again. Some found the rod of iron and kept hold of it until they made it safely to the tree."

Lehi got a peculiar look on his face. "The people at the tree ate of the fruit and tasted of the joy of it. But then they seemed ashamed of what they had done, and they wandered away from the tree, never to return." Lehi searched our faces as if for an answer. "I couldn't imagine what could cause such a tragedy at first. Then I saw a magnificent building, grander in decor and size than the temple in Jerusalem, floating as it were in the air at the far side of the great field. And in that building were the great and powerful ones of the world, shouting and scoffing and mocking those of us standing at the tree." Lehi took a deep breath. "Many, many people were trying to reach that great building. Many, many people were lost in the darkness of the field or drowned in the river before ever getting near the building." He looked at Mori and Gid and their wives then at me and my sisters. "But there were also those who found their way to the tree, who continued to partake of the fruit and stayed."

He dropped his head into his hands. "But two of my sons would not even come and partake of the fruit!" No one moved. Lehi slowly raised his head and, straightening his back until he reached his full height, gazed at Laman and Lemuel intently. "I fear for you, my sons Laman and Lemuel. I fear lest you are turning your backs on the Lord forever, turning your backs on his glory and eternal joy, turning your backs on the chance for repentance. Oh, my sons! There is nothing more I want for you than eternal life and joy in the presence of God forever! I would give my life gladly if it would help even one iota."

Lehi stepped toward his sons as though wanting to embrace them. They remained sitting with eyes downward. Instead, he rested a hand on each of their shoulders. "My sons," he said quietly. "Listen to the words coming from the honest desires of my heart. I know you don't like to have your father forever preaching at you, so I will tell you now what I constantly wish for you, and you will know for always." He took a deep breath.

"The Lord is God! He desires to bless his children but can only do so when they obey his commandments. He has sent prophets to the earth to teach us of his will, of the way of salvation. I have pleaded with him as your father that he would have mercy upon you, and that you would believe and turn unto him. But that is your choice, my sons. You must repent of your pride, of your rebelliousness, of your anger. Be faithful to living exactly the truth that you know! Otherwise, you rationalize and deceive yourselves, and God cannot save you then. Think deeply about these words, my sons, and live."

Neither Laman nor Lemuel looked at their father. He gazed at them sadly, and then embraced both of them anyway. "I want you to know I love you to the very depths of my soul."

Dropping his hands, Lehi turned and walked slowly back into his tent.

Lehi had a habit of gathering the men every afternoon in the shade at the front of his tent to talk and share some of the writings from the plates of brass. Zoram and Nephi were also able to read the writing so sometimes they read for him. The day after telling us about his vision of the tree of life, I was walking past his tent to fill a bag of water from the well when I overheard words of their conversation. I stopped beside the tent to listen, my water bag forgotten.

"The time is very soon when Jerusalem will be destroyed," Lehi was saying. "The Jews and many people from the land about will be taken captive into Babylon."

I sank to the ground in shock. There had been talk when we were still in Jerusalem about different political scenarios. Many believed we should ally with Egypt, while a smaller faction thought we should appease the Babylonians. It seemed we got out of Jerusalem just in time.

"But not to lose hope, my sons!" Lehi continued. "In the own due time of the Lord, the people will return again to the land of their inheritance."

"Then we can return again to Jerusalem!" Laman interjected gleefully.

"Nay, my son, it will not happen in our lifetime. We are to be as a branch broken off of an olive tree and planted in another part of the vineyard. It will be a long time before the House of Israel will be gathered again to the main tree."

So we will never see Jerusalem again, I thought. The realization had not really hit home to me before. We were wanderers in a strange land now.

"But I have good news, my sons!" Lehi exclaimed. "I have learned that in six hundred years, the Lord God will raise up a great prophet in the land of Jerusalem, even the Messiah!"

Laman gazed at his father critically. "So? That will not even happen in our grandchildren's lifetime. Why should this matter to us?"

"Why will this matter to us?" Lehi repeated. "The Messiah will redeem us from our sins, from any mistakes we have ever made! It doesn't matter if we live before his time or after. He can still save us!

Any person in the whole world who repents of his sins can lay claim on his redeeming grace. And now we know when he will come!"

Now Sam spoke up. "Father, how will people recognize the Messiah when he comes?"

"There will be a prophet who will come before the messiah to prepare the way as before a king," Lehi answered. "He will baptize him and bear record that he is the very lamb of God, the one we remember when we make sacrifice unto the Most High. This Messiah will teach the gospel unto the Jews, bless them, and heal them."

"Oh, that we could see that in our day!" Zoram sighed.

"Will the people in Jerusalem accept him?" Eli queried. "Look how they are treating the prophets now, like Jeremiah. They imprison, beat, and even kill them."

Lehi's response was spoken so quietly I could barely hear him. "Alas, many will not accept him. Those who are the most hard-hearted among our people will slay him."

There were gasps in the group. My heart dropped into my stomach. Why would anyone slay the Messiah, for whom we had looked for generations?

Lehi was weeping. Then he wiped his tears unashamedly with his arm. "Then, O my children, the Messiah will rise from the dead and show himself unto his people by the power of the Holy Ghost."

I was so deep in thought that I didn't realize Lehi had finished his discussion. Sam suddenly appeared around the corner of the tent and nearly tripped over me. Before either of us could say a word, Nephi appeared from the same direction and nearly collided with Sam. Sam and I looked at Nephi's confused look, then at each other, and then Sam grinned. When I smiled back, Sam let out a chuckle, and soon the two of us were laughing gleefully, the more so because Nephi still looked confused.

"All right, I give in," Nephi said. "What's the joke?" He looked at me, but I only shrugged and pointed at Sam. He couldn't answer right away.

"I don't know either, actually," Sam finally panted out. "I just didn't expect to run into Didi right here and now, and then the expressions on both your faces . . ." I giggled again and soon both brothers joined in the laughter.

Nephi reached out a hand to help me up. "What are you doing here anyway, Didi?"

"I was on my way to fetch water and got distracted by a very interesting conversation from Father Lehi," I answered truthfully. "I am sorry to eavesdrop, but I couldn't help myself."

Nephi studied me thoughtfully. "What did you think of his words?"

"Exciting and sad at the same time about the Messiah. It gives new meaning to our sacrifices." I paused. "Is your father from the tribe of Levi?"

Nephi looked surprised. "No, we are of the tribe of Joseph, through his son Manasseh. I believe your family is through his son Ephraim. Why do you ask?"

I took a deep breath. "I didn't know that anyone not a Levite could offer sacrifice."

Sam and Nephi glanced at each other. "Anyone with the holy priesthood after the order of the son of God can also offer sacrifice," Nephi explained.

"How did your father get the holy priesthood?" I asked and then regretted it a moment later, worrying that I was being disrespectful.

Nephi smiled wistfully. "The prophet Jeremiah ordained him right after my father's first vision of God on his throne. The priesthood is usually passed from father to oldest son. It is also shared among the prophets. The priesthood can be traced back all the way to Adam. It was soon after his ordination that my father began preaching repentance in Jerusalem."

I nodded slowly. "I notice your father spends a lot of time writing on leather parchment in the evenings with you or Zoram. What is he writing?"

Nephi glanced at Sam who nodded. "We are recording his prophecies and visions. One day he hopes to record them more permanently on metal plates like the brass plates."

I sighed and hefted the empty water bladder. "Thank you for explaining all of this to me. But I suppose I better get back to fetching water."

The next day, Nephi left before dawn to go hunting. At least that is what we assumed since his bow was also gone. But our supply of food was good, and usually he liked some company when he went. I began to wonder if everything were all right, especially when he wasn't back by suppertime. When I was through with the work Mama still was able to dream up for us even in this wasteland, I found a seat in the shade of one of the tents where I could listen to Lehi's sons talking and at the same time look out over the valley toward the hills in hopes of spotting Nephi.

I must have dozed momentarily, for the next I knew, Nephi had returned, and was standing by his family's tent listening to his brothers arguing in the shade just beyond it. I was about to jump up and ask him where he had been all day but was stopped by an indescribable expression on his face: a mixture of exhaustion, sorrow, and yet fulfillment. Usually, he would take advantage of any chance to talk with his brothers about Lehi's teachings. Instead, I watched as he turned and dragged himself into the tent, without saying a word to his brothers.

After a moment's deliberation, I approached the door of Lehi's family tent. "Hello!" I called in. "Nephi? Sariah?"

After a moment, Sariah came to the tent door. "What is it, Didi?"

I hesitated a moment. "I saw Nephi come in from hunting. He looked exhausted. Perhaps I could bring him some cold water from the well?"

Sariah smiled. "That would be wonderful, Didi." She reached up above her head, pulled down an empty water bladder, and handed it to me.

I ran to the well and pulled up a bucket of cold water. I filled the water bladder as quickly as I could, spilling some of the water in the process, and then walked quickly back to Lehi's tent. Sariah led me inside where Nephi lay on a couch, his back to me. Sariah returned to her bedroom deeper inside the tent.

"Nephi?" I asked tentatively.

He did not answer. As I got closer, I saw his shoulders moving in sudden jerking motions. It reminded me of when Noala was crying. I heard a soft sobbing sound. I knelt on the ground behind him and laid my hand on his shoulder.

"Nephi, it's Didi. I brought you some fresh water to drink. Is everything all right?"

His sobbing stopped. He suddenly rolled over and grasped my hand tightly to his chest. I let him cry, his tears dripping onto our clasped hands. I was frightened. I had never seen him weep before. Something terrible must have happened. When finally the sobs quieted some, I pulled his other hand away from his face.

"What happened, Nephi? You can tell me."

He nodded, sat up, and wiped his eyes. "Yes, I'd like that," he whispered. He was silent for so long I wondered if maybe he wasn't going to tell me. Then he began in broken sentences.

"I wanted to understand the vision my father saw of the tree of life," he said. "I prayed to know the meaning and God showed it to me." He paused again. "Didi, I saw the Messiah! He will be born of a virgin in Jerusalem and minister unto the people. I saw as wicked men killed him, and witnessed him rise again."

I listened silently.

"There is more," Nephi continued. "After his resurrection, I saw the Messiah visit our descendants upon the Land of Promise. Imagine that! There were thousands of people upon the land, and he came to visit them!"

"Was that what made you weep like a child?" I finally asked.

He shook his head and his expression clouded over again. "I saw our descendants, Didi, mine and my brothers'. There will be wars and destructions between them from time to time. There will be periods of righteousness and periods of wickedness. After Christ comes, there will be four generations living righteously! But then the people will become very wicked again, and the descendants of our brothers will . . . overcome our descendants." He began to weep again.

My heart felt tight. "What do you mean by 'overcome,' Nephi?"

"They will destroy, annihilate them," he whispered.

"Why would you weep for people you don't know?" I asked, puzzled.

He stared at me. "They are our descendants, Didi, our people. Do you not feel a responsibility for them? What we teach our children will be taught to our grandchildren and so on. We have to get it right from the very beginning."

I had never thought of that before. Suddenly being a parent and grown-up sounded a lot harder than I imagined. "So we teach our children about God and our siblings do the same. That should work, right, Nephi?"

He stared at his hands. "It should work, teaching correct principles, setting an example, encouraging obedience. But our brothers still resist. Why? What am I doing wrong?"

"I don't think you are doing anything wrong, Nephi." I laid my hand on his. "You are a good example to Sam and to me. You love, honor, and support your father and your mother. I believe you will teach your children great things and be a wonderful father to them." I paused. "Maybe your brothers just don't understand the scriptures and Father Lehi's prophecies as well as you do. Share your insights with them. Teach them."

Nephi nodded. "I will try again." He gazed at me a long time until I felt nervous. I lowered my eyes. Nephi put his finger under my chin and gently raised it until I was looking into his eyes again. "Devorah," he whispered.

"Yes?" I trembled.

"You are the most amazing woman I have ever known, Didi. You strengthen me. The burden seems more possible now." He paused. "My father has plans to ask your father for us to be betrothed. But I want to ask you myself. Will you consent to marry me?"

My mind was a whirlwind of thoughts. I liked Nephi a lot. He was a little different now than when I knew him before, much more serious and intense. But I loved that he loved God. And I believed he would treat his wife well and raise his children with good morals. I believed I could have no better choice in a husband.

"Yes, Nephi, I will marry you," I answered softly.

He tilted his head back and laughed. "Yes!" he cried happily.

Sariah poked her head around the corner. "Are you okay out there?"

"Yes, mother!" he responded, letting go of my chin and hand suddenly.

She disappeared again and I cleared my throat. "I better go," I mumbled.

Nephi nodded. "I better go back outside and see what I can teach my brothers about Father's vision. I think they were arguing about something they didn't understand." He stood up and helped me up too. He held my hand and gazed into my eyes a minute longer, smiling joyfully. Then he turned and left the tent.

I returned Sariah's water bag and headed back to my family's tent, my heart soaring. Nephi wanted to marry me!

A few weeks later, Nephi disappeared again with his bow. Again we had no real need for meat, and there was much to do around the camp to prepare for the upcoming trading trip to the seaside city two days away. I could tell Laman was angry at losing another pair of work hands and at Lehi being unreachable while in consultation with Papa and Zoram regarding betrothal arrangements. Mama sat, working, intently embroidering a robe, saying little, and paying little attention to any of our conversation. Sariah was fluttering around nervously, giving instructions and orders whether needed or not. Riddah was laughing and talking almost nonstop, Naola and Mary adding commentary here and there. Bekka seemed withdrawn, expression unreadable. Abisha with her sharp tongue kept the children out of the way, and Kora followed Sariah around, obediently carrying out her orders.

Finally Papa and Lehi emerged from their tents, smiling and arms around each other's shoulders, and Zoram behind them with a contented look on his face, but no details were given about the betrothal arrangements. Mama hovered around Papa, and Sariah tried to ask for the information, but the men gave not a clue. Nephi showed up just in time to eat. Tension continued high through dinner. Finally, Lehi signaled for us to gather around him and Ishmael.

"I understand how difficult it is to wait once certain kinds of arrangements have been made between two families concerning their children's futures. We will delay telling you no longer." Lehi paused a moment while looking around the group. Mary was looking at the ground. Riddah's smile seemed frozen on her face. Bekka was biting her lip while glancing at Lemuel. Naola was watching Papa eagerly. Zoram continued to look calm. Laman was standing, arms folded, feet apart, and expression blank. Lemuel's gaze shifted from his father, toward Bekka and Riddah, to the ground, and back to his father. Sam was fidgeting with a strip of leather. Nephi stood still with his eyes closed. I found myself biting my nails.

Papa spoke, "Zoram, an adopted member of Lehi's household, has asked for the hand of my daughter, Mary, in marriage. I have given permission for their betrothal, upon his word to treat her well." Mary looked up slowly at Zoram, and he gazed back at her, smiling tenderly. A shy smile came to her lips and grew until she was absolutely radiant.

"I have given permission for my second daughter, Riddah, to be betrothed to Laman, first son of Lehi." Laman smiled, unfolded his arms, and clasped his hands behind his back. Riddah seemed to relax, and a light laugh escaped her lips. Bekka was staring at the ground.

"My permission has been given for my third daughter, Bekka, to be betrothed to Lemuel, the second son of Lehi." Lemuel looked toward Bekka hesitantly. She looked back at him and smiled slightly, and a tear escaped the corner of her eye. She did not wipe it away.

"My fourth daughter, Naola, has been betrothed to Sam, the third son of Lehi." Naola clapped her hands silently and seemed to bounce on her toes briefly. Sam grinned and forgot about his strip of leather.

"My last and fifth daughter, Devorah, shall be betrothed to Nephi, the fourth son of Lehi." Nephi opened his eyes and grinned at me. I smiled back joyfully. He worked his way over to me through the sudden commotion and grasped my hand. Before we could say anything, Papa intervened, kissed me on the forehead, and began shaking Nephi's hand energetically.

When I looked around again, Lehi was gazing at me with a mixture of sadness and contentment. Mama was sobbing into her head shawl, with Mary's arms around her shoulders. Papa went over to shake Zoram's hand heartily. Naola and Sam were talking quietly. Bekka had disappeared, and Riddah was laughing with Laman and Lemuel. Abisha and Kora had their arms around each other's waists and looked on silently but contentedly as Mori and Gid talked. I went to the edge of camp and sat down on a little rise, facing the hills where the men usually went hunting, and watched the sun set.

I wasn't sure what the future would hold, but I felt I had crossed a threshold from my childhood to adulthood. I suddenly had a fear that I might not measure up to what Nephi's expectations were of me. Nephi, I vowed, will not regret having me for his wife.

Nephi kept his promise made to me earlier that he would teach me some reading and writing, both Hebrew and Egyptian. I never directly told Mama, although I suspected she knew, but I did feel I ought to obtain Papa's permission. When I finally approached him about it, it was with some dread.

"What is it, Didi?" he asked gently, half hidden in the shade of his tent. I drew closer and sat down in front of him.

"Papa," I began my carefully thought out words. "You and Mama have always encouraged learning and worthwhile activities in your children, daughters as well as sons." I paused; his face was attentive, but an eyebrow was raised. "I have now an opportunity to learn a worthwhile skill from a good and willing teacher, a skill that I promise I will use wisely and appropriately."

He waited but I did not go on. "And what is that skill, Daughter?"

"Reading and writing, Papa." I watched for signs of approval or not. "It would not be a wasted skill on me, Papa. I could read or write for you when your eyes grow too dim, I can teach my sons. It will not interfere with my other responsibilities, and I will not read that which I should not."

I waited what seemed a forever of silence. "And who is going to teach this skill to a woman?" he finally asked.

I almost faltered at the unspoken comment in his tone of voice. "Nephi," I answered.

"Nephi," he said in a low voice to himself. "Nephi does have some strange ideas at times. But he is not a troublemaker, and he has some sense about him, though young. Well." Papa raised his head and looked at me. "If Nephi feels he is doing the right thing by teaching you letters and you are willing, then I can only give my permission to the endeavor."

"Thank you, Papa!" I cried and gave him a kiss atop his balding forehead before skipping off.

It was not easy, learning the symbols of sounds and expression, especially the ones less often used. Nephi would teach me one or two in the morning, and I would practice writing them during the day with the ones I already knew, and he would test me in the evening. Gradually I was able to read and write longer and more difficult words and phrases, and I felt that I was learning how to see a lush green valley that I had always walked past before and not even known was there. My sisters did not feel the same way as me, and this was more difficult for me than the learning itself.

"Our sister is aspiring to become a man," Riddah would joke. "Perhaps she will become our next rabbi."

I usually just turned my back and concentrated on my work, humming a tune to sound nonchalant. But even Naola didn't like it, and that hurt the worst.

"How can you do it, Didi?" she asked once. "Why don't you just tell Nephi 'Thank you' but you've learned enough now?"

I attempted to reason with her. "Do you realize that this is a new world opening up to me, Naola? No longer will I have to depend on someone else to communicate in writing if needed or to read a message. I will not go beyond my bounds knowingly. But I do hope to read the words of the prophet Isaiah myself someday, if that is not improper." I looked at her slyly. "I could even teach you some characters!"

Naola recoiled. "No, thank you, Didi! I have no desire."

Feeling not quite accepted by the women folk, I took advantage of a hunting trip one morning and asked the men if I could go with them "for the fun of it, to keep them company."

"Sorry, Sis," Mori responded. "This is men's work, you'd only slow us down."

Nephi noticed my disappointment. "She won't get in the way, I'll make sure of it. She understands the rules of—"

Laman cut him off with an abrupt cutting hand gesture, and the others followed him down the trail leading toward the hills. Nephi started after them slowly, then turned, and with a wink and a hand-stop followed by a beckoning gesture which his brothers didn't notice, he communicated to me the plan that I should follow after a short wait. I smiled in return then shivered in excitement.

I inscribed a message using some of the characters Nephi had taught me in the sand by my father's tent, then after waiting the allotted time and making sure no one was watching, I followed the course the men had taken.

I climbed the hill enclosing the valley away from the sea and, where the trail dipped into a gully, found Nephi alone, sitting on a rock, fiddling with his bow.

He looked up and grinned. "So you got my message and really wanted to come after all!" He stood up and slung the graceful steel bow to his shoulder. "Since the others didn't care to have you along with them, Didi, we'll just have to pick a different place to hunt!"

I pulled a cloth-wrapped bundle out of my pocket, which I had procured before leaving. "Then I guess they won't be able to share in the lunch I brought," I said in mock sorrow.

We both laughed and bantered lightheartedly as we scrambled over rocks and ditches.

"Tired of practicing your letters today?" Nephi asked.

"Nope," I said and paused. I didn't want him to know how the other women felt about it. "I just thought that with relatively little women's work to do today—"

"Sh!" Nephi warned suddenly. I froze obediently. There was a rustle in the bushes to his left, and Nephi quickly, silently nocked an arrow to his bow and poised, ready to shoot whatever appeared.

There was a sudden thrashing in the bushes, and two frightened hares leaped out and dashed up the hill. He let fly the arrow and one dropped dead. He started up after it.

"Those are the loudest two rabbits I've ever seen, how lucky that they would just jump out like that—" Nephi was interrupted by a scream that tore itself from my throat.

I had felt a sudden hot pain pierce my left ankle, and I jumped back a couple of feet, staring in fascinated surprise at a large snake, slithering around a rock to face me again. There was a *hsst*, and a second of Nephi's arrows went home, stealing life from the startled serpent.

Through a growing haze, I heard Nephi calling my name and I felt his arms around me, helping me to sit down against the rock.

"Are you all right, Didi?" his tortured voice asked. "Oh, please tell me you're all right!"

Sitting down helped clear some of the dizziness away. "I'm sorry I screamed," I said searching his face. "It was a poisonous snake, wasn't it?" I still felt no fear, but my hands groped for my left ankle. And I couldn't stop the childishness of the sound of my voice in my ears. "I never expected to get bitten by a poisonous snake."

I felt Nephi prying my hands off my ankle almost forcefully. "Oh, Didi!" he whispered hoarsely. "It really did bite you." He closed his eyes for a minute then looked up at me with mixed wonder and pain in his face. "This may sound like a strange idea," he told me quietly. "But I'm going to cut open the bite and suck out the poison. Do you think you can take it?"

I nodded to him. My ankle must have been going numb for I hardly felt any pain while he worked. He used his small knife blade to gently slit the skin between the fang marks on my anklebone, then leaned over my extended leg, and sucked and spit numerous times.

After a few minutes, I felt my head swimming with dizziness again. Without a word, I let my shoulders sink to the ground and closed my eyes.

Nephi immediately stopped working on the bite and leaned over me, gripping me by the shoulder until I opened my eyes.

"Say a prayer for me, Nephi," I murmured. "The dizziness . . ."

I felt his hands cradling my head and his voice rising in earnest prayer, but I couldn't concentrate on what he said. In what were disconnected moments of time, I saw him wrapping a cloth tightly around my calf then felt myself being lifted and carried jarringly over rough terrain. After what seemed like hours, I heard the sound of several voices grating in my ears and felt myself being placed against pillows and blankets. I sighed in relief, and complete darkness replaced the grayness of my world.

I spent forever in a timelessness consisting of hot, tormenting dreams before I awoke one afternoon, exhausted but finally fully conscious.

I heard a rustling of skirts, the flapping of a tent panel, then heavier footsteps, and Nephi was at my side, eyes bloodshot and weary, with Mary behind him.

"Nephi," I croaked. "You look like you've hardly slept for days."

"Look who's doing the talking!" he returned, a slight smile of relief breaking over his features. "Scaring us like that and worrying about me getting sleep?" His expression became solemn again as he grasped my hand and squeezed it. "I'm so grateful you came back to us, Didi."

Over the next couple of days, my strength returned slowly. My ankle was swollen and sore for a few days longer, and I limped on it for a while, but soon that, too, healed.

Although we never spoke of it, I shared an undefinable bond with Nephi since the snake incident, which I knew arose from something more than just the gratitude I felt toward him. It was the result of a third party's influence, invoked by the prayer Nephi had offered at my side in the wilderness that day.

One day as I was sweeping out the inside of my family's tent, I heard Nephi's voice at the entrance. I replaced the basket of household items I had just swept under and went to the doorway.

"Oh, there you are, Didi," he was breathing hard. "My mother needs your help for a while."

I tossed the short bundle of sticks that was my broom into the corner by the door and followed Nephi outside and over to his family's tent. Mother Sariah was sitting on the ground, her newborn son, Jacob, swaddled and perched on the rug beside her. She was kneading something pink in a bowl in her lap and laying strips of it out on a cloth in the sun. Beyond her lay another cloth covered with similar pieces, but these were already browned by the sun. My sisters and sisters-in-law stood around her and watched in silence.

"What is this?" I asked, stepping forward to get a closer look.

"Something to do with strange cravings one gets being with child," offered Bekka.

"Not after giving birth," Naola retorted.

"It's raw meat," said Riddah, turning her head to the side and gagging. "Lemuel said this is what we're going to be eating all the time if we ever go deeper into the wilderness."

"It shouldn't be that bad after being browned in the sun," began Naola. Bekka and Kora gave her looks of disgust.

"I can't imagine it would have any nutritious value for the little ones," commented Abisha. "All those spices the meat was dipped in would destroy their little systems."

"It's called basturma," Sariah said, working away.

"The nomads and deep desert traders live on this," said Nephi quietly. "Their children do very well, as a matter of fact. Here, try a piece." He picked up a few that had been sun-browned and popped one in his mouth. "It's delicious," he mumbled, chewing. "Here."

No one moved to take a piece from his hand. He held them out to everyone in the circle until he came to me, then stopped, hand still outstretched. His eyes were pleading. *This is important to him,* I thought. *He really expects that we will eventually have to be eating this stuff, and it would be much better if we ate it willingly.* The thought turned my stomach. I wasn't much one for trying new food, especially food completely foreign to me. But Nephi was my betrothed, and if I didn't support him in this . . .

I reached out and took a piece of basturma from his hand. Trying not to think about it, I brought it up to my mouth, placed it inside, and began to chew. It was spicy but surprisingly flavorful.

"My goodness!" I exclaimed. "This isn't what I expected at all! Are you sure it's uncooked meat?" I looked into the bowl Sariah was kneading in. Then I picked up a few more browned pieces from the cloth at my feet and held them out to my sisters. "You really should try this, you'd be pleasantly surprised."

They looked at me silently. Then Naola picked one from my hand and put it into her mouth. A slow smile broke over her face. "This isn't bad!"

Soon everyone in the group had tried at least one piece. "Maybe the children could handle this after all," said Abisha, sorting through the variety of spices beside Sariah.

"It's really a nice way to keep meat edible for a longer period of time," replied Sariah, putting more strips out on the cloth. Kora reached into the bowl and began to help her lay them out.

"Thank you, Didi," Nephi said in a low voice after pulling me a short distance away. "I was afraid for a minute that prejudice was going to have its way and we'd never be able to introduce this travel food to the women folk. You've done more of a service than you realize."

I looked him in the eyes. "It wasn't easy," I said. "To tell you the truth, I only did it for you. But I'm glad now that I did." I looked at the barren hills around us. "I sense there are going to be a lot of things I will be experiencing for the first time in the near future. But I think I'm ready to face them now."

Nephi nodded then grinned. "Give me some time and I'll think up some really good ones. I must confess though, Didi, that basturma will be hard to beat."

Soon it was time to start preparing for the weddings. It was agreed that all five of us would be married the same day and that we'd have the usual big celebration accompanying it. We decided to invite our desert neighbors and began a good couple of weeks beforehand preparing the food and rearranging the tents to house guests.

The morning before the weddings dawned hot like any other day, but there was an excitement in the air even the little children felt. Before we had quite finished cleaning up breakfast, Mori's oldest boy, Zachariah, often shortened to Zac, came running up to his parents excitedly.

"Mama! Papa! Someone is coming! Coming from that a-way!" Eagerly he pointed toward the hills through which we had first entered the valley.

Kicking up a fine cloud of dust plodded four camels with riders in light-colored robes. As they drew closer, several figures of various heights in long black robes could be seen walking behind them. It was the first of our wedding guests, a desert-living family we had passed several times on our trips to the port town three days away. Lehi and Papa came forward and greeted them, behaving like perfect traditional desert hosts. Soon Mama and Sariah had welcomed the women folk into a sectioned-off area of my parents' tent, prepared specifically to receive the female wedding guests. Lehi's sons led the visitors' camels to the watering trough then secured them in our corral by the small clump of trees beyond.

Through the day many other guests arrived, more than I could count. I wondered how so many people could be living near us and we cross their paths so infrequently. I was awed by the intricacy and colorful brightness of the embroidery on the women's dark robes. The quick intelligence and beauty in the faces of the brown-skinned children running around next to my fair nieces and nephews made me realize what a different world we were a part of now. Would we really adjust to living a nomadic desert life? I thought of all the luxuries we had in our home at Jerusalem and how most of these people had not even an inkling of the existence of such things. How fortunate we were! No, had been. No, still were.

The first day of festivities just about undid me. Going around and speaking with all the guests was exhausting even for me who usually enjoyed crowds; I don't know how Mary, usually quite reserved, survived it. At least there were five of us brides to spread out the effort of hosting and gain a little time for rest. I could tell Mama was feeling the strain of hostessing, but Sariah seemed to thrive on the hustle and bustle, even with having to care for little Jacob.

Finally the third day for the weddings arrived. Early in the morning my sisters and I, accompanied by Mama, Sariah, Abisha, and Kora, entered a back part of the women's tent to dress for the ceremony. I pulled from my bundle of clothing my best dress and head shawl, the one I had brought for the Sabbath. In Jerusalem, I would have worn a new dress bought or made specifically for the wedding and perhaps a head shawl made of lace. I could just imagine the disappointment Riddah was feeling at having to wear a simple Sabbath dress, with Mary feeling pure excitement that she would be getting married at all. Being so tired, I hadn't absorbed that I was really getting married.

"Oh, Mary," Naola scolded. "Stop chewing your nails! You look marvelous. You don't have to worry about a thing! Just do what Hannah did at her wedding last summer: look calm and let the rabbi tell you what to do." Naola giggled. "Just think! By sundown you'll be a married woman!"

I looked up from fumbling at the bodice of my dress and caught Bekka's eye. She was biting her lip. I nodded my head toward Naola while looking at Bekka, then shook my head while rolling my eyes. Bekka smiled and nodded slightly. I looked down at my dress again and heard Naola's words echoing in my ears: "By sundown you'll be a married woman."

Suddenly my hands trembled. Married! Thoughts of what that meant, as much as anyone not yet in that position could know, sent my mind reeling. My fingers felt cold, I shivered, and suddenly I felt faint. Why should I feel this sudden fear? I looked around at my sisters. Well, if they didn't look calm, at least they didn't look terrified. Naola actually glowed. Did she even consider what awaited her, what awaited each of us?

I shook myself mentally. What was I thinking? Every married woman had made it very well through those first days and nights with their husbands, and we would too. To top it off, the men we were marrying were good men, and we could expect to be treated well. At least I couldn't think of Nephi purposefully hurting anyone. Besides, he was someone I wanted to spend my life with. All would be well. The faintness left me, I straightened my shoulders, and found my fingers once again steady enough for the task at hand.

When we were ready, Mama brought out of her wooden chest a gift for each of us, heirloom gifts that she had been saving for just this occasion.

"For Mary, my eldest daughter," said Mama, handing her the first item wrapped in a clean white cloth. "I give you the gold necklace from Egypt worn by my grandmother on her wedding day."

Mary unwrapped the package with trembling fingers and held up the glittering chain in her hand, cradling it. Mori's wife, Abisha, took it from Mary's grasp and placed it gently around her neck. A tear rolled down Mary's cheek.

"Riddah, to you I give great aunt Siri's wedding veil." Riddah unwrapped her package and caressed the lace edged shawl for a moment. Then in one swift movement, she removed her Sabbath shawl and slowly, carefully placed the new one over her hair in its place.

"Bekka, for you I saved a white lily made of silk your paternal grandmother received from her husband from one of his business travels to the east. It will fasten where you wish to wear it." Bekka raised her left hand to her ear, and Kora fastened it into her hair right there. A light smile played on Bekka's lips.

"Naola, this is the ring my mother received on the day of her betrothal. Your hands are small enough, it should fit you." Naola slipped the ring onto her little finger and it fit. It was simple, but added grace to her already pretty hands.

"And Didi, for you I have this box that you can keep treasures in. It belonged to your great aunt after whom you were named. It is rather irregular, but was made by her husband shortly before he died, and was her most prized possession. Her name is engraved inside the lid."

I opened the cloth surrounding it and found a small cedar box with what looked like flowers carved on its worn surface. I loosened the leather clasp and opened the lid. The inside of the bottom was lined with a red cloth, still brilliant after all these years. The letters inside the lid I recognized as spelling my name, Devorah. I thought about what treasures I would keep inside it. The white stone from our yard in Jerusalem? I hurried to find it, placed it inside the cedar box, and then stored it carefully among my belongings. It was now time to go outside.

It was strange holding a traditional Israelite wedding ceremony in the midst of desert guests. But Father Lehi, who married us, carried himself with authority, and the guests were quiet and respectful. It was hard for me to imagine such honor for another's traditions being shown by the people in Jerusalem had it been a desert-traveling family in their midst. I found myself liking these people more and more.

Lehi, standing near the altar he had built for sacrifice, called Mary and Zoram up first. She was radiant, he was nervous, both seemed shy. As they were pronounced husband and wife, Mary began to cry, and Zoram gently wiped her tears with his hand and then kissed her on the lips. Any fears I'd had for Mary's happiness disappeared.

It was hard to restrain ourselves from breaking into cheering and singing, but there were yet four marriages to go. Riddah came forward regally, and Laman, dressed in a handsome colorful desert robe, was looking pleased. The moment they were legal, he gave her a dramatic, drawn-out kiss on the lips, and a few of the guests gave a cheer. Blushing, Riddah rushed to join the group of ladies at the side.

After them stepped forward Bekka and Lemuel. Her mouth was drawn into a smile, but her eyes, I saw, looked pained. Lemuel, also dressed in a bright desert robe, stood looking straight ahead at his father. They disappeared quickly from my view into the groups of guests after their ceremony. I got the sense that Lemuel's heart was toward Riddah, and that Bekka knew it. I prayed that Lemuel would learn to love Bekka as much as she wanted to love him.

Naola, the prettiest of the brides in my mind, gracefully took her place before Lehi, with Sam, dressed in his Sabbath robes, at her side. When Lehi was through, Sam kissed her, took Naola's hand, and led her to the group of women guests where her sisters were waiting before retiring to his place among the men.

Now it was my turn. Looking calm but trembling inside, I stepped forward. Nephi was waiting, smiling at me. I dropped my gaze for a moment then lifted it again and returned Nephi's smile. I barely heard the words of Lehi's joining and blessing. As soon as he was finished, shouts and cheers arose from the guests, and as various musical instruments started playing, singing began. Nephi and I just stood looking in each other's eyes. At seventeen, I still felt very young to be a married woman.

"My wife, Devorah," he said quietly, taking my hand.

"Nephi, my husband," I replied smiling, and squeezed his hand.

Suddenly, we were both being lifted up on the shoulders of guests and paraded around with our recently married siblings. I felt giddy from the turning, but could only lay back my head and laugh. Soon we were put down, and the feasting and dancing began in earnest. Then gifts from the guests were brought forward: food, baskets, embroidered robes, various household tools necessary for desert life, water bladders, and camel hair tent panels. The visiting women were eager to talk and tell of their own marriage traditions. Soon one group of women began to piece together tent panels, many of them obtained from the once large tents of Lehi and Ishmael, and another group of men gathered to erect them into five new tents, small but sturdy. Soon the sun sank behind the hills, and the young children were put to bed; but the rest of the guests continued their lively talking, eating, singing, and dancing.

Never had Mary looked so happy and Riddah so sophisticated, Bekka danced so gracefully, or Naola been more enthusiastic. Mama glowed with quiet pride, and Papa boasted about how many grandchildren he would have. My earlier fears never crossed my mind until it came time to retire to bed.

"Didi," came Mary's voice from behind me as I dragged myself toward the lady's tent. "Where do you think you're going?"

"Inside, to go to . . ." I paused and felt my face flushing hot in the dark. "Oh my! Thank you, Mary, for catching me! How could I forget we have our own tents?" I laughed shakily. "After all, we're married women now."

I felt her hand on my arm give a gentle squeeze. "You'll be just fine," she whispered and was gone. I smiled to myself at the irony of the situation: Mary comforting me for once!

I turned and stepped toward Nephi's and my new small abode. On the way I passed the coals of the party's bonfire and grasped a partially burned stub of wood with some coals still glowing on it.

"Hello!" I called at the tent's doorway. All was silent and dark. I swept aside the doorway hanging and entered. After fumbling for long minutes among the items around the doorway, I found a small lamp left as a gift, and lit the oil inside. A warm glow filled the one room.

Various items that were gifts hung from the tent supports or sat on the floor. A small bed lay in the corner as tidy as if Mama had prepared it herself. My personal items lay next to it on one side, and a couple of bundles I assumed to be Nephi's lay on the other side. I shivered and went over to my things to withdraw my warmer shawl and throw it around my shoulders. With fingers trembling again, I rearranged the pillows on the bed and pulled the coverlet down to the bottom. Looking around, my eye spotted a small water bladder by the door. I eagerly unhooked it, passed out of the tent door, and headed down to the water hole to fill it. I could hear low muffled voices from the large ladies' tent, but all else was quiet. Finished with my task, I headed back up the hill and then paused to gaze at the little tent that was my new home. Nephi came up beside me and put his hand around my waist. My heart began to pound from his touch.

Nephi was silent, and I could think of nothing to say. Then he swept the door covering back with his arm. "Welcome to our new home, Devorah," he said, and his voice cracked. I entered and then turned to face him as he came in.

"I got you something to drink, Nephi," I said and handed him the bladder. My voice trembled.

He took a swallow from its neck and then set it on the ground. "Thanks very much, Didi," he said, licking his lips. He paused again. Suddenly he laughed and his teeth flashed in the lamplight. "Are you as scared as I am?" he asked.

"Yes!" I answered almost without thinking, relief in my voice. Then I laughed too. "How silly."

I felt Nephi take my hand in his. "You don't have to be afraid, Didi," he said quietly. He touched my hair with his other hand once. "You know I would never purposefully hurt you."

I swallowed and nodded. "Yes, I know, Nephi."

He kissed me on the forehead, lightly, and then looked around the room. "I had been dreaming of providing you with a wonderful large house, Didi," he said quietly. "Sturdy and protective from all the elements, and in a nice neighborhood. I didn't quite have a small nomadic tent in mind." He looked at me again, his left eyebrow lifted slightly.

I laughed, glanced away, and then looked up at him again. His face was serious now. "Oh, Nephi!" I said quickly, softly. "The house doesn't matter, what it's made out of. It's the home you make out of it, the people that are inside it, the atmosphere you bring into it, that matters. At least that is what Mama says."

He looked into my eyes without saying a word. Then he kissed me again, lingeringly, on the lips. "The Lord has truly blessed me to give me a wife like you, Didi."

I couldn't, for the life of me, find my voice, but I squeezed his hand firmly. After gazing at me a moment longer, he led me over to the bed, and I sat down upon it. Then he returned to the lamp and puffed out the flame. Enveloped in darkness, I lay back, strangely calm. I heard Nephi rustling beside me and felt his arm touching my shoulder. I took a deep breath, let it out slowly, and then snuggled up against him, my heart happy.

It was only a few days after the wedding guests had departed and things returned basically to normal that Nephi and I were awakened at dawn by a commotion outside, voices calling and footsteps crunching quickly through the sand.

"What is it, Nephi?" I asked, seeing him sit up to listen better.

"I'm not sure," he shook his head. "I'll be right back." He threw on an outer robe and ducked out through the door. I pulled my warmest shawl over my head and followed after him. The other families were gathering outside Lehi and Sariah's tent and whispering excitedly. Nephi pushed his way to his father's side and looked over his shoulder. I stood on tiptoe but could not see over the others' shoulders nor tell what everyone was so excited about.

"My brother Ishmael and my children," I heard Lehi's deep resonant voice above the hubbub. "I have something to say unto you." The noise dissipated to a hush.

"I have had a dream, another night vision," spoke Lehi again. Someone groaned. Lehi seemed to ignore it. "We are to pack our things, and on the morrow, take our journey into the wilderness."

Voices erupted again, and above the noise one voice rang clearly. It was Lemuel's. "Father, not again! This is the wilderness! How can you call anything wilderness besides this? Aren't we far enough from Jerusalem to satisfy you? How far must we go?"

Lehi turned to look at him. "It is not I that desires this, my son. It is the Lord."

"Yes, and let me guess," spoke Laman's voice, "that funny looking exotic metal ball in your hand just appeared from nowhere as a sign that you should go." I could see nothing of what Lehi held, except for a flash of reflected sunlight as the person to my right shifted slightly.

"Son, it was outside the door of my tent this morning. I have never seen this fine of workmanship before in all of my travels. And the timing with the voice of the Lord is undeniable. What do you make of this object, my family?" He held it up and I could just make out a ball of round arches intricately carved in brass colored metal, with two spindles in the middle of it.

Laman said nothing, but his arms were folded, and he was just perceptively shaking his head.

"Look, Father!" exclaimed Sam. "No matter which way you turn that ball, that arm keeps pointing the same way, that way." Sam pointed south-southeast, opposite the direction we had come from Jerusalem. Voices fell silent once more.

"There is a trading route in that direction," spoke Lehi softly. "It travels through many miles of wilderness, with oases interspersed. One branch of the route even crosses a great desert. I have never taken it but have talked with travelers who have. It is a long and rough road. Only the experienced dare traverse it."

"Father," said Lemuel shakily, his joviality gone, "you aren't thinking of going that way, are you?"

A low hum of voices rippled through the group. I knew what Mori and Gid were thinking. Travel that route? Not with our women and children!

"My sons and my daughters!" Lehi's face was firm. The noise hushed. "The Lord back at Jerusalem commanded me to take my family and go with them into the wilderness. We are to raise up unto him a righteous people in the Land of Promise. Do not bring shame upon your heads and mine by dividing up this family. If one can claim no family, what is there in this world to claim?" He looked around the group wearily. "The Lord has promised to lead us to the Land of Promise, even though the way be difficult. If that is the way the ball points, this Liahona, then that is the way we shall go. Anyone who is not with us, now is your chance to speak."

No one moved or spoke. I hoped we would not have a recurrence of the rebellion that occurred on our journey to this valley with the sons of Lehi. But Laman and Lemuel stood with heads bowed, and my brothers and sisters said nothing.

"Well, what are you all standing there for?" Lehi finally broke the silence. "Gather the tents and provisions together to be ready for loading onto the camels. We leave tomorrow at the break of day. And may God bless us in our endeavor."

CHAPTER 3

PLACE OF THE BROKEN BOW

We traveled for four days straight after leaving the Valley of Lemuel, resting for several hours during the hottest parts of the days and during the darkest hours of the nights. I was tired long before we reached the stopping place where we would set up our tents, and wondered how the little children and Papa and Mama managed the pace. But Lehi had warned us in advance that we could not stop long in between water sources, for though we could carry enough water for our own consumption and for our few sheep, the camels would have to go on what they had drunk at the last watering hole. We quickly left the mountains surrounding the Valley of Lemuel, and as we traveled further south-southeast, the flat stretches of land surrounded by low hills offered only coarse clumps of grass and tamarisk bushes. By the men's report from exploration while hunting, there were few other more fertile areas. With any animal but camels, we would have had difficulty traveling this area, not just for the water problem but for the ground becoming increasingly soft and sandy. Though Mori's wife, Abisha, didn't ever actually say she was glad to be traveling by camel, she stopped complaining about the animals fairly quickly.

On the fourth day of travel from the Valley of Lemuel, I noticed my camel pricking up his ears and twitching them back and forth. Suddenly he picked up his pace, and it was all I could do to keep my balance on top. I looked up and noticed the other animals were keeping pace with mine.

I spotted Nephi a couple of yards away. "What's going on with the camels?" I called out to him breathlessly.

"We're near the oasis," he called back between lurches of his own animal. "They do this when they're thirsty and smell water."

The camels must have had an extraordinary sense of smell, for instead of finding the oasis at the bottom of the next hill, it was a couple of hours before we came to it. Needless to say, we were all glad to get off the animals and stretch our stiff muscles while they guzzled the water down.

The oasis consisted of low ground water seepage surrounded by trees and grassy plants. It seemed dry after the green of the Valley of Lemuel, but with its trees, it was lush compared to the dry dirt and brush plains through which we had been traveling. After the tents were erected and the men had a short rest, they took their bows and slings and headed into the nearby hills to hunt. As long as there was game handy, we were hesitant to delve into our supplies of dried fruit, honey, oil, barley, and wheat, or the grain seeds brought for planting.

The stay at the place we called Shazer was sweet, but short. We stayed for a few weeks, just until we felt well rested. In that time, the animals had exhausted the nearby grazing areas, we had eaten all of the fruit the trees offered, and the water source was muddied and insect-ridden. We then packed our tents and traveled on again.

We traveled in the same manner from oasis or well to the next, stopping at each just long enough to rest and hunt again. Occasionally, if the hills we traveled by looked at all promising for game, a couple of the men would slip off from the group to catch something and then rejoin us a little later on. Sariah fussed and worried a lot while they were gone, but those jaunts supplied us with much-needed game. I must admit, it was fun to watch Mori and Gid becoming much better hunters, but I was also much relieved every time the men returned safely.

After several weeks of travel, we reached a long green valley oasis, once again in mountainous territory. It looked as if it were a popular spot, as the remains of other visitors' campsites could be seen in the valley. Pomegranate trees were relatively numerous near the watering hole, with others scattered the length of the valley. As we descended into it, a humid but cooler salty breeze hit us, refreshing after the still, dusty air of past camping sites.

"Oh, how I love this breeze!" exclaimed Kora, opening her head veil and flapping it to fan the air around her body.

"And look how green this valley is!" added Riddah. "Oh, Papa! Please tell Lehi we want to stay here as long as possible!"

The little children were begging to get off the camels and go run amongst the trees. Kora and Naola volunteered to attend to them while the others chose a spot further down the valley to set up camp. Lehi and Ishmael went together to explore the valley while things were unloaded and the animals led to drink. Soon they returned.

"This seems to indeed be an ideal spot to stay awhile," Lehi told the group. "There are areas of good soil that ought to be quite fertile if handled right. I think we ought to plant grain here and rest ourselves until it's harvested." He glanced at Ishmael and then gazed at Sariah.

"I like that idea very much," she said, and all agreed with cheers.

For the next two weeks, we prepared the ground and planted the seed that had been grown in the Valley of Lemuel. With many hands, the work went quickly. It was exciting to think of being in one place for a period of time again. Then the men went into the hills to hunt for food. Two days later they returned.

Several children came running up excitedly, Gid's son, Gad, pulling his little sister, Johanna, along.

"They're back!" Zac pulled on his Abisha's sleeve insistently. "Daddy's back from the hunting trip! Come on, Mama!"

All of us dropped our work and followed excitedly. We were eating the last of our supply of fruits and nuts and were eager to get at the new catches. But as we approached them, it was plain to see they were empty-handed, and the expressions on their faces were not encouraging. We met them silently.

Zac's younger brother, Matthew, broke the silence. "Where's food, Daddy?"

Mori looked away. The others shifted uncomfortably. "There's not much game," he began.

Lemuel could stand it no longer. "Nephi broke his bow. And our bows don't work, their springs are gone and they bend like cloth." He threw his bow onto the ground. The bowstring looked stretched out, and the normal bow curvature was straightened. Nephi held the pieces of his once fine steel bow in his hands, the inside looking rusted and rotten.

"It seems to be the moisture and humidity of this part of the country," Nephi began. His voice was mild, but his eyebrows were knitted together in the middle. He cleared his throat but said nothing more.

I swallowed the urge to state sarcastically that maybe our brothers had not cared for their bowstrings as they ought.

"Even what animals there are, are few and far between," said Zoram. He tried to look calm, but his voice shook. He would not look at Mary. Sam gazed at his father pleadingly. Gid and Mori simply appeared lost.

Laman was gripping the wood of his bow as if he would tear it apart. "If only Nephi hadn't broken that steel bow. I told him he was drawing it too hard. At least we would have had one bow to hunt with. Now we have nothing. We shall all perish here in the wilderness. If we were to perish, at least we could have stayed in our home at Jerusalem." He looked at his father pointedly.

Lehi slowly bowed his head. "I have no answers," he said quietly. He stood unmoving for several minutes then turned and wearily walked toward his tent. Sariah followed after him picking nervously at the cloth wrapped around the child in her arms.

The rest of us turned to look at Ishmael. Mama was gazing up at him steadily. He said not a word but took Mama by the arm and led her away to their tent. She let him lead her, head now lowered. The others silently went to their tents. Nephi was the last one to move. I went up to him and grasped his hand.

"There's got to be a way," he whispered fiercely, and he clenched his other hand into a fist. He looked over at me, and his shoulders sagged. "But what it is I don't know." He let me lead him back to our tent.

The next two days were difficult for all of us. We ate the last sheep that Lehi had been saving for sacrifice. Sariah made a little flatbread from a small bag of grain she had saved. There was just enough camel's milk to feed the youngest children. We rationed out the last of the food and tried to fill ourselves with water from the well. The seed grain had been planted. The pomegranate trees were not in the fruit-bearing season. The sun beat down in the humid heat, and there was no longer any breeze to cool us. Tempers grew shorter, and almost every conversation returned to "if we were at Jerusalem."

Both days Nephi spent a couple of hours in the hills, but each time he dragged himself back looking more exhausted. The rest of the time he either wandered around the valley or sat in front of the tent staring at the ground. I couldn't bear to see him like this, but neither could I tear myself away. I mostly stayed out of sight inside the tent watching him. It was while he was sitting at the tent door that Laman came up to him.

Laman stood and looked down at him a minute. Then he kicked at the sand in front of Nephi, and Nephi looked up. Laman clenched and unclenched his fists. Suddenly he grabbed Nephi by the shirt and raised him to his feet.

"Damn it, little brother!" he hissed, and shook Nephi hard. "Would you do something useful for once?" Laman let go of Nephi and turned away a moment. Then he faced him again, and shook a finger in his face. "If you and Father hadn't dragged us out here into the wilderness we would not be in this fix. Our families are starving! We are starving! What are you going to do about it?" Laman clenched his fists again and shook them at the sky. "Why would you do this to us, God?"

At this Nephi came to life. He grasped Laman's arm. "Do not speak to God that way!" Laman turned to face him, fists still clenched. "Do you not recall all the times the Lord has aided us? Look at how he has blessed us in our journey so far. We, mere city folks, surviving without any mishaps here in the wilderness, with small children even, and we have not even gotten lost. Aren't those great blessings? I know God's purpose was not to bring us out into the wilderness to die, I feel it in my soul. He would have let us die much earlier if that was his purpose. No, we are in this situation because there is something for us to learn."

Laman threw up his hands and turned away. "I knew I shouldn't have wasted the energy."

"My brother!" Nephi grasped his arm again. Laman threw it off. "Have patience with the Lord."

"'Have patience with the Lord,'" Laman mimicked and stalked away.

"Patience and humility," Nephi said to himself. He sat down again and then stood up. "I'm going to talk with Father," he said.

I didn't have the energy to follow him. Inside the shade of the tent, I let my tears run freely. I understood exactly what Laman was feeling.

I must have fallen asleep, for the sun had moved a ways when Nephi returned. He kicked at the dirt at the front of the tent and paced a few steps. "All of them," he said to no one in particular, "they're all angry, all complaining, all speaking against God." He held his face in his hands for a moment. Then he sat down and began digging at the ground with a long stick. "No solutions, no ideas, no trying even. How do they expect God to help?" Suddenly Nephi looked at the stick in his hand. "Didi!" he called to me, urgency in his voice. "Didi, are you there?"

I didn't want to move. "Yes," I croaked.

He almost ran inside the tent. "Tell me my eyes do not deceive me," he said excitedly. "What is this I hold in my hand?"

I looked at him in disbelief. He ran all the way inside to ask about a stick? He's more delirious than I thought. "That's a stick, Nephi," I answered, humoring him.

"Good, Didi. Now describe the stick to me."

"Oh, Nephi. I don't have the energy. Is it really that important?" His eyes were serious, imploring. I sat up and took the stick from him. "It's about the length of my arm," I said. "It has very few knots on it, it's perfectly straight, it looks like it comes from one of those trees out there, and it's hard, probably just the kind Matthew would use to hit Zac with." I handed the stick back to Nephi. "If you think it useful to dig holes with, go ahead, Nephi. I won't stop you."

He grinned. "That's what I thought, Didi. Thanks!" He went outside the tent and disappeared.

About an hour later, I heard scraping noises outside and some whistling. I dragged myself to the tent door and looked out. There sat Nephi, a moderately large, curved tree branch in his hand and several small straight ones by his side. He was vigorously scraping the large branch with a sharp stone, flattening one side. On the ground next to him were some long thin strands of sheep gut and rabbit sinew, drying in the sun.

"Nephi, what in heaven's name are you doing?"

He looked up. "Oh, hello, Didi. Have a seat." He went back to his scraping. "You are witnessing what I think will be a solution to our little problem here."

I didn't have the energy to comment on his use of 'little' to describe our dangerous predicament. I just sat and stared uncomprehendingly. Then suddenly it struck me. "You're making a new bow! Where in the world did you find wood stiff enough . . ." I knew the answer as I spoke. Nephi looked up at me again, and we both began to laugh.

"Pretty silly, eh?" he said, his eyes twinkling. "Here we were surrounded by the solution all the time. This pomegranate wood is amazing stuff, sturdy and strong despite the humidity. Didi, I need your help twisting the sinew strands into bowstring." I nodded and he showed me how to twist and weave the strands into a long fibrous bowstring. We worked into the night by moonlight until bow and arrows were done. Then we slept a couple of hours.

At dawn the next morning, I followed Nephi as he went to his father's tent. I couldn't help but call at the tents of my brothers and sisters on the way and tell them what Nephi was up to. Soon we were all gathered in front of Lehi's tent door. At the noise we made, he and Sariah appeared at the entrance.

"What is it, my son?" he asked, blinking in the sunlight.

Nephi held up the bow in his hand. "I now have something to hunt with, Father. Tell me where I should go to get food."

Lehi only stared at Nephi. "How should I know, my son?"

Nephi gazed steadily back at his father and spoke softly. "You are the patriarch of this family, Father. We all look to you to give us direction from the Lord." He turned and looked at the rest of us, his voice louder, firmer. "Brothers and sisters, we have not thought and looked to the Lord for help in this situation as we ought. Instead, we have complained and blamed others not responsible." He looked down at the ground a moment. "I myself have been guilty of this." Then he looked up again and straightened his shoulders. "It is still not too late to turn now to God for help. In fact, he is needed even more now. I have a bow, but need game. You men have seen how slim the game is in these hills." Nephi turned again to Lehi. "Father, once again I ask you. Whither shall I go to obtain food?"

Lehi cleared his throat. "Perhaps we should pray," he suggested.

Nephi nodded and knelt down, propping himself with his bow, and bowed his head. Mama immediately followed suit, pulling Papa behind her. I knelt simultaneously with Naola and Sam and Mary and Zoram. We were followed closely by Lehi and Sariah. Kora and Abisha followed with their children, and then Bekka and Riddah. Lastly came my two brothers and Laman and Lemuel. We were once again a family united in prayer, something we had not really done since offering sacrifice on our arrival in the Valley of Lemuel. Tears stung my eyes as Lehi lifted his voice in prayer.

Suddenly, in the middle of a sentence, Lehi stopped. After almost a minute of silence, I sneaked a peek at him. He was gazing steadily upward, a look of shock on his face. Tears started flowing down his cheeks. Without a word, he arose and almost staggered into his tent. By this time, others had looked up and were watching the scene in surprise. In a moment he returned, carrying the curious brass ball we had first seen in the Valley of Lemuel. He held it out to us with trembling hands.

"Look," he whispered hoarsely.

The Liahona looked different somehow. Then I noticed that its surface was covered with writing, many small characters. At my distance I couldn't make them out.

"What does the writing say?" I asked.

Lehi did not speak. He handed the ball to his nearest son, which was Sam. Sam rotated the ball in his hands a minute and then began to read the words aloud.

"'If thou do at all forget the Lord thy God, I testify against you this day that ye shall surely perish because ye would not be obedient unto the voice of the Lord. I, the Lord, do chasten you for the murmuring of your heart and your rebellion against the commandment of the Lord your God. Because ye have sinned against the Lord and have not obeyed my voice, therefore is this evil come upon you. And if ye walk contrary unto me and will not hearken unto me, I will bring seven times more plagues upon you according to your sins. I will utterly pluck up and destroy this nation.'"

Sam's voice broke. His face was pale. "The spindles aren't working anymore," he said, holding the ball up and turning it. He cleared his voice twice then once more. He handed the ball to Nephi and then looked down at the ground.

Nephi in turn rotated it in his hands. "Curious," his voice trembled a little. He paused and looked around at us. I felt a cold weight in the pit of my stomach. He spoke again. "There is more writing. Do any of you wish to read it?" No one answered. He began to read in a voice soft but piercing.

"'But if ye obey my voice, I will walk among you, I will be your God, and ye shall be my people. Ye shall walk in all the ways which I, the Lord your God, hath commanded you, ye shall not turn aside to the right hand or to the left, that ye may live, that it may be well with you, and that ye may prolong your days in the land which ye shall possess.'"

Nephi paused and looked up at us. The weight in my stomach seemed less cold. "There is more," he said. "'If ye will be guided by the Lord your God, take ye heed, watch, and pray. Turn to me with full purpose of heart and put your trust in me and serve me with all diligence of mind. If ye have faith and doubt not, the way shall be clear before you. Blessed are they which hear the word of God and keep it.'"

We were all silent. I felt a little ashamed of myself. I had always thought I would be more faithful to God than I had been the past few days. I guess one never knew until in a situation how one would act and think in it. I could have done better, had faith, and not murmured in my heart. I would do better.

Nephi handed the ball back to Lehi. "Where should I go to find food?" he asked yet one more time.

Lehi was gazing downward, started to shake his head, and then stopped. He looked up at us. "The directors are working again!" he exclaimed. He examined the ball again. "The spindle points in that direction," he said, pointing his hand toward the group of taller mountains behind the hills.

Nephi gazed at the mountains a moment. Then he turned to face us. "Who will come with me?" he asked. I knew I did not have the strength to go far and did not want to burden him; I said nothing.

Zoram spoke up, "I will accompany you, my friend."

"So will I, my brother," chimed in Sam. He squared back his shoulders, but I could see them trembling with the effort.

"I don't think I would be of much use to you," said Mori, head lowered. He looked up at Nephi. "Do you mind if I stay here?"

Nephi shook his head. He picked up his arrows from the ground and turned toward the mountains. "Wait, Nephi!" I called. "Let me fill your bag with water before you go." He stopped and gave me a grateful smile. I took the water bladder from our tent and hurried down to the well. While filling it, Mary and Naola joined me to fill bags for their husbands too. We smiled at each other and walked back together.

"May your hunt be successful," I said, tying the bladder onto Nephi's belt again. I gave him a quick kiss. "And may you return safely," I whispered, turning away. I looked back only to watch the men disappear over the rise of the next hill. Then I returned to the tent to await his return. This time my heart was filled with peace and hope, instead of despair and dread. I picked up the bowstring from Nephi's steel bow. On an impulse I put it into my cedar treasure box in case he ever needed it again.

Zoram and Sam returned that afternoon, long before we expected them. "I couldn't make it past the foothills," explained Sam sheepishly.

"Nephi insisted I make sure he got back safely," said Zoram. He shook his head. "I must say, I wasn't exactly in the best of shape myself. I don't know where Nephi gets all his energy. Only God knows."

"I'm glad someone has it," said Sam and gave a brief laugh.

Late the next morning, a cry went through the camp: "Nephi comes!" I hurried outside and joined the others. A lone figure appeared over the hill, carrying a large beast on his shoulder and dragging another behind him. A bounteous hunt indeed! We went to meet him and help him with the animals the rest of the way.

"It was amazing!" reported Nephi excitedly to me. "I thought we'd explored all the ideal places before, but the mountains here are teeming with life!" He tilted his head and gazed at me. "I think in future we should dry and prepare extra meat to carry with us, in case we run into sparse areas again on our journey."

"The trick will be getting our brothers to ration their supplies and save some for later," I responded quietly.

Nephi nodded thoughtfully. "Perhaps they will listen better to Father than to me. I will suggest it to him."

We lost no time in preparing a feast. The majority of meat we had eaten during weeks of travel had been dried and spiced, and the children were absolutely ecstatic over the idea of roasted meat now. There was not much to go with the main dish, but that didn't matter one bit. When all was prepared, we gathered for prayer. Papa offered it, short but full of gratitude. Then we filled ourselves to our heart's content.

One morning I awoke feeling sick to my stomach. I had felt similar stomach upheavals the previous couple of days, but none quite this bad or long lasting. Knowing how much all of us dreaded the idea of getting sick in the middle of nowhere, I swallowed the nausea with some effort and arose to fix Nephi some light breakfast, trying to appear to him as healthy and cheerful as usual. We had both awakened at the first hint of dawn, for the men had planned to go hunting again. Through clenched teeth I "smilingly" waved Nephi goodbye then quickly returned to bed to calm my heaving stomach.

By midmorning, the nausea was gone and I was able to tackle my usual tasks, though without the pleasure of having eaten any breakfast myself. Hungry at last for lunch, I decided the illness had been just a passing thing, and was glad, for I preferred many unpleasant things to an upset stomach.

Things went well until the men returned the next evening. My little nieces and nephews called out their arrival, and I went to meet Nephi, with the intention of helping him clean the prizes. He put down his load in front of our tent and gave me a tender hug and kiss. But simultaneously, the odor of blood and dead animals on his clothing assailed my nostrils, and my stomach lurched threateningly. I couldn't speak; I broke from Nephi's embrace, dashed around behind the tent, and lost my lunch. After a moment Nephi followed, and I felt his hands steadying me as I leaned over the sand.

"Honey," he began gently. "Are you all right? Is there anything I can do—"

"Yes!" I suddenly snapped. "You can take your smelly old raw meat and give it to the wild jackals, then go burn your hunting clothes before going inside and smelling up the tent."

Nephi's hands suddenly let go of me. I was shocked at what I had said. I wondered at the sudden anger I felt, which I thought I had put under control as a young teenager. I couldn't look Nephi in the face, and in a moment, he was gone, leaving me heaving mentally as well as physically.

After recuperating somewhat, I returned to the tent door, but Nephi was nowhere in sight, and the meat he had brought was gone. I went inside and fell onto the bed, sobbing.

A few minutes later a voice called in from the entrance, and Mama entered.

"Nephi tells me you're not feeling well, Didi," she said, sitting down beside me. "Is there anything I can do to help?"

It was just what I needed right then, a caring maternal arm and ear. I put my head into her lap. "Oh, Mama! I've felt so sick to my stomach this week, and I've tried to be so healthy! Then I had to go and yell at Nephi the minute he got home from hunting, and after he's been so kind and understanding too. And here I am crying like a little girl again when I'm supposed to be grown up and responsible now!" I lifted my tear-stained face to her, and with her apron, she wiped my cheeks.

She gazed at me a moment. "Is there anything else not quite normal about your health you ought to tell me about, Didi?" I stared at her without comprehension. "Is it possible this might not be a stomach illness at all but morning sickness? Is it possible you might be with child?"

I could only gape in shock. I stood up and turned away from Mama, wringing my hands in my own apron. Then I turned back. I opened my mouth and then closed it again. "How?"

Mama's eyes twinkled. "How could I ask such a question? How could I tell? Or do you want to know how babies are made?" I shook my head and opened and closed my mouth again. "Let me ask you this," Mama said, now more serious. "How long has it been since your body's been completely normal, since your last womanly cycle?"

"Well," I stammered and blushed a little. "I guess it was, ah, shortly before leaving the Valley of Lemuel." I paused. "I think it was about two moons ago, Mama."

A slow smile came over Mama's face as a tear rolled down her cheek. She came over and gently gave me a hug. "I think we've found the reason for your illness, dear little mother." She patted my cheek. "Won't your papa be pleased."

She turned and headed for the door and I called out to her. "Mama!" She stopped at the panic in my voice and looked at me. "You won't tell, will you? I mean, until . . . until we're sure?"

"I will leave the telling up to you, daughter, when you're ready," she said. I finally smiled. She smiled back, winked, and was gone.

I sat down on the bed, numb. What did I feel? Shouldn't I be ecstatic, joyful, and radiant? I wrapped my arms around my legs and let my head fall to my knees. I, a mother? Was I ready for this? Was Nephi? What if I really wasn't with child? That would be embarrassing! I mean if I had told people I was. I sat up and pushed on my tummy. I didn't feel that different. Well, perhaps sometimes a little nauseated and not quite as energetic as usual. And who was to say I didn't have a stomach illness? Ha! That would be funny after all this talk with Mama! That settled it. I would wait it out a while and see what would happen before getting everyone excited. Besides, I'm the youngest! I shouldn't be the first one of my sisters to announce this kind of news, not in this family (Gid would never let me live it down). I'd just have to apologize to Nephi and tell him I'm not feeling well.

I pulled off my outer dress and folded it carefully into my clothes bag. With still no sign of Nephi, I climbed into bed, vowing to stay awake until he returned. But before he did, I was asleep.

Before I awoke the next morning, Nephi left for one of his one-man hunting trips. I knew he usually spent very little time actually hunting on these trips, but as he took his bow, that's what I told the others he was doing. It gave me more time to ponder what Mama and I had talked about earlier and to decide that this "stomach illness" was not like any I had had before. Mama also seemed to make a point when she could catch me alone of describing other symptoms a woman with child should be having. I had them all.

That night, Nephi slipped in quietly after I had fallen asleep, and I didn't notice his presence until I rolled over and suddenly found him sleeping peacefully beside me. I stared in his direction with a silly grin on my face. I had a sudden insane desire either to hide the secret from him forever, which would never work, or to scream out for him to listen to my confession and apology this minute. In the end, I couldn't bring myself to disturb him.

The next morning he awoke ahead of me and almost succeeded in slipping out without my noticing. I got the distinct impression he was trying to avoid me.

"Nephi!" I called after him in a panic, sitting up. "Please don't go! I've got to talk to you!" He froze, his back still to me. I almost began crying at the thought that I really must have hurt him with my angry outburst the few days before, but I had to continue. "Nephi, I . . . I've got to ask your forgiveness for speaking like that to you the other day. My feeling sick was no excuse, and I'm in torment over it." I took a deep breath. "Will you forgive me?" A couple of sobs escaped my throat, at which Nephi whirled and suddenly gathered me in his arms.

"Forgive you! Oh, my darling, Didi, of course!" his voice cracked. "My thoughts when you spoke then were how insensitive I had been to expect you to help me in a job that's probably sickening to you. Will you forgive me for that?"

"Oh, Nephi! You don't even need to ask! Of course, I forgive you. You have been better to me than any woman could wish." I tilted my head. "Except for leaving me days at a time!" I smiled so he'd know I was at least partly teasing him about that. I suddenly felt a warm bubbling of excitement in my heart, and I felt I couldn't keep back the knowledge about the baby any longer. "Nephi, I-I'm . . ." But just then my stomach heaved. "Oh bother. I'm going to get sick again." I clutched one of the bed coverings to my mouth and quickly lay down. In a moment the feeling passed.

"Your illness is hanging on a long time. I think I better ask my father to come tonight give you a blessing," Nephi told me. "You just lie there and rest. I'll be back."

"No, wait." I began, but he was gone. I sighed in frustration. It was going to be harder than I thought to tell him.

That afternoon my sisters accosted me fetching water. "You've been sick a lot lately," commented Mary. "What's going on, Didi?"

"I think she's caught the stomach bug that was going around a couple of months ago," cut in Riddah. "It lasts forever, let me tell you."

"Mama says that morning sickness can make you sicker than drinking a whole bladder of brackish water," said Bekka.

"Didi!" Naola gasped. "Don't tell me you're . . . you're . . ."

"With child?" Mary finished her sentence.

I ignored them and dropped my water bag down into the spring. They all crowded around eyeing me eagerly, except Riddah who stood back, face pale, clutching her stomach.

"All right," Bekka finally said. "If you won't say yes, tell us you're not pregnant."

I finished fetching the water I needed and heaved the larger, full container to my shoulder. Still I did not respond.

"Still no answer," grinned Bekka. "She must be with child if she won't deny it. Right, sisters?"

Riddah went over behind a tree out of sight. I could hear some retching noises. I continued to walk back to my tent without saying a word. Soon they gave up following me, and I felt all my muscles relax. I didn't know they had been so tight.

My sisters knew the cause of my condition, but I still hadn't informed Nephi of it. How was I going to tell him? And how was I going to tell Father Lehi when he came that I didn't really need a blessing for the sick?

That evening, Nephi suddenly stormed into the tent, which I was cleaning, disengaged the hand broom from my fingers, threw it aside, and faced me, hands gently gripping my shoulders.

"What do you mean by keeping secrets from me?" he demanded. "People have begun talking, and I don't know fact from rumor. Is it true? Your answer could have some dire consequences." At the expression of bewilderment on my face, Nephi suddenly laughed and drew me into his arms. "I'm talking about the baby, hon. Is it true that we are going to have a baby?"

I laughed back in relief. "Who told you? Yes, it's true. And I've had the hardest time trying to figure out a way to tell you." I paused and tried to read the expression on his face. "You're not upset with me, are you? That I waited so long to let you know?"

He smiled reassuringly, and then suddenly his expression went blank. "No, not at all."

"It all seems so exciting"—I paused when I saw the look in his eyes. He seemed to be staring beyond the walls of the tent—"Nephi? Are you all right?"

His eyes refocused on me. "No. I mean yes, I'm all right. I just . . ." He took a deep breath. "I suddenly don't know if I'm ready to be a father yet, Didi. I . . . It's all so sudden."

I grasped his hand with mine. "I felt the same way, Nephi, at first. You'll get used to the idea." I stood on tiptoes to give him a kiss. Nephi only nodded, staring straight out again beyond the tent, a silly half grin on his face.

We called this valley the Place of the Broken Bow. Our time spent there was peaceful and happy. Nephi worked with the other men in making new bows and arrows for hunting. The pomegranate season came on, and the children were constantly entertained by peeling the fruit and picking out the tiny juicy seeds from their circuitous paths inside to nibble on them one by one. The planted crops grew tall above the soil. It took constant work to keep the soil moist, directing or carrying water to the irrigation ditches from the well. The sun often grew wiltingly hot, but I was glad for something to do each day and helped tend the plants as I might my own children. Soon it was harvest time, and I was excited.

We were all out in the fields the first day of harvest, the men cutting the grain, the women gathering. Abisha was watching the youngest children by the tents. I kept watching Kora, recently ill, wondering how long she would last in the heat and humidity, but she seemed to be faring quite well. Then Mary tapped me on the shoulder and pointed to Riddah. She was stopping often to mop her face with her head shawl and was beginning to look not well at all. Mary went over to her and talked for a moment. Then the two of them headed toward the tents, Mary supporting Riddah. Laman stopped briefly in his work to watch them, then lowered his head and kept on.

In a few minutes, Mary returned to my side. "Didi, I don't know what to do. Riddah says her stomach is just bothering her a little bit, but I think she might be in labor. She says she doesn't want to bother

Mama about it. But what if she has her baby? I've never delivered a baby before."

I gazed at Mary while I thought. Riddah had never really made a formal announcement about being with child, but one couldn't mistake the growing belly and ungainly walk. I also knew that babies didn't do well if born too early. This was no time to take chances. "You need to tell Mama about it, Mary," I said firmly. "Riddah might get upset about it now, but I would rather have Mama there to make sure everything's okay than to have something happen to the baby."

Mary fetched Mama, and the two of them hurried back to the tents. They didn't return after what I thought should be ample time if everything were well. By this time, I was working near Naola.

"I'm going back for a drink of water and maybe a little rest," I told her. I finished my bundle of grain, carried it over to the side of the field, and headed for the tents. Out of sight of the fields, I skipped my drink of water and went into Riddah's tent.

Riddah was being supported in semi-sitting position, Mary and Mama on either side, and she was breathing quick deep breaths, eyes tight shut. Mary looked up at me, face pale. "She is in labor, Didi," she said quietly.

Mama didn't look up. "Didi, go get Sariah now. I'm going to need her help."

I ran back out into the field. I didn't spot Sariah right away and then saw her on the far side, giving drinks to a couple of the men. Unable to run any more, I walked as quickly as I could with my own awkward weight until I reached her side. "Mother Sariah, Mama Leah needs your help in Riddah's tent, right now."

I stopped, panting, and watched her quickly cross the field. As soon as I could, I followed. Upon entering Riddah's tent again, a different scene met my eyes. Mary was starting a fire in the cooking area, and Sariah was pouring water into two different basins. When the fire was going, she placed one of the basins over the fire to heat up. Mama had a stash of clean linen by her side I hadn't noticed before.

"Now?" asked Riddah, her voice strained.

"All right, go ahead and push," said Mama.

I didn't want to stay, but I didn't dare leave. I wanted to know what delivery was like, yet I was afraid I wouldn't be able to go through it myself if I knew. But I couldn't leave Riddah until I knew everything would be all right. I stayed but found my head swimming. I sat down.

While Riddah pushed, Mary brought the basins of cold and warm water over to Sariah. Sooner than I expected, the baby came. It was a boy. Sariah grasped the baby expertly by the feet and held him upside down. He remained silent and slightly blue. She spanked his back side and then handed him to Mama, who wrapped him in one of her linens and rubbed him down vigorously. There was no movement. Sariah grasped his head with her free hand and dipped his body into the warm water, then the cold, then the warm again. The baby coughed once. Sariah held him upside down one more time while Mama rubbed him again. One more cough then a faint cry. As Sariah grasped his head again, he took a big gulp of air, turned pink, and wailed. Everyone in the room relaxed visibly.

"You have a son, Riddah," announced Mama.

Riddah said nothing, but tears were running down her cheeks, and she held her arms out toward her son.

Mama grasped a dry linen, swaddled the baby tightly, and handed him to her. Riddah cradled him in her arms and caressed his face.

"He's larger than I expected," commented Sariah as she bent over the basins to clean them up. Riddah's hand froze. "But that should help him do better for being so early."

Mama and Mary were occupied with other parts of the cleanup and didn't look our way. I glanced in Riddah's direction and saw her looking straight at me, eyes wide and pleading. I was confused. What was Riddah trying to tell me? We were about seven months out from our weddings in the Valley of Lemuel, she's had her baby before she has even properly announced being with child, but it's big and beautiful and healthy...

My mouth dropped open at what I was thinking. Riddah was shaking her head and mouthing the word "No, no." I turned my head and struggled to my feet. "I'm going outside for some fresh air," I said to no one in particular.

Outside, I leaned against the tent's corner pole. My palms were sweating but my feet were cold. "I wasn't that desperate to not be the first one to deliver," I told myself. After a while, I had a hold of myself, and I returned to the field to help with the harvest. To those who asked where I'd been, I simply replied, "Riddah just had a beautiful, healthy son."

No one seemed to think anything strange about the event. Riddah never discussed it with me. I never spoke of it to anyone but to God.

I had never thought that pregnancy could be contagious, but before Riddah's delivery, Mary, Kora, and Bekka had announced that they also were with child. I was now nearing my time to deliver. It was an exciting time, but I was starting to get nervous about what delivery would be like for me. Mama and my sisters-in-law coached me in what to expect, and I remembered Riddah's experience. It shouldn't be all that bad, I told myself. I tried not to think about stories I had heard about difficult first-time deliveries, especially if the mother was young.

With so many of us expecting, the families had voted to remain longer at the Place of the Broken Bow and grow another crop. I was finally getting used to the humidity, but the heat was still sometimes difficult to bear. However, I was determined not to let it slow me down.

Occasionally other travelers stopped in the valley for refreshment from their travels, and we tried to welcome them to the oasis while still maintaining a polite distance and our privacy. Then they would move on again, and we would have the valley to ourselves again.

One morning a small caravan of about five camel riders appeared over the hill and into the far side of the valley. But instead of stopping and sending forth an emissary to meet us, they continued riding hard right up to the doors of our tents before dismounting. I was out in the field with Naola and Abisha, and we watched from a distance.

I saw Lehi arise from the shade in front of his tent while they were still a little distant, and beckon to Sariah. She hurried all the other women and children inside one of the smaller tents before the riders drew near, and remained there herself. The rest of the men of our camp gathered around Lehi at some signal I didn't catch, a couple of them carrying their walking staffs in their hands. I held my breath as the first of the strangers dismounted from his camel and stood before Lehi. The other riders held their mounts, which seemed anxious to get at the water hole, tightly in place. Not knowing their intentions, I called softly to Naola and Abisha to join me near one of the pomegranate trees, and we huddled down around it and watched.

The man in front of Lehi, apparently the leader of their group, was gesturing wildly. Lehi moved little but did seem to be asking an occasional question. Then the visitor stopped gesturing, and Lehi pointed toward the water hole. Then the strangers began leading their mounts toward water, and Zoram and Sam went with them.

I turned to my sisters. They looked at me, eyes wide. "What's going on?" asked Naola.

"I'm going to go find out," I said.

"No, Didi!" cried Abisha, clutching at my sleeve as I started to rise. "There's something funny about that group, and I don't like it. You better stay here."

"Out in the open? Where all we can do is watch helplessly? No, thank you! Besides, they didn't act particularly dangerous to me, just in some big hurry. Why don't you both come?"

They looked at each other a moment. Then Abisha said slowly, "You start out, Didi. We'll gather the tools and follow right behind you."

As I walked toward camp, I watched the visitors join our men, sitting down in a circle in front of Lehi's tent. Their leader and Lehi seemed to be the two main ones talking. Then Lehi poured a cup of tea and passed it to the leader of the other group, and he drank deeply. Then they continued talking. As I drew near, I caught snatches of their conversation, but it was in a language I didn't recognize. I went closer and placed my hand on Nephi's shoulder. He started and looked up in surprise, his hand grasping the large stick beside him. His sudden movement caught the attention of the others in the group.

The stranger who had been speaking looked at me in surprise. He said something to Lehi in the language I didn't understand, and Lehi nodded. At another comment from him, Nephi began to grin and his face turned red. The other men from the caravan all laughed.

"What did he say?" I asked, not knowing whether to be offended or not, but suspecting I was at the heart of it.

"He said he didn't know there were women with us," answered Nephi after a pause.

"And he commented on, ah, how beautiful you are," said Lehi, smiling.

I curtsied to the man, and he and his companions laughed again.

Then suddenly they were serious again. The leader began drawing in the sand before him, glancing at Lehi intermittently while he talked. Zoram, who had been standing off to the side, watching out over the valley, came over to me.

"Is everyone in the tents?" he whispered in my ear.

I shook my head. "Naola and Abisha were out with me in the field, and they are on their way in now. What's going on?"

"I don't speak much Egyptian, so I am only catching snatches of it, but I do know that these men are being followed by someone, and have asked for protection from Lehi. As I gather, Lehi could just have easily said no and killed them on the spot. In saying yes, he is now responsible to guard them with his life. I don't know if that puts all of our lives in jeopardy for the travelers or just his alone. Either way, we're in the middle of it now."

I stared at Zoram. "You mean Father Lehi would risk all our lives for strangers?"

Zoram shook his head. "Father Lehi would risk his own life for just about anybody, but not all our lives. No, it sounds like these men happen to be friends of a friend."

"Who is following them?"

"I don't know for sure, Didi. I missed that part at the very beginning. But I think it would be safer if you joined the others in the tent."

The men soon finished their plans and split up to do some very interesting activities. The sons of Lehi took some of our camels out to cover up the tracks the travelers had made as they approached us, and make some diverting tracks toward some harder packed and rocky terrain deeper into the hills. Papa and Lehi helped our visitors unload bundles from their camels and store them among our tents. My brothers started gathering a bundle of sturdy sticks and sharpening the ends for the women to use if it came to our needing them. The women gathered food and water supplies into the tent we were going to hide in, one more centrally located yet inconspicuous behind Lehi's tent. The older children seemed to be more sober and were more obedient than usual.

It was late in the afternoon when the cry rang through the camp: "They come!" The women hurried the stray children into the appointed tent, the visitors inside with us, and our men took up their positions throughout the camp and in the field as though working at their daily chores. I watched through a crack in the tent door panel as about a dozen camel riders circled the valley then gradually worked their way down into the valley toward us, the first rider walking and leading his camel, looking side to side as he came. As they neared, our men gathered together again in a group to meet them, as though greeting fellow travelers come to drink at the well. The air inside the tent was getting stuffy, but my hands were clammy and cold.

Lehi spoke to them as he had to other travelers, giving the polite greeting and statement that they were welcome to what water they needed. The leader said nothing but nodded his head toward the water hole, and half of his company rode past our camp toward it. Then he looked around at our tents, and I held my breath. He spoke to Lehi in words I couldn't hear, and Lehi responded by shaking his head. The leader looked around our camp again, nodding his head, one eyebrow raised. There was a hard look in his eye. I shivered. One of the children behind me whimpered and was quickly quieted.

The men who had watered their camels returned, and the other half of the group went. I wondered how long it would be before those men left. By this time, Lehi, Ishmael, and half of our men were sitting on the ground in front of Lehi's tent, and the new caravan's leader was sitting on the ground facing them. Finally all the animals were watered. The leader stood and made a movement as if to go then turned back to Lehi and said something else. I caught the sounds of his voice, but the words were again meaningless to me. Lehi shrugged his shoulders, pointed in the direction of the inland hills, and then spread his hands out in front of the leader.

The leader spat on the ground then looked at Lehi and spoke curtly, his hand going to something at his waist. Nephi, who had remained standing behind his father, made a slight move forward himself, uncrossing his arms and letting them hang loosely at his side. The caravan leader glanced at the large frame of my husband, Nephi, then returned his gaze to Lehi, still sitting on the ground. He spoke again, and his voice carried across the camp. Lehi responded in a voice so low I couldn't hear it then pointed at the door of his tent with his hand palm upward. The leader moved toward it.

Laman stood in front of the door and did not move as the caravan leader walked toward it. The leader pushed him aside roughly and walked inside. Laman stood outside clenching his fist. Then the leader re-emerged, holding both hands up as though to show they were empty, but grinning and showing his teeth. I could see our men watching his every move.

The leader turned to Lehi and spoke some more. Lehi replied in a firm voice in the words I didn't understand. The leader stamped his foot and walked to the next tent. Nephi followed him and grasped his arm, which the leader shook off roughly before going into that tent. I got a heavy feeling in the pit of my stomach. The tent we were in was next.

The leader emerged from the second tent and walked toward us. Nephi followed right behind him, a pleading tone in his voice. Both our men and the dark men of the caravan seemed to be at a tense state of readiness. It was now or never.

I stepped out quickly through the door, letting the flap drop immediately behind me. I turned to face this man who was invading our privacy and perhaps was a threat to our very lives. "If he wants to see what is within this tent, here I am," I said in as steady a voice as I could muster, and I folded my arms across my belly big with child.

Nephi turned white, and he moved his body to stand protectively in front of me, his hand at his waist. It was then that I noticed Nephi was wearing the sword of Laban. This was the fine sword that Nephi had obtained when he went to Jerusalem to obtain the religious record on brass plates, when Zoram joined the family in the wilderness. The man looked at me from his dark eyes with another toothy grin that made my skin crawl. Lehi seemed to almost smile as he stood and came over and joined us. "This is my son's wife," he said as I found out later. "It is she we were wanting to protect. If you will allow her the privacy of her tent, you may look in any others you desire." The leader nodded, still grinning widely, but turned away from the door.

Then he looked at his men, waiting with their mounts in front of Lehi's tent. Suddenly, while speaking low coarse sounds that could only be a curse, he whirled and quickly lifted the door of the tent beside me. He was met by a huddled group of women and children, many of them pointing hefty sharp sticks in his direction. He paused, gazed at them a moment, then lowered the curtain door. He stared at Lehi a moment then walked purposefully to the other tents and searched them all.

When he was done, he spoke not a word but rejoined his men, mounted his camel, and with a mere signal of his arm, led the whole group of them at a gallop across the valley floor toward the inland hills. In a few minutes, they had disappeared behind the crest of the first hill.

We stood as we were, unmoving, after they were out of sight. Finally registering they were really gone, I breathed a sigh and felt myself slipping toward the ground. Nephi reached out and steadied me.

"Didi, are you all right?" I nodded, and he continued. "I can't believe you actually came out and faced that man. He gave me the creeps." He stopped and stared at me. "Didi, you're trembling."

"I-I'm all right," I said and smiled weakly at him.

Lehi had approached the tent and looked inside. "I can't believe those men didn't see our visitors. How?" Then he stopped and laughed. "Of all the creative tricks!"

I looked too and couldn't repress a broad smile myself. The "women" inside consisted of my sisters, my brothers' wives, and the visiting men. Somehow they had found head shawls and robes to don and were huddling shyly behind the others. If I hadn't known the individual faces of my family members, I would have had trouble telling the difference. Thank goodness that man had not taken the time to look more closely at each member in the group.

Supper that night was jovial on the surface, but the visitors seemed a little nervous about their surroundings. After getting a good night's sleep, with my brothers and the sons of Lehi taking turns with the night watch, the visitors left with the first light of dawn, heading back in the direction they had come. Thereafter, we were always more cautious about the people who crossed us on the trails.

I spent my hours making clothes and bedding in preparation for the baby, performing light chores around camp when Nephi didn't beat me to them, or sitting in a row among the growing crops and removing all the weeds within my reach in between carrying water to them. The work on the crops was actually quite awkward, but it filled a need in me to keep doing something.

One such morning, after the men left to go hunting, I felt particularly in the mood to do some work with the crops. As I waddled past Sariah's tent, she called out to me, and I met her at the doorway.

"Oh, Didi, darling," she sighed, shaking her head. "Surely you're not planning on going out to the fields today? That somehow doesn't seem wise. To me, you look ready to go any minute now."

"Mother Sariah, don't worry about me!" I laughed. "I feel fine. I probably won't be ready for days yet. I won't be far from the encampment. And you know I'll be careful."

"Yes, I know, but . . ." she trailed off and surveyed the sky. "It looks like it could become a really hot day. Come right back if you feel the slightest discomfort."

I smiled and nodded reassuringly then made my way slowly over the slight hill to the nearest field. I picked a spot and began working, singing songs to myself as I dug.

About midmorning I suddenly noticed how hot it really was. I removed the shawl from about my hair to give my head some ventilation and mopped my forehead with it. I took a sip of water from the water bladder I had brought with me and fanned myself with the cloth before reaching up to tie it back around my hair. With my hands half way up, I suddenly felt a ripping pain, like a fiery knife cutting from my stomach to my back. Dropping my head shawl and clutching my back with one hand, I tried to rise but fell back gasping. In a minute the pain passed, my mind cleared, and I caught my breath again.

"What was that all about?" I asked myself. "That wasn't anything like Mama or my sisters described to me. I must have just been sitting funny."

I shifted my position and returned to pulling weeds. I had not been working long when the pain hit again. This time I felt twinges of pain shooting down my legs. At that moment, I felt that something was not quite right; if these were really contractions; they were not like anything I had expected, coming on much stronger than Mama had told me they would. I immediately picked up my things and started back for the tents. Partway there, the pain hit again, and I fell to my knees, dropping everything. Almost in a panic now, I regained my feet and staggered again toward the tents, leaving the dropped items behind and ignoring my slipping head shawl. As I came up next to the first tent, I felt the pain again.

"Ooh, Mama, somebody! Help me!" the cry escaped my lips before I could prevent its utterance. As if in a dream, I saw Mary come to the door of her tent, drop the mending she held in her hands, and hurry to my side.

"Didi, it's all right," she said, helping me to my feet and giving me support toward my tent. "Are you having contractions?" I didn't know what to answer. Mary smiled at me. "Didi, remember other women have been through this before and come through just fine. I'm glad you made it back. Sariah's been worrying—"

"Mary," I interrupted, relieved to have someone else to share my concerns with. "The pains are coming into my back so strongly that I'm scared something's wrong."

"Hush," she said, taking me inside and making me lie down on my bed. "Tell me how long ago the contractions started, how far apart they are coming, and whether your water has broken yet?"

"They started about four or five minutes apart and much stronger than I expected. My water hasn't broken yet, I don't think. But the pain's all in my back." Another wave of pain swept over me, and I writhed on the bed. "It's so different from what I expected," I said through gritted teeth after the pain passed.

Mary seemed at a loss for words. "I'll be right back, Didi," she said and ran out of the tent. In a minute she returned with Mama.

"Mary tells me you're having contractions," Mama said, calm and business-like. I nodded. "Tell me as closely as you can everything that's happened so far, Didi."

With a couple of painful interruptions, I told her when the pains had started and what they felt like. Mama shook her head and patted my hand. "The contractions may have seemed to start unusually close together, but sometimes the first ones aren't felt. And they always hurt more than one expects, especially to those who haven't experienced labor before."

"But the pain is so severe!" I panted. "And it seems to be all in my back and legs, not around the baby." I curled up again with the pain.

Mama began to rub my back. "It's called back labor," she said to me. "The baby's pushing on your back bone from inside." She turned to my sister. "Mary, I need you to get those delivery things from my tent, bring some clean water, and stay on hand to help me."

"Please let this birth be an easy one," I prayed silently between attacks of pain. "And give me the strength to endure it as other women have."

Mary hung a drape in front of the bed to screen us from the tent door, and helped Mama set up. Bekka stopped by to offer brief words of comfort, but her face paled; she began to fan herself quickly, and Mary had to help her back to her tent. Naola brought by a bit of food for Mary and Mama and refilled my water bladder but, otherwise, would not come in. Riddah didn't come at all.

The hours stretched into night. Abisha came to relieve Mary, and the pains only seemed harder and closer together. "Is it almost over yet, Mama?" I asked during a breather.

She wiped the sweat from my face. "You're doing just fine, honey. Do you feel like pushing yet?"

I shook my head as another wall of fire hit my backbone. Mama rubbed my back through the contraction, and then helped me sit up. "We're going to walk around the tent a bit, Didi, to get this baby moving. Just bear with me."

I wasn't able to walk long. Mama tried a variety of other positions, maneuvers, and herbal treatments, which didn't seem to change the pain or move the baby in the least. Why couldn't I have been blessed with Riddah's wide hips?

"Please," the tears rolled down my cheeks with each groan. "Let me rest. Oh, make the pain stop, Mama!"

Abisha and Mama looked at each other. "We're going to start pushing now, Didi," said Mama steadily. "Abisha, get on the other side of her to help. Didi, now listen to me. This is what we're going to do." She explained, and I only had the energy to nod.

Pushing hurt in a new way now, and my head began to swim. Mary returned and Abisha went home to sleep. I could feel the tent warming up again with the heat of day. After what seemed an eternity of tortuous contraction after contraction and screaming push after push, I lay my head back on the pillows and sobbed. "I can't do it any more, I can't, I can't. Why won't the baby come?"

"Hush, Didi. Everything's going to be all right. You're doing just fine. The baby just needs to turn a bit, and then it will be over." Mama readjusted the damp cloth over my head and stood up to stretch and rub her tired eyes. "Just rest now, Didi."

I opened my eyes to see Mama and Mary whispering. I caught none of it. My only thought was to make it until the baby was born. "Please let the baby be all right," I repeated to myself through a half daze.

During one of my breathers, I heard Mary's voice near the tent's door.

"No! You can't go in there!" she cried. There was a whack of something solid meeting flesh then footsteps walking toward the hanging curtain. "Come back here right now!" Mary screeched. "Don't go into the birthing room! Mama, stop him!"

The curtain near the bed was pushed aside, and Nephi stepped into the little room, rubbing his arm and looking undeviatingly at my face.

"You can't come into the birthing room, young man," Mama gasped and stood quickly toward him. "Now you turn around and march right back out!"

Nephi said nothing, pushed her gently but firmly aside, and continued to walk in my direction. I tried to smile at him but could feel the dreaded pains worsening again. I bit my lip, determined to say nothing in front of Nephi; I didn't want him to know what endless agony I was enduring for our child. Nephi knelt at my side and took my hand in his, his eyes never leaving my face.

I couldn't keep silent any longer; a scream escaped my lips, containing more energy than I thought I had left, and I clutched at Nephi as a man dying in the desert would at a mirage.

"Ooh, it hurts! Take it away," I sobbed. "It's going to kill me and the baby too if you don't fix it. Please help me! Mama! Nephi!"

Mama drew near to place a cool damp cloth on my hot forehead and to give me another sip of water. Nephi lifted his face to hers, questioningly. She averted her eyes and turned away. That was answer enough for Nephi.

"There's something wrong, isn't there?" he whispered hoarsely.

Mama was still turned away, but she nodded. "The baby is facing backward and won't turn," she said in a muffled voice.

"Will . . . will Devorah be all right, Mother Leah?"

Mama turned red eyes back on Nephi, held out her hands, and shook her head briefly.

Another scream tore Nephi's attention back to me. He clutched my hand in a death grip. "It's got to turn out all right, Didi. It can't be possible God wants you back with him so soon. You've got to be all right!" Nephi lowered his head, and his body shook. "I can't live without you!"

The pain started to subside and I let out a weary sigh of relief. Nephi looked again at me, and loosened his grip on my hand. "May I give you a blessing, Didi?"

I nodded and closed my eyes. There was nothing better in the world I could have asked for at that moment. Nephi lifted his hands to cradle my head, paused, and then began to speak in a low voice.

"O God, our Father, thou who knowest everything in heaven and on the earth, thou art aware of our plight here at this time. Thou knowest the complications, and thou hast the power to overcome them in our behalf if thou wilst. Grant thy healing spirit here if it be thy will for thy beloved handmaiden." Nephi paused another moment then, his voice more firm, named me by my real name. "Devorah, also known as Didi, the daughter of Ishmael, a descendant of Joseph through Ephraim, I bless you by the power of God that you will be healed of the problem that hinders this birth. I bless you that this delivery will be normal, that you shall give birth to a healthy child, and that you shall live to raise it and take it to the Promised Land. I bless you that your body shall heal normally, that you may with strength bring further children into the world. Thou art a choice handmaiden before God, and he has heard your prayers and the prayers of your husband and extended family. I bless you now with the strength you need to endure the trial ahead, that hidden resources of strength may sustain you. You have an important mission yet to perform in this mortal life, in raising a family, and influencing those around you toward righteousness and godliness. Find comfort in remembering that you will not be tried with more than you are able to bear if you look forward with hope and with the offering of a righteous life. In the sacred name of our God, amen."

I found myself able to handle the pain of the next contraction without screaming. I looked up at Nephi with tears on my cheeks.

"Will you be all right," he asked, wiping one of my tears with his fingers, "if I follow your mother's directions and leave the place where only women are allowed? I promise nothing could drag me further than just outside the door unless you wish it."

"Yes, I'll be all right now. Thank you." I smiled at him, though I felt another contraction coming on. "Go or stay where you want to, Nephi." As I watched him leave, I felt a twisting movement of the baby inside me. "I'm feeling the urge to push, Mama," I said, gritting my teeth.

It was not long after that Nephi, dozing just outside the door of the tent, was awakened by a tiny lusty cry. He jumped to his feet and ran inside then stopped in front of the curtain. "Didi?" he called hesitantly. "Mother Leah?"

Mary poked her head around the drape, a broad grin on her face. "Congratulations, Nephi. You are the father of a perfect, healthy little girl!"

A slow smile lit his face. "A daughter. I have a daughter!" Suddenly he grabbed Mary by the arms and whirled her around. "I am the father of a daughter!" He noticed her red face and let go of her quickly. "When will Mary the doorkeeper allow me to go in?" he asked, his head slightly bowed and his hands now clasped behind his back.

Mary, her head turned away, cleared her throat. Then she looked back at him, and though the corner of her mouth twitched upward, her voice was firm. "We have to clean things up a bit first, and then you may come in. But only for a short while. Didi really needs a good rest. After that the place will again be home for husband and wife and daughter."

CHAPTER 4

NAHOM

We stayed about a year at the Place of the Broken Bow. The men all made new bows from the hard wood there, and became quite adept at hunting with them. All the infants were safely delivered: Mary, Abisha, and Elizabeth had sons; Bekka and Kora had daughters. It was time to move on again. The first few oasis campsites were as humid as the ones just before arriving at the Place of the Broken Bow, but then almost imperceptibly, the air grew drier and hotter. The vegetation at the oases became coarser, and the men had to take the camels farther from camp for grazing. It also seemed as though the wells were farther apart in this part of the country, for it took us longer to travel from one to the next. It was at one of these oasis wells where we stopped for a week that I noticed Papa sitting in the shade of his tent, looking quite tired. He also seemed thinner than I remembered. I went over to him and sat down, picking up my apron to fan him.

He opened his eyes and then closed them again. "That feels quite nice, Didi," he said.

"How are you doing, Papa?" I asked, concern in my voice.

He sighed. "Just a little tired. I'll be fine after a good rest."

Mama came out of the tent with a woven fan in her hand and looked down at us. "I'll do that, Didi. You have other things to do," she said. She began fanning Papa, and I looked at them a moment. "Go on, shoo." She waved her arm at me and I left.

Papa did indeed seem to pick up strength over the week of rest. But the oasis was fairly barren, and we had to move on for the sake of the animals. The next stretch was the longest yet. Papa seemed melancholic, so my sisters and I took turns traveling near his side to keep him company. We talked to him, told jokes and stories, and sang songs to lift his spirits, but he was much quieter than usual. Eli and

Elizabeth stayed constantly near him and Mama, doing all they could to make their journeying easier.

"Something's wrong with my father, Nephi," I commented during one of our short stops for sleep. "He's lost his usual vitality. I don't think he has recovered from the last round of traveling. He doesn't complain, but I'm afraid if he doesn't get a real chance to rest soon, he'll become ill or collapse."

Nephi didn't answer for a moment. "If the next oasis is anything like the last one, we can't stop for long or the animals will die. I can't promise anything about how soon, but I guarantee it that my father will stop at the first hospitable one we come to."

The children became increasingly cranky, tempers were very short, and Kora lapsed into frequent bouts of tears. "I'm just so tired," she would answer to our queries. I must admit I was feeling more than ready to stay put in one place for a while.

We had to spend a Sabbath sitting under makeshift canopies in the middle of nowhere before reaching the oasis. But this one was greener, with adequate vegetation for the animals, and surrounded by good stretches of land that looked possible for planting. Lehi looked around at the plateau-like mountains that surrounded us and then scanned the valley. "This is where we shall stay for a time," he said slowly. Amidst sighs of relief and low cheers, we pulled the packs from our animals and set up camp. Now my father will have a chance to rest, I told myself.

My father, though, did not regain his strength. Nephi tried to prepare me for the worst, but I refused to believe Papa could die just like that. I stubbornly nursed him, cheerfully telling him he would get better soon, that all he needed was rest. At first he smiled back at me when I said this, but later he only sighed and looked away.

One day, Papa beckoned to me as I was bringing him a fresh bottle of drinking water.

"My daughter," he murmured as I leaned closer to him. "You are as stubbornly cheerful as your mother is. That makes it a little harder to say this to you." He paused and I felt my heart chill. "I believe my time has come to go and leave this life. Continue on your journey to the Land of Promise, and know that I do not regret coming on this journey with you. Take care of your mother, Leah, for me. Stay true to the principles I have taught you. Listen to the teachings of Lehi, he speaks great truths. Take good care of Nephi, I couldn't have found a better man for you if I had searched the four corners of the earth." He glanced down at my daughter, Siri, in my arms. "I am sorry I won't in person be able to see my grandchild grow up. But I give you my choicest blessings. Remember I love you, Devorah."

He squeezed my hand and sank back against his pillows, eyes closed, exhausted from his speech. I was frightened; for the first time I realized that he really could die. I stood up quickly and fled the tent, bumping into Nephi just outside the door. He caught and held my trembling body.

"What's wrong?" he asked. "Is it Ishmael?"

"Oh, Nephi!" I began crying. "You were right. Papa is dying. I didn't want to believe it was possible. But now . . ."

Nephi strode into the tent and looked out a moment later. "Go get your mother. I'm going to find your brothers and sisters, Ishmael wants to speak to them."

Papa spoke to Mori and Gid then to each of my sisters in turn. I, though, did not go back inside the tent, for I couldn't bear to see my father again right now, wasted from illness and fatigue. Instead I wandered away from the tents so I could think alone. My mind whirled with questions and anguish. Why did my father have to die now? Would he still be strong and well if we had not left Jerusalem?

When I returned at dusk, Nephi glanced at me questioningly, but I volunteered no answers. I fell asleep that night with fists clenched, back turned to Nephi, too angry at him and myself and the whole situation to look him in the face.

We were awakened in the early hours of dawn by a wailing and crying coming from the direction of Ishmael's tent. We all ran outside. It was Mama, sitting in front of the tent, rocking herself back and forth and tearing at her hair. Elizabeth sat next to her trying to comfort her. She also looked devastated. Through Mama's broken speech, we discovered that Papa had passed away during the night in his sleep.

I walked away from the tents, numb. I could hear Abisha and Kora adding their cries to those of my sisters, but I could give none. I didn't have the strength. I tried to imagine life without Papa, and was met with him in every scene. I felt Papa holding me as a tiny child on his knee, bopping me up and down and singing the donkey song. I saw him waving goodbye to Mama and me as I accompanied her for the first time to the big market in Jerusalem. I heard his deep voice ringing with pride as he modeled to our neighbors the first awkward garment I made for him. And I remembered the deep sense of security that overcame me each time he offered prayer to start the Sabbath. I would not have any of these experiences again, nor would any of my children know them.

I fell to my knees on the sand and leaned against a rock. At last the tears came, trickling at first, and then pouring uncontrollably. Soon I felt an arm around my shoulder. It was Nephi. He said nothing, but merely sat and held me. My sobs quieted. Soon he helped me to my feet, and walked me back to the tents, arm still supportive around my shoulder.

The other women were still wailing in a huddle in front of Papa's tent. The men sat around silently, looking off into the distance or poking at the ground. I went up to Mama; we put our arms around each other, I buried my face into her clothes, and time seemed to stand still. I felt again the security that Papa's presence had always brought me before. It was the security a child feels going out into the big world to play, and turning around, sees mother or father smiling at them as if to say, I'll be here for you always. I lifted my head and saw Mama's unwavering eyes searching my own. Here was great sadness, grief at losing a life companion. Yet here also was determination, courage, and hope. I took a deep breath, stood tall, and returned the look. Mama nodded briefly and stepped back. I turned and went to Mary, touched her on the arm, and hugged her. Next to her were Naola then Bekka, Riddah, Kora, Abisha, Elizabeth, and lastly Sariah. In turn, I embraced them all. Then I lowered my head and managed a low wail for tradition's sake. Then it grew in volume till my heart was in it, crooning my grief. Hands touching, the other women chorused in after me. It was therapeutic.

While my brothers prepared the body with what spices and ointments we had on hand, and the women gathered cloths to bury him in, the sons of Lehi searched the land for a burial site. When they returned, they had some interesting news to tell.

"There seem to be burial caves in the rocks of the nearby hills," Laman told the group. "We actually met a nomadic group there visiting the site. They were suspicious at first as to why we were there. Apparently, it is a desired spot for burial. We are welcome to use it. It is called Nahom. I think that means to sigh or moan among these people."

Nahom. It sounded like Nahum in Hebrew, or consolation. The name seemed to laugh at me. How could they call it that? I felt no consolation at all. Apparently, my siblings felt the same. Talk again arose of Jerusalem, wondering what would have happened had we stayed there. We all felt the hard traveling had been a major contribution to Papa's death. How many more deaths would there be? The talk was the same as it had been every other time some hardship came our way. Why couldn't we have stayed in the Valley of Lemuel? Why couldn't we go back there or to Jerusalem? Why had we even left Jerusalem in the first place? I was tired of their complaints, tired of the wilderness, tired of the whole situation. All I wanted was time alone, some moments of peace, and one place where we could stay put.

When all was ready, we made the trek by foot up to the burial ground, one camel pulling father's body on a makeshift bed on poles. Sariah walked with her arm around Mama, whose face was blank and eyes distant most of the way. My sisters cried quietly. The men were silent. I felt numb again.

Among the hills in a small cave which Mori and Gid had chosen, the prepared body was placed in a shallow hole. Mori, as the oldest son, offered a prayer. As the men began piling rocks over him, Mama began softly singing a psalm about God strengthening us in times of trial. The rest of us joined in. Soon the body was covered, and the men created a stone pile at the head to mark the grave. We stood gazing at the spot in silence.

"Goodbye, Papa," said Naola, and she started weeping again.

Mary put her arm around Naola, and turned her away. The rest of us followed, Mama and I last.

"Now he'll have, at last, the rest he wanted so much," said Mama, weeping. I nodded. She put her arm through mine and together we walked back to the tents. When we moved from this place, we would never again be able to return to Papa's gravesite; he would be alone forever in this barren wilderness.

The first week after Papa's death, my sisters and I spent a lot of time around Mama at her tent, keeping her company. We didn't dare bring up the subject of Papa unless Mama did first. So we would bring our mending, or do our meat drying and spicing there to keep her company as the children played around us.

One morning the men came back from a hunting trip well loaded down with game. All of the women gathered together to help the men clean the animals and prepare the meat. Nephi and Lemuel produced bags of spices they had obtained from a caravan on their way back from the hunt in exchange for a couple of their beasts. We would be able to make another big supply of basturma and sun-dried meat.

After helping us clean the carcasses, the men left to sleep in their tents. Mama also retired to her tent for a short rest. The sun became hotter as we worked. We kept the unprepared meat shaded behind one of the tents, and the children had fun gathering palm leaves to wave the flies away. Cloths were laid out on the ground in the sun for the cutting and drying of meat, and periodically a toddler would run over the cloths, laughing as his or her mother scolded and chased the child off.

"Oh, pshaw!" exclaimed Riddah, after chasing her son Raoul off the meat cloths for the third time. She sat back and wiped her forehead with her headscarf. "What gives our men the right to sleep in the tents while we labor out here in the hot sun saving the meat?" She gazed longingly at the shade of the adjacent tent.

"Well," offered Naola mildly, "they did hike around in those hills the last three days, stalking these beasts and dragging them back to us. They haven't exactly been lazing about, have they?"

Mary, Kora, and I looked at the piles of meat around us and laughed, shaking our heads.

"There's enough, I think," Bekka nodded. "It may last us a week or so."

Abisha snorted.

"Oh, all right," said Riddah. "I'll give them that. But I bet they rested in the heat of the day anyway. I can't imagine Laman, or Mori and Gid for that matter, running around in this heat." She glared at Kora and Abisha.

"There's nothing stopping you from going and resting right now, Riddah," commented Naola. "You have to put Raoul down for a nap soon anyway."

"Right," sniffed Riddah as she continued working. "There's nothing stopping me."

"Except guilt," giggled Bekka, poking Riddah in the ribs with her elbow. "While we're all sweating and slaving in the hot sun to keep your family fed . . ."

"And to keep your family fed, Bekka," interrupted Abisha. "Keep working, girls, or we'll all be hungry next week."

"We could wake the men to help us," I offered. "Then we'd all be in this together, and no one could complain."

"Oh, no, not me," protested Kora. "Gid will kill me if I interrupt his sleep! I don't mind really."

Bekka laughed. "That's right, Kora. Step one to a happy marriage is adequate uninterrupted sleep for the husband. Second is a full stomach."

"Third is keeping the children quiet and out of his way," panted Riddah as she chased Raoul off the food cloths for the fourth time.

Elizabeth merely smiled to herself. Her older son, Seth, seemed quite content to sit and hold his new baby brother.

I glanced down at Siri, playing quietly by my side. I decided I was glad she had a calm helpful personality. Would a boy have been quite different?

My thoughts were interrupted by seeing Abisha's daughter, Anna, running screaming after the other children, waving a leafy branch. Perhaps being male or female wasn't the deciding factor after all. I smiled down at Siri. She grinned up at me and then tossed a handful of meat chunks up in the air, giggling while I tried to keep them from falling in the sand. Unsuccessfully I tried to brush the sand from those that missed the work cloth.

"Go play with your cousins, Siri," I told her, perhaps more harshly than I needed to. She scooted off after her cousin Anna, giggling happily, the two of them throwing sand at each other.

"And then he expects a really nice dinner and a perfectly clean tent while he lounges around in the evening talking to your husbands," Riddah was saying. "After a hard day of work, and when I finally get Raoul down to sleep, I'm ready to collapse myself, and he wants me to still have all this energy for him." Riddah's breath hissed out between her teeth.

"Some days I think I need two of me," Kora nodded.

"I would refuse to let him take another wife," said Abisha firmly. "I know some of those desert families do that, but I will not allow that here in my family."

"Oh, I don't know," commented Mary, a half smile on her lips. "Just think of all the extra work you could command other wives to do, the cooking, the washing, chasing the children."

"Humph!" said Abisha.

"Oh, stop it, sisters," I said. "Our husbands work very hard to provide for us." The other women looked at me, waving eyebrows up and down. "Oh, you know all that they do, hunting for meat, caring for the camels, trading for spices and tools, planting and harvesting the crops."

"Yes, then leaving the weeding and watering for us," said Abisha.

"Yes, Didi, and when your husband goes on his little hunting trips, how often does he actually bring something home for you to eat?" asked Riddah.

My anger flared. "Often enough," I answered.

"Come on, sis. You've married the perfect husband," challenged Bekka. "Tell us he never does anything wrong."

I gazed at Bekka a moment. Her lips were pursed, but her eyes gazed at me intently, searchingly, accusation gone.

"Nephi's not perfect," I answered, my anger gone. "Perhaps being married to him I see more of his faults. I get frustrated with him at times, like when I wish he would see my needs and help me out more, when he leaves his pile of clothes on the ground, and yes, when he goes on his little hunting trips. But I also know he's trying to be a good husband and father, and he listens to me when I'm struggling."

Riddah tossed her head. "Just what I thought. You do-gooders are always trying to look better than the rest of us. Be real."

Mary shot her a stern look and then turned back to me. "Didi, I was thinking. It must be easier to do what's right with Nephi right there all the time."

Bekka smiled again half mockingly. "I bet he shares with you divine secrets and mysteries. How would it be to bask in the glow of his spiritual presence?"

I looked at Bekka and laughed a little bitterly. "Like basking in the glow of some distant star! I can see how bright he is way up there, but my path still feels dark where I am. He doesn't share any secrets with me unless he tells all of us. And I don't feel any more spiritually gifted than the rest of you or any closer to God. Sometimes I'm ready to give up and turn rebellious, just to be different." I looked up at the late afternoon sky. "I can see where Nephi is, like the North Star, always pointing the way I should go, but it doesn't make it any easier to get there myself. It just shows me how far I have yet to go." I laughed again shakily. "The only good thing is that at least we are both trying to go in the same direction."

Mary nodded slowly. "I guess that makes sense. Each of us has to follow God's laws for oneself and at one's own pace. I can't be blessed for Naola's righteousness if I have been wicked myself. It is that way with the Abrahamic Covenant: every man must be circumcised himself to be numbered among God's covenant people."

Riddah suddenly snorted, gathered her meat chunks into her food cloths, and stood.

"Where are you going, Riddah?" Mary looked up at her, squinting against the sunlight that now framed her.

"Somewhere else. I can't stand these questions you're asking. Can't you talk of more practical things than this wishy-washy spiritual stuff, Didi?"

Naola, Mary, and I watched her leave and then looked at each other in surprise. "What was that all about?" asked Naola.

"Did you ever stop to think how spiritually fanatical you sound," Abisha blurted out. "Always crying repent here and repent there? Have you ever stopped to think about how the rest of us feel? Come on, Kora and Bekka. Let's go."

Abisha and Bekka gathered their things and followed Riddah's tracks. Kora remained bent over her meat supply, spicing and mixing. Suddenly she looked up at us. She spread her hands before us and shrugged. "I'm sorry," was all she said. Then she gathered her work too and followed the others.

We who remained worked in silence for several minutes. Then Sariah, who had been listening the whole time without comment, spoke, her voice barely audible, "There is a bitterness that has been growing in our midst. It may divide us one of these days."

"Is there anything we can do?" Naola asked impulsively.

Sariah sighed deeply. "I do not know. I do know there is not an easy answer. I can only watch and hope and pray."

"Mother Sariah," I asked suddenly, "have you always found it easy to support Lehi in his prophesying?"

She gazed at me in silence a moment. "No, Didi. I was often afraid, afraid for him, afraid for me and my children. And then when it came time to leave Jerusalem and live in the wilderness, it was very hard on me. I like the comforts of living in a real house. I have had to learn a whole new way of life." She sighed. "I confess I criticized him for sending our sons back to Jerusalem to obtain the brass plates. I was afraid for their lives and was without faith until he shared with me his impression that all our sons would come back safely. And when they did return successfully, I felt the love of the Lord and knew that He answers our prayers." She laughed a little. "It also helped that I told Lehi he cannot keep me in the dark anymore when he knows something!"

I nodded, understanding a little more the loneliness of being a supportive spouse.

We had planted crops again while Papa was ill. The several weeks after Papa's burial were very difficult for most of us. But life soon settled into a pattern of daily activities, and time began to heal us. In fact, promise of new life became apparent, as Riddah and Bekka grew with child again. They were excited to be first in the second round of children, and giggled about it a lot. A couple of times I heard them making snide remarks about those who refused the responsibility of bearing children and caught them looking at Naola. She appeared to shake it off, either ignoring them or making some smart retort back.

Then I noticed that Mary was more quiet than usual at these times, glancing from Naola to her other sisters with sadness in her eyes. It was then I became aware that her abdomen was just as pregnant as the others.

I went over to her. "Mary," I said, "you haven't told anyone your good news. You—"

"*Shh*!" she hissed. Kora glanced our way, and Mary smiled innocently at her until she looked away. "I don't want anyone to know right now. Okay, Didi?" And she turned and left the scene. I stared after her, puzzled. Was this just to protect Naola's feelings? I felt sure Naola would be delighted in Mary having another child.

Shortly after this discussion I discovered I, too, was expecting again. But perhaps because of Mary's example, I didn't tell anyone, except Nephi, and I made him promise to keep silent about it too, at least for a while. Mary's reasons became clear to me several weeks later.

It happened when I took a trip to the well while my daughter, Siri, was napping in the tent. Every once in a while I could hear a strange sound, like a wounded animal. I kept pausing between pulling bags of water up, but I couldn't identify location or creature. Then the sound took on a new tone, one that sounded like crying, human crying. I fastened the rope of the well bag securely to the hook on the side and went to investigate. The sounds led me around a hill of sand and rocks.

It was Naola. She was sitting, back against a rock, knees curled up to her chin, and arms hugging her legs to her. Tears streamed down her face, and every few seconds a sob escaped her throat. She made no effort to wipe her tears. Her eyes were closed, and she didn't notice I was there.

I stood for a moment, wondering if I should leave her alone or try to comfort her. Then I decided. I knelt down and touched her shoulder. She jumped, and her eyes flew open.

"I'm sorry to disturb you, Naola," I said softly. "But I wanted to know if there was anything I could do for you."

She threw her arms around my neck. "Oh, Didi," she sobbed, tears flowing anew. "I am glad you're here." For the next five or ten minutes she just cried in my arms, with the intensity that sympathy suddenly releases. Then the sobs quieted and she finally lay still in my arms. I thought she must have fallen asleep, and had begun wondering how long I could stay here before my daughter would wake up, when Naola suddenly raised her head.

"I'm sorry, Didi," she said, wiping her cheeks with her hands. The sand from her hands stuck to the moisture on her cheeks, and she looked like she had just been rolling in the dirt like a child.

"That's all right, Naola." I hugged her and kept my observations to myself. "Is there anything you want to talk to me about?"

"Well," she sighed deeply, and another sob caught in her throat. Then the tears started pouring again. "Didi, I . . . well, they make me feel so . . . I just want . . . to have my own baby!" She crumpled again, head on her knees.

"Oh, Naola! I didn't think . . . I didn't know." I found I could only hug her.

She looked up. "Didi, am I being punished? Riddah said that, well, being barren, I must have done something horrible. Only I can't think what it might have been. And, Didi, will it last forever? I just don't think I could stand that!"

I was silent a minute. "I think . . . I think Mary would say it's a condition of nature. It just happens and can't be helped. Mama would probably say there's a reason for every trial, and there's something that can be learned from all this. I keep thinking of Abraham's wife, Sariah, who was blessed by the Lord to overcome her childlessness when she least expected it. Maybe you, too, can have that blessing."

Naola laughed bitterly. "I think Mother Sariah has taken that blessing. She's bearing children the ages of her grandchildren." I raised my eyebrows at her use of the plural *children*. "Yes," she told me, voice still hard. "Sariah, too, will bear another child soon."

I just looked at Naola steadily. When she caught my gaze, she lowered her eyes, and her shoulders drooped. "I didn't mean it like that," she whispered. "I guess I just get envious sometimes, and it hurts so much. It's hard not to get a little bitter. I really do want to take this like a mature woman."

I nodded and squeezed her shoulders. "So what are you going to do about it, Naola?"

She was silent a while. "I think I'll focus on where I can be of service. Mother Sariah does get tired trying to keep up with a toddler, and I can be kind of a second mother to Jacob, let the urges work out of my system in useful ways. And maybe I'll ask Father Lehi for a blessing."

We smiled at each other and hugged. Then Naola washed her face at the well and helped me carry my water bags back to the tent.

While we were in Nahom, we occasionally noticed some of our nomadic neighbors traveling to the caves in the hills. Some were burying their recent dead, others were paying their respects to loved ones previously buried.

We took advantage of the proximity of these groups, often trading goods, sometimes just trading news. Lemuel was particularly good at sorting through the various dialects of the common trade languages, and loved to spend hours discussing whatever topic arose. Gid was often at his side. They took weekly trips into the hills hunting for game to trade, Mori and Laman often with them. They discovered a little settlement two days' journey away, where the men found wonderful trinkets and household items with which to please their wives. A few times Naola and I sent our husbands along for some things, but a comment from Nephi made me suspect that he and Sam were unwelcome on these journeys.

One afternoon as I emerged from laying Siri down for a nap in the tent, I saw Lemuel storm out of Father Lehi's tent and stomp off in the direction of his own. On my return from fetching a fresh bladder of water, I saw Father Lehi in the shade behind his tent, rocking and praying intently. He seemed to be weeping.

Late morning, about two weeks later, a group of four black-gowned visitors and one white-robed man approached our settlement. Laman and Lemuel seemed to know them and welcomed them in their dialect. Riddah and Bekka brought out some bread and camels' milk while their children hovered nearby, staring at the visitors curiously. Soon Mori and Gid with their families joined the group.

The visitors were young nomadic women with cloths draped across their faces under their head scarves, only their eyes showing. Their black robes were plain, no embroidery to denote any wealth. Shortly after their arrival, they dropped their face scarves, revealing beautifully shaped facial features, brown skin, and intelligent eyes. The man appeared older, middle-aged. He brought gifts which he gave to Laman, Lemual, Mori, and Gid. They spent the next couple of hours talking in the shade of the tents.

With Siri in tow, I approached the group. "Ah, Didi! Come join us!" called out Bekka. "Let us introduce our neighbors!"

I smiled, held out my hand to the first, and she grasped it shyly.

"Oh, crumb," Bekka giggled. "I can only remember Miriam."

"Mirimi," the second visitor corrected, pointing to herself.

"Hagadah," offered the one whose hand I held.

"Yadeesh," nodded the third.

"Jagadesh," stated the fourth.

Their names were unusual but beautiful. "Welcome," I smiled. "I'm Didi, and this is my daughter, Siri."

The women tried to pronounce our names, with hilarious results. When we all finished laughing, the men began talking to them again in their dialect. The nomadic women responded animatedly, their body language showing interest and mirth. Riddah and Abisha were whispering to each other. I felt rather left out. When I looked up, I noticed Bekka seemed a little forlorn too.

"Bekka," I whispered, scooting over to her. "Where are these women from? Who are they?"

"They are staying at the settlement our husbands have been trading with," she answered. "These women are three sisters and a cousin. The older man is the father of the three sisters. An uncle died recently, bringing them here for their period of mourning. That's all I know."

I watched them closely. The first three seemed about our age, maybe a little younger. Jagadesh, the fourth, seemed more reserved and mature in her responses. She also had a different tenor to her voice, making me suspect that she was the cousin.

Soon evening approached. The five visitors spoke as though saying goodbye and stood up to go.

"Wait!" called Lemuel, and then spoke another word in their language that stopped them in their tracks. He turned to Bekka then the rest of us women. "It's a two-day journey for them, they should not start back in the dark. Is there a way to make sleeping arrangements for them?"

I thought of how we'd shift tents and realized Sam and Naola, without children, were the most flexible. "I'll see if Sam and Naola would be willing to sleep with us and give up their tent for the night."

Lemuel smiled at me. Sam and Naola were agreeable to the plan, and the switch was made. Our five visitors were most grateful. They played with the children during dinner preparations and helped with cleanup. After the children were put to bed, the adults stayed up another couple of hours visiting. Finally everyone retired to bed.

Early the next morning, the man and four women were up, faces draped and ready to leave. Lemuel and Gid offered to escort them back home, and they accepted. At Abisha's urging, Mori and Laman went along as well.

After the visit from the four neighboring women and their father, everything continued as before. Lemuel and Gid continued to hunt together, perhaps for longer periods of time, Mori and Laman often accompanying them. A couple of times Nephi, Sam, and Zoram tried to go along, and were informed in clear language that they were not invited.

One night Siri woke up vomiting, and by midnight, I had washed her up and changed her five times. The water bladders were completely empty. I shook Nephi semi-awake and instructed him to listen for Siri. Then I grabbed all the bags I could find and stumbled groggily out to the well.

The night was clear, the stars bright. A feeling of calm began to settle over me. I could hear the crickets singing, and a camel snorted in its sleep. As I neared the well, voices wafted over from it. I paused in the darker shadow of a tree, and listened.

"I tell you, Abisha," said Bekka's voice, "Lemuel seems really distanced lately. Even when he was trading with those nomads, his trips weren't two weeks long, and he stayed home longer in between. He doesn't say as much to me, unless it's to demand I change how I'm doing something." Her voice became even softer, and she looked down at her pregnant belly. "He's not wanting to be intimate as often either."

Abisha sucked in her breath. "Now that you mention it, there is something odd going on . . . with all of our men."

There was silence now, broken only by the sloshing of the water bucket rising up from the well and filling water bags. I wondered if I dare approach the well.

Bekka broke the silence again. "I'm going to follow them next time and see what he's up to."

"Bekka, don't!" commanded Abisha. "What if they catch you out there? Do you know what the nomads do to unfaithful or disobedient women? Do you think a similar thought wouldn't cross their minds?"

"Then what do I do?" Bekka asked miserably.

I found my feet carrying me forward to the well. My sisters would know I had heard their conversation. Sure enough, they stopped talking and stared in my direction.

"I'll send my husband after them," I blurted out.

"Didi," breathed Bekka.

None of us spoke for a moment. Then Abisha spoke. "No, Didi, that would put his life in danger. We can't ask that of you or him."

Bekka grasped Abisha's arm. "Then we do nothing to . . . to find out what is wrong?" She was crying now.

Abisha only stared at the well.

My heart ached for my sisters. What were their men really up to? "I can at least ask Nephi what he would suggest, maybe he can find a third option." I paused. "With your permission of course."

Bekka gazed at Abisha, who nodded. "Yes," Bekka breathed.

None of us spoke while we finished filling our bags. Then on impulse, I turned and hugged them both together. When I returned to the tent, Siri was asleep in Nephi's arms, and we slept peacefully the rest of the night.

Early the next morning I rehearsed my sisters' conversation of the previous night. Nephi pondered for a minute.

"Abisha is right," he said. "It would be dangerous to send any of you women out there. I could, however, track them at a distance, they wouldn't even know I was there. If it is anything like they fear," Nephi's jaw tightened, "I could wait until they return to sort it out."

When Laman, Lemuel, Mori, and Gid returned from their current trip, Nephi and I observed a little more closely their interactions with their families. They seemed natural and loving with them. But I kept packed a travel bag of supplies for Nephi.

About two weeks later, Nephi rushed into the tent just as Siri and I were waking up. "They've gone hunting," he said tersely. "Where's my travel bag?"

I found it quickly and handed it to him.

His eyes met mine. He kissed me and was gone.

Nephi returned a week later. I was out front preparing supper while Siri played in the sand, when he strode up. He nodded to us, threw his bag into the tent, and then turned to Father Lehi's tent without saying a word. I followed him with my eyes. Mother Sariah exited the tent, saw us, and came over to play with Siri. We said little, she ate supper with us, and still Nephi did not return. Sariah helped me put Siri to bed, and then we sat in front of my tent holding hands. Finally Nephi came out and walked toward us. He looked weary.

I ran to him and embraced him. "I have some supper for you, Nephi."

He nodded and smiled briefly. As I brought him his food in front of the tent, Mother Sariah said "Good night," and slipped back to her own tent.

I sat down beside Nephi. "What happened?" I asked carefully.

He chewed a few times and shrugged. "I found out what I went to find."

"And?" My eyes followed his face.

He looked at me, but there was no mirth in his eyes. "Father will talk to them when they return."

It didn't sound very good. My heart was heavy when I thought of my sisters. What were their husbands up to?

Upon the return of Laman, Lemuel, Mori, and Gid, Father Lehi stepped out of his tent and beckoned to them. Laman shot a dagger look at Nephi as he followed his father in. A moment later, Lehi called to Nephi, Sam, and Zoram to also be present. They talked for over an hour, then Sam was sent out to fetch Riddah, Bekka, Abisha, Kora, Mother Sariah, and Mother Leah. Mary, Naola, and I gathered in front of my tent where we could watch all the children playing, and waited.

"What's going on?" Noala whispered to me.

I knew something was terribly wrong but did not know what. "We'll have to wait and see," I answered.

Another hour went by, during which we fixed a simple supper for the children and tucked the younger ones into bed. Finally the door panel to Father Lehi's tent opened. Bekka left first, stumbling out and running to her own tent. She had been crying and looked awful. Riddah walked out next, stoic and stiff, ignoring Laman and Lemuel who were following behind her. Kora, near collapse, was supported by Abisha while Gid and Mori walked behind.

"I was tricked!" Mori called after Abisha. "I didn't know the gifts were a marriage contract. I didn't know until it was too late!" Abisha ignored him.

All of them went straight to their own tents, their older children following.

Ten minutes later Zoram exited the tent, followed by Mama leaning on Sam, and then Nephi.

"Naola," Sam stated. "Your mother should stay with us tonight." Naola nodded and hurried off to prepare a bed for her.

Zoram took Mary in his arms in an intense embrace. Then he led her silently to their tent.

Nephi stopped in front of me, placed his hands on my shoulders, and gazed deeply into my eyes. Then he drew me close in a long embrace. "I will never, ever be unfaithful to you, Didi," he whispered fervently in my ear.

I pulled back and searched his face. He didn't offer any more information, and I didn't ask. He turned and guided me into our tent.

The next morning Laman, Lemuel, Mori, and Gid left again, taking extra camels with them. During the week they were gone, everyone, it seemed, was miserable. Bekka and Kora cried a lot, Abisha was harsh and stern, Riddah lost her temper often, and Mama spent most of her time with Mother Sariah in her tent.

When the men returned this time, they brought with them Mirimi, Hagadah, Yadeesh, and Jagadesh. Additional camels carried loads of goods and tents, and they brought a small herd of goats. Everyone came out of their tents or in from play to welcome or gawk at their arrival.

While many hands reached up to help the women down, Father Lehi approached and held out his arms to each of them in an embrace.

"Welcome, daughters," he said while Laman translated for him into their language.

My breath caught when he used the more familiar term for "daughter." I looked over at Nephi, who was studying his brothers and their wives.

Lehi continued, "Let the men unload your things while you refresh yourselves." He beckoned to Sariah, who brought forth fresh water for them to drink. My sisters and I brought them dinner while the men unpacked, watered the camels, and set up four new tents. After we all had eaten, Lehi called the entire camp together. When all were seated, he arose to speak, again Laman translating for the nomadic women.

"My family," he began, "you multiply beyond my fondest dreams and even expectations." He raised an eyebrow at his two oldest sons, but they made no visible response. "We welcome you, Jagadesh, Mirimi, Yadeesh, and Hagadah, fully into our family." He paused to let the news begin to sink into our minds. "Tonight we have set up your tents, and on the morrow, we will officially celebrate your marriage union with our sons."

I heard Mary suddenly suck in her breath. I looked at her, and her eyes were wide with surprise and a bit of horror. Naola was merely staring at Father Lehi uncomprehendingly.

"My sons," Father Lehi was saying, "would you introduce your new wives to the rest of us?"

He sat down, and no one moved for a moment, except for Kora's infant crying and being comforted. Lemuel nodded his head to Laman and Laman finally stood up.

"This is Jagadesh," Laman said, reaching out and pulling her to her feet. He finally looked at Riddah. "Jagadesh, my wife Riddah."

Riddah merely nodded at Jagadesh, barely looking at her. Jagadesh quickly went to Riddah and knelt before her, bowing her head almost to her knees.

"You are first wife," Jagadesh spoke in broken Hebrew. "I follow your wishes."

Riddah looked at her in surprise. Jagadesh remained bowed before her, obviously meaning to stay that way until told otherwise. "All right . . . Jagadesh," Riddah stammered. Jagadesh still didn't move. "Uh, you may rise."

Jagadesh nodded and returned humbly but gracefully back to her place. Riddah remained staring after her in astonishment.

Lemuel stood next. "Everyone, this is my new wife, Mirimi."

When Mirimi arose awkwardly, I suddenly noticed that she was with child, perhaps five months along. Bekka went to meet Mirimi, grasping her hands. "Welcome to our family," she said graciously. Mirimi smiled, and she too bowed her head deeply. When Bekka turned away, her fixed smile was broken by the sound of a brief sob, which did not reassert itself again.

Mori stood next. "I present to you Yadeesh. Yadeesh, this is my wife Abisha."

Abisha stood, looking at Yadeesh as though she were studying how to carve the dinner meat. Yadeesh knelt at Abisha's feet and murmured, "Abisha."

"Yadeesh," Abisha nodded at her.

When Abisha made no further comment, Yadeesh returned to her place without looking directly at Abisha again.

Last of all Gid stood. "My wife Hagadah," he said, helping her to her feet. "And my wife Kora."

I wasn't sure, but Hagadah also appeared to be with child. However, Hagadah moved easily over to Kora and knelt before her.

"I will serve you, Kora," she spoke in Hebrew and touched Kora's foot with her hand.

Kora raised Hagadah up and tried to smile. Then she collapsed back to the ground and turned her face into Abisha's shoulder sitting beside her. Hagadah reached out a hand as though to touch Kora's shoulder, paused, let her hand drop, and returned to her own place.

Father Lehi faced all of us. He looked stern. "What is done is done. I would not have my sons forsake an oath of marriage however it came to pass. I have prayed earnestly over this. At times the Lord will approve of plural marriage that he may raise up posterity until him. But hear this: the Lord God has decreed that we should have save it be one wife, to cleave unto her and none else. Let this law be followed from this time forth and forever. I have spoken."

After Father Lehi offered family prayer, we retired to our tents. I did not sleep well that night, thinking about my brothers having multiple wives, like the nomadic families we had passed in our journey.

Early the next morning, Mama woke us to begin preparing for the festivities. The men had left early to hunt, and Mother Sariah declared that today we would roast the meat over a fire. The children were sent out to find any burnable material (dried grasses, tree branches, dried camel droppings), while the women prepared bread, sauces, grains, and brought out all varieties of fruit. By then the men began arriving with their game, cleaned and ready for cooking. Soon there was not much more to be done but get ourselves ready.

Mama had volunteered Mary, Naola, and me to help dress the new brides for their formal Hebrew weddings. We gathered together in Jagadesh's tent. They each pulled out an intricately embroidered colored gown to put on. They pulled off their black robes and hoods, revealing their hair, Jagadesh with shorter and the other three with longer sets of straight long black hair falling over lovely smooth brown skin. These girls were beautiful, and I could begin to understand my brothers' interest in them.

I brought Jagadesh a fresh container of water for washing. She brought out vials of oil to soften her skin, and perfume. Then I helped her pull on her red embroidered dress. She handed a comb to me, and I combed her hair until it glistened. Though her hair only reached partway down her back, it had a thickness that her cousins' hair didn't have. I envied how the comb went so easily through it compared to the tangle of natural curls I struggled with.

Jagadesh showed me how to braid part of her hair to decoratively hold the rest in place. As a finishing touch, she put on earrings, bracelets, and anklets that flashed multicolored jewels on gold. Then she covered herself with a matching red head scarf that she pulled across her face, leaving only her eyes showing.

"Only husband see hair and face tonight," she told me, with a golden peal of laughter.

I turned around to see the finishing touches of the other three brides. Mirimi was dressed in blue, Hagadah in gold, and Yadeesh in green. They, too, were adorned with jewelry that beautified their bare ankles and wrists.

"Well," sighed Mama, leaning back from straightening Yadeesh's dress. "I don't think we can make you four any prettier. Our sons will have to take you as you are."

The four brides giggled. Naola impulsively leaned over and gave Mirimi a hug.

Jagadesh spoke, "We must prepare tents for husbands. You go now." She waved the rest of us out. Soon after we left, the three sisters peeked out to ensure no men were around, and scurried to their tents.

Mary looked at Mama. "Mama, what about Riddah, Bekka, Abisha and Kora? What do they do tonight?"

Mama breathed deeply. "I don't know, Mary."

"Let's do something special for them, Mama," pleaded Naola. "Do we have any oils or perfumes for them?" Mama smiled and nodded.

"Oh, yes! An evening of making them lovely, complete with an herbal foot massage!" offered Mary.

Inspired by Jagadesh's creativity, I spoke, "I'll do their hair for them!"

"We'll do it in my tent," suggested Naola. "Bring all your softest cushions and a couple of extra lanterns."

"Let's make it a surprise for them," said Mary. "I'm sure our husbands will help with their children."

Smiling with our secret, we parted for the final feast preparations.

Soon Father Lehi was calling us for the ceremonies. The families of the new wives had arrived. It reminded me much of my own wedding, and I caught myself smiling at Nephi. He smiled back, reached over, and held my hand. I picked Siri up in my arm and hugged her.

After the weddings, we feasted then tucked our children into bed. Then, while the guests and newlyweds continued to party, we "kidnapped" Kora, Abisha, Riddah, and Bekka into Naola's tent.

"What are you doing?" Abisha demanded. "This wasn't on the schedule of events."

"Maybe not on yours," smiled Mama. "But your sisters seem to have something special in mind."

"But my children—" began Kora.

"Will be watched over by our husbands while you're here," Naola told her, pushing her down into the cushions. "This evening you will spend with us."

Protesting half-heartedly, the women let us seat them on the cushions, Mary with Riddah, Mama with Abisha, Naola with Kora, and I with Bekka. We began by washing their faces, hands, and feet. We oiled and softened their skin, applied perfume, massaged tired muscles and feet, and combed and braided their hair. As we ministered to them, they talked and we listened. They spoke of their families, their hopes and dreams, and their daily challenges. We dried a few tears and gave several hugs. And then we returned them to their tents, clean, relaxed, and loved.

The next morning we sent off our wedding guests then began to settle into the routines of our new family dynamics.

At first, Riddah, Bekka, Abisha, and Kora made a special effort to be kind to Mary, Naola, and me. But soon real life took over, and we found ourselves chasing kids, feeding husbands, and keeping camp cleaned up.

It came to my attention that progressively on our journey since the Valley of Lemuel, our encampment arrangements divided more and more into two distinct groups. The tents would be arranged so that the oasis or well took central position in the camp, but Laman, Lemuel, Mori, and Gid's tents would be clustered on one side, the others grouped near Lehi's tent on the other side. Family members of Laman's group would join us for meals increasingly late or not at all. Several weeks after the weddings, they stopped joining us at all. They kept much to themselves, their children playing off on their own, the men hunting separately. They would eat in their encampment at different hours than we, breakfast later in the morning and supper later in the evening. As I would fall asleep at night, I could hear their voices, drifting across the night air well into the late hours, talking and laughing and occasionally singing. Sometimes I would jerk awake to what I thought had been yelling or crying, but then all would be silent. I would look at Nephi, sleeping soundly beside me, then turn over and go back to sleep. I could not help but wonder how much of my siblings' personal lives I was missing by this division. I also began to sense that this division was not what God wanted in our family. After much prayer, I felt that I needed to make more of an effort to bridge that gulf.

Naola and I decided one evening to visit them at suppertime on a peace envoy, Naola with some dried fruit goodies for the children and sun-baked bread cakes and I with my daughter, Siri. As we walked into their circle of tents where they were noisily making meal preparations, I called out a greeting. In an instant, the group fell quiet and turned to look at us. I almost lost my power of speech.

"We . . . we wondered if we could join you for dinner tonight. We've missed you from our group the last several weeks."

Naola broke in to help me out. "We brought some fresh bread cakes and fruit for the little ones. Where shall I put them?"

Abisha was the first to respond. She came forward and took the cakes from Naola. "Thank you, my dear Naola and Didi. You are welcome to join us. Have a seat, and we'll be ready in a moment."

Most of the children eyed us from a distance, as if we were strangers. But Mori's oldest sons, Zac and Matthew, came up to Naola and sat down in front of her. Siri shrank behind me and peeked at them around my shoulder.

"What do you have in your apron?" Matthew asked Naola, reaching toward it.

Zac nudged him hard with his elbow. "Shh! Don't pester her! It's rude!"

Matthew drew back, abashed, and Naola laughed. "You'll see after supper!" She folded her arms and looked at them with one eye half closed and the other eyebrow raised. "What story shall I tell you tonight?"

The boys argued for a minute but couldn't decide. By then Gid's children, Gad and Johanna; Mori's daughter, Anna; and a few of the other children stood closer by.

"I know!" spoke Naola solemnly. "I will tell you a story about a slave baby who was found in the bulrushes of a river by a princess—"

"Dinner is served!" called out Riddah, followed by Hagadah carrying a big bowl of spiced meat, maize, and bread cakes over to the children. They bolted over to the food, grabbing bread cakes and stuffing fistfuls of maize and meat into their mouths. Jagadesh took another large dish to the circle of men, who ate with little more restraint. Yadeesh brought a third large bowl over to where Naola, Siri, and I were sitting, and the other women joined us, dipping bread or fingers into the dish, conversing between bites. The food looked wonderful and smelled of spices I didn't quite recognize.

"What about prayer on the food?" Naola whispered to me. Everyone was eating away, giving no indication that they planned to pray.

"Say a silent one," I whispered back and bowed my head slightly.

Abisha looked at us briefly and then stared at the food a moment. Suddenly she stood up and clapped her hands. The hubbub of voices quieted down. "We have guests with us tonight, and we welcome them! We hope you feel comfortable, Naola and Didi, and will come visit us again. But first, my husband, we need a blessing over this food." She shot him a look and sat down again.

Mori, next to Laman, looked uncomfortable a moment. Then he stood, looked around the group, and bowed his head. "Thank you for the food, O God. Bless it. Amen." He sat down again and returned to his conversation with Laman.

The nomadic wives chatted quietly in their native tongue. Riddah, Bekka, and Abisha tried to make some small talk, and Naola answered back as best she could. I could not keep my mind on the conversation enough to help it out. Something about the atmosphere here seemed off, and I couldn't quite place it.

Soon supper was finished. The children ran off to play in the last bit of daylight, and Siri followed at Matthew's beckoning. The men remained together near one of the tents playing some kind of game in the dirt. Naola and I helped the other women clean up, sand washing the dishes, and getting things put away as dusk deepened. Then we all collapsed in front of Kora's tent.

"Tell me what your children are up to these days, Abisha," I asked her. It was the right topic. She went on and on about the escapades her two oldest boys got into daily and occasionally dragged their dainty younger sister into also. We laughed in delight at her telling. Almost before she finished, Riddah jumped in telling about her toddler's antics. Kora said little but smiled broadly whenever others mentioned her children. It was obvious these women were proud of being mothers.

"What about your daughter, Didi?" Bekka asked. I glanced at Naola. She was looking at her feet. I looked back at Bekka and gave her the updates, trying to mention the funniest incidents I could. My daughter, in comparison, almost seemed boring, at least in what I could remember to report. Where were all those wonderful questions and insights my Siri came up with almost daily? Questions like "where does God live, Mama?" and "what does he look like?" Questions only Nephi could answer.

Bekka turned to Naola. "When are you and Sam going to have children, Naola?" It was the inevitable question.

Naola gazed up at her steadily. My heart cried out for her. This was the one question she herself had sobbed out to me earlier and had prayed to God unendingly in the secret of her tent. What a brave, sweet soul! "When it is God's will," she said simply.

Bekka looked down, embarrassed.

Riddah commented half out loud, "You have to sleep with a man first." Bekka snorted.

Abisha hit Riddah on the arm. "Shush! You ought to be ashamed of yourself!"

Riddah and Bekka both giggled, and Kora followed suit. Naola stared straight ahead but blinked quickly a few times. Everyone fell silent again.

Kora broke the silence, "How many Jewish men does it take to set up a nomadic tent?" she asked, looking at Naola.

Naola's gaze suddenly focused on hers. "I don't know. How many?" she said after a moment.

"At least four and then only if a Jewish woman is telling them how to do it." We all laughed.

The men at the next tent looked up. "Hey, no jokes without us!" called Gid.

"Hey, wait, I've got one!" said Mori. "How many women does it take to satisfy one desert-traveling man?"

The other men hooted. "How many?" "I give up!"

"No more than one, if she's a Jewess, and it only takes one night," answered Mori. "At least four if they're nomadic women, and then it takes his entire life!"

The men could barely contain themselves. Riddah and Bekka giggled. Abisha looked disgusted. Naola glanced up at me, puzzled. I shook my head.

"Enough jokes for tonight," Abisha said firmly. "It's about time you men finish up that game and water the animals for the night. It is your turn."

"Just a moment, Abisha. We'll be done in a minute," Gid answered.

The other women left to gather the children. Abisha turned to Naola and me. "It'll take the men hours before they get to the animals. Do you care to join me at the well?"

We nodded and walked with her in the moonlight. She carried two large water bladders in silence. At the well, she let down the first bag, and I helped her lift it out again and pour its contents into the water trough. The camels sucked it up thirstily.

"Naola," she finally spoke, "I'm sorry about Riddah and Bekka's behavior tonight."

"It's all right." Naola gave her a quick smile and helped her pull up the next bag of water.

"Didi, Naola," Abisha seemed to be struggling to choose her words, "how do you deal with your husbands?"

Naola and I stared at each other. "What do you mean?" I asked.

Abisha shrugged. "I don't know. Men just frustrate me so sometimes. They never do what you want them to."

I helped her with the next bag but said nothing. Abisha didn't speak for a minute. Then suddenly she couldn't stop.

"I have been thinking a lot, Didi, since the conversation you had with Mary way back after Papa died, about what it is like being married to Nephi. I have thought a lot about what it is like being married to Mori. When we first married, it was all a glorious dream come true. Not only was he an upstanding man in the community, but he was handsome and strong. He was perfect in my eyes, almost a god. But gradually I realized that deep down there was another side to him, one not so perfect at all. And no one else seemed to see it or care about it. Some of the things he said and did would shock and anger me. They hinted at a past or inner life that was foreign to me. And then he had to go and marry Yadeesh." She gritted her teeth. "Now he grows distant from me, communicating with me less and less often, leaving more of the childrearing to me, going off with the men or Yadeesh every chance he gets. I feel I hardly know who he is anymore." She had stopped pulling up water and stood with tears running down her cheeks. "Didi, is Nephi really the righteous man he seems, or is it all a front as Laman says? It's been so long since I've known Nephi, and then he was just a little boy. But you would know. Or are you still in the honeymoon period of blind belief?"

I was shocked. Could Nephi be just pretending, creating a certain glamorous image for some reason known only to him? I could not imagine him that way. I had never sensed it, but neither had I ever looked for it before.

"No!" I protested. "Nephi could never be like that! He is a good man down to his very soul. I believe he really has seen the vision of Father Lehi's dream and many others. What you see on the surface is really what you get inside!"

Abisha looked at me sadly. "I only hope you are right, Didi," she said. She picked up her waterskins and walked back to her tent. I stood and stared at the stones of the well.

"Didi," Naola whispered, tugging at the sleeve of my dress. "Didi, are you all right?"

I looked up. "Yes," I said simply. We collected Siri and turned back toward our tents.

I held up well until I got inside and had tucked Siri into bed. Then the complete meaning of the question Abisha had asked hit me full force. Was I still in the blind honeymoon period? Was it possible Nephi hid some terrible dark side of himself from the eyes of even his wife? Could he be lying about the visions he told us he had received? Could this all be part of a plot to gain control of all of us as his and my older siblings kept suggesting?

I shook my head. No. It was as I had told Abisha. Nephi was a good man, trying hard to balance his search for God with raising and supporting a family and keeping peace with brothers that persecuted him. There was no dark hidden side to him.

As I undressed for bed, doubts again filled my mind. I thought of the times I had been frustrated with him: his not always seeing what needed to be done without my telling him, his throwing his dirty clothes into a corner of the tent for me to find days later, his always going away on those long hunting trips. I suddenly realized I was lonely, lonely that he could not share his deepest thoughts and most treasured experiences with me, lonely that I could not measure up to the standard of goodness he seemed to set. I was tired of constantly trying to keep my outlook positive for him, tired of keeping up the energy to meet my family's needs in this desert. I was tired of always struggling for answers and guidance, never to find an outstanding spiritual experience, only just strength enough to carry on one more step or one more day.

Where did Nephi get all his energy to constantly be teaching his extended family? Why was he the one to receive all these marvelous spiritual experiences as opposed to someone else? How could he be so unfailingly righteous?

By the time I reached these thoughts, I was on the bed and sobbing. I paused to wipe my face with my apron and heard a sobbing cry. I had waked Siri. Pulling myself to my feet, I went over to her lying on her little bed of soft woven blankets. I picked her up and, going back to my bed, cradled her in my arms, caressing her hair. At this moment, her face showed complete contentment, trust. She was unaware of the complications of the world around her, innocent of what sin meant. Perhaps she even remembered what it was like to be in the presence of God before coming here. The tears started flowing again, but this time my sobs were silent.

Nephi came in while I was still in this state.

"Didi! Whatever in the world is wrong?" he asked, hurrying to kneel at my side. Putting one arm around my waist, he wiped my tears away with the other.

I could only laugh and cry at the same time. "It's so silly!" I managed between breaths. "Really, Nephi, you'll just laugh at me."

At that, he smiled slightly. I guess I must have looked and sounded pretty comical. But, as he usually did, his facial expression and words let me know he really did care about what I thought and felt. "Try me," he said.

It all poured out: the visit with my sisters, the conversation with Abisha, my own thoughts and fears. By the time I finished, I was laughing and sobbing again, and this kept waking poor Siri up.

Nephi remained quiet after I finished and shifted his position from crouching in front of me to sitting on the bed beside me, his arm around my shoulders. "I didn't know you felt all that," he commented quietly.

I shrugged and sniffled. "I didn't either."

"I, too, feel lonely a lot," he said. "And tired. Bone tired. I think God gives me just enough strength when he needs me to speak or do something for him." He looked at his hands, then back at me.

"I don't know why God shares with me the things he does, Didi. I would be just as happy with much less in answer to my questions." He paused. "Perhaps God needs someone to witness to my father's words. Perhaps he needs someone to carry on the spiritual leadership of our people after Father is gone, and Laman or any one of my older brothers should really carry that leadership. Laman and Lemuel don't seem to care enough about spiritual things, and Sam is always afraid to say anything that would hurt other people. Your brothers, I'm afraid, Didi, are like my two oldest brothers. And no one would listen as easily to Zoram or Eli, who are not true family, or to you women." He sighed and looked heavenward a moment. "It is a heavy, heavy responsibility." He looked at me again. "But I would choose to carry the burden again for how important it is."

Siri had finally gotten to sleep again. Nephi picked her up from my arms and carried her gently, now sleeping, to her bed. He pulled off his outer robe and joined me again on our bed.

"Didi, you and your sisters expressed a feeling that I represent to you some standard of righteousness, of perfection even." He laughed. "Oh, I feel so far from it! I see before me so clearly my own faults and weaknesses: feeling anger with my brothers, harboring occasional thoughts and feelings I shouldn't have, getting impatient even with you sometimes."

He saw the look on my face and gave me a gentle kiss. "Then I realize, Didi, how often I do things that upset you, and I'm able to forget everything that bothers me. In fact, sometimes I even find myself missing your little mannerisms and gestures when I've gone hunting." He grinned. "You are all I expect and more. I wouldn't trade you for all the wealth in Jerusalem!"

"But I'm not even close to perfect, Nephi!" I cried. "I've never had a revelation, or seen a vision, and often I go through a whole day hardly thinking about spiritual things. Sometimes I wonder if I'm even going in the right direction. You need a spiritual giant for a wife! I'm just plain me. I don't even know if God is really there!" There, it was out.

Nephi gazed silently at me a moment. I dropped my head into my hands and started crying again. He put his arms more tightly around me and just held me until I stopped. I looked up at him again. He searched my face, as if trying to find just the right words to say.

"I didn't always know either," he told me finally. "It came gradually at first. I would have a small experience here or another one there. The key for me was learning to recognize the Holy Spirit as it touched my life. Do you know how the spirit speaks to us, Didi?"

I thought about it a minute. "I've always heard about God's Spirit speaking in dramatic ways, like to Moses in the burning bush or in the cloud. But then there are other prophets who seemed to just automatically know God's will or words, like Isaiah or Elijah, as if God spoke to them in their minds and hearts. And then there are the people who believed and followed the prophets, even through famines and persecution, they must have had a testimony, some feeling deep inside that the prophets spoke the truth."

I looked up at Nephi again. "I've thought a lot about what made my family leave Jerusalem with you and your brothers. Some of them say they've regretted it time and again. But others keep following your family, as if there is something deep inside telling them it is the right thing to do. I know I felt something like that the day you came to our house. I just felt that this was what God wanted us to do. I think that is the Holy Spirit." Nephi nodded. "And then there have been a couple of times I have had ideas that just seemed to drop into my head." I thought of when I was trying to get out of Jerusalem past the soldiers and when the rough camel riders were looking in our tents for the travelers under our protection at the Place of the Broken Bow. "I like to think that was God helping me."

Nephi smiled. "Those are all excellent ideas. I also have found that God communicates through feelings."

I remembered the unease I felt when Nephi's brothers bound and left him in the wilderness on the way to the Valley of Lemuel, the peace and excitement about the prospect of even beginning this journey out of Jerusalem, and the rightness of being chosen as wife to Nephi. I nodded my head vigorously.

"Now," said Nephi. "Let's look at testimony again. Do you know what the definition is?"

I thought a minute. "I think it is the knowledge one has of something spiritual. I also think of the testimonials one gives in courts of law, stating a fact of something witnessed. Does that sound right?"

Nephi nodded. "But remember, a testimony of spiritual things must include the feelings of the heart bearing witness of their truth, not just the head knowing facts. That's what many people don't understand. If they can't make sense of it with their reason, they won't believe it. But before they can 'see' or feel the truth of spiritual things or principles, they must want to believe in them first. Then can come the faith that gets them to act on the principle in question, which opens their soul to the Holy Spirit's witness, creating personal knowledge or testimony of that principle. But the whole process takes some work. And a lot of people would rather not do the work it requires, which is to live the principles of God and to humble the heart enough to hear the Spirit."

Nephi paused a moment and his eyes gazed into mine. My heart started pounding at the clarity and joy that shone in his eyes. "Devorah, I want you to know that God lives, that he wants us to succeed, that the laws he gives us are meant to teach us how to live lives of joy. And though the way is longer and harder for some, he wants each one of us to feel the witness of his Holy Spirit in our hearts. The Messiah will come, and he will redeem us from our sins and from the imperfections of our mortal existence. And, Didi, until you can feel and know it fully for yourself, be at peace that I know, and Father knows, and Sam, and many people and prophets before us. I promise you will find it for yourself if you keep seeking the truth."

I melted in his embrace, my earlier doubts about him and myself diminished. I was grateful that he did not consider my lesser faith as a barrier in our relationship. This time my tears were of relief and joy.

"Did I say something wrong?" he asked, eyes wide.

"No, Nephi. What you said is right, all right. It was just what I needed to hear." I sounded ridiculous. I looked up at him, and our laughter mingled with my tears. But deep down inside a cold knot of . . . doubt remained.

Over the next few weeks I felt that knot try to resurface several times, sometimes even in my happier moments. While tickling Siri, my laughter stopped cold. How can I find joy in this little girl or our next baby when life is so uncertain? At any moment, death or illness could find us. How can she be so happy, only believing simply that there is a God and trusting that her parents know what life is about? And what is life about anyway, truly? Some people seek wealth or power or control over others. Some people live for their families or spend life seeking that God who is forever just out of reach. And others are lost, just living one day at a time, not knowing what to live for or perhaps wishing for death and too afraid to embrace it.

I couldn't tickle Siri anymore. I wasn't sure I knew what the purpose of my life was. My daily goal was to keep my family fed and healthy. But long term? Many societies based their stability and structure on valuing the family as the end all. Trying to get along with my extended family took so much effort, and I wondered, *What was the use*? Nephi's life purpose was to bring his brothers to God, and this desire kept him going despite rebuff after insult.

Suddenly it hit me. Having a purpose for life, a true one, depended on a belief, even a knowledge that there is a God. Only then did family matter, only then did trying to be good matter. Without God, life was full of pain, of the powerful treading down the weak, of despair and loneliness and darkness. I had always believed there was a God, but had anything happened in my life to prove to me that he existed? I searched the memories of my life. I had had no visions, no miracles or experiences that couldn't be explained away somehow. The feelings of testimony were likely only the emotions of others affecting me in the excitement of the moment. My heart grew darker.

"Mommy!" Siri's voice broke into my reverie. "Come play wif me, Mommy!"

I went over to where she was playing with her rag dolls, and sat on the earth beside them. She was playing house. But my heart wasn't in it, and I just moved the doll Siri had handed me wherever I was told to. Then with the Mama doll, she set up the other dolls to teach them to pray. I felt tears pricking at my eyes, and the cold lump hit the pit of my stomach again. I couldn't do this anymore without knowing.

I stood up. "Come on, Siri," I said, trying to keep my voice steady. "Bring your dolls. We're going to visit Aunt Naola."

At Naola's tent door, Siri called in her greeting. Naola came to the door, and at sight of her, my tears burst forth.

"Whatever is wrong, Didi?" she asked, embracing me. "What can I do to help you?"

I pulled back and looked at her. "Can you take my Siri for the afternoon, Naola? I need some time alone to think."

Naola nodded eagerly. I knelt down in front of Siri.

"What's wrong, Mommy?" Siri asked, a serious look in her eyes. "Was I bad?"

"No, Siri," I smiled through my tears and hugged her. "You are doing everything just right. I just need a little time alone to sort some things out myself."

Naola gathered Siri into her tent, and I turned toward the desert hills around our encampment. As I walked, I let my mind go blank, and my heart started feeling calmer. *Now I know why Nephi spends so much time in the wilderness,* I thought. *It is peaceful here.*

After an hour of walking, I started feeling a little thirsty. It was then that I realized I hadn't thought to bring any food or water with me. I would have to be careful to shade myself. It looked like I would be doing a little fasting during this soul searching. The cold rock hit my stomach again full force. I would need the fasting spirit to get through this, I knew.

The weight of what I was seeking slowed my brisk pace to a meandering walk. Did I dare ask the question? The course of my whole life hung on what the answer would be. But without the answer, I didn't know if I could continue trying, certainly not as a woman of faith.

This was the question: was there a God up there? If yes, then it was worth the effort to try and be good, to try and keep the extended family together, to teach my children about him. If He did not exist, then I could no longer support my husband in his life's direction toward God. I would no longer expend the energy to try to make peace in the family, and I might as well leave the caravan and move to the nearest wealthy town to live a life of pleasure and greed. Without a god, my life would just be surviving, lost, dark, and afraid, without hope of a better life after this, without reason for living.

I fell to the earth and sobbed. I was afraid that I might find there was no God. I was afraid of being a lost soul. But now the question was asked, and I couldn't return to where I was before. If I did, it would be a sham, a cover up, an act. I knew that I could only live according to the truth I found, that I could do or be nothing else.

Now came the problem of how to prove to myself that there was a God. I laughed to myself. People had been trying to prove the existence of God for centuries, and couldn't do it. Maybe it would be easier to prove that God did not exist. And what would that take? Someone saying there is no God, someone from the other side? But that would only prove that creatures exist in another realm, and would only give more evidence to the possibility of God. It seemed like a ploy Satan would use. The only thing I could come up with was doing all I knew and had been taught to entice God to communicate with me and then not to receive an answer. But how long should I wait? I knew of people who searched for years for an answer, and I knew I could not wait that long in my condition. Under all this doubt, I might be able to go on a few weeks, maybe a couple of months, before breaking. But even if God never answered while I was alive, that still didn't prove he wasn't there. It was his choice to answer me or not, and he could choose to wait until after I was dead and had returned to him.

What about proving there was a God, if not to the world, at least to me? *Simple,* I thought, *a vision or angelic visitation would do it.* Then I thought of Laman and Lemuel. They had seen an angel and heard him speak. But did their subsequent actions show they were convinced to believe in God? Hardly. Or else, even worse, they knew of God and willfully lived in disobedience to his will. No, that wouldn't do for me. External signs alone weren't proof enough, or else they could be explained away if one tried hard enough: for example, madness and hallucinations. It would have to be something that touched me internally, something I knew without a doubt did not come from me. I didn't need anything spectacular, just convincing. Like foretelling the future; I knew I couldn't do that.

I sat up and wiped my face with my apron. Then I laughed. *Who am I,* I thought, *to think God will answer my prayers on this?* True, I've tried to live my life as he has asked, and I don't have any major sins that I can think of to stand in the way of hearing his spirit speak to me. But it is a big request, and I'm only one young woman, not very significant in the big scheme of things. I guess I could be patient for the answer to my question.

I stood up and realized that the sun was getting lower in the sky. I'd have to hurry to get home before dark. Then a voice spoke to my mind: "Siri will be scared, a close call, but she will be well." I stopped in my tracks. What was that all about? I almost ran the rest of the way back to the tents.

I reached Naola's tent breathless. "Naola! Naola!" I practically screamed. "Where is Siri?"

Naola came out of the door of her tent. "Calm down, Didi!" she smiled. "Siri is all right. Come on in."

"B-but . . ." I stammered. "I thought . . ."

I followed her inside. Toward the back of the tent, Siri was playing quietly with Naola's scarves and robes. She looked up, and a smile lit her face. "Mommy!" she cried, jumping up. Her hand clutched the most recent scarf she had been tying to a chain of others. As she jumped forward, the scarves caught around the corner pillar pole supporting the back of the tent and jerked the foot of it forward. Amidst Siri's screams, the back of the tent collapsed, pottery hanging from the roof crashing down around her.

I screamed myself and rushed forward, frantically trying to untangle items holding the heavy tent down around my only daughter. Naola worked beside me. As I paused to wipe wild damp hair from around my eyes, I noticed that all was quiet from where Siri lay.

I nearly panicked. "Siri! Siri! Are you all right? Baby!" I started digging away shards of pottery again.

"Mommy!" cried a muffled voice.

"Oh, my Siri!" I sobbed. "Mommy's coming. Don't move, baby!"

Pretty soon we had untangled enough of the hanging pots that Naola was able to press her back against the roof of the heavy camel hair tent and lift it somewhat. I crawled into the space she had created, and my fingers found Siri's hand. I reached over her body, pulling away a few more heavy items until she was free. Then I touched her face, stomach, and each limb to make sure she was not broken.

"Up, please," Siri finally begged. "Want hug."

I grasped my child to me, and we rocked for a wonderful blessed moment. She was all right!

"Didi," gasped Naola. "I can't hold up the tent much longer. Can you get her out yet?"

I scooted back, still holding Siri in my arms, until we were free of the fallen portion of the tent. Naola collapsed next to us, and we just sat looking at each other.

"Is she all right?" Naola asked tentatively. Siri and I looked up at her and nodded.

Suddenly two figures came crashing in through the front door of the tent. "Naola! Are you all right?" asked a panting Sam.

Nephi was right behind him. "Didi! What happened? Where's Siri?"

Naola and I gazed at them in relief. "Daddy, tent fell down on me!" sang Siri, smiling up at Nephi.

"What?" He looked from me to Naola and back again.

"It was a close call," I began. "It mainly scared her, but she is well." The meaning of my words, and their familiarity, hit me full force, and I jumped to my feet. "Nephi, I was warned this would happen. God told me something would happen, but that Siri would be all right! Nephi! God just answered my prayers!" I found I was crying with joy as bright almost as my earlier despair had been dark. I hugged Siri, hugged Nephi, then pulled Naola to her feet and danced around the part of the tent that was still standing.

I started singing. "Make a joyful noise unto God, all ye lands: sing forth the honor of his name: make his praise glorious. I love the Lord because he hath heard my voice and my supplication. Because he hath inclined his ear unto me, therefore will I call upon him as long as I live."

My heart was full. God was real! He was really there! Instead of wandering the earth in despair, there was a purpose to my life: raising my daughter to believe in God, supporting my husband, working to keep ties open with our siblings and their families, and trying to be a righteous daughter of God. I felt peace and joy and excitement. God had answered me and in a single day! Then I stopped my singing and dancing. Sam, Naola, and Nephi were all staring at me. I laughed. "Oh, don't mind me. Let's just get this tent back together again, shall we?"

Time passed near Nahom as we nurtured a second round of crops and the new infants began to arrive. Riddah and Mary delivered daughters; Bekka, Mirimi, Hagadah, and Sariah had sons. Despite my anticipated fears, my second labor was tolerable, and our second daughter, Zenna, was born. I discovered it was harder to take care of a newborn with a toddler, but I soon found a rhythm to balance it (with Naola's and Mama's help). Zenna was also a peaceful child, which helped.

Then the difficulties started. Areas that had once produced game were barren, the hunting trips grew longer, and we once again found ourselves eating more sparingly to try and make it until our crops ripened. Nephi several times went to Lehi for hunting directions from the brass ball but with no better results.

"It's funny," he remarked to me after one of these unsuccessful trips. "It's almost as though the compass were leading us to the most desolate places instead of the most fertile. I could almost do better myself. I examined the ball carefully the last time. It looked like it was working, and there was no particular writing upon it either. I just don't understand. Are we being tested again, Didi?"

I had no answer for him. Nephi continued hunting, with his brothers and alone, unsuccessfully.

Tempers grew shorter among my oldest siblings and their spouses. Complaints about our hardships and talk of Jerusalem were almost constant, at first. Then suddenly the subject was dropped. My hope was that their attitudes were improving, but there was no change in sour looks and keeping to themselves. I enjoyed the quiet, but Nephi was more pensive than usual and more restless at nights.

"Nephi, what is it?" I asked one day. "Something seems to be troubling you."

He looked up from his scant meal, blinked his eyes, and squinted at me. "You asked what's troubling me? I don't know, Didi. Something just doesn't feel right around here. It has to do with my brothers, but . . ." He drifted off into his thoughts again.

More support for Nephi's fears came from an unexpected source late one evening while Nephi, Sam, and Zoram were on an overnight hunting trip. I was just drifting into sleep when I heard a rustling at the tent door, and a dark figure slipped quickly inside. It stood about a foot from the door, panting rapidly. I didn't move a muscle, but my mind came quickly alert, and my heart started pounding heavily.

"Didi?" A barely audible female voice came from the figure.

"Who is it?" I asked, struggling to sit up, and making sure the baby was still asleep. I didn't quite place the voice.

"Oh, Didi! Thank goodness you are there!" The figure took a step toward me, hand outstretched. "It's Naola."

I pulled myself to my feet and went toward her. Then she seemed to see me, and suddenly she was in my arms, trembling and crying, arms tightly around my neck.

"Oh, Didi! It was awful! I was so scared! I thank God you are here!" She sank to the ground, her arms around my knees. I unpeeled her arms from around my legs and sat down beside her, my arm around her shoulders.

"Naola, calm down. It's okay. Tell me what you're talking about. What frightened you?"

She took a deep breath and shuddered. "I couldn't sleep. I went out walking beyond the camp for some fresh air. It was then I heard them." She stopped.

"Heard who? Are there robbers out there?"

"No." She shook her head violently. "No! It was Mori and Gid, with . . . with Laman and Lemuel." She began to weep again.

I almost laughed. "What's so frightening about that?"

Naola lifted her face in my direction. I couldn't see her expression, but the tone in her voice echoed to my very soul and left me hollow. "Their words, Didi, their words of bitterness and hate. Laman and Lemuel. I have never imagined such words before. I have never imagined even such thoughts before. And Mori and Gid just sat and listened."

I stared at the tent wall I couldn't quite see. My hands and feet felt cold. "What did they say?" I asked tonelessly.

"Oh, Didi. I dare not repeat it. I could not. Such awful things against Nephi and Sam . . . and Father Lehi. Their own family!"

"And we are among the more righteous of Jerusalem?" I said to myself. "Is this what Nephi was feeling all along?"

Naola wiped her face with her skirt. "They accused Nephi of trying to rule over his older brothers and the rest of us, telling us how to live our lives and what is right or wrong. He uses tricks and cunning, they said, to brainwash us into following him into the wilderness, and to make us believe that God has told us to go there. And Father Lehi is part of the plot and the tricks with Nephi. Sam, they said, is easily deceived by them. We are all blind sheep walking into the trap. We are being led deeper into the wilderness, deeper into their power so they can play with us as they want, or deeper into the jaws of death, they said. We will all die . . . like Papa." Naola lowered her head into her lap and began to sob again.

"No wonder the directors are not leading us to fertile hunting ground," I murmured. I grasped Naola by the shoulders. "Does anyone else know of this?"

She shook her head. "You are the first, Didi."

I calculated quickly. "We cannot tell their wives. I hesitate to burden Lehi and Sariah with this all over again unless we have to, they being at the brunt of it. Mary would be hurt deeply by this as you are, Naola. Of those here, Mama would be the only one I dare tell." I paused. "Naola, did they say anything else when you were there?"

She remained silent.

"Naola, was this just talk, or would Laman and Lemuel do something with their hate? This could be important!"

She clutched at my arms. "Don't go near them, Didi! Leave well enough alone. They will cool down eventually. They have before. They are good men at heart. No one could be wicked enough to . . . to . . ." She broke down in sobs again.

I stared at her dark form. "They have also gone a bit too far before." I stood and pulled Naola up with me. "Come on, Naola. We're going to tell Mama and go warn our husbands." I grabbed my warmer head shawl and wrapped it over me. "Or do you want to stay here while I go alone?"

Naola stood motionless. "Don't leave me alone, Didi." She grasped my arm. "I'm coming with you."

Outside, the wind was blowing, and I could hear the branches of nearby bushes and trees being blown against each other. Clouds had blown across the moon. Naola and I half felt our way across the sand to Mama's tent and inside.

Mama listened in silence as I related Naola's experience. "This is true, Naola?" she asked when I was through.

"Yes, Mama, it is true."

"Then do what you have to do to warn them," she said firmly. "Didi, I'll take care of your girls and will watch for your husbands to give them warning. And I think Lehi and Sariah ought to be told. I will tell them." She gave each of us a kiss on the cheek. "I will pray for your safety. Return with Godspeed.'"

Naola and I crept out of Mama's tent. The wind had picked up and blew strong cold tendrils through our dresses.

"Let me stop and get a warmer shawl, Didi," whispered Naola.

I waited for her outside her tent, and then we headed onward. As we passed Mary and Zoram's tent, the deeper darkness of a figure at the door caught the corner of my eye. I stopped.

"Who is that?" I asked in a low voice.

"It's Mary," came the reply. "Didi, is that you?"

Naola and I stepped toward her. "What are you doing up, Mary?" I whispered.

"I couldn't sleep with all that wind. What are you doing up?"

"We're going to find Nephi and Sam," cut in Naola before I could think of an alibi. "We have to warn them—"

"Mary, may we come inside?" I interrupted.

Once inside, I repeated Naola's story to her. When I finished, Mary didn't move.

"I heard Laman say they ought to slay Father Lehi and Nephi," said Naola in a barely audible voice. She trembled next to me. I put my arm around her and she began to weep again.

"You are going to warn our husbands that their lives may be in danger," Mary's voice came out of the darkness. Her voice was steadier than I expected it to be. "I wish that I could come with you. But my infant is sick, and at night my eyes are useless. I will pray for you though. I can do that."

"Thank you, Mary," I said. I didn't hear Naola crying anymore, and I turned to her. "Naola, are you ready to go?" She paused, straightened her shoulders, and then nodded. "Then, Mary, farewell." I pulled Naola outside after me.

On the edge of the encampment facing the hills our husbands had headed toward the day before, I stopped. "Where was it you found

Laman and Lemuel?" I whispered hoarsely into Naola's ear, trying to speak just above the wind.

Naola pointed off to our left. I pulled her toward our right, planning to make a wide circle away from them before taking a straighter course toward the mountains. I only had a general idea where to find those who were hunting. I said a prayer in my heart that we would find them before anything happened.

The wind was really fierce. As we walked away from the frequented ground of our encampment, sand and small debris blew into our faces. Naola and I walked gripping hands, our free hands keeping our head coverings in place across our faces. I could barely see with the sand stinging my eyes in the darkness. I could hear a low rumble from the clouds over the mountains. This was going to be a terrific storm. I went as far as I dared in the right-hand direction before turning slightly to the left toward where the mountains ought to be. We were heading up the side of a hill. If only we had the light from the moon! I thought how dark it must have been for Nephi creeping down the back streets of Jerusalem when he went back for the brass plates, and shuddered. I felt a little bit safer here . . . a little.

Suddenly, Naola stopped. "I hear voices, Didi," she said into my ear.

I listened. I could only hear a low roll of thunder coming from the distance. I shrugged and started to pull Naola forward again, when a brilliant flash of light lit the night followed by a crack of noise. The next thing I knew, Naola had pulled me to the ground.

"It's Laman and Lemuel!" she cried, and started trembling all over again.

Was it possible? I was sure I had headed as straight toward the mountains and away from their direction as we could have gone. Naola was so shaken by her experience with them earlier, she could have imagined anything. Or perhaps we had come upon the hunting party returning early. I dragged myself forward on hands and knees, peering into the darkness and sand for any hint of movement or shadow.

Another streak of lightening lit the sky followed by a clap of thunder. I saw four figures in the little valley before us, a large ditch actually, one huddled on the ground, three staring into the sky above them. I didn't move. Was what Naola told me all truth, or was this a nightmare of our own imaginings?

I heard a voice carried on the wind, but the words were lost to me. Another flash of light revealed now three people prostrate on the ground, and the fourth had his arms raised above his head in defense. The earth rumbled. Naola crawled up next to me. I felt a drop of moisture then another and another. The mountains rumbled again, louder now. A low whooshing sound grew louder, and the rain came, soaking into our dresses. The wind no longer picked up the sand. Distant lightning flashes revealed the valley before us, now empty.

I waited a while to be sure. The wind softened into quiet occasional gusts, and the rain became a sprinkle. The moon came out briefly from between the clouds. We were alone.

"Naola," I nudged her. "They're gone."

She looked up and then sighed. "I'm cold," she said simply.

I looked at her. Should we really go on in this weather to meet the hunting party? But would it be safe now to go back to camp? "Come on, Naola, it's time to go." I pulled at her hand, but she drew it back.

"Let me sleep," she said, and pulled her shawl over her face.

I sat down beside her again. I was tired too, exhausted. I lay down next to her, huddling up to give her warmth, and soon I was asleep too.

We were awakened by voices and warm sunlight.

"My! What have we here? Angels sleeping in the middle of nowhere! Come over and look, boys!"

Naola and I sat up, rubbing our eyes and clutching each other, hearts pounding. Zoram's grinning face met us.

"You two look as though you've seen ghosts!" he commented, helping us to our feet. "Actually, you both could be mistaken for ghosts yourselves."

Nephi and Sam came into view, the latter carrying one hare. "Hey!" Sam called. "What a surprise to have you come meet us!" He gave Naola a hug then stepped back and stared at her. "You're all wet. What did you do, stay out all night in the storm?"

Naola and I looked at each other in silence. Somehow, the whole episode of last night seemed silly now in the daylight.

The three men stopped grinning. "What happened last night, Didi? Naola?" Nephi asked, looking from me to her and back again. Naola lowered her eyes and looked at the ground.

I took a deep breath. "Nephi, do you remember your concern the other day about whether the compass was working, about whether we were being tested again? I think Naola and I discovered what happened."

Sam and Zoram looked at Nephi and me, not comprehending. Nephi nodded, his brows knit together.

"Some members of our group apparently have been disobeying the spirit of the Lord, acting contrary to the words of the compass," I said quietly.

Naola lifted her head. "Your brothers . . . and mine . . . were talking about . . . about slaying you and Father Lehi. They wanted to return to Jerusalem, and they said you were trying to . . . to deceive . . ." She broke down in tears again, and only Sam's catching her prevented her from sinking to the ground.

"What does that have to do with your being outside all night?" asked Zoram.

Nephi looked at me, waiting.

"We came out to warn you," I explained. "We got this far then ran into them. They were in that gulch below us. But they didn't see us that I know of. Then near the end of the storm, they left. By this time we were so tired, we just stayed here."

Nephi paced in a circle, looking at the ground, hand over his eyes. Then he stopped and stared toward the mountains they had just come from, then toward the camp, then back at me. "Did they go back to camp or into the mountains, Didi?"

I started to shake my head and then stopped. Their behavior had been so strange last night, almost as if they had been suddenly afraid of something. Almost as if they had seen or heard something, something greater than the storm. No, I was reacting to my own fears. "I don't know, Nephi."

Sam, still holding up Naola, looked at us. "Wherever they are, I think we better get the women back to camp. If we happen to run into Laman and Lemuel anywhere, I would rather it be there in front of everybody."

Nephi nodded. Zoram picked up the hare Sam had dropped. Sam half carried, half led Naola down the slope we had climbed the day before. Nephi put his arm around my shoulder, and we headed back in the direction of camp.

We were met by the normal sounds of a camp waking up, children's voices, women preparing breakfast, the camels snorting on the far side of the tents. Our brothers were nowhere to be seen. Sam and Zoram looked at Nephi, who shrugged back.

"I'm going to get Didi back to the tent," Nephi said simply. "I'll meet you both after that."

Suddenly, pregnant Kora came lumbering up. She stopped in front of Nephi, panting. "My husband wishes to speak with you, Nephi," she said.

Nephi's grip around me tightened, and he looked toward Sam and Zoram. Zoram shook his head almost imperceptibly. "Where is he?" Nephi asked.

"In my tent. He is ill." She looked at Sam, then Zoram, then back at Nephi. Her body seemed to sag. "He said to tell you he will come out to meet you if you do not want to come to him." Her voice was pleading. "But I do not think he has the strength."

"I will come, Kora," said Nephi.

We watched him follow her to the door of their tent then stop outside as she went in. After a minute, the door curtain parted, and Gid slowly stepped out. Even from this distance, he looked pale and stooped. He eased himself to the ground and Nephi followed suit. After several minutes of talking, the door curtain of the adjacent tent moved, and Mori appeared and joined them sitting on the ground. Eventually the three men stood, Nephi embraced Gid, then Mori, and then held up the doorway to Gid's tent for him as Mori went back into his own. Nephi started to walk back toward us but was stopped by Laman and Lemuel in front of their tents.

"Oh, no," murmured Naola next to me. Sam tightened his grip around her waist.

I watched as Nephi spoke to his brothers, his hand reaching out to them palm up in supplication. Suddenly Lemuel stepped forward and embraced Nephi, and Laman followed suit. Then they, too, returned to their respective tents.

Nephi returned to us, a smile on his lips. I grasped his arm and it was trembling. "You were right, Naola," he said. "But you need fear no more. The plotting has changed to repenting."

Naola sighed and relaxed visibly. She looked exhausted. Sam helped her back to their tent, and Zoram went back to his own, Mary meeting him at the doorway. I turned to Nephi.

"Nephi," I began, "you don't really believe that they have stopped wanting to hurt you, do you? After all, every time before—"

"Hush," said Nephi, putting a finger to my lips. "I believe they are really sincere in their apologies." He stopped and looked up at the sky. "Gid and Mori spoke of hearing a voice, a voice from the heavens. It berated them soundly for their plotting and rebellion. I'm sure Laman and Lemuel heard it too, though they did not mention it." He sighed. "What miracles does it take for them to stay committed to righteousness?" He looked back at me and I shivered. "You're still wet, Didi. Let's get you into something dry and give you a chance to rest."

Naola was slow in recuperating from that night out in the storm. She developed a deep chest cough that lingered, and then she began throwing up everything she ate or drank. Hagadah offered an herbal drink to settle her stomach without success. Even Mary had run out of ideas and herbs to try to help her. I feared we would lose her too here in Nahom.

We took turns tending her, trying to get her to drink sips of lightly salted and sweetened water to keep her hydrated. Then she developed a craving for fruit, and when we found she could keep down little bites of dates and figs, Sam left on the fastest camel to search for other fruits. A few days later he was back with a load of pomegranates and cactus fruits, which she also devoured. Coconut, however, made her sicker. Soon she was able to also keep down sunbaked biscuits and nuts. But the dried spiced meat and camel's milk and cheese she would not even look at.

"Just the thought of those things turns my stomach," she'd say, rolling over to rest again.

Gradually she regained her strength enough to slip out of her tent door to sit under the shaded canopy in the cooler mornings or evenings. After a few minutes of sitting, she would have to lie down again. Sam would join her, pull her head onto his lap, and stroke her hair, talking quietly as she listened. Her eyes would close and he would just sit, looking down at her. Then he would carry her gently back inside to sleep.

Personally, I loved to watch Naola and Sam together like that, perhaps with a twinge of envy. Laman, however, was not pleased. One evening he came over to their tent and stopped in front of them, hands on his hips, looking down at them.

"You haven't done your share of the hunting lately," he said gruffly to Sam.

Sam looked up, surprised. "No, I haven't," he answered softly. "Nephi has been taking my place on the longer hunts, and I've taken his share of the field work so I could remain closer to Naola."

"No one consulted me about it," Laman scowled.

"I am sorry," answered Sam. "But we didn't think it would matter as long as the work got done." Sam shook his head. "Besides, Nephi's quite a bit better at the hunting than I am."

"That does not matter. I am in charge of organizing the work duties around here. From now on, you will inform me of any duty changes before implementing them!"

Sam gazed at Laman steadily but said nothing. His hand, however, had stopped stroking Naola's head. She still appeared to be sleeping.

"I do believe Naola has been sick long enough," Laman spoke softly, but his eyes were hard. "It is time she pulls herself together and performs her share of the womanly duties. Or does she plan to be like her mate and shirk all the harder work?"

At this, Sam lifted aside Naola's head, placing it carefully on the ground. He stood up and faced Laman, his hands clenched and trembling slightly behind his back.

"Laman, my wife nearly died!" his voice was intense. "You will not speak of her as a shirker! She has done her share and more of the hard work, growing crops, loading camels, pitching tents, and all without complaint. She has done everything . . . nearly everything . . ." A shadow of pain crossed Sam's face. "She has done all that she could that your wife and the others have done. When she has the strength to put one foot in front of the other, she will be at it again. But meanwhile, I will remain here at her side to make sure she does get back on her feet again. That is all."

Sam remained standing, glaring at Laman, clenched hand still behind his back. Laman gazed evenly back at Sam

"I will be watching," Laman finally said then turned on his heel and walked away.

Sam watched until he disappeared into his own tent and then stooped down by Naola. Tears were seeping out of the corners of her eyes.

"I am so sorry," she said to Sam. "I am trying so hard to get better."

"I know," Sam responded, kissing away a tear on her cheek. "Don't you worry about Laman. He just likes to make a scene." Sam slipped his hands under Naola, lifted her up, and took her inside the tent.

The next day when I brought Naola her supply of biscuits and fruit and water, she was sitting up in bed already, waiting for me.

"I'm practicing," she said. "I feel so out of shape with all this lying in bed. I've really got to get moving more."

I handed her the drink, and set the food down beside her.

"Oh, gross," she said, closing her eyes. "I just think I'd rather dry up than drink any more of that salted water." She opened her eyes, stared at the cup I poured her, and then finally took it from me. "Oh well, here it goes." She took a swallow and then opened her eyes wide.

"It's regular water, the delicious, clear, sweet good water directly from the well!" She tilted up her cup and drank it all. "More, Didi!" she commanded, handing the cup back to me.

"Oh, no!" I laughed. "You may not be throwing up everything anymore, but Mary still wants you to stick to small amounts at a time. After some fruit and biscuit, you can try some more."

She peeled a pomegranate and picked out some of the juicy seeds. I noticed how thin her arms were and her face. She really had been ill.

When she was done, she looked up at me. "Didi, I need some help getting to the pot."

Supporting her as she stood, she did feel very lightweight. Yet her stomach seemed strangely swollen to me. I thought of the swollen bellies of the starving beggar children on the streets of Jerusalem.

"Naola," I asked very carefully. "I know Mary has been more your medical consultant, but has your stomach been hurting lately?"

She looked down at herself as I laid her back on her bed. "No-o," she said slowly. "It used to whenever I got sick all the time. But now I just feel weak and tired and nauseated." She looked up at me and grinned. "Otherwise, I sure am skinny though, aren't I?" She giggled a little. "The best part of being sick is that my cycles have stopped!" She picked up a biscuit and contemplated it. "I sure would like to find a way to make a moister biscuit." She dropped it on the blanket and looked up at the tent ceiling, breathing heavily with her recent efforts.

I had a sudden wild thought. "Naola," I asked, not daring to think. "Are you . . . could you possibly . . . be pregnant?" Our eyes met and held a long time.

"Didi, I can't . . . get pregnant . . . can I?" Worlds of longing, of hope, and of despair flitted across her face.

I took a step forward, then another, and then knelt at her bedside. I drew the blanket down over her legs, and my hand hovered over her belly. Her eyes held mine, pleading.

"Oh, God," I pleaded in my mind. *"Please let this be a baby for Naola."* I dropped my hand on her belly and gently pushed. A firm roundness met my hand below her middle. It was the right size and shape, especially as I counted back to when her illness started.

Something bumped my hand from inside her belly. I pulled my hand back.

"Oh!" cried Naola, pulling back too. "What was that?"

I gazed at her, a slow smile spreading across my face. "Congratulations, Naola! You're with child!"

She shook her head slowly, not daring to believe. "But . . . but I can't . . . You mean, I can, Didi? You mean, I did? I mean, I am?"

I nodded vigorously, grinning.

"Oh, Didi! I'm so excited! I've got to tell Sam!" She jumped up and took a step then fell back on the bed. Her face was white, and she lay down, holding her head. "I shouldn't have done that," she groaned. "I'm going to be sick—"

We both reached for a bowl at the same time. When she was done being sick, she lay back again, breathing hard, face now flushed. "In a minute, I want more of that delicious water," she said then looked at me. "I'm going to kill you if you're wrong, you know, about . . . about why I'm sick." I looked at her in mock shock. "Actually, I couldn't do it. But Sam might." We both giggled, and then I went to pour her another cup of water.

Fortunately, Naola truly was with child, and in a day, the whole camp knew about it. Laman said no more to Sam about "shirking" or "duty." Riddah did not use the word *barren* again, but she also avoided talking to Naola directly. Everyone else, however, took a moment to congratulate Sam or Naola at some point during the week. Though Naola was slow in regaining her strength, she did help as much as she could around the camp, turning sun baking biscuits, meats, and nuts, and holding fussy infants to free up busy mothers. She still couldn't face camel's milk products, but she did begin chewing on meat jerky again for her protein. Her stomach remained sensitive enough that Sam had to make two more scavenging trips for fruit, but she did slowly gain weight and did not get so dehydrated again. Kora had hard pregnancies, but Naola's had been worse. I stored a piece of pomegranate rind in my treasure box to remind me that God does answer our prayers, even if it is in his own time.

CHAPTER 5

THE GREAT DESERT

We stayed at Nahom until Kora, Naola, and Yadeesh delivered their sons; Mary, Elizabeth, and Jagadesh, daughters; and the next crop had been harvested. Our crops here fared better than the ones at the Place of the Broken Bow, giving us a bounteous harvest. This was fortunate, considering the difficult travel that lay before us, though we didn't know it at the time.

A small caravan of traders visited us one day at Nahom, weary and ragged. They had just come from across the great desert from the east, along a barely visible trail that followed a string of isolated wells, the only way of crossing the desert alive. There was also another route out of Nahom, one that continued southward following the coasts of the sea that led to established villages and larger cities. I could sense my sisters' excitement when they heard about civilization just down the road: tree-shaded homes, markets overflowing with goods, home-cooked meals, clean water for baths, never to see another camel again. We fed the weary travelers, watered their animals, and after a week-long rest, watched them leave again, on their way with frankincense and other spices to trade in Jerusalem and other western countries.

Then came the news. The compass once again was directing us to move onward again. But not southward as we had anticipated. The spindle was pointing directly eastward, toward the direction the traders had come from, through the great desert.

I walked back to my tent after hearing the news, carrying Zenna and leading Siri by the hand and shaking. Was God really asking us to cross that great wasteland with women and little children? I felt I could do it, though pregnant again, but frail Kora or older Mama and Sariah? And what about the babies and young children? Why not travel through more verdant and civilized lands to reach the same destination? Actually I could answer that last one; once we reached villages and cities, we would be sure to have a tough time convincing Riddah and Bekka and my brothers to leave again. I could see a reason, but I was still fearful about our surviving the desert route. Nevertheless, within a week, we had packed our tents, loaded our supplies and children on the camels, and resumed our journey.

Before we had traveled far on the trail heading due east, the land became absolutely barren. Compared to what we were now traveling, the trail behind us was a veritable paradise. Now no plants underfoot were to be found, and the ground became soft and sandy, making progress on foot difficult here. We would stay camped at each well until the camels had drunk their fill and we had rested a couple of days, then move on to the next one. The goats died one by one, and we dried and spiced their meat at the campsites. Jagadesh showed us how to catch and eat locusts for sustenance. The weather grew hotter and drier. Between wells we traveled in the cool nighttime and rested under canopies only a few hours during the worst heat of the day. The complaints grew louder. I wondered how long it would take to reach the end of this desert trail.

One morning while traveling, Lehi stopped the caravan. He walked to the top of the hill in front of us and stood still, hand raised, looking over the hills of sand ahead. Yadeesh climbed up after him to look too. The rest of us watched him silently; one of the camels pawed the sand, another snorted and shook his head, slapping his lead rope against his neck. All was quiet in the hills except for a faint murmur in the wind.

Yadeesh spoke something to Father Lehi. Suddenly he turned around to face us. "Unload one of the tents quickly. And gather the camels into a circle. There's a sandstorm coming."

We jumped quickly into action. While we women gathered the children and tied the camels into a group, the men set up a large tent, and Mama and Sariah unloaded some food items. In moments, we were all safely huddled in the single room tent, listening to the wind gradually rising in tone and strength. The men sat against the tent poles to ensure their sturdiness in supporting the tent panels against the whipping wind. We listened wordlessly to the sound of stinging sand hurtled against our protective covering. I moved to the corner of the tent to sit next to Nephi as he leaned against one of the poles; the sound of the beating sand was louder here than in the middle of the tent.

"Will the camels be all right outside?" Naola's voice broke the spell of silence that the moans of the wind and creaking of the tent had put us into.

It was Lehi who answered her. "Yes, Naola. Camels can survive sandstorms even better than people. You don't have to worry about them."

"Will we be all right?" Kora asked, voice trembling. Gid put his arm around her. "The sand could cover us up, and we'd run out of air and not be able to dig ourselves out—"

"And our fate would be the same as many another luckless traveler," Sam's voice came from his corner of the tent with an eerie timbre in it. "Many have been caught in desert sandstorms, only to be buried beneath tons of sand, and their bones only uncovered hundreds of years later when another sandstorm blows the sand away again."

Kora's daughter Hannah squealed and hid her face in her mother's lap. Kora herself put her head on Gid's shoulder, eyes closed, her face ashen.

"That's enough, Sam," Lehi cut in sternly. "Remember how you felt in your first sandstorm."

Zac, Matthew, and Gad huddled in front of Sam, staring up at him excitedly.

"You've been through one of these before, Sam?" Naola asked in awe. "Oh, please tell us about it! It must have been such an adventure!"

"No! Let's not talk about such horrible things," Abisha cut in. Bekka and Riddah nodded their agreement. "I think we ought to talk about something much more pleasant."

Jagadesh and Hagadah exchanged smiles, and Mirimi giggled.

"Oh, please tell a story! Any will do," Mary spoke up. "You're such a good storyteller, Sam, and it would help to pass the time while we wait for the storm to quit."

"All right, I'll tell one," Sam decided and rearranged himself to a more comfortable position against his pole.

"Oh, no. Not again," I heard Laman mutter.

Nephi leaned close to me. "It's interesting to see how each person reacts in a problem situation," he whispered just above the sound of the wind. "What each says and does is a pretty good reflection of his or her character." I nodded my agreement and snuggled up against him, Zenna curled up in my lap, and Siri lay with her head on her father's. Nephi put his strong arm around my shoulders, and I suddenly felt much more secure against anything the elements could do.

"Many years ago," Sam began, "there was a wealthy merchant who had two sons. These two did not get along very well but not for lack of trying. It seemed the younger could never do anything the right way to please the older one, and their interests were too varied for their paths to cross much.

"The merchant's older son loved to travel, and often went with the traders across large wildernesses, delivering the merchant's goods into foreign lands and bringing back great treasures. It was an exciting life, but lonely. The younger son was learning the merchant's trade in the city and had settled down and started a family. His life was definitely not as exciting as his brother's, but he was happy and content.

"One day the younger son noticed that his father was troubled.

"'What is the matter, father?' he asked.

"'It has been three years since I have seen or heard from your older brother,' the merchant replied. 'I fear something may have happened to him.'

"The younger son suddenly realized this might be his chance to make peace with his older brother. 'Do not fear, my father. I will go search for him,' he said.

"So, entrusting his family into his father's care, he began the search for his lost brother. After months of investigation, he found that his brother was last seen in a caravan crossing the great desert. It seems that caravan never reached its destination; only one man survived by clinging to one of the camels as it struggled through a sandstorm. The identity of that man was unknown; he had gone crazy and did not know who he was. The younger brother decided to find this crazy man in hopes it would be his brother. He traveled across that great desert himself with another caravan and searched until he found the man. It was indeed his only brother.

"These two brothers had been rivals so long that the younger one had been uncertain how he should greet his sibling when he finally found him. But now, as he gazed at his brother's thin face and raggedly clothed body, his soul was filled with compassion for him. Though the older brother did not recognize him, the younger dressed him in his best cloak and fed him with his best food. The next day, he started back across the great desert to take his brother back home.

"The journey started off well. However, as they passed the halfway point, a large storm arose, a sandstorm. The younger brother had never been in such a storm and did not know how to prepare for it. His supplies were lost, and he became disoriented in the sands and winds, still clinging to his dazed older brother. They were doomed.

"Suddenly, the older brother came to life. He began calling with camel-like noises, over and over again. In a moment, a camel's bray was heard over the sands and wind, and the older brother began dragging the younger one toward it. Soon they had found one of their lost camels, and clinging to it through the sandstorm, followed wherever it went until the storm was over.

"The next morning, when the older brother awoke, he remembered who he was and recognized who was beside him. The two embraced warmly for the first time in their lives. Realizing where they were, the older brother led the younger through the rest of the desert homeward, using his survival skills from experiences past. No trace of their equipment or the rest of their caravan was seen again. However, the two made it home again, reaching their sorrowing father on his sickbed. The two brothers ever after supported each other in their work and family lives, friends at last."

All of us were silent as Sam finished his story. The littlest children were sleeping, lulled by the sing-song of Sam's voice mingled with the pulsing of winds overhead. Kora's eyes were still tight shut; she was gripping Gid's arm as it encircled her, daughter Hannah curled in her lap, Johanna leaning against her while Hagadah caressed her hand. Riddah looked bored and was picking at the sand beside her; Laman pretended to be asleep, head in Jagadesh's lap. Yadeesh tried in vain to calm her baby and keep him from waking Abisha's toddler. Lehi was looking upward, head cocked to one side, listening to the wind. Naola, nursing her son, Benjamin, leaned against Sam contentedly. Mary's eyes looked thoughtful, gazing down at her sleeping son, Jonah, and daughter, Eva, her lips parted in a half smile. Bekka was playing with her daughter, Shanna's, hair. Zac, Matthew, and Gad still sat wide-eyed, gazing at Sam. Nephi seemed to be enjoying watching the others as I was. Our eyes met, and he winked at me as though to say, "Isn't this fun?" I almost laughed.

The winds went on and on, and the little light filtering through the blowing sand and the tent panels above us began to fade. It looked like we'd be here all night. We all ate the light supper Mama and Sariah passed around. Then I curled up with my head in Nephi's lap, Zenna and Siri leaning against me, and fell asleep.

Suddenly I awoke. It seemed much lighter inside the tent; it must be morning. But something seemed different, almost wrong somehow. Then it hit me: the winds had stopped blowing. I sat up quickly. Nephi opened his eyes and groaned, Naola's baby whimpered, and Zenna started to cry. In a moment the whole tent was awake, several voices crying in unison, voices mumbling sleepily. I looked up at Nephi sheepishly. So much for it being quiet.

"Quiet please!" Lehi called out. Everyone stopped talking and listened a moment.

"The winds have stopped!" cried Lemuel, and he jumped up to lift the entrance panel.

It was a different world out there. We had originally set up the tent on a plateau halfway up a sand hill. Now we nested near the bottom of a mountain of sand, the hill sloping up steeply just in front of the doorway. It seemed as though the tent had traveled down to the bottom of the hill, but the only movement I remembered was a trembling of the tent walls in the wind. The camels were huddled together a short distance away, blinking their sand-laden eyelashes at us.

We all piled out of the tent, stretching, drinking in big gulps of fresh air. Mama, Sariah, Abisha, and Mirimi dug into the packs in the tents and got a light breakfast ready for everyone. The children, led by Sam and Naola, ran, calling and shouting up the hill of sand, and had races rolling and sliding back down the hills. The men started pulling apart the tent and repacking it onto the camels.

Before starting breakfast, Lehi offered a prayer of thanksgiving for the sunshine, for the fresh air, for the food, but most of all, for our protection through the storm. I felt a lump growing in my throat and was glad that I was not the one giving the prayer at that moment.

After breakfast, we gathered our camels and traveled on again toward the next oasis.

I hoped I would not deliver my next child between oasis wells. The wells would vary from four to seven days apart, the latter taxing our water carrying capacity. At times I thought I preferred walking to riding, as the baby and I were jarred less, but my lumbering through the sand was so slow and hurt my hips, so I decided I was better off riding the camel, carrying Zenna in front of me. Siri rode with her father, singing little tunes her uncle Sam had taught her.

My wish for site of delivery came true, but just barely. We had thoroughly exhausted what plants the last well site had to offer, and had to move on, despite protests from Mama that we ought to stay for my sake. The distance to the next well seemed interminably long. The jarring seemed worse, and it was about all I could do to keep riding. But neither did I have the energy to walk. Nephi would constantly watch me whenever he thought I wasn't looking. The sixth morning I couldn't get out of the saddle, and he had to pull me limply to the ground. I slept in that spot that day, and Nephi put up our shelter right over me. When it was time to move on again, I didn't think I could bear the sight of another camel. But I let Nephi boost me on anyway, anxious to reach the next well.

The contractions started on that stretch of ride. At first I could deal with them easily. Then they became stronger, and I had to concentrate hard not to make a sound. The last thing I wanted was to stop here. Then Nephi slowed his camel's even pacing to follow at my side. I knew he had seen my last grimace.

"Didi, what's wrong?" he asked softly so no one else could hear. I didn't know what to answer. He knew at once what was wrong. "Didi, if the baby's coming, we'll stop right here. We'll send scouts on ahead to bring water back from the next well. Just say the word."

"I will not let our group get separated," I said through gritted teeth, breathing with the pain.

Just then the camels' ears began twitching, and their speed picked up. "Water!" cried several voices at once from the company. I sighed in relief as much from freedom from the last pain as the news of nearby water. I held on as my animal moved forward.

Just when I thought I'd have to call for a stop, water well or not, cheers came from the front riders. "There it is!" came Gid's cry.

"Now, Nephi," I breathed. "Get me off this camel now!"

His response was like lightning. "Sam! Zoram!" he cried as he lifted me off. "Get a tent set up for us immediately!"

Mama and Mary's responses were just as rapid. Almost before the tent was set up, they were ready for me. Naola arrived a minute later with the first-drawn water from the well. Much more quickly than with my first, I delivered my third daughter into the world. She was beautiful.

Nephi brought in Siri and Zenna. Both girls gazed in wonder at this young life, their new sister, so recently come from heaven. Siri reached out a finger and stroked the baby's head and then touched her hand. The little fingers curled around Siri's larger one. Siri giggled.

Zenna, not old enough to understand much except that her place as the youngest was now taken by another, looked lost. "Mama!" she suddenly wailed and fell to the ground sobbing. Nephi attempted to pick her up and hold her, but she wriggled out of his grasp.

"Zenna," I said quietly, soothingly. She paused a moment and looked up. "I have two arms, Zenna. One for you, and one for little Leesha." I held out my empty hand. She looked at it but did not move. Then suddenly, she ran into my embrace and lay there, trembling. I held her close. "Zenna, I need you to be Mama's helper and teach Leesha everything you know. It's a big job, but do you know what? You're a big girl now and know a lot of things. Do you want to show her how you can give a big kiss? Right there on her forehead, just like you give to me."

Zenna puckered up her face and touched it to the baby's. Then she looked up proudly.

"That was perfect, Zenna! The best kiss ever! I'm so proud of you." I leaned over and gave Zenna a kiss on the forehead too. Her little arms clung to my neck, and I felt her tears on my cheek.

It seemed an eternity that we traveled from desert well to desert well. I didn't think about much except our survival. Wake up, feed the family basturma and some sun biscuits made at our last stop, make sure the girls were protected from the hot sun or cold night for the next stage of travel, one step after another, pause to eat and sleep, and move on again. At the wells, I'd air freshen clothes, make another batch of sun biscuits, attempt to keep the girls covered from the sun as they ran and played, rest a bit myself, draw water for the ever thirsty camels and people, and then refill water containers. Then we would move again. I could think enough to be grateful that no one got sick, making the risk for dehydration worse, that I had enough milk for my baby, that the girls became very obedient in following the rules of the caravan, and that no one had the energy anymore to argue very much. It was in this phase of the journey that Laman and Lemuel's desert travel experience became obvious, and they delighted in teaching Mori and Gid their skills.

Thus, it came as a total surprise to me when we came to the end of our journey. I heard Mori's sons at the head of the caravan shouting from the top of the next sand hill. As each family reached the top, they began shouting too. I was afraid something terrible had happened. Had we ended up going in circles and returned back to the western edge of the desert? Was there another caravan ahead in trouble? Were we about to be set upon by robbers? Ahead of me, Nephi called to the camels, and they eagerly pulled forward. Siri and Zenna hung on tightly as their mount broke into a careening gallop. I clutched tiny Leesha to me as my camel ran, pounding up the hill to keep up.

As our mounts stood, panting and sweating at the top of the hill, I looked at the slope below us, hunting for the tragedy that awaited us. I could see nothing but another sand hill.

Then the specific words being said sunk in to my consciousness: "Look! How beautiful!" "Are we really there?" "I can't believe it!"

Then Siri's voice came to me. "Mama, Papa! What is that?"

My gaze finally lifted high enough. On the horizon stretched a blue-gray ridge larger than an oasis, and it appeared to be mountains. Could we be nearing the end of this desert journey after all?

Already the front camels were racing down the hill, eager to reach the promise of cooler air, water, and vegetation. Nephi brought his camel to my side.

"Are you ready to run?" he asked, his eyes twinkling, looking back and forth between me and our two older girls on the other camel.

We were. He faced forward and nudged his mount. We were off, careening down the sand dune. All my attention was focused on holding on to the camel and to Leesha. I hoped my other girls were doing all right. But then they had been riding camels their whole lives.

The mountains were farther than they looked, and night fell before we were near. But we pressed on as eager as our mounts to reach fresh water and a real camp and rest. The children rode on bravely, though tired. Nephi took Zenna with him so he could hold her while she slept, but Siri was able to stay awake, and I continued carrying Leesha.

About midnight we reached the foothills. The ground became rocky and unpredictably treacherous. We were forced to stop and make camp. We fastened the camels securely and slept where our bodies collapsed. At the first light of dawn, we awoke, all of us eager to reach the end of our journey. Gulping a quick breakfast, we were off again. Following the directions of the Liahona, we found a pass through the mountains. From the desert side, they were as barren as the wilderness outside of Jerusalem. As we passed the summit, the scene changed dramatically. Before us were slopes green with dense vegetation. Moist, cooler air hit us as we descended, and soon we were engulfed in the humid foliage. Though I had not as yet drunk of any fresh water, my throat did not feel as parched any more.

The children were excited; none but the oldest had seen any vegetation so dense and green. It was all we could do to keep them on the camels as we descended. Suddenly the sound of water touched our ears, and in moments we met a stream. Following it down a short distance, it tumbled onto a meadow loaded with green grass. At the far end of the meadow, through some palm trees, could be seen the sparkling of sun on a blue body of water.

The camels stopped and drank and drank from the stream. Enthusiastic children and equally excited adults slid off camels' backs, ran, stretched stiff limbs, and washed eagerly in the stream. As the camels' thirst abated, they moved into the meadow to eat and eat. It seemed like an abundant and peaceful place. I hoped we would get to stay here a long time.

CHAPTER 6

BOUNTIFUL

After we had rested a few hours, Father Lehi counseled with the men. He planned to send Laman and Lemuel, Nephi and Sam out to explore the area the next day. Then the men put up tents while we women unpacked our other belongings.

When the explorers returned later the next evening, we gathered to hear their findings. They reported that we were on the southern end of a crescent-shaped area of fertile land, curving around a large body of water. Further southwest, the land ended in mountains and cliffs overlooking the sea. Nephi and Sam held up samples of fruits and honey they had found in the hills in this southern area. A couple of miles to the northeast of us, the valley gave way to more hills and mountains. They promised to be rich for hunting and were nestled around meadows and flatter land that would grow crops well.

"There was something else," Lemuel began. Laman shot him a look, and he fell silent.

Laman cleared his throat, building up the suspense, until everyone's attention was focused on him. "We saw a fishing boat," he began. "It was moving northeast along the coastline, fishing. Usually these boats are not built for long ocean voyages. We figure there must be a fishing village not too far northeast of here, perhaps only a couple of days' journey."

Everyone was silent while the meaning of their words sunk in. Suddenly, everyone was talking in excitement. I knew most of the women wanted to visit that town, and I even looked forward to finding some pretty dresses for my girls, experiencing civilization, and tasting some real variety of food. The children, on the other hand, having seen little of towns or even villages, were more enthralled with tasting of the fruits and honey that were immediately available in our valley.

The next day, several of the men went hunting while others looked for a good place to plant crops and start clearing land. The meadow we had originally found did turn out to be the best place for our tent settlement, and the lower end of the meadow valley was chosen for the planting of the garden produce. North of the settlement was chosen for the grain crops, and work was started, preparing the soil there too.

When the hunters returned that evening loaded down with game of all varieties, a fire was built, and we had a celebration feast. Many of the children had rarely tasted roasted meat before, and I had to laugh at their wondering eyes at the new flavors. I savored every bite of the roasted meat myself and felt that I was in heaven!

We didn't do any more exploring for nearly a month till we had the crops planted. Then finally Lehi told us we could send a few of our men to discover this northern fishing village. Of course, Laman and Lemuel wanted to go, and Nephi felt he should go to keep them out of trouble. Zoram decided to go with them while Mori, Gid, and Sam stayed to take care of the camp. They packed a few days' food supplies and their hunting gear onto their camels, planning to return within one to two weeks. As we said our farewells, we hoped the village would be found close enough that we could travel there ourselves.

It was a long ten days before they returned. They did find the village, four days' journey from our valley, through three days of desert travel. They described the village nestled among farmed valleys and herds grazing on the surrounding hills. There was a port, mostly for local fishing vessels, but occasionally trading boats stopped there to get supplies and trade goods at the small but colorful local market. The men described a wide variety of goods we hadn't seen for eight years, spices we had never even heard of, and foods that were as foreign as the language spoken in the village.

There really was a village! But it was so far away. Would we ever be able to go visit it? I could tell that was the question on everyone's minds. I heard Riddah and Kora in particular encouraging their husbands to talk Lehi into letting us go see it, if even only once. When Nephi approached me, I only gazed up at him longingly. That evening the men gathered in Lehi's tent to discuss if we had any future with the village.

After several hours of discussion, some of it heated (we could hear their voices and occasionally their words from outside), the men dispersed. Nephi only told me that Lehi would think about it and let us know.

We went back to tending the crops, hunting and gathering food, and keeping the children out of trouble. The days passed, and no word either way came from Father Lehi's tent. Nearly a week later, I stumbled upon Riddah talking to Laman in the trees uphill from camp, where I was returning from gathering some fruit. I stopped rock still, and at first they didn't notice me.

Riddah was speaking. "It would be so easy," she said to him. "Bekka and Lemuel would cover our chores so we're not missed, and we'll hurry right back. Then we cover them while they—" Riddah looked up and saw me. "I don't think . . ." She stopped speaking.

Laman turned and saw me. His eyes narrowed.

I pretended I hadn't heard as much as I had. "Sorry!" I said, smiling. "I didn't mean to interrupt a romantic moment. I won't tell anyone you're here." I slipped away as fast as I could.

On arriving back at camp, I searched for Nephi. I found him studying the brass plates in the shade in front of Lehi's tent.

"Nephi," I panted. "I need to talk with you. In private."

He carefully wrapped up the plates and set them back just inside the door of the tent. Then he followed me back inside ours. Our girls were still off in Naola's care. I pulled Nephi down beside me on our bed.

"Something peculiar just happened," I told him. "I just encountered Riddah and Laman talking as though they're planning a trip to the village." I repeated what I had heard.

"I was afraid they might try something like this." Nephi thought a few minutes. "It sounds like they will go to the village whether Father gives them permission or not. We'd be better off all going together, so we make sure they come back. I will go talk to Father."

Lehi gave his permission the next day for us to go to the village, but with strict instructions that we return promptly. Lehi decided he would stay with the tents and camels, and Sariah and Mama stayed with him. Naola and Sam offered to take Lehi's youngest sons, Jacob and Joseph, with them. All the rest of us prepared to go, taking a few light tents and several days' food and water. We packed our nicest garments, gathered together any items we felt were tradable, and set off on the camels. Four days later, we reached the village.

Virtually all of us headed straight for the market to see what they had. The tools and boots on display fascinated the men and boys. The women oohed and aahed over the fabric and clothes. Children watched, fascinated, as toys were modeled to them. Everyone salivated over the varieties of food and spices available. Unfortunately, the items we had brought for barter seemed poor and worthless in comparison to the fine things offered in this village. After my initial disappointment, I had to laugh when I realized how small this market was compared to the fine stores and markets in Jerusalem where my sisters and I used to shop. What a different life we were now living compared to my childhood!

After visiting the market, we wandered in groups around the town. Being a fishing village, some of the men and even a few of the women were rougher than I liked. I was glad I understood none of the swearing. But through their looks of curiosity and sometimes disapproval, I knew we didn't look too fine to them either. So when Nephi seemed drawn to the docks to look at the fishing boats and trading vessels, I left him for a few hours. Mary and her children joined my girls and me on the beach south of town, where we could play in the water and rest. Some children from the village joined us, and though we couldn't understand their words, they made friends with our children through smiles and body language. Eventually the other children in our group joined us, and we played until dusk. Soon everyone gathered, and we set up the tents and fixed a light supper. Then the more social of our group (my brothers, Laman and Lemuel, and their wives) went back into town to see what the nightlife was like.

The rest of us put the children to bed, looked at the stars awhile, and then went to sleep ourselves.

The next morning Nephi headed off to the docks again, and Sam, Hagadah, Mary and Naola proposed to take the older children on a hike into the hills beyond town to look at the animals and scenery. I didn't feel like carting my little Leesha up and down hills, so I stayed behind. However, I was not excited about the prospect of staying on the beach all day with nothing to do. So when my other sisters finally awoke and invited me to join them going into town again, I accepted.

I didn't know what might interest me there at first, but I found myself back in the market, eyeing the foods and spices. The women chattered at me, probably trying to sell me their goods, but I could only spread my empty hands at them. Soon they lost interest in me, and I watched them sell to other customers. As I wandered around, I bumped into Yadeesh and Jagadesh eyeing the food area too. My sisters found their favorite wares at the market: Riddah the jewelry, Abisha the many-colored cloths, Bekka and Elizabeth the baskets and pottery, and Kora and Mirimi the musical instruments. I passed Gid examining leather belts and shoes. Laman and Lemuel seemed to be trying to make conversation with a group of men lounging in the shade of a larger building at the edge of the marketplace. Mori spent time with the fishermen. Zoram and Eli I didn't see, but found out later that they spent the day wandering through the village studying how the homes were built. Our smaller children wandered from aunt to uncle, loving the new exciting environment, and occasionally getting momentarily lost.

When we met back at camp that evening, the children who had gone on the hike talked excitedly about the animals they had seen, new to all of the younger ones: donkeys, cattle, sheep, chickens, and dogs. From the outskirts of town they could see the big desert to the west, and green coastal communities to the northeast. After seeing the quality of goods in this village's market, I suspected that these communities had a thriving trade with each other.

The next morning we headed back toward home. Reactions to our trip were mixed. As we traveled, excited voices chatted about the wonders we had seen. The children all were impressed. But those of us who had lived in Jerusalem, more than eight years ago it was now, seemed more subdued. I heard some wistful reminiscing of our life at Jerusalem, and I found I missed it too, especially the clean floors, soft beds, cool porches, and kitchen luxuries. But I also realized I liked my life now, with my loving husband and beautiful children, where the simple joys brought us such pleasure.

Back in the valley, we spent our days tending the crops, mending garments, adding to the tent panels, trying different food recipes, and watching the children play with endless energy. I discovered that Riddah and Bekka, Kora and Abisha, and the nomadic wives were on a secret mission to discover what items they had or could make that might be of interest to the villagers for trading at the market. When their husbands discovered they were doing this, they joined in too. I didn't think much of it, until Nephi and I were talking one day as we rested in the evening shade of our tent.

"I'm worried about some of our families, Didi," he said to me. "We've been away from Jerusalem a long time. Now we are near a village that represents civilization to them, and I worry that we might lose them. We barely got them away from the city in the first place, and we might not get them to leave this part of the country either."

I was startled. "What do you mean, Nephi? Aren't we going to stay here? Isn't this the Promised Land the Lord promised?"

Nephi sighed. "I don't know for sure, Didi. But I don't think so. This oasis is small with very little room for generations of descendants. There is too much risk of our children intermarrying with the locals, and they do not believe in our God. Our religion and the pure blood of our descendants would be thinned beyond recognition. I think God has chosen another place for us, one where there will be no temptation to intermingle our blood with strangers, a place where our line, a branch broken off from the tree of Israel if you will, can become strong as a tree itself." He grinned at me. "Scriptural metaphor. Do you recognize it, Didi?"

I wrinkled my brow. "Oh dear, Nephi. It's been such a long time since I've thought about . . . Oh, I know! Isaiah, isn't it? He's the one always talking about Israel and the dispersion and gathering."

Nephi put his arm around my shoulder. "That's right! You remember well. Zenos in the brass plates particularly talked about the grafting of the olive branches in other parts of the vineyard. Anyway—"

Just then Leesha beside me woke up, crying for her supper. Nephi didn't speak until I got her nursing and quiet again.

Then I was the first to speak again. "I think I have to agree with you, Nephi. About our siblings, I mean. It didn't occur to me until now to be concerned, but"—I paused, sighed, and then filled him in on their activities recently—"it seems harmless, but it is a little materialistic. Do we need to tell Father Lehi?"

Nephi thought for a while. "There are some dangers, I must confess. But there are also a lot of advantages. We don't know a whole lot about building houses or boats, or fishing, or making cloth except out of camel hair, or many other skills that we might need settling a new place. Perhaps we can take advantage of this situation." He grinned again and laughed. "I can just see how they would react to Father ordering them to spend time in the village! We'd have to drag them to get them to go! It might just solve our problem yet!"

It didn't turn out exactly the way Nephi predicted. But it did remove the idea of secret visits to the village and allowed all of us a chance to go. Lehi sent us in groups of two to three couples, and required that all but the infants stay behind, to ensure that everyone returned.

We all found ourselves learning new skills as well by our interests as by Lehi's encouragement. Mary and Hagadah worked with the local midwives; Abisha and Naola became adept at spinning and cloth weaving. Nephi focused on learning about sailing and shipping. Sam learned as much as he could about the care and breeding of herd animals. Lemuel spent his time listening to the locals, learning their myths and stories, and softening their mistrust of our group. He and

Laman were the first to pick up the local dialect and teach it to the rest of us, enabling us to communicate better as we learned their skills.

I was amazed at first that the villagers would allow us in on their territory. But then I saw how many foreigners came through to trade, rough men of the desert caravans or trading ships, or less often, elegant visitors from the north countries trying to obtain spices at a cheap price. We, on the other hand, were an intriguing and different group. We were a family of nomads, poverty-stricken and looking to the village for our survival and cultural refinement (or so we appeared), and carrying with us a strange assortment of supplies. We started bringing in camel haircloth and camel's milk to trade at the market as our camels were able to produce it, and we were able to obtain a few more living necessities and niceties this way. Naola and Sam worked on breeding extra camels and traded them for sheep, chickens, and goats. Now we had our own wool supplies, eggs, and extra milk for cheese making.

Time passed pleasantly for most of us in this bountiful green land on the shores of the sea. Several of the women became pregnant again, and though Naola did not, she had her Benjamin and was content.

Nephi, however, became quite preoccupied. Whenever he was in the camp, he walked without really noticing his surroundings or the people he passed, and I'd have to speak to him two or three times before he'd hear me. After a couple of months, he started going into the mountains. From before sunup to after sundown, he would be there, and he'd come back dirty and exhausted.

"What are you doing in the mountains?" I asked him once as we were going to bed.

"Making tools to build a ship to take us to the Promised Land," he answered. Then he promptly turned over and fell asleep.

The news travelled fast that the Lord had directed Nephi to build a ship. The information was received with mixed reactions. Naola and

I were probably the only adults excited about the prospect of a boat voyage, but the older children thought it would be very romantic.

A couple of times early on, I saw Nephi approach his brothers to ask them to help him. Laman and Lemuel scoffed and turned their backs. Gid and Mori quietly disappeared and avoided him. Sam, Eli, and Zoram agreed to go with him, and they, too, spent most of their days in the mountains.

Then one day, Sam, Nephi, Eli, and Zoram set up shop in the valley, cutting down trees from the nearby forest and hauling them to an open area near the shore. Laman and Lemuel, Mori and Gid stopped frequenting the shores and spent noticeably more time hunting in the mountains. Naola, Mary, and I started spending our days with the men, helping cut off the branches from the trunks, and holding the logs for the men to split. Our older children made it their job to take the branches and wood chips back to the camp for the cooking fires. Sariah and Mama brought food down to us regularly and brought the babies when they needed to be fed. But even with our added help, it took the men weeks to get the needed lumber ready.

Then they began building the framework of the ship. This was the trickiest part, as it required great lengths of wood to be pressed into shape and nailed into place with cross pieces of wood. We women were often not strong enough to hold the timbers in place. Mary was unable to aim well enough to hammer effectively, and Naola's strength was not enough to drive the wooden nails into the beams. I found I could only drive a few at a time before I needed rest, and I ended up splitting almost a quarter of the beams or cross pieces I hammered, and we had to get new pieces of wood and start again.

Nephi's temper grew shorter. I did my best to keep the girls out of his way, and help him with the building too, but I was exhausted, physically and mentally. Several times I cried myself to sleep while he was out late at the ship site.

One early afternoon, the men were working on an upper-level section of the ship frame, with Nephi hammering and Sam, Eli, and Zoram bracing a beam. My back was half turned from them, where I was comforting Zenna with a skinned knee from a game of tag.

Suddenly I heard a loud crack and a shout. I turned in time to see Sam clutching at a broken piece of a cross support, then fall from the framework with a thud onto his right shoulder. No one moved for several long seconds. Naola gave a strangled cry, dropped her pot of lunch soup, and ran over to him. Nephi helped Eli and Zoram ease the beam they were holding down onto supporting framework, then they scrambled quickly down from their perches. As they reached him, Sam groaned and tried to sit up but fell back, clutching at his right arm with his left.

"Sam! Sam! Are you all right? Speak to me, Sam!" Naola cried. She reached forward as if to embrace him, but caught herself, her hands fluttering above him.

"Naola," he gasped, but could say no more.

"Mary! Where's Mary?" Naola turned, searching for her sister. "Tell me what's wrong with him, Mary. Hurry!"

Mary was at his side in moments. "Sam, listen to me," she said quietly, gently. "Tell me where it hurts."

Sam lay still, moved his left hand up his right arm to his shoulder, then inward toward his neck. Suddenly he gasped and began rocking in pain again. "Sh-shoulder," he finally breathed out.

"Do you hurt anywhere else?" she asked.

Sam shook his head. "I don't think so."

Mary reached out a hand to touch his forehead. "Sam, I want you to hold still a minute. I need to make sure everything else is all right." She started at his legs, moving them at each joint, and then checked his left arm. Finally she felt up his right arm, pausing a moment at the collarbone. She touched gently. The bone shifted under her fingers.

"Aaah!" Sam cried and pushed her hand away. His pale face became more ashen, and suddenly he was throwing up on the sand.

"Sam!" Naola cried and reached out to cradle him in her arms.

"His collarbone is broken," Mary said. "We need to stabilize his arm." She looked around at the others, then down at herself. Quickly she untied her apron and, as soon as he finished being sick, used it to tie his right arm against his body. Feeling somewhat better, he sat up for a few minutes, and then Naola and Zoram helped him back to the tents.

The rest of us stood looking around at each other and at the structure of lumber that didn't look like much of anything. Then Nephi spoke, "That's enough for today." He turned and headed into the mountains.

I didn't see Nephi until suppertime. He ate in silence and then sat just outside the tent, staring at the nearby trees while I put the girls to bed. Then I joined him at the door, laying my hand gingerly on his knee.

He grasped my hand and held it tightly. His eyes were closed, and his other hand was shaped into a fist. Suddenly he pounded his other knee with it. "Damn it, Didi! I can't do this alone anymore! It's wearing you out, it's wearing me out, others are getting hurt." He turned to look at me. "What does it take to get my brothers to help me? They do the opposite of anything I ask or need, they have to be dragged, protesting before they'll do anything useful." He threw his arm up in the air. "I've always believed the Lord would make a way that I could do whatever he asked, but I'm finding no solutions! We can't build this ship alone, and I can't get those brothers of mine to lay a finger on this ship." He let go of my hand, crossed his arms on his knees, and laid his head upon it.

I looked up at the sky. I wished I were stronger and could be of more help to my husband. I wished that my powers of persuasion could affect Laman and Lemuel or even Gid and Mori. Maybe I hadn't tried hard enough. If only I had an angel's power to persuade them, some thunder and lightning and . . . My gaze swung back to Nephi.

"Maybe you and I can't persuade them, but the Lord can."

He looked up and stared at me a moment. "Perhaps I have been trying to do it all myself. I just hate having to ask the Lord to motivate them again and again and again. He must get tired of hearing from me."

I laid my hand on his arm. "I doubt that. Or else he wouldn't keep asking us to come to him or keep putting us in situations that give us that opportunity. Try him again, Nephi."

After a moment, he nodded. "I will, Didi." He stood up. "But first let's get a good night's rest."

The next morning he was up early and gone into the mountains. We did no work on the ship while he was gone. It was actually a much-needed rest for us. I was used to Nephi being gone like this, but when two days and nights had passed, I began to worry about his safety. Oh, he could take care of himself very well, but I couldn't predict what his brothers might do. I left my two older daughters with Naola and went to visit Bekka. On learning that Laman and Lemuel had left on a hunting trip the previous day, I tied Leesha to my hip with a cloth sling, grabbed a water bladder, and headed into the hills.

As I walked, I talked and sang softly to Leesha, explaining the scenery to her as we passed, pausing occasionally to find a stick, plant, or rock for her to play with. I was alternately emotionally distraught, thinking the worst, then calm when I remembered God's words that he would support the faithful.

Midmorning I stopped under a shady tree to nurse her. We had climbed well into the foothills. I could see in the mountains above me a cliff area that overlooked the sea. I decided to detour by there and get a view of the lands below.

Another hour brought me to the level of the cliff area. I started pushing through the brush and trees to move toward the cliff edge. Before I got far, I thought I heard something. I paused and listened then heard it again. It sounded like voices, speaking alternately louder and softer. I glanced down at Leesha. She was asleep, head resting against my breast. I pushed ahead as quietly as I could, pausing intermittently to listen for the direction of the voices. I stopped as I came to the edge of a clearing. I could see Nephi facing Laman and Lemuel. Beyond them the cliff dropped away to sky and ocean far below. Nephi was speaking.

"Look, brothers. The Lord worked through Moses to lead His people out of slavery in Egypt, and Moses was not an articulate man. Not only that, but God fed the people manna for forty years and, when there was no water to be had, brought it out of a rock. He saved them from a pestilence of poisonous serpents, and all the people had to do was look upon an image of a serpent to be saved. Then the Lord brought his people to a rich land, a Promised Land for them, and aided them in driving out the wicked inhabitants before them. If the Lord can do all this, working through one mortal man, why can he not instruct me how to build a ship?"

Nephi paused for breath, and Lemuel spoke up, "Yes, but I still don't see why we had to leave Jerusalem at all. Look how much our wives have suffered, barely surviving in that wilderness and bearing children under horrible conditions. I would rather we had died before leaving Jerusalem and making them go through that."

Nephi spoke softly, "Then you, too, would be destroyed with the wicked of Jerusalem—"

"There you go again!" Laman cut in. "You and Father both! How can you say the people were wicked? They kept the Law of Moses—"

"Ah, but look again, brother!" Nephi's voice was still soft, but more intense. "Outwardly they appeared to be. But behind closed doors was greed and theft, remember Laban? Violence and abuse, adultery and murders abounded, don't you remember the news proclamations? They even tried to murder our own father for speaking out against all this! How could the Lord have managed to look at our sins even this long? For all we know, Jerusalem is even now on the eve of its destruction and captivity."

Nephi sighed deeply and held out his arms toward his brothers. "My soul fears for you, my brothers. You too have sought to take away our father's life. You, too, have hardened your hearts that you cannot hear the soft, still voice of the Spirit of the Lord as he tries to guide you. You can hear only the voice of thunder and earthquake. And despite having seen an angel and heard his voice many times, you still run to do iniquity and ignore God's directions." He drew a deep, quavering breath. "I fear that you will be cast out of God's presence forever, and the thought pains and weakens me." He let his arms fall to his sides, and hung his head.

Laman and Lemuel exchanged looks and then suddenly lunged toward Nephi as he stood with his back to the cliff. I cried out involuntarily. Nephi looked up quickly and held out his right arm.

"Stop, I command you!" His brothers hesitated. Nephi drew himself up to his full height and his eyes flashed with intensity. "In the name of Almighty God, do not touch me! I am filled with the power of God, and if you lay your hands on me, you shall wither like a dried reed!" He stopped speaking and looked his brothers directly in the eyes. Lemuel had stepped back. Laman looked a bit pale from my vantage point. Nephi spoke again, quieter, but even more firm, "God has commanded me to build a ship and instructed me how to do it. You are to stop murmuring and complaining, and are to help me build this ship." He paused. "Now go, return to the camp. After the Sabbath, we will begin."

Laman and Lemuel stood unmoving for a minute then quickly turned and fled down the hill, crashing through trees and bushes. Gradually all grew quiet, and still Nephi stood, back to the sea, staring off into the mountain's higher peaks. Then he seemed to shake himself, and he looked around for a minute, glancing once briefly over the edge of the cliff, then away again.

"You can come out now," he called in my general direction. "Whoever you are, I heard you cry out earlier." He walked forward as though to search the brush himself.

I pushed forward the last few feet into the clearing. "Here I am Nephi. It is I." I reached my arm out toward him and the ends of my hair stood up. An odd sensation wrapped around my body and I heard or felt a quiet buzzing.

"Stop!" Nephi cried out. He looked at my hair and stepped back from me. My hair sank down again and the quiet buzzing stopped. "I do not know if it is safe for me to touch you, Didi," he said then grinned sheepishly.

I smiled crookedly back at him. "That's all right, Nephi," I said. "I'm just glad you're safe."

Nephi looked behind him at the sea far below. "That was a close one." He looked up at me. "At least I think they'll help us build the ship this time."

Leesha awoke with a start. She whimpered and rubbed her eyes. Then she saw Nephi. "Da," she said, starting to reach out her hand to him. Then she stopped and looked at me. "Ma," she whimpered and hid her face in my shoulder. Then she peeked out at him from time to time, watching his every move. I had never seen her act this way toward him. I looked at Nephi, raised my eyebrows, and shrugged.

"Never mind, Didi." He laughed quietly and then sighed. "Well, let me take you both back to camp."

It seemed odd to be walking with my husband without holding his hand. But as long as neither of us knew whether it was safe for me to touch him, though I had no intention of harming him, we wanted to be on the safe side. A withered wife can't do very much.

On our return, we told the girls we were going to play a game of "don't touch Papa" for a few days to see how good their memory was. Nephi made his own bed in a corner of the tent so we wouldn't accidentally touch in our sleep. It was quite a challenge to keep our distance. But the game made it much more tolerable, and we'd blow Papa kisses and give him air hugs.

After the Sabbath, the men began working on the ship again. This time Laman and Lemuel, Gid and Mori were there to help. Sam came too, his right arm still tied to his body, and helped as much as he could with one arm.

The first week, as I helped bring drinks and lunches to the men, Laman and Lemuel worked along silently and obediently. The second week, their expressions were more sullen, their actions more reluctant. Helping bring lunch one day, I heard Laman swear out a complaint against Nephi under his breath. He looked up startled as my shadow passed him, but I walked on as if I'd heard nothing, his eyes following me until I reached the lunch place.

"Lunchtime!" I called, setting down my basket of food next to those the other women, including Riddah and Bekka, had brought. The men needed no prompting. With hoots and hollers, they laid aside their equipment and jumped down from the ship's frame. Soon all were busily eating and talking, children running and playing around us. I sat down near Nephi as he ate near the edge of the group.

"Laman is complaining against you again, husband," I said quietly between bites of bread.

His shoulders drooped. "I thought as much. Their attitudes show in how they work and treat the others." He sighed. "Will this never end?" He glanced at me. "Don't worry, Didi. I'll find a way."

That evening Nephi was a little later than usual coming home. Knowing his brothers, I always was nervous not knowing where Nephi was, so I was glad when he showed up at the tent door.

"Didi," he said and stayed standing there. At the tired tone in his voice, I turned, dropped the dress I was folding, and ran to him, stopping myself at the last minute from touching him. "It's all right now," he said, reached out, and folded me in his embrace. It felt like heaven to feel the touch and warmth of his body after the previous long two weeks.

I looked up at his face, now serene and smiling. "What happened?" I asked between his kisses.

"Laman and Lemuel are finally convinced God wants them to help build this ship, and Mori and Gid will follow their lead. I don't think we'll have to worry about them . . . at least until the ship is done."

Nephi's prediction was correct. It was through Naola, who had been told by Sam, that I found out how Nephi had touched his brothers, and they had been shocked and shaken into following his directions again. I watched our brothers work, if not as intensely as Nephi, at least consistently. Finally, months after the building project was started, it was complete. The men sent the children around to spread the news.

"Mama, Mama!" Siri was the first to alert me as she bounded in the tent door. Zenna stumbled in breathlessly behind her. "Come see the ship! It's all done!"

I gathered up Leesha and followed Siri and Zenna to the ship. On the way, we were joined by Joseph, Sariah's youngest son, dragging Naola and Mary with him. Soon all had arrived, including Mama, Sariah, and Lehi led by Jacob, their next youngest son. The ship rocked slowly in the water, a wooden walkway leading out to it from the shore.

"Father," Lemuel approached Lehi. "Isn't this a fine ship?" He looked with pride at the finished creation. "Come, let us give you a tour through it."

The style was like no ship I had seen before, nor confessed Nephi to me, had he with his exposure to sea life. The workmanship was good, sturdy. The ship seemed spacious, huge, until Nephi reminded me that not only family members, but our supplies, equipment, small animals, and food stores must fit on this ship. I thought of the crops we had been growing and storing in this bountiful land and of how much we could eat in just a week. Yes, our ship would have a lot of cargo to carry.

After the tour, we gathered on the beach again. "You have done well, my sons," commented Lehi. His gaze included Mori, Gid, and Zoram. "This is a beautiful ship. We should give her a name. Let's see, what shall we call her?" He looked up at the ship thoughtfully

A couple of suggestions were made that didn't seem quite right. Then Sam spoke up almost shyly. "Father, how about 'The Liahona'?"

Others nodded their heads approvingly. Sariah grasped her husband's arm and looked up at him, smiling. Laman, scuffing his sandal in the sand as he looked down, was the only one who didn't seem excited by the name, but he said nothing.

Lehi looked around at everyone and then smiled. "Well, if no one disapproves, then I suppose we'll call her the Liahona!" His face became more serious. "Actually, it is a very meaningful name to give to our ship." He looked up at it and raised his arm. "In the name of our God, we ask thy blessing to be upon this ship as she takes us to the Land of Promise. We give her the name the Liahona." He lowered his arm. "As soon as all is made ready, we leave for the Promised Land."

Everyone cheered, except for Laman. As everyone else mingled and hugged, I saw him grasp Riddah's arm and say something to her, an angry expression on his face. Then he walked off toward camp. As he passed, I heard him mutter, "The Liahona. Hah!" As soon as Riddah and Jagadesh had gathered their children, they followed. Lemuel's family left soon after, followed by Mori and Gid's.

The next day I met Riddah at the stream where we were fetching water for our families.

"The ship turned out all right," I commented to her, not knowing what else to say.

"Humph!" she grunted, tilting up a full pitcher, one of Becka's better clay baked models, and she lifted it to the stream bank. But she said nothing more as she lowered a camel bladder bag in to fill.

"I understand the men are going to sell the camels on their next trip to the village," I tried again. "I think I'm going to miss those rude creatures after all, with all the time we've spent depending on them. I wonder if we'll have horses or donkeys where we're going, or some new creature of burden?"

Riddah dropped her second full container to the bank, stood, and turned to look at me. "Really, Didi. You are so naive. What makes you think we are all going with you on that ship?" She leaned forward a little, cocked an eyebrow, and laid her hands on her hips. "I hear tell there are cities further north where they wear silk for work clothes and have even finer cloths for their party wear. And such fine foods that even Mary would feel she had died and gone to heaven!"

"Yes!" I shot back. "They also speak another language, keep their women subservient in harems, and likely would make any of us foreigners into slaves, lower than their lowest class. Is that what you want, Riddah?"

"Humph!" she said again, picked up her water containers, and walked away without another word.

My next chance to see Nephi was that evening after supper, and I told him of my encounter with Riddah as we sat in the evening shade of the tent. He looked appropriately concerned.

"Yes," he said. "I rather expected they would do this. I expect they'll disappear permanently the moment father gives the word to board the ship...or sooner." Nephi remained thoughtful a while. "One advantage we have is that Laman would have no political clout in any town he settled in around here, being a foreigner, nor would small town politics satisfy him for long. The only way he could be lord or leader is with his own family." Nephi looked at me and laughed, but there was some pain in it. "He's been trying to be patriarch of our group behind Father's back most of our living and journeying in this wilderness. But the problem is he's been trying to force half our group to follow him opposite of our own consciences, our father, and God himself. We're just not very obedient in that!"

He stood up and stretched then looked down at me. "Don't worry, Didi. I'll figure something out. At least with the Lord's help, we will. He needs all of us to people this Land of Promise, and he'll show us the way."

I watched for signs of trouble the next day. All were busy with travel preparations and getting ready to sell the camels, but there was nothing obvious, other than the usual noncommunication between the two halves of the family. However, I was now aware of the intents of the other half of our group, and I could feel the tension growing like a weed. It was a bindweed, wrapping itself around our eyes and hearts so that everything we saw we interpreted through our own intentions and desires, hopes, and dreams. My husband's brothers seemed nervous and jumpy, as if seeing traps everywhere and trying to avoid them. Their wives and my brothers and sisters-in-law said almost nothing where any of the rest of us could hear, and kept their children involved in tent-bound tasks. I could tell Lehi, Sariah, and Mama sensed the tension, for they tiptoed through all their interactions with the nervous parties. Mary secluded herself with her family and the task of drying the last of her herbs, ever sensitive to vibes of tension, even if not knowing all the causes. Naola was blissfully ignorant of the tension even being there.

"Didi!" she called to me, bounding up, pulling her new pet sheep behind her to take it to water. "Sam tells me we're not taking most of the animals on the boat with us. Why ever not? Do they think more animals will grow on trees or something?" She grinned, letting me know she was half joking.

"I don't know," I responded, half distracted because Abisha was herding her two oldest truant sons back to camp, and the two boys were looking in our direction with expressions of longing I couldn't begin to fathom. "Maybe Father Lehi has been told of herds or other creatures already waiting for us. Maybe you should ask him if he'll make an exception for your Perky." I knew how much she had suffered giving up her pet sheep, Dan, at Jerusalem, and I didn't want to see her go through it again.

"Oh, thank you, Didi! That's a wonderful idea! And maybe he'll let me pick a mate for him so we never run out of wool cloth for Abisha to sew!" And she left, pulling Perky away from the tuft of grass he was about to devour.

"I'm sure Abisha will be eternally grateful!" I laughed after her. *"If she comes along to the Land of Promise,"* I thought to myself.

That night it happened. I was awakened sometime before dawn by the sound of Nephi rummaging around for something near the tent door. I sat up on my elbows and stared at him, trying to orient my mind. "Nephi, what is it?" I asked softly.

Nephi found what he was after, a large water bladder, and turned to his pile of clothes by the bed. "Our brothers and their families are gone," he whispered. "Sam and Zoram and I are going after them. Sam was on watch and dozed a bit and we missed them leaving. But I don't think it was more than a couple of hours ago." He found his old desert robe and threw it over his head. "The problem is, they took all the camels, so we're on foot." He shook his head. "I was hoping to get a lot of supplies in exchange for those camels." He sighed and then looked at me. "I don't know how long it may be before we're back, hon. But we will be back!" He gave me a quick kiss and left.

Needless to say, I could not sleep any more. It was almost a relief when Leesha woke up wanting her early morning meal, so I cuddled with her in my bed longer than usual. My heart went through many versions of the same prayer: *Please let my husband return safely, and with our siblings too.* Finally it was dawn.

Mary, Naola, and I met each other shortly thereafter with our children in front of Father Lehi's tent. Sariah stepped out, expecting clear passage to the edge of camp to relieve herself, and stopped, surprised to see us there.

"What is it?" she asked, looking from one of us to the other.

We all looked at each other. Finally I spoke. "Laman and Lemuel with Gid and Mori have taken their families by camel out into the desert. We think they are on their way to the village and onward. Our husbands have followed them on foot. We thought you and Father Lehi ought to know."

Sariah nodded. We parted to let her pass. Mary went to waken Mama, and the three women returned to the tent at the same time. Sariah went in to get Lehi. When he came out, we rehearsed the story again.

"Please, Father," begged Naola. "Will you pray for them?"

Lehi nodded and spoke a very beautiful though simple prayer. Then we went about to feed the children and continue packing for our sea voyage. We watched all day, hoping and praying all would be well. When there was no sign of them that night, Mary had Mama join her in her tent, and I brought Naola and Benjamin into mine, and our prayers continued. The next morning, Naola suggested we fast, and the other adults agreed. My Siri decided she wanted to join in too. We spent another day packing and looking toward the north. I felt we could survive in this valley with our current group, but there was no way we could attempt an ocean voyage and keep a settlement alive alone. It would be difficult even if our three husbands returned but without our other four brothers and their families.

We passed another lonely prayerful night. The next morning our fasting continued, but little work was done. About midmorning, we heard voices calling through the trees, and much to our joy, two of our husbands burst through into view.

"We've returned!" called an exuberant Sam, and Naola rushed toward him. He dropped the packs he was carrying and gathered her into his arms.

Zoram was right behind him, similarly loaded down. At Mary's questioning face, he grinned. "The others are right behind us," he explained. "They'll be along soon."

In a few minutes, the rest of our family came through the trees. The littlest children rode on their siblings' shoulders, while the adults carried or dragged their packs and goods. Every person was accounted for, my Nephi drawing up the rear. But there was no camel in sight, no tents, and no extra supplies.

I greeted Nephi with a tight hug. Then I stood back and looked at him. He said nothing, but the corners of his mouth showed the signs of a smile. "Where are all the camels?" I asked.

He laughed. "That story will be told shortly," he said. "But first, where is Father?"

Lehi and Sariah were welcoming the families they had thought they would not see again. Water bladders were being filled and drained by thirsty travelers, and the children chatted excitedly. The adults, to my assessment, seemed glad to rest, but did not seem as joyful as the others to be back here.

"Enough visiting!" cried Lehi. "I wish to hear the story of your recent travels, my sons. Humor an old man and tell me!"

Everyone was seated on the ground near the stream to listen. As Nephi had made a point of sitting down, Laman remained standing. He did not speak for several minutes. Lemuel started to stand, but Laman waved him back down. He raised his head, squared his shoulders back, and began.

"Seeing that this part of the world was a green and bounteous land, several of us desired to remain. Accordingly, we packed our worldly possessions and set forth across the desert. It would be a simple trip, for we had traveled this way several times before. But we did not count on the twists that fate might bring." Laman glanced in Nephi's direction, but Nephi's calm expression did not change in any way.

"We traveled until the sun grew hot, and then set up our shade tents to rest. We were awakened by a commotion outside, a stomping and crying from our camels. Rushing out, we were horrified to see the last of our beasts running off northward into the desert, chased by a group of robed strangers on horses." Laman stared at Nephi again, as if to accuse him of the theft.

"It was a bad time for all of us. We were stranded in the middle of a barren land, without a source of water beyond a couple of days, during which time we had no hope of reaching the northern village on foot, even if we left all of our equipment behind. It was the little children who would suffer most in the desert heat." Laman paused as if reaching an even more painful part of the story.

"Soon after this my brothers arrived." Laman again glanced at Nephi. "They offered to help us carry our gear back here to Bountiful. We had no other choice but to accept." He looked at his wife Riddah a long time and then sat down. "That is all."

I noticed Nephi nodding his head slightly, and his shoulders seemed to relax. Considering who had told the story, I thought Laman had told it fairly well. I couldn't help but wonder though at the timing of those desert men driving away the camels. It felt like providence, like the hand of the Lord helping us solve a difficult problem. I poured out a prayer of gratitude in my heart.

"Well told," said Sariah, standing up. "But I believe there are many hungry stomachs in this group that we need to feed. Girls, let's go to work and make a feast for the returned travelers!"

We needed no further urging. With renewed strength, we put together some of our quicker favorite foods and created a feast worthy of a holiday. The men roasted some of the last of the fresh meat. I suspected it would be a while before we would eat this way again until we reached the Land of Promise.

CHAPTER 7

The Sea

Over the next few days, our time was filled with drying and spicing the last of the meat, packing up all of the remaining tents and supplies, the final gathering of wool, fruit, herbs and spices, seeds and grain into woven storage bags, and pouring honey and water into clay, wooden or skin containers. Then the day came. We loaded our final belongings, five sheep, three goats, and some chickens on the ship, and gathered on the shore one last time. Father Lehi offered a prayer for good journeying and to say farewell to the part of the world we had called home. Then we boarded the ship, Father Lehi and his family first with Mama, followed by the married sons in order with their wives and children: Mori, Gid, Laman, Lemuel, Zoram, Eli, and Sam. Nephi and I were last.

As my foot left the ground to step onto the wooden planks leading to the ship, I looked over my shoulder and paused. "We shall never return to Jerusalem, shall we, Nephi?" That thought had never seemed absolutely final to me until now.

He shook his head. "No, Didi. I feel that we never shall."

I gazed at the trees lining the shore, at the mountain peaks above them, pictured the desert behind them, and great distances beyond that, Jerusalem. It had been close to ten years since we had left, and the memory of my home was vague and fading. My children had never seen the city; they knew only the nomadic life. I turned to look out beyond the ship where sea met the sky. Nephi had had no answers to my questions of where we were going, only that God had reserved a special land for us, a blessed land. I pictured a land where I could raise my children in a house, among good people with no fear for the safety of my children, in a land verdant and green. I ran back to the shore and picked up the first unbroken seashell I could find for my treasure box and then hurried back to Nephi's side.

I looked up at Nephi and smiled. "I am ready. Let's go!"

Nephi grinned. "All right! Let's race!"

He took Leesha from my arms and grabbed Siri's hand while I grabbed Zenna's. We ran, hooting and shouting, out to the ship. Waiting hands pulled us on board. Zoram pulled up the anchor as Lehi shouted instructions to the men. They heaved up the great sails and turned them this way and that as directed. The ship creaked, leaned one way, and then another for several minutes while the men figured out how to set the sails, then the ship finally turned and started moving away from shore. Shortly thereafter, Lehi turned the handling of the tiller over to Nephi.

The rest of us crowded to the railing of the ship to watch her progress. Soon we left the protection of the inlet where we had camped the past many months, and the water became rough. Sail adjustments were made to compensate for strengthening winds. I hurriedly went to find shawls to wrap the girls in. I hadn't felt this cool except in Jerusalem on early winter mornings. I hoped we'd find enough clothes to keep warm this journey.

It wasn't until after the girls were bundled that I saw Father Lehi standing beside Nephi, holding the Liahona, with Nephi glancing at it from time to time. I had not seen it since our arrival in Bountiful. Seeing it being used on this stage of the journey was calming, comforting to me. God was guiding us again, east-southeast.

It wasn't long before the constant rolling of the ship on the ocean waves started bothering us. Riddah was the first, suddenly rushing to the side rail and throwing up over the side of the ship. Kora and Mirimi joined her there not long after, gripping the rail with closed eyes, a distinctly green hue to their faces.

The children overall tolerated the ship's motion well; in fact, Abisha's boys had started playing "pirate" and "shipwrecked" the moment land disappeared from sight. The older children quickly became involved, hooting and running here and there, but careful to stay away from those working the sails. The adults, however, all seemed more reserved than usual, and most of us not employed on the decks retired to our quarters. I thought I was doing fairly well until

Zenna came up to me, put her head in my lap, and promptly threw up. I wiped her face a bit, holding back some lurches of my own stomach, and then suddenly found myself following her example. Needless to say, by evening over half of us were lying in our bunks, not wanting to even think about food. Only two or three of the adults were up and moving to get dinner for the children and those adults who had any slight interest. I was not one of them.

Late that night Nephi's face appeared above mine. "How are you doing, love?" he asked, and planted a kiss on my moist forehead. I could only turn my head and groan. "That bad, huh?" He sat on the edge of the bunk to take off his shoes. "Don't worry. In the morning, you'll either feel worse or better. It takes no more than a week for most people to get their sea stomachs."

I had no idea how he could smile and told him so. "And I bet you never went through this yourself, mister," I hissed.

He paused and then looked at me. "Actually, Didi, I was horribly ill the first time Father took us on a boat out on the open sea on one of his merchant trips. Two days into it, an old sailor made me drink a cup of some bitter old tea that I thought would kill me. But the next day not a trace of nausea was left." He scratched his ear a moment. "Now what was in that stuff?" He shook his head. "Maybe I'll remember it in the morning."

I was greeted next morning by a cup of something that smelled strong and earthy. "Here, Didi," Nephi said, thrusting the cup toward me again. "Drink this, and you should feel lots better."

"What is it?" I asked, wrinkling my nose. I took the cup from him and stared into it. I didn't know if I'd be able to keep any of it down.

"Just drink it," Nephi grinned. "It's an herbal concoction to help the seasickness go away. The others are getting their doses too."

Between the swells rocking the boat, I swallowed it. It was bitter. But somehow I managed to drink most of the cup and keep it down. Then I lay down again and groaned.

"How long does this take to work?" I asked weakly.

"One to two days." Nephi grinned again. I would have punched the smile off his face if I'd had the strength. "At least by the end of the week."

"That's how long you said it would take without this stuff," I moaned.

He shrugged. "Mary and I had to improvise a little. I can't promise any miracles."

I rolled over in my bunk and pushed my face into the pillows, groaning, only minimally exaggerating my misery. At least Nephi was well enough to take care of the girls for me, except for nursing Leesha, which at least I could do lying down.

After a long midday nap, I awoke actually feeling well enough to get out of bed. I suddenly wanted some fresh air. I dragged myself to the nearest ladder and pulled myself up to the upper deck. The cool salty sea air struck me as I emerged, but this time it felt invigorating. I sucked in deep lungsful, and sat down near the railing. Little Zenna ran up to me, a doll in her hands, motherly Siri close behind carrying Leesha.

"Mommy, Mommy!" Zenna cried and threw her arms around my neck. "Are you all better now?"

"Much better, my little one," I replied, tousling her windblown hair, noting that she looked much better too. I smiled at Siri. "Thank you for watching the little ones, Siri. You are truly a lifesaver." She smiled and gave me a hug, partially in relief it seemed.

It took longer for Nephi and Mary to convince our seasick siblings to down their bitter tea than it did for it to work. At last we were all up out of our sick beds, and if not actually enjoying the constant rolling of the boat, at least we were able to keep some food down. Within another week, most of us were able to walk around the boat with only an occasional loss of balance from the swells, and life settled down to a routine.

The men took turns at the tiller where the Liahona had been fastened into a special box, its directors visible to all. Occasionally the man at the tiller called for help in making sail adjustments. The others would be checking the fishing lines and nets for food or mending the equipment. The women mainly stayed below deck, mending clothes by the light of the porthole windows, preparing meals, and passing the time. The children would spend their time in the larger eating room, or petting or teasing the animals in their stalls at the aft end of the living level, nearest Nephi and Sam's quarters. Tiring of this, they would find their way up to the decks to watch the sea, and the women would be regularly pulling them out of the way of the men.

I was glad for the chance to spend more time with my sisters-in-law and their children. They had done so much growing up in the desert without my realizing it. Mori's oldest boys especially, Zac and Matthew, seemed like nice young men. All the older girls adored them, chattering at them while they worked with the men, trying to dominate their free time, and yet they were still polite and friendly.

I can't say we were always happy about being in such close quarters with each other though. I began to realize some advantages of having had Laman and his following camped somewhat separately from us in our latest travels. And it did not have to do with bumping into them more often in the close air below decks. I found I had to be careful which of their colorful conversations I let my girls hear. Fortunately, the girls were usually tired early in the evenings, and I could put them to bed early, thus avoiding the worst of it.

Many weeks passed in this manner. Daily routines took on the feel of daily survival. It was getting difficult to keep the children from bickering over little things. I would have given almost anything to have a long stretch of meadow in which to take the kids running and playing. It seemed whenever they forgot themselves and started running around the ship's decks, the men working above would chastise them and send them below until they could stay out from under foot. If they played at all loudly on the living deck when the small children were napping, invariably a baby would awake crying and a mother would be cross. And the children were not the only ones frustrated by the lack of space. Everyone's tempers were adversely affected, including mine, much to my shame. I expressed my concerns to Nephi a couple of times. We talked about some strategies for increasing patience, and that helped some. I truly empathized with

Patriarch Noah and his family, being cramped on a boat together, but with a boat full of animals too, and for nearly a year! I hoped fervently our voyage would not last as long as theirs.

One advantage we had over Noah though, was that the first half of our nautical journey took us periodically close to land where we could pull to shore and resupply with fresh water, fruit, and vegetables. We tried to stay away from obvious settlements, yet we managed to find enough food to keep us supplied.

One afternoon when the girls were especially restless, I got a sudden inspiration. Grasping Zenna by the hands, I swung her around the dining table area in a dance step I mostly remembered from my girlhood days in Jerusalem while humming a merry tune. Siri lifted Leesha into her arms and swung around with her right after me. Soon many of the other children and their mothers joined in. As I turned around the room, a hand on my arm interrupted my step, and I looked up into the face of Nephi.

He smiled and took my hand. "May I have this dance?" he asked.

I nodded, and he started humming a different tune to a line dance. Others followed his lead, and we stepped sideways, back and forth, the children trying to learn the dance steps. After a wonderful half an hour of exercise, we all collapsed onto chairs or the floor, smiling and giggling at our efforts.

"We should do this more often," Nephi commented.

I couldn't have agreed more. The dancing lifted my spirits as nothing else had on this ocean journey.

It became the habit for my brothers, Laman, Lemuel and their wives to gather in the evening in the main eating room after putting their children to bed. At first Mary, Naola, Mama and I stayed with them. But gradually the women's conversation became more gossipy and exclusionary. The men began playing gambling games, bragging about the fine ship they had built, and telling borderline stories and jokes. By the time I noticed how uncomfortable I was being there, I realized Naola and Sam, Mama, Sariah, and Father Lehi were seldom there much after dinner. Mary, finally one evening after trying several times unsuccessfully to change the conversation into a more positive direction, put down her sewing and stood up with an exasperated whoosh of air. She breathed deeply a few times while wrapping up her things, then walked out through the curtained doorway toward the sleeping quarters. I stitched a little longer, trying to absorb what had happened, then put away my things.

"Good night, sisters," I said and followed Mary's example. I stood outside the camel hair curtain to her family's quarters for a moment. All was quiet. I was about to walk on when I heard a quiet sob. I called softly to her. All was silent again. Then I heard footsteps, and the curtain opened. Mary stood with a tear-streaked face.

"Are you all right, Mary?" I asked. "May I come in?"

She wiped her cheek, smiled briefly, and stepped back to let me in. Then she shut the curtain after me. Her children were asleep, but Zoram was absent, probably taking his shift above deck.

"What happened?" I asked.

Her face clouded over, and she hit her left palm with her right fist. "Ooh, I'm so mad! Why can't they—" She suddenly stopped and laughed harshly. "Maybe they're trying to tell me something. I guess I should realize when I'm not wanted . . ." She raised her chin upward, but her eyes were squeezed shut.

I went over to her and hugged her. She stood unresponsive for a minute and then suddenly hugged me back hard. We stood that way for a long time. Then Mary let go and stepped back slightly, her hands on my shoulders.

"Oh, Didi," she sighed. "Is there anything we can do to make a difference?"

I was silent a moment. "If there were another gathering room, I would start a group of my own with upbeat conversation and activities."

"That's it!" cried Mary joyfully. "We start another gathering group and attract the others to it one by one!" I gazed at her evenly. Then her face fell. "But where would we meet? We can't move the animals further below or they'd eat all the grain. The upper deck is outdoors, our sleeping rooms are too small, and the lower decks are dark and full of storage. No one would want to spend their time in a dungeon."

I snapped my fingers. "No, Mary, wait! You do have it! We may have eaten enough of the food supplies, that with a little rearranging we'd have enough space! We can use some of the storage items for sitting and work surfaces. It could work, Mary!"

That night we presented our ideas to our husbands. They agreed to help move some of the heavier items, but the rest of the arranging would be up to us. Their work with the running of the ship and obtaining seafood and sleeping in between shifts was keeping them busy. The next day we started, in between fixing meals, airing out clothes, and caring for the children. Naola joined us, in addition to three or four of the older children who were big enough to move things. We planned and moved what we could, moving less needed items out of the middle of the storage deck and packing as much as we could away in nooks and crannies fore and aft. Then we found Sam and Zoram to help with the bigger items, making sure nothing overbalanced the ship to port or starboard. It was a couple of days before we had everything possible out of the way, and we stepped back to examine our work.

Naola rubbed her aching back, and I massaged my left shoulder. Mary sat down and put her hand to her forehead. "It's still so small," she sighed. She raised her eyes and looked at us. "Maybe six of us could squeeze in here, hardly enough for an exciting evening get-together."

Naola looked around. "It's too dark to sew by, even with a couple of candles burning. I doubt Father Lehi would let us use candles both here and in the dining hall, given the unknown length of our journey."

I stood with my hands on my hips, and looked around one more time. "Maybe we'll just have to wait a little longer into our journey," I said. "I think our problems will be solved once we use up more of the supplies, and we save up a supply of old candle stubs. At least we have a place started."

We resigned ourselves to putting up a little longer with the company upstairs. When the sun went down, I would bid good night to any family mingling in the main room, then take my girls to bed, and retire myself. Nephi usually took his second shift in the middle of the night after helping me tuck the children into bed, and I missed his company sorely during those later evening hours. I cursed my wakefulness, but also refused to take part in the borderline conversations.

Over the next several weeks, the only ones who stayed in the big room in the evenings were Laman, Lemuel, Gid, Mori, their wives, and occasionally their older children. Several times I found myself awakened by their loud voices, laughter, singing, and dancing, and was certain it was deep into the night. A couple of times I thought I heard Father Lehi's voice asking them to be quieter in respect for those sleeping, and it almost seemed they became louder immediately after. Though my sleep was often interrupted, and occasionally my daughters', I found I enjoyed going into the main room in the early mornings when it was filled with our parents, Naola, Mary, and happily playing children, without the strain of having to see the exhausted and often ill-tempered night revelers.

One evening I was awakened by a loud crash, followed by a screech, then coarse laughter. Stunned by the suddenness of it, and trying to clear my mind from sleep, I was startled to hear a small voice near my bunk.

"Mama!" it sobbed. I reached out and gathered in Zenna beside me. She was shivering despite the robes around her. I wrapped her in my blanket, hugged and rocked her, humming a lullaby. Slowly her shivering stopped. I thought she had returned to sleep, and I sought to do the same. Then I heard another screech and chorus of laughter, and her little body started shivering again.

"Mama! Why do they laugh so loud?" she started crying again. "It scares me! Please make them stop!"

"Hush now," I whispered. "It's all right. You're safe. The sounds won't hurt you." I listened to the wind and water splashing outside, and felt the swelling waves rocking the boat soothingly. I hummed another tune in time to the swaying of the ship. When I heard her even breathing return once more, I gently unwrapped my blanket and lifted her back to the bunk above mine that she shared with Siri, and tucked them both in together. I looked at Leesha sleeping peacefully on our lower bunk, and sighed. Some of the sounds that came from that room scared me too, I had to admit. It was time to say something to them out there. I wrapped a robe around me and slipped through our room curtain.

I wasn't the only one with that idea. Mary came out of her room a split second after I did, and we looked at each other a moment. Then we entered the eating room together to face the noisemakers.

"We need you to please keep the noise level down," Mary started. "It wakes the children and—"

"It wakes the children!" repeated Laman nasally. "Are you accusing us of being too loud? Of purposely trying to 'wake the children'?"

"Please," she begged, her voice a little shaky. "I didn't mean you were doing this on purpose. It's just that your voices carry—"

"Ah!" Mori grinned. "Isn't that a quality one desires in a voice for singing? Come, Abisha, pleasure us with a song!"

"Really, Mori," she shook her head, "I don't think this is the time." He looked at her sternly, and she took a deep breath as if to begin.

"Excuse me," I cut in hurriedly. "There's not a whole lot we can do to block the sound even with our curtains closed. We just didn't know if you were aware—"

"Oh, for God's sake, Didi!" chimed in Riddah. "We're not fools. We're only trying to pass the time during this interminable cruise. I don't know why you have to be so self-righteous about it, you not joining us anymore and all. You'd think we were leprous, the way you all have been acting." She sniffed and wiped at her cheek, but the corner of her mouth turned upward slightly.

"Good night, all," I said firmly and turned back to my door. Out of the corner of my eye, I watched Mary do the same, and breathed a sigh of relief. I did not want to start a family fight at this moment, just to have a little uninterrupted sleep. What I really wanted was for Nephi to finish his shift and return to cuddle with me in our bunk.

I went into our room, pulled the curtain closed behind me, and lay down again to struggle for sleep.

The hooting and calling and singing continued moderately loudly that night, but my girls stayed asleep, and I did not attempt to quiet the revelers again. I did hear Mary's baby crying one more time, and at one point Riddah's toddler awoke too, but an older sibling quieted him down. I hoped other nights would be less raucous. I was beginning to get short on rest.

However, over the next couple of weeks, though an occasional night was quiet enough to get some sleep, the overall tone became even more loud and wild. Nephi must have been able to hear the noise above deck because he asked me how I was able to get any sleep at all. I just shrugged my shoulders and joked that I probably wouldn't know how to sleep anymore without background noise. His mouth smiled in response, but his eyes probed me in a way that I knew he guessed the strain I was under.

Finally one night my patience snapped. The reveling had spread from the eating room to the hallway of the families' sleeping area. Drinking, dancing, and singing had gone on for several hours, and now some sort of shouting chase game was going on. Leesha had been crying in my arms for nearly an hour, exhausted but unable to fall asleep. Suddenly two bodies fell in through our door curtain, and landed on the floor, one struggling to escape the other's grasp. It was Riddah and Lemuel.

"Let me go!" giggled Riddah. "I did the dare part, now you have to give the truth part!"

Lemuel's response was slurred and incomprehensible. He was definitely drunk. He picked himself up, tried unsuccessfully to help up Riddah, then they both fell to the floor again, giggling uncontrollably. By this time all my girls were awake and had scrambled to the far side of their bunks to get out of their way. I pulled the blankets around me to hide my nightclothes. I suddenly realized that the two beings on my floor were barely clothed themselves. I had had enough. Nightclothes or no, I was going to have my say.

I got to my feet, finding one of Nephi's robes to pull around me. I stood towering over the two on my floor, hands on my hips. "Mister Lemuel and Mistress Riddah," I said in my most acid voice. "Will you two please have the courtesy to evacuate my last vestige of private space and return to your own quarters?"

Lemuel pulled himself onto my bunk just in front of Leesha to get closer to my eye level, and burped. "Shishter! How nishe of you to drop in. Have a drink?" He pulled a bottle from his waist pocket and offered it to me. Riddah giggled.

I raised my arm and pointed out the door. "Leave! Now!" I ordered.

Riddah grasped my arm and pulled herself up with it. She stood swaying in front of me. I tried not to look at her nearly bare chest. I felt an intense sickening in my stomach. I wished my girls were not seeing this.

"Sister," Riddah breathed in my face. "You're missing a hell of a good time. Really, you should leave that stuffed-shirt husband of yours and join us. Or are you too good for us too?" She hiccupped. I gagged at her breath.

"I order you both to leave now!" I cried as firmly as I could. I wished there were a way to call for Nephi.

As if in answer to my wish, the curtain moved aside again and another figure entered. But it was not Nephi. It was Laman. Riddah giggled again and leaned against her husband. "This little sister of mine is ordering us to leave, my husband," she pouted. "What are you going to do about it?"

Unlike Lemuel, Laman was not a nice drunk. He grasped Riddah around the shoulder, pushed past Lemuel, and stood over me threateningly. "I do not take kindly to insults to my family," he growled. "Apologize!"

I stood my ground. "I think it is you and your family that need to apologize!" I returned his gaze angrily. "Night after night you have disturbed our sleep, awakened the children, and forced us out of your company by your insults. And now you come into our private quarters and demand our apology? I do not think so, Laman!"

His hand slapping across my face came so unexpectedly that I staggered back against my bunk and almost fell. I just stared at him.

"That is for speaking against your elder," he roared. "Now apologize!"

"I will not!" I hissed.

His hand was raised to strike me again when the curtain opened and Nephi walked in. Everyone froze. Nephi took in the situation and then faced Laman. "Leave," he said quietly but with a force I had heard only twice before.

Laman lowered his hand. "We will discuss this outside, Brother." Then he pulled Riddah out with him. Lemuel followed with a hiccup.

Nephi looked at me, and I sat down suddenly on the bed. My cheek burned, but I doubted Nephi could see it in the darkness. "I-I'm all right," I said, but my voice shook. He grasped my hand a moment and then turned toward the curtain. The girls scrambled in a cluster around me, and I hugged them tightly. Nephi lifted the door curtain and went out.

I could hear Nephi's voice rising and falling in the eating room, with regular outbursts from his two oldest brothers, and occasionally from mine. From snatches of words, I could tell the gist of his message, similar to his past exhortations: shape up and repent. The girls and I remained cuddled together in the narrow lower bunk to help them fall asleep.

Suddenly I heard a shriek that sounded like Kora's voice. I disentangled myself from the girls and hesitated just inside the curtain, listening. There were no further voices. I pushed the curtain aside and stepped out.

Inside the eating room I saw Abisha, Hagadah, and Kora huddled together against one wall. Jagadesh and Yadeesh sat at one end of the table holding hands, while Bekka sat at the other end, head down, shaking slightly, Mirimi caressing her back. Riddah faced the opposite wall, arms folded and scowling. No men were in sight.

"Where's Nephi?" I asked, my breath catching. Riddah stuck her chin higher into the air, not looking at me. Bekka did not raise her head, but her shoulders froze momentarily. Hagadah looked up from

Kora, face tear-streaked, and glanced up the ladder at the front end of the room leading up to the outside deck. It was then I noticed the fore hatch was open. "Thank you," I said, and started up the ladder leading to it.

I was met by a cold breeze at the opening, but I continued on. Once outside, my eyes had to adjust to the predawn darkness. I heard low deep voices coming from the center of the ship, where the main mast stood. As soon as I could see enough to move without stumbling over things, I crept in that direction.

Four shadows moved around the mast over some combined task. I could not see Nephi's figure . . . at first. Then I saw him, and a cold shaft of fear shot through my belly. They were tying him to the mast. Occasionally I could hear a grunt as one of the men tightened a rope, and once or twice I heard a muffled groan. This would only elicit a verbal curse and a kick from one of his captors, mostly Laman. I had had enough.

"Stop what you are doing this instant!" I stepped in front of Laman as he reached for another piece of rope. "I demand that you free my husband right now! He has done nothing to deserve such treatment!"

In answer, Laman shoved me aside with another vile curse and placed this new rope around Nephi's neck. I could hear Nephi gagging. "Speak up again, Little Sister, and I tighten this rope around your dear one's neck!" Nephi choked as the rope tightened again. "Leave now, and I might just decide to let him live to see daylight. See?" He loosened the rope slightly and I could hear Nephi's breath coming more easily. "I do not think you are in a position to bargain, my dear. Go back to bed and dream of all the ways I just might kill your tyrant husband!"

I looked from Laman to Nephi's figure. Faint traces of light were beginning in the eastern sky. Nephi's head hung slightly. It occurred to me that he was barely conscious. What had they done, beat him too? There was nothing I could do now while they were all drunk. I would come back later when that poison had worn off, and see if they would listen to reason. I turned and walked away to the sound of hoots and catcalls. It sounded like my own brothers were entering in. Where was Gid's past protection of his little sister? My brothers had changed under the influence of my husband's brothers, and for the worse. I did not know if I would see again the kind, thoughtful brothers I once knew.

Back in the eating room, the other women had disappeared to their respective rooms. I returned to my girls, now sleeping peacefully in a huddle on the lower bunk. I stretched out on the upper bunk, but I could not sleep. I just listened and prayed and tried not to think about the things Laman had hinted at.

When the girls awoke a short time later, I said nothing of where their father was. I wanted to protect them as long as I could from the truth of the situation. As I brought them breakfast in our quarters, my mind continued to ponder ways to free my husband. When Siri asked where her Papa was, I changed the subject and sent the girls to go play with Mary's children. Then I went to collect some breakfast for Nephi.

The boat was starting to roll in a strong wind and growing waves. In the eating room, I only saw Mary and Naola. Lehi and Sariah lately had been sleeping in later in the morning, and Mama would come in a little later to fix their breakfast. I did not see any of the midnight actors of last night's horror, nor did I expect to, as usually only the two handling the tiller and sails the last shift of the night stayed up. But neither did I see Sam or Zoram. They must be sleeping still or above deck already. I gazed at Naola and Mary's faces to see if they were aware of any problems. Their banter was light and cheerful. They were not aware. I took the dish of food and climbed up the ladder to the ship's deck.

It was a dark morning, with clouds being blown thickly overhead. Increasingly larger waves were splashing against the sides of the ship. The deck appeared deserted except for Mori at the tiller at the back of the ship. Nephi was awake now and gazing out over the ocean. I drew near. "Nephi," I whispered. He turned his head slightly, and I noticed for the first time a rag was stuffed in his mouth and tied in. But his eyes brightened when he saw me.

I put the dish of food down between my feet to keep it from sliding away, and tried to untie the rag holding in the gag. The knots were tight, and it took me a couple of minutes to loosen them. Finally they came free. Nephi opened his mouth, stretching all the muscles, and sighed. "Are you all right, my love?" I asked as I picked up a spoonful of cereal for him.

Before the spoon made it to his mouth, it was knocked out of my hand. Mori stood there, frowning. "Laman!" he yelled toward the open hatch near Laman's family's quarters. "Topside, quick!"

I tried to pick up the spoon, but Mori's foot stomped on it. I picked up a morsel of food with my fingers to put it into Nephi's mouth, and Mori knocked the whole dish out of my hand. The contents spattered irretrievably across the deck. I threw my arms around my husband and shut my eyes tightly. Almost immediately I was jerked back by a pair of strong arms, and I looked up into the angry face of Laman.

"What are you doing here, little lady? I thought I made it clear to you last night to stay away from here. Do I need to persuade you further?" He turned around and slugged Nephi in the stomach, hard. Nephi coughed and gagged a moment but said nothing. "No one feeds the prisoner, no one unties the prisoner, no one approaches the prisoner!" Laman stuffed the gag back roughly into Nephi's mouth and retied the rag holding it in place tighter than before. "You can inform the others so. Every effort to help him will hurt him more. We keep him here until he learns his lesson and pays for his insults to us. And pays for yours."

Laman took a piece of rope from his robe and wrapped it around Nephi's neck, pulling it tight. As Nephi gagged, a look from his eyes pierced to the center of my heart, letting me know he loved me. I tried to tell him with my eyes that I would not give up until he was free.

Sam was coming up the ladder from the eating room as I was starting down. I waved him back down, and he waited at the bottom until I was down. As I turned to face him, the fatigue from little sleep the night before, combined with the emotional trauma I was under, hit me all at once. I burst into tears and clung to him, even as I sank to the floor. In a moment, Mary and Naola were there, lifting me to a seat at the table. Then I saw the faces of Mama, Zoram, and my girls. I reached for Siri, Zenna, and Leesha, and sobbed.

"Mama," Zenna asked, nearly crying herself. "Why are you crying?"

I took a deep breath. I didn't know yet how to tell them. "Your papa, he . . . he's . . ." I looked up at Sam. The look on his face told me he half guessed what had happened. "They have him tied up to the main mast outside." I explained to Sam as much as to anybody. "I can't get near enough to feed him, let alone free him. I just don't know what to do." I hugged my girls again, deriving as much comfort from them as I was giving.

By now Father Lehi and Mother Sariah had arrived from their room, led by Naola. Sariah's face was ashen. Lehi and Zoram helped her to sit down. "Why?" was all she could manage to say.

"I think much of it was because he chided them for their night reveling," offered Mary. She turned to me. "I heard most of the whole thing last night," she explained. "Give them a few hours to calm down, and then we can reason with them like we've done before."

I shook my head. "I don't know if it will work this time, Mary," I shuddered. "They almost killed him last night." I glanced at my girls. "They're threatening to hurt him every time we try to intercede. We have to tread very carefully."

"Maybe this would be a good time for a prayer?" offered Naola hesitantly. Sam nodded.

Lehi nodded. "I'll say it." Those of us with young enough knees to kneel did so. When Lehi finished, we all arose. Riddah and Bekka were in the doorway of the room now watching us.

"They think they can free their man with a prayer!" Riddah laughed. "He'll need more than that this time, fools. In fact, I'm not so sure anything will free him unless my husband chooses to!" She sneered. "Chew on that!" She turned back down the hall leading between the sleeping quarters and climbed up the aft ladder to the upper deck. Bekka followed. We could hear them laughing about something.

We all looked at each other silently. Then we dispersed to our various tasks without saying a word.

I was unable to approach Nephi all that day, nor was anyone from Lehi's, Sam's, or Zoram's families allowed up on deck.

It was early afternoon the next day, the wind blowing rain and the seas increasingly rough, when Siri came to me in tears. Zenna followed close behind, her face solemn. "Mama, we went to see Papa. Why do they want to hurt him? Aren't they his brothers?"

I held her in my arms. "Yes, they are his brothers. Sometimes people let anger cloud their judgment. We must keep a prayer in our hearts that they'll free him, and that God will forgive them." Suddenly I had an idea. "Siri, let's see if we can soften their hearts another way. What do you think would work?"

Siri furrowed her brow. Zenna spoke up. "Mama, make their favorite food for them!"

I laughed. Zenna was my most eager eater. But her idea was a good one. "All right. How about some of Grandma's best fish soup and sun-dried biscuits?" The girls nodded and grinned. Our plan was begun.

As we combined ingredients and got the biscuits ready, we sang some of our favorite songs. The boat was lifting and diving in bigger swells as we worked, making it a little more challenging. I ended up fastening Leesha into the child swing in the room so she wouldn't keep falling over and hurting herself. We finished the meal just as Mama came in.

"You better put things away soon, Didi. The storm is getting worse, and we can't have things sliding around while we're trying to stay afloat."

Siri helped me clean and put everything back in fastened-down containers or hanging bags. I bundled the girls in their shawls and brought them with me up to the deck. No one was guarding the hatches now.

The skies were indeed looking bad. It was dark, though perhaps only late afternoon. Flashes of lightning could be seen in the skies on the horizon. I could feel heavy raindrops spattering in gusts around us.

The men were busy tightening ropes and canvas sails. I could hear a couple of voices at the helm beyond us.

"It is pointing us in that direction more than half of the time, but I really think it is acting inconsistently right now," came Sam's voice.

"Then fix it," growled another. I think it was Laman.

"I have no control over this compass. You know as much about it as I do. When you have a problem I can solve, call me." Sam jumped down from the platform and started working on some rigging.

Laman cursed and pounded the wheel in front of him. Then he called for Mori to replace him. "Just keep the ship straight and upright," he said and jumped down himself.

By then I was near Nephi. He heard me coming and turned his eyes in my direction. I saw they had his head bound motionless now against the mast. Gid was standing nearby and approached me.

"Sorry, Sis. I can't allow you to feed your husband. Wish it were otherwise."

I smiled engagingly but ignored his comment in my response. "I brought some food for you hungry workers. Good stuff too, Mama's own best recipe."

Gid's eyes looked longingly at the dish and he sniffed at it. "That does smell good."

Laman stepped by. "You're relieved," he said to Gid but looked at me. "What's that?" he asked me as Gid left.

"Dinner for all of you," I said. Siri offered him a bowl of the savory stew.

He took it and scooped up a big spoonful. "Wait," he said. "How do I know you didn't put something in it?" He scratched his beard. "You have a bite first," he said.

I did, and so did each of my daughters. Laman called over Sam and Zoram to eat first, and watched all of us for anything unusual. Satisfied, he then ate, then had Lemuel, Mori, and Gid eat. There was nothing left when they were done. I gazed at my husband sorrowfully. He smiled briefly with his eyes and then closed them.

"Please, Uncle Laman!" said Zenna suddenly, tears running down her cheeks. "Let Daddy go! Please?" She tugged at his sleeve.

Tears stung my own cheeks as I hugged my daughters and gazed at Laman pleadingly. For a moment, I thought he might relent, but then his face hardened, and he jerked his sleeve from Zenna's grasp, upsetting her balance. She fell to the deck, but did not cry out.

"Go!" cried Laman. "You will not speak to me of releasing him again, do you hear? Anyone else who talks to me will meet his same fate, child or adult!"

I clutched Zenna to me, and we all backed away. Nephi watched us with his eyes as long as he could. My heart nearly broke. I had trouble focusing on the ladder, but I kept blinking away the tears until my girls were safely down. Mama, Naola, Father Lehi, Sariah, and Mary and their children were waiting for us when we got down. They looked at us silently. I shook my head. Sariah turned her head into her husband's shoulder and started shaking. Mary and Mama came over and hugged me. Naola hugged Zenna, who was now crying.

"It's hopeless," I sobbed. "I don't know what more I can do. I cannot endanger my daughters."

"I will speak to my sons," said Lehi in a husky voice. We all looked at him. He had had a lot of trouble getting down the ladder when boarding the ship with his arthritic knees, and hadn't attempted it again. I didn't know how he would see Laman and Lemuel though unless he went up on deck; they certainly weren't going to go to him in his quarters.

Father Lehi started for the ladder. Mother Sariah caught at his arm as he passed her. "Don't go up out there, Father. Your joints are not strong enough, especially in this storm."

He shook his head determinedly. "I must," he said, and went to the ladder, grasped it, and started slowly up. Mary and Naola came to his support, stabilizing him as he went up. Together, all three of them went out on the deck, leaving the rest of us below. Sariah collapsed at the table and I held her. We listened to the howling winds and held on as the boat dipped and rose with the ever-increasing waves.

It seemed an eternity before Lehi returned. When he did, Eli and Sam came with him, Eli coming first and mostly carrying Father Lehi's body, with Sam supporting from above. Mary and Naola followed. Lehi seemed stricken, almost stiff, and was staring off into space, mumbling. The two men stood him on his feet at the bottom of the ladder, but his legs took very little of his weight, and Sam and Eli had to continue mostly carrying him.

"They would not . . ." I heard Father Lehi mumble as they walked him past me. "Their father commands them, and they would not." Sariah followed them, weeping, to their room.

We all looked at each other in silence again. The fear, the worry, the loneliness for my husband hit me, and I started sobbing myself. I felt Naola's and my girls' arms around me. *"I must be strong for them,"* I thought. But I didn't know if I could be strong any longer. I should have faith that God would deliver Nephi, but I didn't know if I had enough faith left. Finally I stood, and I felt suddenly very tired. "Keep praying for us," I whispered to my sisters and their families and then turned to retire to my quarters with my girls. Zac, Matthew, and their siblings were at the door to the common room, watching us, but as we came toward them, the younger children disappeared again to their quarters. Zac and Matthew went up on deck to help their father.

In our little room, we huddled in prayer. Each of the girls said a prayer for "Papa," then I added my own fervent prayer after the example of my girls. Then Siri and Zenna huddled in the upper bunk while I held Leesha, and we went to sleep.

The third day as the storm raged on, the women and children stayed mainly in their quarters, only coming out to get water and basic food items. Mostly we were trying to keep from getting seasick again. The men spent most of their time out on deck, only coming in for bites of food, a little rest, and to warm up from the frigid rain and wind. I couldn't imagine the storm getting worse than this.

I was awakened in the night by a sudden lurch of the boat and a thump. Siri had fallen out of her bunk, and Zenna clung to the ledge, halfway off herself. As Siri held her arm and whimpered, I staggered up to replace Zenna. The floor was on a deep slant, and I found I could only hold her from falling off further. Then the boat lurched again the other way, and Zenna found herself against the far wall of the bunk. By this time, Leesha was awake and crying from the rolling, and items I had thought were secure were scattered all over the floor. I could hear other children crying, and voices calling out in alarm. I checked Siri's arm. It was not broken. I settled the three girls together in the bottom bunk against the wall, and stepped through the curtain to see what was going on.

Zoram and Gid were running past to go above deck, shouting orders to the women and children to stay put. Zac, Matthew, and Seth pulled on coats and went above with the men. Soon a group of women and a few children gathered around the eating table.

"What's going on?"

"What are they doing up there?"

"That was quite a wave!"

"Is the ship going to sink?"

I looked around, but not everyone was present. "Where are Father Lehi and Sariah?" I asked. Everyone stopped talking and looked at each other.

"I'll go check on them," Mary offered. It was a few minutes before she returned. There were tears on her cheeks. She sat down and just stared off into the distance.

"How are they? What's going on?" Naola asked.

Mary looked up. "Father is just lying there, not answering anyone. Mother just cries, and neither will eat anything. Jacob and Joseph are scared and will not leave their mother."

There was another big lurch of the boat, and a voice called down from above, "Fasten down everything! Make sure the children are secure! We're in for a big storm!"

We all scurried to our various tasks and then returned to our quarters to huddle in families. I saw Naola with her son, Benjamin, enter Sariah and Father Lehi's quarters to be with them and their two youngest sons. I thought we had been in a big storm before but found out differently now. The boat was rocking side to side and up and down violently. Leesha threw up, but I didn't dare move anywhere, so I used my apron to wipe up the worst of it. I could hear rain pouring down outside, and the crash of the waves against the side of the boat.

"Mommy, I'm scared," cried Zenna.

Siri looked up at me with wide eyes. "Are we going to die, Mama?"

I looked at my girls. "I think heavenly Father means for us to get to the Land of Promise safely. Just hang on and keep praying."

It felt like hours that we rolled and bounced in our bunks. The storm, if anything, was getting worse. Finally I decided I had to see what was happening above deck, and if we had anyone left guiding the ship. I pulled on my warmest cloak, left instructions for Siri to hold tight to her sisters, and went into the hall toward the aft ladder. Water was splashing down the ladder through the closed hatch above, and the floor had enough water to thoroughly soak my shoes. I staggered across to the ladder and looked up. Did I dare go above? I just had to know how my husband was doing!

I climbed up the slick ladder, almost falling off halfway up. At the top, I pushed against the hatch door, but it didn't move. I looked for the latch to release it, but it was unlocked. Then I pushed again with all my might, and managed to lift the door open.

I was immediately hit with a gust of the coldest, wettest wind I had ever experienced. I kept my grip on the ladder and climbed out, shutting the hatch behind me. Suddenly a wave of icy seawater hit me in the back, and I was thrown across the deck. Near the railing I caught hold of some ropes holding barrels in place against the side, and I pulled myself to my feet. As I looked around, I caught my breath.

Half the sails were torn to shreds, and the ones the men had managed to roll up before the brunt of the storm hit were beginning to flap in the wind where ropes had broken. My inner sense said that it should be morning, but the sky was only slightly lighter than at midnight. Dark figures were struggling to hold and refasten ropes guiding the booms and holding the masts. Occasionally another rope would snap, and a boom would swing around wildly until someone could stop and fasten it again. A couple of times it looked as if a figure or the group of them would be tossed or washed out to sea, but all of them managed to hang on somehow. Then I looked at the base of the main mast. Nephi's figure was still there, still fastened tightly. His body hung limply in the ropes, and I didn't know if he was still alive.

I set myself a task, and slowly, carefully found my way to the main mast. The last stretch was a walk with nothing to hold on to, so I watched for the moment when the boat was most upright, between waves and gusts of wind, and made a dash for it. As the boat lurched, I almost missed. Flinging out my arms, my hand caught hold of Nephi's clothing, and I pulled myself to him and the mast, clinging tightly. He groaned, and I felt a wave of relief.

"It's okay, it's just me!" I called through the screams of wind. I didn't know if he heard me. The gag was still in his mouth, and my thought was to loosen it so he could get a drink of rainwater.

As my hands struggled with the tight, wet knots of cloth, an arm grasped me around the shoulders and pulled me away. It was Laman. "What do you think you're doing, you crazy woman?" he screamed. "You leave that man alone, he's mine!"

I grasped for the mast again and looked him straight in the face. "Can't you see he's almost dead and needs a little water?" a sudden thought struck me. "Besides, do you think that will matter when we've all sunk in the depths of the sea?"

Laman laughed harshly. "You don't give up, do you? I will not fall for your tricky words, little sister."

"Look around you, Laman," I called, my words strangely clear in the storm raging around us. "Do you know where we are in this vast ocean? Do you know when this storm will end, or how to steer us out of it? It seems to me we are circling endlessly in the worst of it. Perhaps it is the only way our God can reach your ears and your heart as with the voice of thunder he had to use in the desert! Could it be that the only way out of this is to untie your brother, rather than let him die? You are his oldest brother, and should be protecting, not hurting him!"

Laman stared at me. "How did you know about . . . but you couldn't—"

"It is your choice, Laman. We all, including your own wife and children, will perish or live with your decision." I turned away from him and buried my head on my husband's shoulder.

Laman made his way to where the compass was fastened. After staring at it a few minutes, he banged his fist on the stand it was fastened to, and swore. I was glad most of the words were lost in the wind. He called orders to the men to face the boat again into the wind then stared up at the sky. I looked up too, but could see no clearing of sky or moon or sun to give us direction. It seemed to me that the winds were swirling around us, and I could not tell from which direction they came.

I was shivering violently and thought I should get below deck now, but the boat was heaving so wildly I didn't dare cross the deck. I hung on, waiting for a momentary lull. Before I had a chance to move, the ship, now turning a circle in the wind, gave a huge creak and groan and heaved over nearly to its side. I clung tighter to the mast and prayed I had the strength to hang on. Waves washed over the deck, and I saw with horror that the fore hatchway had opened and water poured into the lower decks. Laman was screaming at the men, who could do little but hang on for dear life.

"This is it," I thought to myself. *"We're going to die."* My shaking fear became more of a resolute calm. My only qualm was that I wasn't near my girls to comfort them. Poor Siri, having to be a little mother long before she was grown herself!

Slowly, almost imperceptibly, the ship righted itself. But enough water had washed in that it settled deeper in the water. One more tipping like this and it would probably sink.

Just then Riddah managed to crawl up through the hatch. Together with Lemuel, Gid, and Mori, they approached Laman. After some gesticulating among them and dagger looks from Riddah toward him, Laman staggered across the heaving deck in my direction. When he reached Nephi, he pulled out a knife. I held my breath. Then with the knife, he cut the cloth covering Nephi's mouth and the ropes holding him to the mast. Nephi groaned, collapsed in my arms, and both of us fell to the deck.

"Take him below," Laman growled.

"Wait," Nephi croaked. "Fetch me the compass."

In a minute, Sam appeared with the Liahona. Nephi, head now cushioned in my lap, took the Liahona and gazed at it a few minutes. Then he raised his face, eyes closed, to the sky. After long enough that

I wondered if he had fallen asleep or was unconscious, he opened his eyes and gazed at it again. Then he handed it to Sam. "You can put it back now," he said.

Sam looked at the ball and yelped in joy. "It's working again! It's working!" He staggered off to refasten it at the helm.

"I'm ready to go now," Nephi whispered.

In a moment, other arms were helping me lift him. I looked up into the faces of Gid and Zoram. They carried him to the aft hatchway, down the ladder, and into our quarters. They laid him gently on the lower bunk, which my girls vacated for him, and then Gid and Zoram left us.

"Mama," Siri said, and she looked questioningly at me.

"He'll be all right," I said, and I hoped it would be true.

While Siri fetched a flask of water, I removed the wet clothing from Nephi's cold and wrinkled flesh. He groaned as I did so. His wrists and ankles were red and very swollen from the ropes that had held him. I found some salve and soft cloth to dress his wounds. After layering him in dry clothes, I changed out of my wet things. When the water came, I gave him sips, and sent Siri to bring some soup and dried meat. It suddenly occurred to me that no more was the ship rocking violently, and the rain outside seemed to be lessening. Indeed, the near pitch-blackness of our room seemed lighter. I creaked open the shutter of our little porthole and peered outside.

The clouds were beginning to disperse, and I could see that morning was well under way. As I looked, the last raindrops spattered into the ocean below, and the waves were splashing evenly against the side of the ship in the brisk wind that was driving the storm clouds away. I pulled in my head from the porthole and heard feet running in the hall past our room.

"Sam and Zoram, go check the storerooms!" I heard Mori call. "Matthew and Zac, gather all the buckets you can find. Get the older children to help in bailing the water out of the lower levels. And check on the animals!" His voice faded as he climbed above deck again.

I looked over at Nephi. His eyes were finally open, but his body was shivering. "It-it's c-c-cold," he chattered.

I climbed under the blanket with him and held him close. "In a minute we'll have something nourishing for you to eat," I said. I looked him deep in the eyes. "Nephi, I'm so glad to have you back." Tears started running down my cheek, and a sob escaped my throat.

He reached out a still very cold hand and laid it on my cheek. "I'm glad to be back too, Didi." He closed his eyes and I just held him, concentrating on warming him up.

Siri returned with the meat and soup. We fed him small bites until he finally lay back satisfied, the shivering gone, the color returning to his cheeks. "Many thanks," he sighed, closed his eyes, and slept. Zenna and Leesha curled up around his legs and slept with him.

Siri and I looked at the three of them then at each other. Siri grinned, and I hugged her tight. "I'm so glad to have you here to help me, Siri." We quietly slipped out to let them sleep.

In the main eating room, Kora and Abisha were sitting at the table, holding hands and talking. Yadeesh and Hagadah were mopping up the water off the floor, and Mary was mixing a big pot of soup. A couple of infants were playing in a recently cleaned corner with some cups. We could hear calls of laughter from the deck below.

Mary turned from her pot. "How is he?" she asked me.

Yadeesh and Hagadah paused in their cleaning but did not look up at me.

"He's finally warm, and his stomach is full. But he's exhausted. I don't expect to see much of him until tomorrow." Mary and I looked at each other, then she glanced at Yadeesh and Hagadah. They were busily mopping and squeezing out rags again. When Mary looked back at me, her face concerned, I gave her a smile, and then went over and gave her a hug. "It's okay," I whispered.

Kora looked up at me. "I'm sorry," she said quietly. "About everything. I wish—"

"That's all right," I said again. "It's in the past now."

Abisha looked up. "I'm sorry too. This whole thing got out of hand. No hard feelings?"

I looked at the floor. "It was a very difficult experience. It will always hurt. But if Nephi can forgive his brothers, I can forgive all of you too." I looked up. "But part of saying sorry is not doing it again. I hope they remember that." I grasped Siri's hand and we went out to the ladder leading down to the storage rooms.

We helped the others finish scooping out the last of the water and cleaning the floors. Then they started sorting through the stored items looking for water damage. As Sam passed me with a wet bag of seed to either dry out for using later or to discard, I stopped him.

"Where's Naola?" I asked. "I haven't seen her all morning!"

"Oh. She's taking care of Father and Mother, and Jacob and Joseph again. The boys seemed to perk up when she took over, and I think she's finally coaxing Mother and Father to eat. If she and Benjamin can't do it, nobody can!"

The next day, Nephi indeed felt much better. His wrists and ankles were still red and tender, but the swelling had much subsided. He ate a double breakfast, though he had eaten heartily the night before too. Then he went up on deck to check on the ship's progress. The men were doing pretty well, splaying ropes back together, retying lines, and patching together what was left of the sails. The women were given assignments of finding fabric to make new sails to replace the ones irretrievably damaged. But Nephi refused to leave the helm. I had to bring his meals out to him, and finally Sam convinced him late that night that he needed at least a couple hours of sleep in his bunk, and he personally would watch over the guidance of the ship. I made sure once Nephi was down that he got a good night's sleep before allowing anyone to wake him. He stayed at the helm for the rest of the journey, and in his determined frame of mind, I was glad no one else fought him for the task.

Interestingly, our raucous siblings spent quieter evenings the rest of the journey. Oh, we heard them often enough, but nothing like the rude behavior of earlier. We found we could spend some of our evenings with them without the insulting comments, though perhaps the atmosphere was cooler than before. We never did need to use the dark storage room as a meeting place.

One afternoon as I was trying to put Leesha and Zenna down for naps, I heard a cry from above deck. The shouting of many voices followed it, but I couldn't make out what they were saying. My girls were fully awake again, so I picked up Leesha and grasped Zenna by the hand, and we made our way to the ladder. Everyone seemed to be trying to get above deck. The ship was not tossing any more than usual, so I knew it wasn't a storm brewing. Finally we were all up on the deck. I found Siri standing by Nephi, looking out over the railing. Nephi picked up Zenna so she could see too.

"Look! Way out on the horizon," he directed. We looked out where he pointed, and I saw a dark thin line steadily growing between sky and sea.

"Is it . . . could it be . . . land?" I whispered.

"That she be!" Nephi grinned at me.

"Yippee!" shouted Siri. "Land! We're at the Promised Land!"

"Land!" echoed Zenna.

"Aann," chirped Leesha.

I laughed and hugged Nephi and my girls. All around us were cries of joy and celebration. Soon cups and wine were passed around and we all joined in.

"A toast!" called Laman. "To our arrival at the Land of Promise!"

"Hear, hear!"

"Amen!"

"Praise to our Lord!"

It took several hours to get near shore, but all of us stayed on deck to watch. With Lehi looking over his shoulder, Nephi stayed near the Liahona mounted on its stand at the helm, and guided the ship, occasionally calling out directions for sail adjustments. It seemed a long time that we slid along the coastline looking for the right place. It was dark before we were there.

"Go to bed," Nephi finally told us. "I don't think you'll see much until morning. I promise I'll wake you all if anything happens."

In twos and threes we reluctantly went below, a couple of the men staying to help with the sails. In our excitement I don't think we slept much that night. As in the past, Sam made Nephi take a couple hours' rest, but Nephi was back at the helm as soon as he awoke. At dawn, most of us were above deck watching the coastline again. About midmorning, we approached a large inlet that made a nice harbor. Nephi beckoned Lehi over.

"Father, I think you should take over now," he said

Lehi's hand was no longer shaky as he took the helm. He steered the ship in. The land was green with vegetation, and hills could be seen farther inland. A small river flowed into the harbor beyond us. It promised to be a bountiful land. We approached the far side of the cove where a rocky outcropping seemed to make a natural pier. We dropped anchor, and the men stretched out the wooden plank that we had used to load the ship. It held firmly.

As when we entered the ship, we exited in order of age of families. Father Lehi took Sariah by the hand and, with Jacob and Joseph right behind, walked down the plank onto the rocky outcropping. Then they walked the rest of the way to the beach. Other families followed. When it was our turn, I looked at Nephi, smiling. Then we hurried down the plank and onto the shore. The only time I had been more grateful to arrive anywhere was when we found the meadow in the land of Bountiful at the end of our long desert journey. I fell to my knees like others around me and let the tears flow. My full heart joined gratefully in the prayer of thanksgiving Father Lehi offered for our arrival in the Land of Promise.

CHAPTER 8

THE PROMISED LAND

The first night in the Promised Land the families set up their tents among the trees near the shore. The next day was spent exploring inland for more permanent places to settle. Father Lehi had a special mission, which he revealed at supper that night.

"My children," he announced, "I have found a hill where we will build an altar so we may offer sacrifice to the Lord. On the morrow we will build it."

True to his word, Lehi awoke us at dawn. After a quick breakfast, the entire group followed him inland and up a large hill that had a view of the seashore, river, and land around. Lehi directed the older boys and men in gathering large stones for building the altar. The younger children and women cleared vegetation from the immediate area and gathered dead wood to make the altar fire.

After the men hefted a large flat rock to make the top of the altar, Lehi stood back and nodded. "It is done. Sam, go fetch me a lamb for the sacrifice."

Sam and Naola hurried off back to camp. Lehi and Nephi arranged the wood on the altar, and then we sat down and waited. After what seemed longer than necessary, Sam and Naola returned, leading a sheep with a rope. Sam took the creature over to Lehi, while Naola sat down beside me. She sniffled once, and I looked closer at her. Her eyes were red like she had been crying. I looked back at the sheep that Lehi was preparing. A shock went through me.

"Naola," I whispered, "that sheep is your pet, Perky!"

She nodded once. "Yes. He was the only one without blemish."

I turned and stared at her. "How could you give up your pet for the sacrifice?"

She returned my gaze through her tears. "We are supposed to give our best to the Lord, aren't we? What sacrifice is greater than God giving up his Son for us?"

I had no answer to that. I could only hug her as we watched Lehi offer Naola's sacrifice on the altar in gratitude for our safe journey to the Promised Land.

Our next task was clearing land to plant crops. There were several valleys lining both sides of a little river that promised to be fertile and needed minimal clearing. The men found that the surrounding hills and woods abounded with a variety of fruits and animals, and for the first time in months, we ate until our stomachs were full. While the crops were being planted, a centrally located well was dug. Then we set to work planning the layout of our settlement. There were some disagreements, of course. Some wanted to live near the ocean, others preferred the view higher in the hills, and some wanted to settle further inland, upriver. After much discussion, Father Lehi decided to let us settle pretty much where we wanted.

Nephi chose a place for our house on a hill with a view of the ocean in one direction and inland in the other. "So I can keep an eye on all my siblings," he told me, winking an eye. Mori and Gid chose sites in the hills on the opposite side of the river from our hill. Lehi and Sariah wanted to settle near the river inland, with Mama in her own little place nearby. Eli and Elizabeth settled near them. Sam chose a site between them and our hill, at the edge of the main valley where our crops were planted. Laman and Lemuel moved quite a bit further inland upriver. Zoram chose a site in a fertile valley located partway between Sam and Lemuel's sites. Two more wells were dug, near Mori's and Laman's homes. I felt that this arrangement of homes could work quite well, close enough to tend the crops and visit each other as desired, but far enough from each other to allow some privacy and maybe cool some of the tempers heated during our close proximity on the ship.

The families now set to work using skills acquired the past several years to build homes. Zoram's and Eli's expertise was especially in demand, showing others the varying advantages and techniques of wood versus clay brick construction. Nephi went to work, making enough tools for the building projects. Everyone, including children, did what they could, making bricks and cutting and carrying wood. Once thatched roofs were set upon walls, each set about more specialized tasks. Bekka and Elizabeth worked with both reeds and clay for making cooking instruments and baskets, teaching some of the older girls their skills. Abisha and Naola pulled out the wool saved the past year, and began coloring, carding, spinning and weaving it into warm cloaks and shawls for the cool evenings, again with daughters' and nieces' help. Boys were given tasks of whitewashing walls, helping their fathers build furniture, window shutters, and real doors to replace the hanging camelhair cloths. The women enjoyed calling instructions to the men and children on how to build and arrange everything in their homes.

A few weeks after our arrival, a hunting party returned with an interesting find. There were horses in the hills! Plans were immediately made to catch and tame some of them, and corrals were built to hold them. Shortly thereafter cattle, goats, and asses were found, and the families caught and worked to tame some of these as well. With these animals, the sheep and chickens we had brought and new real homes, life was beginning to look more and more luxurious.

Finally life settled into a routine. After building the homes, Nephi proposed building a meetinghouse or synagogue in a central location of our settlement. Nephi's oldest brothers stalled at his request to help him build it, whether at the idea of a synagogue or because Nephi proposed it instead of them I couldn't tell. Nevertheless, Zoram, Sam, Eli, Mori, and Mori's oldest sons set to work, and finished it just before the weather turned rainy, though it was still warm and humid. It was wonderful having an indoor place for our Sabbath gatherings!

I was only too glad with this wet weather to settle down inside my dry house and practice the weaving skills Abisha was trying so hard to teach me. Siri was getting very adept at carding and spinning the wool from Naola's flock, and was constantly chiding me about keeping the loom strung tight enough. I finally gave the seat of the loom up to her to devise her own zigzag designs, which resembled the décor on

Bekka's pottery. I shook my head and smiled. My girls were developing skills and talents faster than I ever dreamed possible. Zenna busily crushed grain from our first harvest in the hand grindstone bowl, her hands working a steady rhythm as she hummed a catchy melody. Leesha squatted at her side and watched, then helped bring her more handfuls as the grain reached the fine flour stage and was poured into the storage pot. Yes, I was very blessed with these girls!

After the rainy season, we discovered we were not the only people inhabiting the land. We were working in our fields when a group of men approached. They carried bows and stone hatchets, wore leather loincloths, had travel bags draped across their shoulders, and carried some small animal carcasses across their backs. They looked like a hunting party, traveling cross-country.

The children ran to their parents, while the adults stood still watching the strangers approach. Laman walked up to their leader, always the first one interested in other cultures. Lemuel and Nephi followed behind him. After some gesturing, the hunters pointed south, and Laman made motions like a boat on the water. Then Laman made gestures like putting food into his mouth. The hunters smiled and nodded.

Laman turned to the rest of us. "Prepare some food. I believe these men are hungry. Riddah, come meet and welcome them."

Riddah joined him. They seemed to be making introductions, pointing to themselves and laughing at each other's attempts to mimic name sounds. Then Riddah brought them to sit down in the shade of some trees while the rest of us ran to bring some food.

The men ate and stayed for about an hour trying to communicate with Laman, Lemuel, and Nephi. Then they stood up and motioned they must go. One of the men handed Laman something, bowed slightly, and then they left heading inland along the river. Laman handed the object to Riddah. Bekka, Abisha, and Kora gathered around her to look.

"It's gold!" Abisha remarked.

"Didn't you notice?" Riddah replied. "They had gold and silver on their necklaces. Crude, but unmistakable."

"Oh!" the other women sighed.

Nephi went back to his work in the fields, looking thoughtful. I took my hoe to work beside him.

"What are you thinking, Nephi?" I asked.

He was silent for a minute, digging in the soil. "I've been wrestling with a concern lately," he finally confessed. "I have felt the desire to record our journeys and Father's prophecies on more permanent material, but there is no room left on the brass plates. If there is ore in this part of the world, that would solve the problem."

"Then you must find it," I answered.

It seemed our brothers had the same idea. After finding out the neighboring people had found gold, they took every opportunity to go hunting in the hills and look for it themselves.

One day after a hunting trip, Nephi came home very excited. "Didi! I found ore in the mountains!" He grasped me around the waist and swung me around.

"Nephi!" I gasped. "What kind of ore? Silver, gold?"

"Yes!" he grinned. "And I think copper too. We can make metal plates to permanently record father's prophecies!"

"That's wonderful!" I responded. "But doesn't that take a lot of work to collect the ore?"

"Yes," he replied more soberly. "It will take a team to dig it, sort it out, and refine it. I wonder how my brothers will react?"

Surprisingly, everyone seemed excited at the prospect. Even Riddah encouraged her husband to be involved. Personally, I thought her motivation was to have some silver and gold jewelry. I wondered if the men were motivated by the idea of wealth. They divided themselves into two teams to alternate workweeks: Laman, Lemuel, Mori, and Gid and their families were one team; Sam, Zoram, Eli, Jacob, and Joseph and our families comprised the other team. Nephi didn't argue, figuring men who got along together would work well together. Nephi periodically checked in on Laman's team but mostly worked with Sam's.

While the men and older boys dug rock, women panned the dirt away in a nearby stream while the children sifted through and picked out the flakes and nuggets of gold. Laman's team was intent on keeping the gold they found for jewelry. Sam's team willingly donated all they found to Nephi to make plates for their holy records. After weeks of alternating teams, Nephi made a very interesting observation to me.

"Didi, I have noticed that the weeks Laman's team works, they don't find as much gold as Sam's team. At first I thought it was the difference in their intensity of work, but everyone seems intent on finding the gold. It is almost as if God is helping Sam's team find the richer sources. Yet we are working in the same location."

"Don't tell anyone," I half joked. "Our brothers will then try and work on both teams."

Nephi nodded. "I almost have enough gold for our records. Then we can turn our attention to the silver and copper. That involves more chipping of rock and smelting out the impurities."

"Where did you learn all of these skills, Nephi?" I marveled. "Ship-building, ore-finding, tool-making. Surely it wasn't all from that little village by Bountiful."

He grinned. "Benefits of following my father on his merchant trips to Egypt when I was a lad. Laman and Lemuel stopped traveling with him when he began to travel farther, and Sam and I were old enough to go. Father admired their civilization and felt it enriched his understanding of Father Abraham and Joseph of Egypt. That's probably why he gave Sam and me Egyptian names and made sure we were fluent in Egyptian characters. It is much quicker and more precise than to write in Hebrew."

I nodded, understanding more about his family. "Perhaps that is another reason Laman and Lemuel feel a gulf between you. You and Sam are more Egyptian while they are more Hebrew."

Nephi stared at me. "I had not thought of that before, Didi. It would certainly explain some things."

As soon as Nephi had successfully created and linked together a book of metal plates, he took it to the tent of his father to present them. Lehi was ecstatic. He pulled several papyri from his trunk and employed Nephi every evening in transferring his writings onto the plates. Then Lehi dictated to Nephi to engrave details of their journey in the wilderness. It took several months, but both Lehi and Nephi seemed pleased with the results.

Soon after our arrival in the Land of Promise, it became apparent that both Naola and Sariah were expecting again. Naola was ecstatic, for her Benjamin had been longing for a sibling. Fortunately, she was not as sick this time around as the first, and fresh fruit, again her craving, could be found in abundance.

Sariah, however, seemed to be having a harder time with her pregnancy. She was much more easily fatigued, and her sons, Jacob and Joseph, spent more time at our home to allow her to rest. Lehi did what he could to help her, but despite his protestations of being self-sufficient, Mother Sariah always seemed relieved and more relaxed when any of the women brought in meals and helped with the household chores. I was surprised Sariah was still having children at her age, and concerned that Lehi, several years her senior, would be up to the task of raising yet another youngster. Jacob and Joseph were well-behaved children, but they could easily outpace their father in work or play.

Another concern became apparent. Sariah's baby was growing faster than expected, or at least Sariah's belly was. Mary worriedly ran through with Mama and Hagadah all the possibilities she could think of, and some of them looked grim. However, other than fatigue, Sariah felt well, and we could only wait. Then after an examination later in her pregnancy, Mary discovered what was happening, and she came running up to our house.

"Didi! Mama!" Mary burst in through our door and found me just starting to prepare lunch. "Didi, where's Mama?"

Mama had been visiting with us for the day. I pointed out toward the courtyard where my girls were giggling over a string game Mama was teaching them. Mary raced out toward the courtyard.

"Mama, Mama!" she called. Mama looked up at her. "Please come with me to Mother Sariah's house! I need you to check something for me."

Mama dropped the string and stood up from her log stool, pausing to make sure her joints were loosened before moving again. I looked at her questioningly, and Mama beckoned me to follow her if I desired. I motioned for Siri to stay with her sisters, and the three of us women made the trek down the hill to Sariah's house.

We found Sariah resting in a cloth and wooden chair Lehi and Abisha had built for her, fanning herself under the veranda that ran along the front of the house with a view of the hills and ocean. She watched us hurry up her walkway and waved.

"Mother Sariah," Mary panted as we approached, "I'd like Mama to check you too, if that's all right with you."

"Of course," Sariah smiled, putting her hands on the sides of the chair to lift herself out. "From the expression on your face earlier, I thought you'd be back. Come inside."

She waddled in to her bedroom, and we followed. If I didn't know better, I would have said she was eight months pregnant instead of six. She lay down on her bed and smoothed out her dress. Mary put her hands on Sariah's stomach, pushing here and then there. Then she pointed out two places in particular for Mama to feel. Mama put her hands on Sariah's belly and also pushed one place then another. Then suddenly her eyes widened. "I don't believe it! Yes, you are right, Mary. There are two heads here. Twins!"

Sariah gasped and pushed on her own belly. Mary showed her where to feel. "Yes, yes, I feel that," Sariah nodded and laughed. "That would explain the simultaneous kicking in the bladder and the ribs!"

Mary turned to me. "Do you want to feel, Didi?" I nodded and then looked questioningly at Sariah. She nodded her approval.

I put my hands high on her belly where the others had and felt a hard round lump; next to it, her belly was soft and something kicked my hand. Then I felt lower down another hard bony lump, and next to it, something else kicked my hands. It sure felt like two little bodies, lying head to foot.

"Amazing!" I said, wonderingly. "I've never seen twins born before!'

Mama smiled. "I guess you'll get your chance, Didi. We'll need your help and everyone else's when the time comes."

Over the next month, we watched Sariah closely. Mama went to live with her in case of immediate need, and to care for Jacob and Joseph. Sariah's legs started swelling, and Mama made her go to strict bed rest.

The next week Naola delivered her baby boy six weeks early. Mary spent most of her time with her to help care for the tiny newborn. He needed to constantly be wrapped against Naola or Mary's body to keep his body temperature up. And they had to drip Naola's hand expressed milk into his mouth to keep him fed, as he was tired of sucking after only one to two minutes each feeding. It was touch and go for a couple of weeks, but he finally seemed to be getting stronger.

Sariah managed to reach nearly eight months, so hopes were high that the babies would do well. Then she went into labor. Joseph arrived at our house, panting from his run up the hill.

"Didi, come quickly!" he panted. "Mother's gone into labor, and Aunt Leah, I mean your mother, needs you to come right away. I'm to go get Abisha and Hagadah. Jacob's fetching Mary and will tell Bekka and Riddah. And Aunt Leah says 'don't dawdle'!"

As Joseph's legs carried him quickly back down the hill toward one of the little boats that would take him across the river, I suddenly realized that though he had grown a lot, he was not yet big enough to row that boat against the river current. I ran outside to stop him and then saw that Sam was meeting him at the river's edge. I turned back inside to give last minute instructions to Siri. Then, gathering up my skirts, I, too, ran down the hill.

When I arrived, Mary was already there at the house, helping Mama set out the last of the warm soft blankets Abisha had woven for the babies. Mama asked me to check the water warming on the fire pit while she washed and laid out a knife and several pieces of string. Then I went and sat down by Mother Sariah's side and massaged her back. She smiled at me gratefully.

When Mama returned, she examined Sariah, making sure the baby that was head down was still in position to come first. Mary told me that Mama had been maneuvering that baby slowly into position the last three weeks because a twin delivery could be much more dangerous if the feet-first baby was born first. Mary trembled as she told me of the delivery of a feet-first baby she had seen in the village by Bountiful, a single baby, and not a twin. Its head had gotten stuck, and by the time they got it out, it was dead. I suddenly realized how scary this delivery was going to be. Two early babies, one of them a feet-first one. I thought of Naola's early baby; Sariah's babies, too, would need a lot of care. Hopefully they would be born alive.

I looked over at Sariah. She was concentrating on a contraction. Mary had told me the story in whispers while Mama attended Sariah, and we were across the room, so I was sure she hadn't heard it. But my head felt light, and the room was muggy.

"I'm going out for some fresh air," I said to no one in particular. I walked slowly outside, making sure that with my swimming head I didn't faint. I sat down in Sariah's cloth chair, picked up her fan, and waved it at my face and neck. I felt better already. I leaned my head back and closed my eyes.

I was startled alert by Hagadah, Kora, and Abisha coming up the front path, talking and laughing.

"Hello, Didi!" Kora called. She had her youngest infant bundled to her back, born soon after our arrival here. They had left their younger children in the care of Yadeesh. We all hoped to be back to our homes soon, as Sariah usually had quicker deliveries. I wondered if Bekka and Riddah would make it here before the babies came.

As we entered the house, Abisha looked around and saw that Naola wasn't there. "How's Naola's baby?" she asked me in a whisper.

"Well, he is able to finally suck through a whole feeding and keep his own body temperature up a little better. But he's still very tiny, and

Mama says he's not out of danger yet. Naola's supposed to keep him isolated just a little longer."

"All right, ladies," said Mama in a calm firm voice. "It's time."

Hagadah hurried to Sariah's side. Kora suddenly sat down on the floor and put her head on her knees. Abisha and I each grabbed a blanket at Mary's instruction and waited nearby.

The first baby Mama delivered just as she had all of our others. "It's a girl!" she announced. She put this child gently in Abisha's arms, and as the infant cried, Abisha rubbed the moisture off her body and wrapped her up. Mama immediately turned back to Sariah, and Mary stood by Sariah's side.

I watched with curiosity as the next infant came out feet first. Then the head seemed to get stuck, and though it was only a minute, it seemed an eternity. Then it was out.

"Another girl!" Mama cried out and handed her to me. She gave a lusty cry as I dried and wrapped her little body. She would do well.

Kora now came over to gaze at the little girls Abisha and I held in our arms. They both blinked up at her, and she laughed. "Oh, they're darling!"

We went to show off the babies to their father, Lehi, who was waiting in the hall outside the room. On our way back in, I noticed Mama, Hagadah, and Mary hovering over Sariah.

"Massage a little harder, Mary," Mama instructed. Sariah groaned. "There, I think I've got everything cleaned out." There was another pause. "The bleeding's slowing down now. Let's get the babies over here to feed."

Obediently, Abisha and I brought our bundles over. Sariah smiled as we showed her the babies. "Which one was born first?" she asked. Abisha held up her bundle. "I'll start with little Leah first," said Sariah, taking the infant from Abisha. When Leah finished her first meal with her mama, Sariah returned her sleeping to Abisha. "Now for little Mary." She smiled as my sister beamed at the namesake.

When baby Mary, too, finished her meal, Sariah sighed. "I'm exhausted," she said and immediately closed her eyes. Mama shooed

Kora, Abisha, and me out with the babies, and Mary followed soon after.

"Kora and Abisha," Mary spoke quietly. "Zoram will be happy to row you across the river so you can get home to your families tonight. Didi, I need to go home and feed my youngest, and be with the children just until Zoram gets back. Would you mind staying here with Mama and Hagadah until I return? It shouldn't be more than an hour."

I smiled and took Leah from Kora, who had been holding her. "I'd love to. You all go ahead. I'll wait here until you get back, Mary."

After they left, I sat down in Sariah's soft chair that Mary had pulled indoors for me, and held the sleeping twins in my arms. They looked so peaceful and trusting. I found myself wishing for another little one. *A boy this time would be nice,* I thought. Someone for Nephi to take hunting and fishing.

Lehi came out of the other room where he had been resting with Jacob and Joseph, and sat on another chair next to me. I handed him Leah, and he gazed at her contentedly. After a long while, I gave him little Mary and took back Leah. He gazed at her too for a long while. Then he looked up and smiled at me.

"Sariah has wanted more daughters for a long time," he said. "Now she has them."

Mary returned and slipped back inside the house to spend a few minutes checking on Sariah. Then she reemerged, took Leah from my arms, and kissed me on the cheek. "Go home, Didi. Thank you so much." Her eyes looked dark, serious. I paused and looked at her with some concern. She pushed me gently toward the door. "Oh don't worry about me. I'll get some sleep right now. Mama, Hagadah, and I will take turns with Sariah and the babies."

I bid them goodnight and slipped outside. The night air was cool and I wished I had remembered to bring a warmer shawl. As I walked briskly home, I realized I hadn't seen Riddah or Bekka arrive yet to see the twins, but shrugged it off. There would be plenty of opportunity in the morning to see them.

Nephi and the girls were all asleep when I got home. I crawled into bed, snuggled up against Nephi's warm back, and thankfully closed my eyes in sleep.

Early the next morning shouting at the door awakened us. It was Sam, and his eyes were red.

"Nephi," he began, then stopped and just looked at Nephi standing behind me at the door.

"What is it?" I asked. "Naola and the baby, are they all right?"

Sam looked at me briefly. "They're fine, Didi. It-it's Mother." He looked back at Nephi. "She . . . she passed away in the night."

I drew in my breath quickly, and grabbed the doorframe for support. Nephi stood stock still for a minute, staring into space. "How . . . what happened?"

"Hemorrhage," said Sam. "They tried everything." His voice cracked, and Nephi stepped forward. They embraced for a long time. When they parted, Nephi had traces of tears on his cheeks.

I had a sudden thought. "What about the twins?"

Sam looked at me again, not quite comprehending my question. Then he smacked his hand to his forehead. "The twins! I'm supposed to tell Kora to get over here to help Naola feed them!" He turned on his heel and was gone down the hill toward the river.

I turned to Nephi, held his arm, and gazed into his eyes. He returned the look, and then we, too, embraced a long time. I felt a tugging on my dress. I suddenly realized the girls had heard Sam's news.

"Mama! Mama!" called a little voice. I turned to look. It was Leesha. "Will Grandma Sariah be all right?"

I knelt down and hugged her. "She's up with God now," I replied. "I . . . I guess that means she will be all right."

"Can we go see her?" Leesha asked again, her eyes filling with tears.

"She's dead, silly," said Zenna. "We won't be able to see her anymore."

I looked up at Nephi then back at my girls. "I think we'll be able to say goodbye to her one more time. She'll just listen to us this time though, like she's asleep."

We packed the girls up and made the trek down to Lehi and Sariah's home. The rest of the family had begun to gather. Zoram was holding his wife Mary, who was weeping loudly in his arms, their children huddled about them. Naola was trying to feed one of the twins, while Benjamin held his own tiny brother, and Lehi tried to calm his other crying baby daughter. Soon Kora came running up to take the other hungry twin from Hagadah; Gid and the children came behind her. With the next boat ride, Abisha with Mori and their family arrived. Then came Laman and Lemuel and their families. Riddah looked stone-faced, while Bekka stroked each of the feeding twins' heads and wept quietly. Laman and Lemuel looked truly mournful. Jacob sat in the corner, his arm around Joseph who was trying not to cry.

Mama came out of Sariah's birthing and death room, her eyes red and shadowed, strands of hair sticking every which way, and her head shawl gone. She looked as if she hadn't slept all night. She went over to Lehi, who was looking a little lost without a baby to hold.

"Come, Father," Mama said gently, touching his arm. "She is ready for you now."

Nephi hesitated and then stepped forward to his father's side as his brothers held back. Nephi and Mama escorted Lehi into the room, Laman, Lemuel, Sam, Abisha and Kora on their heels, the rest of us following. Sariah lay on the bed, face pale but serene, covers drawn up to her chest. At the bedside, Lehi looked and reached out a hand to grasp Sariah's. Then he collapsed to his knees, laid his head down on her body, and sobbed. Mama laid her hand on his shoulder and left it there. Lehi's four oldest sons stood, their faces showing their own grief. My girls clung to me, and Siri started weeping. Then the women in the room started keening the death cry.

After a long time, Father Lehi raised his head. After a moment of trying to push himself up to his feet, Laman and Nephi grasped his arms and helped him up. He turned to face us and took a deep breath.

"My children," he said, his voice still a little shaky, "on the morrow we bury her on the altar hill." Then he shuffled out and went to be alone in another room.

Each family in turn passed by Sariah's bed then went outside. I could hear their keening cries continue. Nephi and I hung back after the others. I held her cold stiff hand a moment. "Thank you, Mother Sariah," I whispered. "You accepted me as your own daughter and taught me much of fortitude, love, and faith. I am glad my girls had a chance to know you."

I looked up at Nephi and noticed a tear coursing down his cheek. I grasped his hand and squeezed it a couple of times.

"Goodbye, Grandmother," said Siri.

"Bye-bye, Gran'ma," said Leesha, and she stood on tiptoes to kiss her cheek.

Zenna held back and cried. "I don't want Grandmother to go!" She hid her head in my arms.

"I know, Zenna," I caressed her hair. "We'll all miss her."

"But where did she go?" Zenna sobbed. "This isn't Grandmother!"

Nephi knelt down beside her. "Zenna, darling. Grandmother is in heaven with God. This is just her body that she left behind so we could tell her goodbye. Someday we'll see her again when we go to live with God."

Zenna raised her tear-streaked face. "Where is God?"

Nephi hesitated. Then he pointed upward. "God lives way up there, beyond the sky, where He can look down and watch over us. Grandmother can watch over you too in just the same way."

Zenna looked upward, though all she could see was the ceiling of the room we were in. But her tears had stopped. "She can see me here, now?" she asked.

"Yes," nodded Nephi. "Here and now."

"Hi, Grandmother," Zenna waved skyward. "I love you. I miss you. Tell God hello for me." Then she grasped Leesha's hand and skipped off to play with her cousins.

"Bye, Mother," Nephi said, laying his hand on Sariah's. "Thank you for . . . everything. I, too, love you . . . and miss you." He sighed. "But Father will miss you more. We'll take good care of him for you."

After the burial, we all went back to our homes subdued. Kora took baby Leah home with her, and Naola took baby Mary. Mama spent most of her days at Father Lehi's house to help care for his youngest sons, and help him through the transition of losing his life companion. No one spoke much at Sabbath services the next day, so after Sam read the scriptures for the day, and no one offered much discussion, the families departed to their own homes.

The next day, Gid's oldest boy Gad, and Mori's son Zac were grazing their cattle in adjacent fields and some of the cattle got mixed up. When it came time to herd them home, neither could agree on whose were whose. Over the next couple of days, various head of cattle began disappearing from one family's fold to end up in the other's. Gid and Mori themselves began arguing, and soon Lemuel's and Laman's families were involved. Midweek Gad and Laman's son Raoul got into a fight in one of the grain fields, crushing a large area of the tender plants. By the time the fight was stopped, no one quite felt that the loss of the crop was worth the fight over the cattle. One thing was clear, some rules in the community needed to be made. Nephi went to talk to his father, Lehi. Lehi did not seem to want to intervene.

"Let them work it out between themselves," he counseled.

Nephi tried to obey his father, but I could tell the unresolved tension between the families bothered him greatly. Finally he went to talk with Laman about it.

"If it bothers you so much, call a family meeting," Laman told him.

Nephi did so. We gathered the next night at the synagogue, Mori's family sitting with Laman's on one side, Lemuel's and Gid's families sitting on the other side. The rest of us sat in the back rows.

Nephi stared pointedly at Laman to start the meeting, but Laman just sat, arms folded, and nodded at Nephi. "Have a go at it, little brother."

Nephi stood up. "I've called this special meeting tonight to discuss some rules we should make for our community to protect livestock, property, and personal safety. I want all of your input." He took a deep breath. "As you know, there was a recent disagreement that resulted in the destruction of some of our crops. There may be times our very lives may depend on our crops, on our animals, and on our homes. These need to be protected. Our community is small now, but our children are growing up, and we will soon be many people. Specifying what modes of conduct are expected and what will happen when these rules are broken is vital to our peace and security." He paused and looked around. "Zoram will be our scribe for recording these rules." He nodded over to Zoram, who was ready with ink and parchment.

After some discussion, Nephi raised his hand. "It sounds like the first rule should be something like 'There shall be no destruction or theft of another person's property.'" All heads nodded, and Zoram recorded it.

"It seems a second rule should involve a way of solving disagreements, such as 'All disagreements that cannot be solved by the involved parties should be brought before a mediator.'" Again many heads nodded.

Mori raised his hand. "Who would this mediator be?"

Nephi shrugged. "Perhaps it is someone both parties agree to, whom they feel can judge fairly."

Sam spoke up. "The community leader could be mediator."

"And who is that?" asked Gid.

"Father Lehi," said Sam.

"He won't be for long," said Mori.

"Do we need to specify right now who would be the mediator?" asked Zoram. "It seems to me that could be decided at the time he is needed."

There was agreement on this, and Zoram recorded rule 2 as Nephi had proposed it.

"Are there any other issues at this time?" Nephi asked.

Laman stood and looked around the room, with an air of authority. He seemed very much in his element. "It seems to me that a precedent was started that could lead to chaos in our community. I agree that rules and laws are needed to keep order." He glanced at Nephi. "However, if anyone in the community could propose and pass a law, we could end up with laws not everyone can live with, or that may be foolish, harmful ones." He paused again to let his words sink in.

"What I propose is a process for establishing laws, perhaps a hierarchy of representation, a process for prospective law proposals that would enable each law to be evaluated, all the consequences considered, and then presented in an orderly manner to the people for their approval."

I wasn't sure exactly what Laman was talking about, but it sounded like a good idea.

Zoram raised his hand. "Laman, in my observation of the elders in Jerusalem, they would hold a vote. A unanimous or majority vote would then establish or change a law."

Laman nodded. "Shall our community establish laws by vote of the people? All in favor say yay." Everyone said 'yay.' "All opposed say nay." No one moved.

Laman looked out over the families. "We need to establish a voting age. I do not think children understand enough to vote. Shall we say all men over the age of eighteen shall vote to establish the laws?"

Many voices said 'yay.'

"Any opposed?" he asked.

Naola nearly shouted, "Nay!"

Laman looked at Zoram. "Please record the first rule, 'All men over the age of eighteen—'"

Naola stood up. "I think women should be allowed to vote too," she announced. I smiled proudly at her.

Laman frowned. "Does anyone agree with this?" he asked.

I stood up. "I agree that women should vote with the men. We have as much vested interest in the outcome as they do."

Lemuel looked down his nose at me. "But how many women understand the nuances of politics enough to vote accurately? Or have the time to even become educated about the issues? How much of politics did you follow in Jerusalem?" I shook my head slowly. "I thought not. Sit down, sister."

Naola looked unhappy, but we both sat down. Nephi laid a comforting hand on mine.

Laman nodded approvingly. "Men voting over the age of eighteen it is." He glanced at Zoram, who bent his head over the parchment and recorded the rule.

Then Laman spoke again. "There is a process for making laws: (a) recognition of the need for a new law, (b) discussion of the issue, (c) a proposal stating the law in clear wording, (d) a vote upon it, and (e) its institution."

Zoram raised his head. "There should be a specific punishment affixed to each law for anyone breaking it."

Laman nodded. "We'll add (f) a punishment for breaking the law. All those in favor?"

All the men said 'yay'. None were opposed. Laman looked over Zoram's shoulder while he recorded the second rule.

"Are there any laws we should put in place tonight?" Laman asked.

Sam raised his hand. "We initially talked about a rule that there should be no theft or destruction of another's property. I think this should be a law."

"Is there any discussion about this?" Laman asked. All shook their heads. "Everyone in agreement say yay." All the men said 'yay'. "Any opposed?" No one spoke.

"What punishment should be given for destroyed or stolen property?" Laman asked.

Again ideas were brought up and discussed. "It sounds like the best idea is the return or replacement of the said property, plus a restitution fee," said Laman. "Is this agreeable?" All the men said 'yay'. No one dissented. Zoram recorded the law.

"Should it be specified who acts as mediator for disagreements?" asked Laman.

"The community leader!" called Gid.

"A judge!" said Zoram.

"The priest," said Eli.

Laman gazed at them thoughtfully. "These are all good ideas. Let's leave the title unspecified for now. I propose that a community leader be chosen, a president, governor, priest, judge, king, or whatever you want to call him. This leader can mediate disagreements. He will be responsible for evaluating the issues involved with each law proposal, which proposals are wise and should be voted into laws, and which are foolish and should be tossed out. He will make sure the laws are enforced, and the punishments for broken laws are carried out justly. He should be able to make hard decisions and lead his people bravely in times of danger or tragedy. This leader should be well versed in leadership skills, social dynamics, and human personalities." Again Laman paused and looked around the room. "I propose we accept nominations for who this leader should be."

There was a commotion of voices around us. My mind was awhirl, trying to understand the nuances of what Laman had proposed. I was a little confused. Didn't we already have a leader, in our father Lehi? Then I realized that his years were many, and that he would not be around much longer. But wouldn't he pass on the birthright to one of his sons, making him the patriarch of the community? That birthright traditionally went to the oldest son, unless for some reason there was a serious contention between the father and that son, or the son had dishonored his father, or was disinherited.

I suddenly looked up. Nephi had been observing his siblings through the course of my thoughts, and now his gaze fell on me. "Laman must be afraid of losing the birthright," I whispered to him hoarsely.

Nephi nodded grimly. "I think so too," he said. "Else why would he try to wrest the leadership power from Father before it is time? But I don't think Laman understands the full sacredness and the spiritual responsibility of that birthright. I think he just sees the inherited wealth, and the priesthood part of it as a title of power. I would hope otherwise, but I have had more than two decades to observe my eldest brother's tendencies."

Gid stood and clapped his hands to silence everyone. "I nominate Mori, as the eldest man of our generation, to be our new leader." Mori's and Gid's families nodded.

Mary stood. "I think Zoram should be considered. He studied the laws in Jerusalem under Laban and the elders, and would be an impartial mediator should disputes arise." Nephi and Eli nodded their heads.

Lemuel stood. "I nominate Laman, eldest son of Lehi. Laman has traveled far with Father's business, and has had a chance to study the politics of various communities. He would be a strong leader." Laman's and Lemuel's families nodded their approval.

Then Sam stood. "I nominate Nephi, as the one who has many times led our group safely through dangers in the wilderness, showed us how to build the ship that brought us here, and has been conscientious in giving us spiritual guidance as well." Sam's, Zoram's, Eli's, and Nephi's families murmured and nodded.

After more discussion, Laman proposed a vote of the candidates. There were two votes for Laman, two for Mori, three for Nephi, one for Zoram, and one abstention.

"Can we narrow this down any further?" Laman asked the group.

Mori spoke up. "I would be willing to follow Laman, and step aside as candidate for community leader."

Zoram also spoke. "Thank you for the nomination, but I am not interested in the leadership responsibilities. I will willingly follow someone else."

Laman nodded. "Fine. Let's vote again."

Now there were four votes for Laman, four for Nephi, and one abstention.

Laman looked at Father Lehi. "Father," he said softly, intensely, "we need a clear majority in our vote to settle this debate tonight. What is your vote?"

Lehi looked up, almost startled. "Eh, what?" he mumbled and looked down at his lap again. "Oh yes, the vote, the choice for succession. Whom to choose?" he fell silent.

"Do you perhaps need more time to decide?" Mother Leah asked him.

His face brightened. "Yes, I need more time. More time to choose the successor. I must evaluate their qualities, their strengths, their characters. Yes, more time."

Laman gazed long and hard at his father. "Then we will give you more time. When you are ready, we will have another vote. I have nothing further to discuss this night. Meeting is adjourned."

Everyone left for their own home in silence.

As we neared our house, I opened my mouth a couple of times before I spoke. "I imagine it will be a strain on Laman the next little while to be on his best behavior for Father Lehi," I finally commented.

"Yes!" Nephi laughed, and then he was quiet. When he spoke again, it was a little bitterly. "So it comes down to another face-off between my oldest brother and me. Nothing better for deepening the rift between us, is there, Didi?"

I could only squeeze his hand, and silently wish things were different between them.

The following day Sam's son Benjamin came down with a bad cold caught from one of his cousins. Naola immediately sent him to stay with Mary for a few days until he was feeling better. Only when all his coughs and sniffles were gone did she allow him back in the house. So far her tiny Joshua and little Mary seemed well. But two days after Benjamin returned home, Joshua and Sariah's little Mary became congested. Naola watched them like a hawk. When the symptoms deepened into coughs, Naola consulted her sister Mary and Hagadah about what herbs she should use. Religiously she cared for the infants, administering the herbs they had suggested, carrying one or both of the infants almost constantly. Sam spent many hours assisting her, and even Benjamin ran errands for them. By the third day, Joshua was drinking very little, spending most of his energy coughing and trying to breathe. Naola went back to expressing milk and dripping it into his mouth with a spoon.

About this time, I went to visit her, leaving my girls in Siri's care. When I arrived, Sam had just gotten little Mary to fall asleep on his shoulder, and Naola was trying to feed Joshua. He lay weakly in the crook of her arm, his little chest heaving in and out rapidly. After swallowing the liquid she dripped in, he gave some shallow coughs and then rested again. Nearby a pot of water over the cooking fire gave out a scented steam. I went over and sniffed it.

"The babies seem to breathe better with that going," Naola commented.

I nodded then took Joshua from her arm and held him semi-inclined for her. She fed him a few more swallows, and then he closed his eyes and went to sleep. Naola sat back in her chair, rubbed her left shoulder, and sighed.

"Why don't you and Sam go rest?" I directed. "I'll watch the babies for a couple of hours. You both look tired."

"I sure could use it," she smiled wearily. "All right, you've talked me into it." Naola stood up and stretched. "Oh, in an hour he gets half a spoonful of the medicine in the red bowl. Thanks, Didi." She disappeared into her room, Sam trailing behind her after laying Mary in the basket near the cook fire.

I sat back in a cushioned chair, little Joshua still cradled in my arms. His skin was hot and damp, and even in his sleep his little heart and lungs worked furiously. Suddenly the congestion in his airways choked him up and he awoke coughing. I held him upright in my lap as he coughed and wheezed and then threw up mainly mucus. Then he lay exhausted and panting in my arms. I was worried: I had never seen any of my girls this sick. I hoped his tiny body could fight it. I looked over at little Mary sleeping in her basket. She weighed a little more than Joshua, and seemed to be fighting this illness better. She rattled and snorted some in her sleep, with an occasional cough, but she wasn't breathing as hard as Joshua.

I reached for the cup of milk Naola had saved for Joshua and spoon-fed him a little more. His mouth was dry and he swallowed the milk hungrily. Part way through I gave him his medicine. Then he fell asleep again. I leaned back, closed my eyes and slept too.

Another fit of Joshua's coughing awoke me, and this time Naola came from her room, looking more refreshed. "Thank you, Didi. I can carry on now. Mary will be by soon to check on them."

As I left, Naola was feeding Joshua again. I was amazed at Naola's ability to care for two sick infants at once, and without complaint!

Later that afternoon Zoram came by to inform us that Joshua was doing worse, and asked if we would fast for him. Father Lehi had just finished giving him a blessing. Siri and Zenna both wanted to join in the fast, but Leesha was too young, so I fed her a snack. We spent part of the evening praying and singing for the sick babies. Zenna was particularly concerned this time.

"Will Joshua die like Grandmother Sariah?" she asked mournfully.

"I don't know, my darling," I said, hugging her. "I hope not. But he was born so little, it's harder for him to fight off illness."

"Will he go to heaven if he dies?" she asked again.

"Yes, he will," I answered with confidence.

"Then Grandmother will take care of him," she said, and went off to play.

The next morning the news was grim. Joshua no longer would drink much, even sweetened water, and his lips were blue tinged. Nephi and I continued our fast, and we went to visit them.

Naola collapsed in my arms. "Didi, I can't bear to lose Joshua," she wept. "It took so long to get him here."

I looked over at my sister Mary trying to get some liquid to stay down in his stomach. "I know, Naola," I said soothingly. "I know."

We didn't stay long. But late that afternoon we got word that Joshua had passed away in Naola's arms as he slept. We all went over to their house and found Naola weeping in Mama's arms. Others in the family arrived that evening to grieve in the traditional manner, then leave. Mary and I and our families stayed on, mainly just to be there. Much of the time Naola held little Mary and just wept.

"Sam, Nephi, why did this have to happen?" she asked between tears. "Papa was old when he died and had lived a full life. But Mother Sariah didn't get to raise her girls, and Joshua . . . his life hasn't even really begun."

Sam and I didn't have an answer for her. Even Nephi was pensive. "Naola," he offered, "my heart tells me that God has a plan, and that through our challenges we can be strengthened and learn something, even if it is just to have faith and trust that God will heal us and help us go on."

Naola hid her head in Sam's shoulder. "I don't know if I want to go on," she mumbled, and began crying once again.

At the burial service at the synagogue the next day, I noticed that Naola kept looking over at Kora holding little Leah. Kora seemed overwhelmed, trying to manage her own six children plus Leah, arms full of two young infants. After one particularly long stare, Kora looked over at Naola, who then dropped her eyes and buried her face in little Mary's hair. Kora went back to shushing her children. Benjamin sat between his parents, alternately patting his mother's back, then leaning his face into his father Sam's chest. After one such pat, Naola smiled down at him, and he hugged her back. Sam's arm never left touching Naola's arm or back.

Joshua was buried near his grandmother, Sariah. After lowering his little body into the ground, Naola turned her face away. Benjamin knelt down and tossed in a flower blossom he had been holding.

"I'll miss you, Joshua," he said, then followed his father taking his mother home.

I took supper over to them that night. Naola was just sitting staring at nothing but refusing to give up little Mary to anyone. The infant looked better and sounded much less congested. I was glad. After they ate, I sat and played a rock game with Benjamin. Sam sat next to Naola, whittling a stick silently. The evening darkness settled in around us, and I got up and lighted a candle. Just then there was a voice calling at the door. It was Kora, carrying a bundle in her arms.

"Where's Naola?" she asked. We brought her inside. Naola looked up at her without expression. "Naola," Kora began and faltered. Then she thrust the bundle at Naola. It was baby Leah. "Naola, I can't . . . I need you to take Leah. I can't care for her right now as well as you can. My milk is running low, and my other children are a lot for me to handle right now. She needs her sister too. Can you, would you, take Leah?"

Naola at first didn't seem to comprehend. Then her face broke into a smile, and she reached out her free arm for Leah. "Oh, Kora! Do you really mean it? I may keep her?" Kora nodded. Naola gazed down at the sleeping twins. "This feels so right somehow. My arms got so used to holding two babies, I didn't quite know what to do when—" Her face became stricken again for a moment. She looked over at Sam, and he nodded. She looked at Kora again. "Thank you, Kora. I will care for her well."

Kora nodded, her shoulders relaxed, and she turned for the door. "Good night, Naola," she said quietly and was gone.

When I left, Naola was contentedly cooing over her two daughters.

One day as my girls and I were approaching Mary's house to visit, we met Abisha, Hagadah, and Kora coming out. Abisha and Hagadah were supporting Kora, who was limping, her right ankle wrapped for support.

Mary's voice called out after them. "Remember, Kora, to stay off of it for a few days. It's just a sprain, but it's still an injury."

Kora nodded then looked up and saw us. Her right eye and cheek were black and blue, the eyelid was puffed shut. She quickly pulled her headscarf lower across her face.

"Hello, sisters," I greeted them cheerfully.

Abisha nodded but didn't look at me straight, and Kora kept her head bowed as they limped past us. Hagadah smiled slightly and then looked away.

"Mama, what happened to Aunt Kora?" Siri asked me as they left.

"I don't know," I told her.

Mary welcomed us in, and our younger ones ran off to the courtyard to play. Siri stayed by my side. When I didn't immediately pass on her question, she went up to Mary and tugged on her sleeve.

"Please, Aunt Mary," she asked quietly. "What happened to Aunt Kora?"

Mary looked at her and hesitated. "She fell on something and sprained her ankle."

Siri still held her sleeve. "And how did her eye get injured?" she persisted.

"I guess she hit a rock," Mary said vaguely, and we returned to our conversation of children and the challenges of running a home, as we prepared some lunch.

Siri sat beside us, picking at the vegetables she was supposed to be preparing. Suddenly she broke into our conversation again.

"Her eye looked like Zac's did when Raoul socked it in their fight. It looked like someone hit her."

Mary and I stared at her in shocked silence. Why would Siri come up with something like this? I started to chide Siri and then saw Mary's face. It was pale, and a tear was sliding down her cheek.

"Mary, what is it?" I asked, dropping my spoon and reaching to touch her shoulder. She leaned her head onto my shoulder and sobbed.

"Oh, Didi, I don't know what to do! I think Siri's right. Kora also had a bruise on her chest and arm. I think she has been hit. What do I do?"

"Anna says her parents fight a lot too," Siri volunteered, speaking of Abisha and Mori. "But I think they just yell a lot."

I didn't know what to say. I couldn't imagine anyone hitting Kora, least of all Gid. However, I had seen his temper at times drive him to throwing things. Then he would be very gentle and thoughtful for a while. I could imagine Laman being rough. I had seen that happen a lot but mainly with his brothers. I had never seen bruises on Riddah, but then I hadn't seen her real often lately either.

"I'm going out with the other children," Siri suddenly said and disappeared out into the courtyard. Mary and I looked at each other a moment and then started working on the food again.

"Would it do any good to tell someone about it?" I asked Mary, deciding to think out loud.

"Who would I tell?" she sighed. "Abisha already knows. I doubt Mori would do much about it. He would just say, 'Isn't it the right of a husband to discipline his wife?' Gid would listen to Laman, but I don't think Laman cares what happens in others' homes. He rather likes hierarchical power plays, I think." She looked up at me, and laughed painfully. "Father Lehi is the only one that could say something to the others, but I don't know how much they'd listen to him."

I sighed and nodded. Her evaluation was as good as mine. Nephi would have something to say about it, but that would only anger the culprits. Sam wouldn't want to say anything that would hurt someone's feelings, but he just might want to punch someone over this. Zoram could talk all he wanted, but he wasn't truly family when things like this came up requiring honor and respect. Nor was Eli. A woman could speak all she wanted, but what man would give up his traditional patriarchal position at her mere request? Certainly he would never listen to her demands.

"I don't know what Father Lehi can do about it, Mary, but you are right that he is our best option." I looked up at her. "I'll watch your children whenever you want to go."

She stood up, brushed off her apron, and took a deep breath. "If I don't go now, I may never have the courage to do so," she said. She grabbed her shawl, threw it about her shoulders, and slipped out of the house.

When Mary returned, she didn't want to look me in the eye.

"Nephi was there with Father Lehi," she said. "I had no choice but to let him listen in." She sighed and looked at me at last. "I think he went off to chastise Gid." She raised her hands and let them fall. "I'm sorry, Didi."

I had a sick feeling in my stomach. "Thanks for letting me know, Mary." I kissed her and headed for home, a prayer in my heart. But despite my worries, Nephi returned home in time for supper and seemed his usual pensive self.

The next Sabbath was Father Lehi's turn to lead the scripture reading and discussion. He sent Jacob and Joseph with messages to every family to make sure they attended. I had noticed that some of the more distantly located families had not been attending as regularly lately. However, Mori's second son, Matthew, seemed to show up weekly whether the rest of his family did or not. Nephi made it a habit of inviting him to our home afterward with Jacob and Joseph, and the four of them would discuss further the topic presented at worship services. Matthew often accepted, taking the opportunity to talk with Siri before and after discussions.

On the morning of Father Lehi's reading, everyone came, although Laman's and Gid's families were a little bit late. Father Lehi, who had already begun his reading from the brass plates, barely lifted his eyes to acknowledge their presence. When he was finished with the reading and his brief commentary, he covered the plates with their protective cloth but remained standing. His shoulders were stooped, but his eyes were sharp as he looked around the room at each of us.

"My sons and daughters, my grandsons and granddaughters, I feel to share with you the joy in my heart because of the Lord's bounteous blessings unto us. For we were directed out of the land of our fathers, the land of Jerusalem. We were guided across stretches of wilderness difficult for seasoned men to travel, and with women and children we survived, and at times even thrived. Yet there were times of rebellion, of chastisement, and of hardship, and still the Lord preserved us in his mercy, bringing us to a land of beauty and plenty."

Lehi paused and looked around at each of us again. "There were times when many of us desired to still be in Jerusalem. But I have seen a vision, terrible to behold, and I saw Jerusalem destroyed with fire and the sword. The Lord's prophecy has now truly been fulfilled, and had we remained, we also would have been destroyed." He shuddered and wiped a hand across his brow, leaning his other hand on the stand holding the brass plates. When he looked up again, his countenance seemed brighter.

"And yet, my children, despite our times of wickedness, the Lord has seen fit to bring us to this bounteous land. It is a land preserved for the most righteous of the Lord's people, for their inheritance and their children's. When we are righteous and obey the Lord's commandments, he will bless us richly. But when we are wicked and reach the fullness of iniquity, we will be destroyed off the land, and others more righteous will inherit it."

Lehi gazed intently, pleadingly into our faces, particularly Laman's and Lemuel's. "I talked today about the people of the Lord and how they prevailed over their enemies to attain their Promised Land, through the power of God and the armor of righteousness they spiritually put on."

Lehi straightened his shoulders and his voice gained strength. "It is now time for us to awaken to the battle, the battle against evil, to root it out of our hearts and the hearts of our children that we may all prosper in the land! The night has ended, the dawn is upon us. Awake, my sons! Arise from the dust where you slumber in sin, and gird yourselves! Take upon you the armor of God that ye may not fall into captivity. Wear the helmet of salvation that ye may know what ye must do to be saved. Fasten on the breastplate of righteousness that your whole heart and soul may choose to serve the Lord. Gird truth about your loins that you may recognize what is error, and live with virtue and confidence before the Lord. Shod your feet with the gospel of peace that you may run with strength unto the four corners of the earth with joy and love, and your children will know of the goodness of God. Grasp always the shield of faith that you may unfailingly and without fear deter the fiery darts and temptations of the evil one that would wound and weaken you. And keep in hand the sword of the spirit, God's voice unto you, that ye may know how to protect your beloved ones and conquer the enemy."

He took a deep breath and looked at us one by one, his gaze finally resting on Gid and then Laman. "And now, my sons, I exhort you to heed the words of your brother Nephi, whom I place as your spiritual leader. He has with unfailing energy taught you in the way of God, and kept this family on course to this Promised Land. He does not speak to you to anger you or to rise above you, but because the Lord's word is in his heart and he cannot stop its utterance. Follow his counsel, and I will leave upon you my blessing for peace and prosperity. Heed him not, and it shall be taken away from you. The choice is in your hands. But remember your happiness and that of your children depends on the choice you make. I am finished."

Lehi grasped his walking stick and moved back to his seat, each step becoming slower and more halting. When he sat down, his lips pursed tight, and his face slightly pale, I thought he looked exhausted. The families dispersed, Laman angrily talking to Lemuel as they walked away. Lehi remained sitting, slumped over his stick perched in front of him. My daughters and I went over to him.

"Father Lehi," I said quietly, then rested my hand on his shoulder. He hadn't seemed to hear me, but at my touch, he jumped slightly and looked up.

"My daughter," he said and sighed, looking at the ground again.

"Come, Father, may we walk home with you? You look like you could use a hand." We helped him to his feet and started off slowly, Siri and I supporting him on either side, Leesha and Zenna skipping around us.

He didn't seem to be paying much attention to where we were going and nearly fell over a stone in the path. After he balanced himself and moved ahead again, I noticed his lips were moving silently as he looked up toward heaven. I leaned my ear closer to his mouth.

"I've said what you asked me to, Lord. I always have," he mumbled. "But this time I have little hope that anything will be different." He stopped speaking and looked over at me. "Oh, I am so tired," he sighed.

When we arrived at his house, Mama met us at the door. "Thank you, girls," she smiled. "Lehi, I have some lunch for you, and then you will rest."

"Yes, Leah," he said, letting her lead him inside. Then he stopped and turned to look at Siri and me. "Bless you, my daughters," he said, then followed Mama in the rest of the way.

A few weeks after Father Lehi's sermon, he sent Jacob early in the morning to bring Nephi to his house. I was instructed to tell no one that Nephi was there. He was gone all day, came home late, and fell almost directly into bed. I was unable to get any information from him the next day, for when he awoke, he took his bow and headed inland. I knew that look on his face, something was on his mind and he had to ponder it. All around me everyone else was working and living life as usual, nothing unusual was happening for them. When asked of Nephi's whereabouts, I reported only that he was hunting.

When Nephi returned two days later, he stopped by our house briefly and then headed straight for Lehi's house again for the rest of the day. When he finally returned for a late supper, I met him with a warm embrace.

"Welcome home, my love," I said, wrapping my arms around him. "Supper is waiting for you."

He smiled. "I am hungry," he said, hugging me back.

As he ate, I talked of the girl's antics of the past couple of days, of Zenna climbing a tree and scraping her knees, and other lighter topics. Nephi ate with an occasional nod and grunt. Then Siri came in.

"Welcome home, Father," she said, giving him a kiss. "Mama, the girls are in bed. I'm going to sleep now too. Good night."

"Good night," we both responded. After she left, we both looked at each other in silence.

"Intense week?" I asked, beginning to gather the dishes to put them away. Nephi put his hand on mine and I stopped. As I looked in his eyes, something about him seemed different, a greater brightness and intensity, but also a greater burden. I dropped the dish I was holding. "What is it, Nephi?" I asked, my voice catching.

"Didi," he paused, and drew a deep breath. "Father gave me the priesthood birthright. I have been promised the patriarchal and prophetic keys. He will give the Liahona and the brass plates into my safe keeping."

I just stared at him as his words swirled in my head trying to make sense. I wasn't sure I grasped it all. But I knew one thing. This was what Laman sought, and now Nephi would have it. "What will Laman do when he finds out?" I whispered.

Nephi shook his head. "He won't like it for sure," he said ruefully. "Father has asked that we say nothing for now. It will become known soon enough, I think. And then life will become much more difficult, I'm afraid."

I was still pensive. "Does this mean Father has chosen you as the family community leader too, Nephi?"

Nephi got a funny look on his face. "You know, Didi, I'm not sure. He never really mentioned that. He seemed primarily concerned that the spiritual leadership is appropriately taken care of. I don't know what his plans are for the community leader."

"Can the two positions be separated?" I asked.

"I suppose so. They were in Jerusalem." He looked thoughtful and then shook his head. "Our group is too small for two leaders. Two bulls in one herd would cause chaos."

What a silly question I had asked. Jerusalem was so long ago and far away, and having two types of leaders in our small community would be a challenge, especially with so many opposing views among our families. In a larger community it might work, but not for us here and now.

A couple of weeks later, there was a knock at our door. It was Jacob.

"Father wants all of you to come this afternoon. He is gathering the family at our home," he said.

"What is it about?" I asked, a little concerned.

He paused. "I think he may be giving his last blessings," Jacob stated quietly.

At the tone in his voice, I looked at him again. He was still young, fourteen years old. But there was an element of maturity in his voice. It wasn't the slight deepening of adolescence. It was a touch of solemnity, the steady gaze of the eyes that spoke of an understanding of what the giving of Lehi's "last blessings" meant. Lehi would not be with us much longer.

I put my hand on Jacob's shoulder. "Tell him we'll be there," I said. I watched him walk briskly down the hill toward Mary and Zoram's house. Then I went to fetch Nephi from irrigating the fields.

When we arrived at Lehi's house, everyone was there before us, including for once Laman and his family. Mama ushered us into the courtyard with the others, which by now was quite crowded.

Shortly thereafter, Jacob came out to call Laman and his family back into Lehi's bedroom. Laman returned with Riddah and Jagadesh about fifteen minutes later, a slightly puzzled expression on Laman's face. Their children came out twenty minutes after him. They looked somber and were unusually quiet. Lemuel and his family similarly were called in to Lehi's room, the parents leaving first, followed by the children. In this manner, Mori and Gid's families also visited with Lehi.

At this point, Mama called a pause for us all to eat the supper she had prepared. She sent a bowl back to Lehi with Joseph, who stayed to help him eat. Soon Lehi was calling to continue the blessings, and Zoram went back with his family.

Mori and Gid left at this point with their families, pulling tired children after them. Soon Riddah was begging Laman to go too. When he persisted on staying, she and Jagadesh took the children and left with Lemuel's family. Laman stayed on, pacing the courtyard at times, or sitting with his elbows on knees and hands propping his chin. We had little to say to him, so he was left mostly to himself.

Zoram's whole family came out together. Zoram smiled at Nephi and Sam. Laman watched him intently. When Zoram's gaze met Laman's, Zoram's smile faded, and he dropped his eyes. He turned to take his youngest child from Mary, who then bent over to wipe another child's nose with the corner of her apron.

Next Eli and his family were called into Lehi's rooms for blessings. Elizabeth shared with me later that they were told that their descendants would be numbered among the righteous descendants of Nephi. She felt that was a blessing to be considered family in such a manner.

Then Jacob called in Sam and his family, and Laman watched them until they disappeared into Lehi's room.

I tried to imagine why Laman was still here. Had Lehi said nothing to him about the birthright blessing, and was Laman trying to figure out who was going to get it? I began to fear again for Nephi's well-being, especially once Laman discovered that Nephi had been given the birthright before this day.

When Sam came out, he purposely avoided looking at Laman. Naola was quiet but looked peaceful. Laman again watched them intently. Then it was our turn.

We gathered up our girls and entered Lehi's room. He was sitting up at the edge of the bed, propped by several pillows. His face, which had looked haggard for a moment, brightened into a smile as we entered.

"My ever-faithful son, Nephi," he said, reaching out his right hand to him. As I neared, he grasped my hand with his left. "My daughter, Devorah." he said.

After I quieted the girls, Lehi had Nephi kneel down on the floor before him, and placed his hands on his head. Lehi blessed Nephi, reiterating the giving of the birthright blessing, and the responsibilities of leadership accorded to him because of it. Lehi spoke again of the blessings of the land if we live righteously on it, and charged him to teach his children and his people about the Lord and the laws of God. Nephi was promised that the Lord would be with him to guide him, and was given many other great blessings and promises if he continued to live righteously.

When the prayer was completed, Nephi stood and embraced his father tenderly. Then Lehi asked him to go to a carved wooden chest beside his bed and open it. Inside, wrapped in silk cloth, lay the Liahona. Next to them lay the metal record that Nephi had made for his father and helped him engrave upon.

"My son, Nephi," Lehi said quietly. "It is now your responsibility to care for the Liahona, Laban's brass plates, and this record of my prophecies and journeying in the wilderness on the plates you forged for me. Care for them well. Pass them on to one who will care for them and teach your descendants the word of God."

"Yes, Father," Nephi bowed his head in acknowledgement. He reverently folded the Liahona back into the silk cloth and tucked it carefully into his tunic. Then he wrapped Lehi's plates inside one of Leesha's blankets, and placed it with our things.

Next, Lehi instructed me to kneel before him, and he laid his hands on my head in the same manner as he had Nephi. His blessing to me told me of the Lord's pleasure in my obedience to him, and that I was a chosen handmaid in his kingdom. He spoke of my responsibilities as wife and mother, and the importance of supporting Nephi in his prophetic and leadership calling. If I did well, the blessings saved for the righteous would be mine, including eternal life and an eternal bond with my husband and children.

When he was finished with me Lehi blessed each of our daughters, reiterating many of the same promises I had received, if they kept the commandments of God. I got an insight into each of their personalities that I had not sensed before, each one vibrant and beautiful in her unique gifts and life calling. When Lehi finished with Leesha, he called in his sons, Jacob and Joseph. We were privileged to hear the blessings Lehi gave to them. When he finished with them all, he leaned back and sighed.

"I have blessed each of my posterity, from my eldest son, to my two sons born in the wilderness, to the youngest grandchild," he murmured. "Some of the parents would not understand the blessings given to their children that the children need not be cursed for the wickedness of their parents, but may be blessed according to their own righteousness."

I had wondered that the children of Laman and Lemuel, Mori and Gid had been blessed without their parents present, while Zoram, Eli, Sam, and Nephi had been allowed to remain. I, for one, was grateful to have heard the blessings of my children.

Lehi looked up at us and smiled. "Go in peace," he said. "I must rest now."

Nephi helped his father lie back on the bed, adjusting the pillows for him. As we gathered our things and tiptoed out, Lehi had already closed his eyes and was breathing evenly.

We were met outside the bedroom door by Laman. He stood right in front of Nephi and glared at him. "What did Father say to you?" he demanded.

"Well," Nephi began, "he said if I kept the commandments of God in this land, I would be blessed—"

"No, no, no!" cut in Laman. "He said that to all of us. I mean, did he give you the birthright?"

I held my breath. Nephi gazed calmly at his brother, casually holding Lehi's plates hidden in his daughter's blankets in the crook of his arm. After what seemed a very long agonizing moment, Nephi opened his mouth. "Yes," he said simply.

Laman's hand shot out but stopped just before striking Nephi's face. "Aaagh!" Laman turned away, hands digging at his hair. "This is not fair! He names you the spiritual leader and gives you the birthright!" He looked back at Nephi, still standing calmly. "You . . . you usurper!" Laman shook his fist at Nephi and then stomped out of the house, violently slamming the door behind him. I could hear him cursing as he strode down the path.

As Nephi turned to me, I realized I had gathered my girls around me protectively. Leesha was hiding her face in my skirts.

"Let's go home," Nephi breathed. We bid farewell to Mama, who was about ready to return to her own tiny cottage nearby.

All was quiet amongst the families for the next two weeks. Then Jacob and Joseph came around to tell the families that Father Lehi had passed away. Joseph seemed lost, quiet. Jacob held his arm protectively around his brother and did the talking. Then they went down the hill together to tell the next family.

The families spent the day mourning and keening at Lehi's house. Then that night Nephi joined Laman, Lemuel, and Sam to prepare their father's body for burial. Mama took Jacob and Joseph over to her place during this time, feeling they were still a little young to join in.

When Nephi came back that night, he seemed peaceful. "It was a good evening," he reported. "Sam got us reminiscing about Father, what things we had learned from him, and memorable experiences. It was healing."

"Who's giving the funeral address?" I asked.

Nephi stopped and stared at me. "We didn't talk about that," he said. He thought for a minute. "We probably better not leave that to chance. Maybe this will be an opportunity to heal some hurt feelings. I think Laman would be the appropriate choice as main speaker. I'll ask him tomorrow."

The next day Nephi made the trip over to Laman's house. When he came back, he looked discouraged. "Laman was not very appreciative of my approaching him about the topic of funeral speaker. 'It is inappropriate for the younger brother to remind the older one of his duty.'" Nephi laughed harshly. "I don't know whether he had been planning to speak or not before I asked. He certainly didn't tell me whether he plans to do it now. I wish Father had not named me the spiritual leader."

"Maybe he was hoping you could find a way to work it out with Laman," I suggested.

"We might be able to if he would talk to me." Nephi shook his head. "I surely don't want to spend the rest of my life telling my relatives what to do and trying to keep them straight. I'd like them to use their own initiative." He shrugged his shoulders. "Anyway, I guess I better prepare that sermon just in case Laman chooses not to."

The next afternoon was the funeral service. Laman's family was there, but I didn't see him. Finally Nephi stood up to open the service.

Several of the grandchildren stood up to sing a Sabbath hymn, and then Nephi began his speech. He spoke of the kind of man Lehi had been, husband, patriarch, and prophet, and related some of his own memories of his father. He told us how he hoped we would all honor him and the sacrifice he had made bringing us here by living the laws of God in this land. We should love each other and take care of each other. Then Nephi invited anyone else who wanted to speak to come up front and do so.

Laman, who had come in to the synagogue partway through Nephi's speech, sat in the back, scowling. When Nephi was done, Lemuel, Sam, Zoram, several of the daughters-in-law, and a few of the older grandchildren also shared their memories and feelings about him. Laman, however, sat stone-faced and said nothing.

After the last person spoke, Laman strode up to the front and glared at Nephi. Then he stared out over the congregation. "Father Lehi is gone. He was a visionary man who led us to this land to make a new life. It has not been perfect, but it has been adequate."

He paused. "As the oldest son of Lehi, I claim the right of leadership over this people. What I say now will become law." He stared pointedly at Nephi. "As of this day, no one uses the synagogue without my permission."

There was murmuring among the family members. Some showed looks of shock and concern, but others appeared pleased. Nephi stood up and faced Laman.

"You know Father gave me the priesthood birthright," Nephi told him quietly. "He charged me with the responsibility of leading this people in religious worship. We need access to the synagogue every Sabbath and on special occasions. You know this."

Laman grinned viciously. "I will lead this community from now on. You will sit and listen to me."

Nephi did not back down. "We will continue to worship God as he commands," he stated firmly.

"You were always one to fawn over Father and be his puppet," Laman accused him.

"You never listened to his teachings, Laman. You would rather rebel and lead others astray."

"Better that than blindly following a dreamer!" Laman's voice had risen.

"You dishonor our father's name and memory," Nephi said quietly.

Laman grasped Nephi by the front of his shirt. "Do you want to fight me for the right to lead this people, young Nephi?"

The room was hushed, the mood strained, the tension high. My knuckles tightened as I gripped my skirt. Siri laid a calming hand over mine.

"This is neither the time nor place for this discussion," Nephi stated.

"Oh, I think it is the perfect time and place to set things in the right direction." Laman waved a hand toward his family. "Is that not right?"

Mori stood and raised his fist. "That is so!" he shouted. "Laman is our rightful leader! Hear, hear!"

Laman's, Lemuel's, Mori's, and Gid's families all stood and cheered.

Zoram, Eli, and Sam looked at Nephi with concern. Nephi carefully peeled Laman's grip from his shirtfront. "I am concerned for the welfare of your soul," he told Laman. Nephi turned and walked down the aisle toward the door, where he stopped and looked back over his shoulder. "We will talk about this again another time, Laman." He quietly left the synagogue.

Laman's gaze turned to me. "What is your choice, Devorah?"

Limbs trembling, I stood and faced him. "Laman, you can never stop us from following our Lord and God." I grasped Zenna and Leesha's hands and led them out of the synagogue. Sam's, Eli's, and Zoram's families followed me.

We watched from a distance while Laman, Lemuel, Mori, and Gid buried Father Lehi next to Sariah's gravesite. Late that night after they had gone home, Nephi, Sam, Eli, and Zoram slipped out to give a dedicatory prayer over his grave.

When Nephi returned, he just sat on the edge of the bed, leaning his forehead into his hand. I sat up and put my hand on his shoulder.

"Nephi, what do we do now?" I asked.

"We carry on as normally as possible. We will still attend worship services, if not in the synagogue, then on Altar Hill. We will try to avoid contention." He looked up at me, his expression grave. "Be careful, Didi. Watch the girls closely. I don't know quite what to expect next, but I feel the tension building again. It could erupt anywhere." He drew a deep breath. "I just pray that Laman learns to see the light."

The next Sabbath, Laman's, Lemuel's, Mori's, and Gid's families stayed away from the worship meetings. But neither did they stop us from entering the synagogue. It was to be Gid's turn at reading from the brass plates; but with him absent, Zoram led the service. Joseph sat with Mary's family, and Jacob with ours, sitting between Siri and Zenna. The two of them kept Jacob smiling, with their finger games and toe drawings in the dirt on the floor. I had to keep hushing them to hear what was being said.

Partway through the reading, I noticed Mori's son, Matthew, slip into the back. Siri paused in her play and looked back. Matthew quickly ducked his head and would not look at her. Jacob glanced back a couple of times, watched Siri, then shrugged his shoulders and continued his attentions with Zenna. At the end of the meeting, Matthew slipped out quickly before anyone else could reach him, and was gone.

The next morning, Nephi headed out of the house at dawn to go hunting. He came back in a minute later.

"Didi, you need to come outside and see this," he announced.

The girls awoke at the sound of his voice and followed us outside. He led us out to the garden and we stared at it. The garden had been destroyed.

Whoever had done it had gone to some effort, bringing in horses to crush the underground plants, and uprooting the vine and bush plants thoroughly. When I saw the damage, I sank to the ground in shock.

Nephi didn't say a word, but the look on his face spoke volumes. Emotions flitted across his face—disbelief, anger, determination. He pressed his lips together tightly and turned into the house. When he emerged again, he had strapped Laban's sword in its scabbard around his waist. His eyes locked onto mine for a moment.

I shook my head firmly. After a moment, he loosened the sword scabbard and dropped it to the ground. Then he strode off in the direction of Laman's house.

I started sobbing. I felt arms around my shoulders. My three girls all were trying to caress and hug me.

"No cry, Mama," begged Leesha, placing a wet kiss on my cheek.

"We'll help you replant," offered Zenna.

"Yes, Mama," added Siri. "The weather here is mild enough. We should be able to get a late harvest in. We still have some seed, don't we?"

I nodded and wiped my eyes. The delay would still mean some meager meals meanwhile, where we'd have to depend on Nephi's good hunting and my sibling's generosity. Then a thought struck me.

"Siri, go check on Aunt Mary and Aunt Naola. Make sure their gardens have not been damaged!"

Siri was off like the wind. Meanwhile, Zenna and Leesha helped me remove the crushed plants to a pile on the side and start creating new rows again. Siri returned with Naola, each of them carrying an infant, Benjamin trotting at their heels.

"Oh, Didi!" Naola fell into my arms. "What a mess! I am so sorry. But you mustn't fret. Sam and I planted more than we could ever eat, and you must share it with us."

"Then your garden is untouched?" I asked, relieved.

"Correct," Naola answered. "Mary's is all right too. Now where do you want me to start?"

"Start?" I asked, confused.

"Yes. Don't you have to replant? We're here to help you do it!" She grinned.

"Oh, thank you!" I smiled back. "What a blessing you are, dear sister!"

Nephi returned that afternoon to help us finish getting the garden cleaned up and replanted. He didn't speak of his encounter with Laman until bedtime and then only to say that they ended up in a shouting match. He admitted it was probably a good thing he hadn't taken his sword. He vowed he would stay within a few hours' distance from home on his hunting trips and not leave us for more than half a day at a time. I worried how he would get the bigger game we might need for food, but I said nothing out loud. It was a relief to know he would not be gone far or for long at a time.

I struggled inside to figure out a way to heal the gulf between our families. Maybe Nephi could do little with his brothers, but I might have a chance with my sisters. I didn't know who had been involved with our garden trampling, but I didn't think I wanted to know. I didn't want that knowledge to taint my reaching out to them. I wanted to truly forgive and forget as God would have me do.

What could I do for them? I was a pretty good cook, but I had to be careful of our food supplies. I could still cook a little something, and then offer my services mending, watching children, or weeding. Yes, that would work! Meanwhile, the girls would have fun playing with their cousins, and Siri was good at keeping young ones out from under foot.

I made the trek to Riddah's house first. She seemed surprised to see us at the door, but let us in. Jagadesh greeted us, then she and the older children left the house, leaving Siri, Zenna, and Leesha to play with Riddah's little Elisa. Too young to understand adult politics, Elisa came running up to greet her Aunt Didi and her cousins with hugs and kisses. Riddah and I could only find superficial topics to discuss, such as what the children were learning, how green the crops were growing, how plentiful the game was this time of year, and how Riddah's pregnancy was going. Elisa interrupted us periodically to tell me of her newest discoveries of plant or animal around the yard and to show me how she could skip and hop and do somersaults. Riddah declined any of my services, so I left the batch of biscuits I had made, and we departed.

The next day we went to visit Bekka. Instead of distant neutrality, I was greeted warmly and was invited in. She accepted my offer to help with the mending while Siri took her children outside to play games in the courtyard. Mirimi joined us as we updated each other on our families and the antics of our children. Yes, their marriage was good. Their children were healthy and well-behaved. I noticed a few times as I looked up from my sewing that Bekka was watching me, hands idle, mouth parted as if on the verge of asking something. A shadow lurked behind her eyes.

"What is it, Bekka?" I finally asked.

She glanced at Mirimi and stuttered a trivial question about the mending. I could tell something was on her mind, something that really bothered her, but that she couldn't talk about it yet. I hoped it would come when she was ready.

When it was time to go, Bekka escorted us to the door. "You will come back, Didi?" she asked.

"I would love to, Bekka," I smiled. "You find some more mending to do, or grow some more weeds in your garden, and I should be able to give you a hand." I placed my hand beside my mouth as though telling a secret. "Actually my girls have been begging to play with their cousins more, so torn clothes and weeds or no, we just might have to get together again, your place or mine!"

Bekka smiled and waved us on. As we walked home, I shook my head at my poor attempt at humor and familiarity. I hoped she wasn't just being polite to invite me back because I fully intended to take her up on it.

My visit with Kora and Hagadah was fairly chaotic. Their children were very energetic and frequently interrupted our conversation and attempts to clean house. When the fourth quarrel broke out, Kora threw up her arms and looked at me hopelessly.

"I'm sorry, Didi. This just isn't a good day to visit. I hope you understand?"

I nodded, gathered my girls, and we left. I didn't know if their household would ever be calmer for visiting. Maybe I'd be better off borrowing two or three of their children to play at our house as my service to them. Yes, that's what I would do.

When I approached Mori's house a day later to visit Abisha, Mori met me out front. I could see Yadeesh and some of the children working out back in their garden.

"I'm sorry, Didi," Mori said. "I don't know what you are trying to do with this visiting house to house, but Abisha and Yadeesh have got too much to do to spend time chatting. You can save your time and go home."

I just looked at him. He obviously was not going to let me by. I thrust forward the sweetcakes I had made for his family. "Uh, Mori, these are for you and your family anyway. Enjoy." I looked at his unreadable face a little longer, then turned with my girls and headed home again.

It soon became apparent that Mori's compound was off limits to half of the extended family. I asked Naola to be a part of my good will team, and go visit Abisha for me. She was not allowed on the property either. For the following month, Matthew did not come to Sabbath services, as was his custom.

Early one morning, Matthew showed up at our house. "Aunt Didi," he said breathlessly. "I can't stay long, Mama's expecting me home soon from an errand. But I wanted to get from Uncle Nephi the Sabbath topics discussed the last few weeks and what he'll be discussing the next while." He paused and pushed some dirt with his foot. "I want you to know I'm still studying. Papa doesn't know, but Mama doesn't seem to mind much."

He looked over his shoulder toward the river, and I hurried to get Nephi. After a brief chat with Nephi, and after Siri had a chance to "happen" by the door to smile shyly at Matthew, he slipped away again.

I could tell many of us felt the strain of our dissolving family relationships. Mama spent more time alone in her little house, Naola walked without a bounce, Sam's lighter hair got a hint of gray speckles around the temples, Eli and Elizabeth stayed more isolated in their little house, and Zoram spoke less frequently. Mary was one of the few who grew stronger under it. She was following in Mama's footsteps as the family matriarch. Somehow she was able to get into any of the homes, asking about the health of the children, bringing useful herbs or food gifts. I could see her mature and toughen with the struggle, but she also glowed, having something unique that she could offer, and a desire to share it with all of the family.

Nephi, I knew, felt the strain the most. I could see new lines appearing in his face, graying of the hair above his ears, and his expression was more often serious. Our girls made it their duty to tickle and tease him daily until he would laugh and wrestle with them and relax. I found I was happier at these moments too and was glad for their diversion. I realized I must have been a sourpuss lately too if it took my girls to even make me smile.

It was soon after Matthew visited us that our corn and barley crops burned. A pounding on our door awakened us in the middle of the night. Mary was there with her three younger children wrapped in shawls.

"The fields are on fire!" she announced breathlessly. "Zoram, Eli, Sam, and my son Jonah have gone to fight it, and try to create a firebreak between the fields and our homes. Naola has gone to warn Mama, Jacob, and Joseph."

Nephi grabbed a cloak, ax, and shovel. "I'm gone," he called as he ran from the house and down the hill.

I could see flames coming from the direction of our nearly ripened cornfield. The smell of burning stalks and brush even here nearly choked me. I wrung my hands and paced the hall.

"I've got to do something," I muttered. "I can't just let another crop be destroyed." I looked over at Mary, who had just stretched her children out to sleep on the floor of our main gathering room. "Mary," I said. "I'm going out to help them."

Siri, who had awakened and was observing the commotion, now spoke, "I'll come too, Mama."

I was about to command her to stay when I saw the determined look in her eye. She was nearly my height, and could work as well as any full-grown woman. She would be a much-needed asset. "All right," I acceded. "But wear a head shawl and cloak to protect you."

We grasped water bags and buckets, and some tools that might help us, and ran down the hill. We met Naola hurrying up with her two infants and Benjamin.

"Go on in," I called to her. "Use my bed for the children." And we continued on.

The smoke became heavy as the wind blew it our way. We found it easiest to go up along the riverbank, where we filled our water containers, and then cut over to the fields. I was glad for the shawls to cover our faces. I hoped the wind would not carry the fire up the hill where the children were; they could easily be trapped there.

I stopped and looked back at the hill. "Siri," I caught her arm and motioned back toward our house. "You need to go back and get everyone out of our house. It's not safe enough there. Get them down by the beach, or if necessary, across the river."

Siri nodded, put down her bucket and tools, and ran back toward the house. I heaved a sigh of relief that my perfect, beautiful daughter would not be in immediate danger of fire burns after all. Then I picked up two of the water containers and headed back to the blaze.

Zoram, Eli, Sam, and Nephi were digging a trench at the downwind side of the fields. Mama, Jacob, Joseph, and Jonah were uprooting and cutting plants along both sides of the trenches to create a firebreak. Sam showed me where to pour the water, and Mama helped me go back for more. Soon Mary joined us. I was beginning to wonder if we'd ever be able to keep up when unexpected reinforcements arrived: Abisha, Yadeesh and Matthew, and Kora and her two older children, Gad and Hannah. Shortly Bekka and her daughter, Shanna, arrived to help. Mama fetched more bags and buckets from her place for a water carrying line. It was starting to look as though we'd contain the fire after all.

All of a sudden, I heard screams coming from where Bekka and Shanna were working. Flames were rising from the skirts of Shanna's dress, and she was whirling around, slapping at them with her hands. Sam, the nearest to her besides Bekka, leaped to her aid. All in one swift movement, he pulled her to the ground, yanked his shirt off to wrap around her legs, and rolled her over and over. In a moment, the fire was out. By this time, Shanna was sobbing, and Bekka was at her side.

"My legs! My legs!" she cried. "They hurt, ooh, they hurt!"

Mama had now arrived. Lifting Shanna's skirts, she could see red blisters rising on her legs. "Bekka, let's get her to the river quickly." Mama instructed. "We've got to get her legs in the cold water."

Mama and Bekka half carried and half dragged Shanna to the river. The rest of us continued fighting the fire.

The firebreak held, and soon we were standing, exhausted, watching the last of the field crops crackle and fall. Only now as I rested did I wonder how we were going to feed our families this winter. Of course, we had been through hunger before and survived, but it hadn't been pleasant. We would have to depend on good hunting and the grace of our siblings to share the fruits of their crops.

Remembering Shanna, I raced down to the river's edge. Bekka and Mama were lifting her out of the water.

"Didi," Mama instructed, "fill one of the water buckets at the river and bring it to my house."

I dashed back for a water bucket, filled it, and lugged it to Mama's house. Mama and Bekka had just arrived with Shanna. We sat her in a chair, placed the water bucket in front of her, and put her legs in again. Shanna sighed with relief as the cold river water soothed the burning of her legs. She leaned back in the chair and closed her eyes.

Mama was gathering clean rags and mixing a special salve. "We're ready, girls," she said. "Bekka, get Shanna's legs out of the water and dry them off. Gently!"

I helped support Shanna's legs while Bekka patted them dry, Shanna wincing and whimpering slightly. The skin was covered with large and small blisters mostly from the knees down, some of them starting to drain a little. Mama covered the blisters with her salve, which Shanna said was soothing. Then Mama wrapped her legs with the cloth dressings. As she worked, Mama was giving Bekka instructions on how to do the daily dressing changes at home, always with clean cloths. Then Mama gave her a covered dish of the salve.

"When the men return, someone will take you and Shanna home, Bekka," she said.

"We're fine, really, Mama," Bekka protested. "Our horse is somewhere around here, I'm sure."

I went back to the fields where the work crews were cleaning up, stomping out remaining embers. Dawn was starting to light the sky. We found Bekka's horse tied lightly to a tree near the river, upwind from the burned fields. Zoram took it back to Mama's place, insisting he would accompany Bekka and Shanna home. Abisha, Yadeesh, Matthew, Kora and her children, Jacob, Joseph, and Jonah returned to their homes. Sam, Nephi, Mary, and I went to look for our families down near the beach. They were huddled in blankets, tired and a little cold, but safe. Then we returned to our homes to get some much-needed sleep.

That afternoon after we had rested, Zoram's, Sam's, Eli's, and Nephi's families gathered at the fields to survey the damage. My girls picked through and found some partially ripened ears of corn, but they were burned black and were inedible. The men were discussing whether it was too late in the year to replant.

"Let's wait a little bit," Nephi recommended. "We can prepare the ground now. But our seed supplies are low, and if this next crop fails, we'll have nothing to plant next spring. I need to think this over first."

The other men nodded, and we returned to our homes.

The next day Nephi went into the nearby hills to meditate and pray. He returned that evening after I had tucked the girls into bed.

"What did you decide about the crops?" I asked Nephi as we climbed into bed.

"We're not going to replant this year," he responded.

I just looked at him. "What is going to happen to us?" I finally asked.

"I don't know yet," Nephi commented grimly. "We're to wait and watch."

In the morning, Mary and I went over to visit Bekka and Shanna. Bekka answered the door. Her eyes were red as if she had been crying. But she greeted us cordially and ushered us in. Shanna was propped up in her bed, two of her younger siblings playing around her on the floor.

Bekka shooed the younger children out, so Mary and I could change Shanna's dressings and check on the burns. While we unwrapped, Shanna hid her face in her mother's lap, squeezing Bekka's arms tightly. Only an occasional groan escaped her throat.

The outer layer of blistered skin was coming off. While I supported her legs and Mary cleaned them and applied new salve, I told Shanna one of Sam's recently created adventure stories. By the time I was done with the story, Mary had her legs wrapped up in clean bandages.

"Thank you for coming to change her dressings, Mary," smiled Bekka. "I'm having a hard time doing it myself right now."

"You'll have to watch her carefully, Bekka," Mary told her, pulling her aside as I rearranged Shanna's pillows for her. "These legs could easily get infected. Send someone for me if she gets a fever or looks ill. And make sure she drinks a lot of water."

Bekka nodded, her eyes betraying a hint of fear. "Yes, Mary," she whispered.

I grasped Bekka's hand as we were leaving. A thought struck me, so I spoke it. "Do you want me to send Nephi to help give her a blessing, Bekka?" I asked.

Bekka drew in a breath, gazed at her daughter, then back at me. "I don't think Lemuel . . . But I think Shanna and I would like that. I'll let you know," she smiled and squeezed my hand back.

A few days later Gid showed up at our house with a deer carcass. The girls had seen him coming and ran to get Nephi and me. We both arrived at the front of the house at the same time. We just looked at the deer and at Gid.

"This is for your family, and Eli's, Sam's, and Zoram's," mumbled Gid. "It was an extra from today's hunting trip. Sorry that your grain fields burned."

"Why, thank you, Gid," I smiled. "This was very thoughtful of you."

Gid shrugged, but a smile was now playing on his lips. "Yes, well, I've got to go now."

We watched him trek back down the hill toward the river. "Does that mean I don't have to try requesting restitution under the law for our burned grain fields, Didi?" Nephi asked softly.

I sighed. "Would it do any good? We don't know who was responsible for starting the fire."

Nephi shook his head. "They would all deny doing it. They might say the deer was restitution enough. Well, let's go clean it."

We dragged the carcass around back to clean it. That night we had a little feast for our four families around the hill. Every scrap that was left over was smoked and dried for future use.

The next couple of weeks were relatively quiet. Sabbaths came and went again, and only Zoram's, Eli's, Sam's, and Nephi's families and Mama attended Sabbath meetings.

Then Kora's daughter Johanna called Mary to come across the river. When Mary returned, she came up to our house to talk with me. At a look from Mary, I directed my girls out to the courtyard so we could talk alone.

"Didi," Mary finally spoke. She was looking down into her lap, twisting a corner of her apron with her hands. "I was brought to Kora's house today. She's been injured again, and I fear it was . . . the same cause as last time. Didi, her hand is broken."

I gasped and reached out for her hand. She squeezed it and looked up at me. "Are you sure?" I whispered.

"Yes," she said. "It wasn't crooked, but I could feel the bone shift. Her hand is splinted now."

"I mean, are you sure . . . of the cause of her injury?" I persisted.

"Well," she paused. "Kora and her daughter avoided responding to my direct question of how it happened. But I could see finger mark bruises on her hand and arm." She stopped and looked me in the eye. "We need to do something about it this time, Didi."

I went and fetched Nephi, who was working with the animals. He joined us, and Mary repeated her story. When she was done, Nephi leaned back on his stool and gazed upward. Then he looked at Mary again.

"I will go and talk to Gid again," he said simply. He picked up his cloak and left.

When he returned an hour later, Nephi didn't say much.

"What happened?" I asked.

"Gid wouldn't talk to me. Gad has a black eye, but Hagadah and the other children seem to be unharmed. I never got to see Kora." Nephi took a couple of bites of his lunch and then looked up at me. "I am going to talk with Laman and appeal to his leadership desires and comradeship with Gid. I am hoping he can influence some change in this situation." He shook his head forcefully. "This kind of behavior must not continue, even if we have to make it a law." He ate a few more bites and then grabbed his cloak again. "I am planning to be back by dinner time, my dear." He kissed me and then went to the corral to get his horse.

I watched him gallop off, and started another prayer in my heart. The physical and spiritual health of my siblings was always my concern, now again included was the safety of my husband.

Nephi did return in time for dinner, but he appeared discouraged and frustrated. "I don't know, Didi," he pounded his right fist into his left. "I don't think Laman is going to do much. It just makes me so angry sometimes, their attitude of laziness and rebellion. Sometimes I think our siblings would act better if we weren't living around them anymore." He put his hands over his face. "Why do I sin? Why am I always so angry because of my enemy?" He dropped his hands onto the table.

We stared at each other silently. I didn't think being angry at injustice was sinning. A mixture of emotions stirred inside me at the thought of leaving. It certainly would be much easier if we didn't have to keep taking care of our siblings. But what about my life purpose I had chosen, to keep our extended family together? And who would protect and help Kora and others like her who would suffer from the sins of our brothers?

Nephi shook his head and sighed. "I'm just dreaming, Didi. We have a responsibility here. We won't leave."

If Nephi was dreaming, it was fast becoming a nightmare. The next morning Nephi's favorite horse was found dead in the corral, its throat slit. All of our horses and cows were gone from their holding pens and were nowhere to be found. Nephi immediately called a meeting with Zoram, Eli, Sam, Mama, and our families.

Nephi raised a hand to quiet us. "I think the time has come to take action about the destruction happening to our animals and property," he stated. "If it were just me being targeted, I would keep my mouth shut a little longer. But all of us are being affected. It was the crops belonging to all of us that burned, and you have told me of your animals disappearing as well. I do not know but that it might be one of us or our children targeted next. What do we do about it?"

There were some whispers among the families, but no immediate suggestions. Then Naola stood and raised her fist. "I suggest we take our animals back and give them a taste of their own behavior!" She sat down again.

Everyone fell silent. This was so unlike innocent, gentle Naola. Was this what the stress of this family was doing to us, turning us bitter and unhappy ourselves? Soon we would be no better than our resentful siblings, and God could have no place with us then.

Words of complaint and anger were being expressed. I was afraid that if this were not halted now, we would end up doing something we all would regret. I stood and clapped my hands. The others quieted and listened to me. I looked at them and realized that this was going to be one of the most important speeches I would ever make.

"My brothers and sisters, look at us. Listen to what we have been saying. What have we been thinking? We have been speaking words of anger and hate and revenge. Is this not what we were trying to escape by leaving Jerusalem? Are we any better than those we are angry against? What is this teaching our children? Can God forgive us if we seek revenge against our own flesh and blood?" I looked each person in the eye. "No. I will not participate in this thing. I have made a promise to myself and to my God that I will rise above the pettiness of others, and try to bind us together through love and forgiveness. If we do not have our family, where is the meaning in life?" I held my breath and tried to gauge the impact my words were having on my siblings. I couldn't tell. "I have made my choice," I declared and sat down.

Again there was silence. Naola was sitting with her head bowed. Siri, who always had an excellent sense of the right spirit and way before God, was smiling at me.

Naola raised her head and glanced at me. "Didi is right," she stated. "I will choose with her to love . . . and forgive."

Sam raised his head high. "I, like Naola, will choose to return kindness for injury."

Elizabeth smiled in relief. "Forgiveness is my choice also."

Zoram, Mary, Mama, and all the older children spoke their assent. Nephi stood again.

"I am pleased with your decision, my family," he said, but his voice was still somber. "You have chosen the better, though harder way. I, too, have struggled with anger, which has threatened to tear my inner peace away. Follow that anger, and sin follows easily behind it. Replace it with forgiveness, attempt to love as God loves us, and the Lord's joy will fill your soul." He smiled. "May God be with us as we strive to make this Promised Land plentiful in emotional as well as temporal goodness."

We returned to our homes and tasks of living. Nephi refused to take one of Sam's horses or any of his cattle, preferring instead to find and tame more of his own. Thus, Sam, Jacob and Joseph accompanied Nephi on a trip to where the herds of wild horses had been found, leaving Eli and Zoram with us to protect the families. Mary continued her visits to all the families and at last was able to talk a little bit with Abisha, Yadeesh, and their children. My girls and I continued tending our garden, hoping to obtain some produce before the rainy season arrived. We also discovered patches of wild berries in the less explored hills inland, and were able to collect a good supply of edible roots and bring back more herbs for Mary. It was also at this time that I discovered I was pregnant again. I dearly hoped it would be a son this time so Nephi could have a namesake and male heir.

A couple of days later as Siri and I were digging in the garden, we heard in the distance some voices calling and the neighing of horses.

"Papa's back!" cried Siri, and rushed to get her sisters. They stood watch from the garden patch as Nephi, Sam, Jacob, and Joseph herded the new group of horses into Nephi's corral. They were a wild bunch, running against the fences, rearing and neighing. Finally they were all inside and Joseph closed the gate.

"Whew!" exclaimed Nephi as he came up to give me a kiss. "That was real work! I am glad to be home." He looked over the horses. "Tomorrow I'll start training."

"Go take a bath, my dear," I teased him. "Then you can have your proper welcome home hug!"

The next morning Nephi was out early working with the horses, trying to get them used to him, the girls watching him from the fence. We could see Mama trudging up the hill to visit with us. I went to meet her.

"Good morning, Mama," I said, kissing her on the cheek.

"Didi," she spoke. "Do you really think that's a good idea, letting the girls watch so close to those wild horses?" She pushed past me and hurried up the hill.

As we neared the corral, we saw a horse inside suddenly rear up on his hind legs, scream, and come down on the horse next to him. The second horse neighed, jumped, and bumped into the horses next to him. In a moment, all the horses were bucking, kicking, and galloping about the corral. Nephi, who had a rope around one horse's neck inside the corral, backed up against the fence, trying to regain control of his animal. The girls, straddling the fence, hurriedly tried to climb off. One horse running by bumped against Zenna, and she fell shrieking into the corral.

Mama herself screamed, and before I could reach the fence myself, she had climbed inside the corral to rescue Zenna. As she lifted the child out, another horse reared and landed, his feet against Mama's back. She lay groaning on the ground as horses trampled and stomped around and over her. By this time, Nephi had given up holding onto his horse and had made his way around the corral to our position. Together we dragged Mama out of the corral under the fence, and laid her on the ground. Zenna and Siri hovered over her as I checked her over.

"Mama! Mama!" I cried, trying to wipe away the dirt and blood on her face with my apron. "Mama, speak to me. Are you all right?"

She groaned and opened her eyes. "Don't move me again." She sighed and closed her eyes again.

"Where's Leesha?" Nephi suddenly asked, looking around.

I caught my breath, not daring to look inside the corral, yet fearing the worst. Siri and Nephi ran over to and around the corral, calling her name. Zenna remained huddled by Mama, watching over her last remaining grandparent, occasionally stroking her cheek.

"She's not in with the horses," Nephi called out to me. I found myself breathing again. In another minute, I heard him call again. "We found her!" Nephi returned shortly, carrying Leesha in his arms, Siri right behind him.

"Where was she?" I asked, running over to take her.

"We found her just up on the crest of the hill, looking into the trees," Nephi responded.

"What were you doing there, honey?" I asked, stroking the hair out of her eyes.

"Unc' Lemuel," she said, pointing in the direction she had been.

"What does Uncle Lemuel have to do with anything?" I asked, looking between Leesha and Nephi.

Nephi scratched his head and looked toward the trees himself. "I'm not sure," he answered.

"We saw someone by the trees just before the horses acted up," Siri offered. "I really didn't get a good look at who it was; I was busy watching Papa. But I did notice that a rock or something hit that horse that first got frightened."

Nephi looked angry. "And now the children are in danger," he began, his voice hard.

I stared at him a moment, fear piercing my heart. Then I remembered Mama. With hot tears running down my cheeks, I knelt down again at her side and grasped her hand. "How are you, Mama?" I asked.

She groaned again and squeezed my hand. "I think my back is hurt, and my hip," she whispered. "Go get Mary."

I looked at Siri, and like the wind, she was off running down the hill. I gazed imploringly at Nephi. "Nephi," I asked, "would you please give Mama a blessing?"

Nephi nodded and knelt at her side, laying his hands on her head. After a moment's pause, he began. Calling her by name, he told her that God loved her for her faithful support of the Lord's cause in establishing a branch of his people in the Promised Land. He blessed her that she would be comforted, that the pain would be tolerable, and that she would see her beloved husband again. Then Nephi ended the prayer.

"What about healing her?" I asked, a bit of panic in my voice.

"Didn't I say that?" he responded, a bit puzzled. "I'm sure I intended—"

Mary arrived on the scene just then with Siri and Zoram. Mary knelt down at her mother's side. "Mama, I'm here."

Mama opened her eyes. "My back . . ." she murmured.

Mary felt along her limbs, none of which seemed to be injured. Mama's face and head though scratched were fine. Her abdomen was bruised and tender. But when Mary felt along her spine, Mama grimaced. And when Mary touched her right hip bone, Mama screeched and her face turned pale.

Mary looked up, concerned. "We've got to get her inside, but I don't dare move her spine and pelvis. Any suggestions?"

"We could make a portable bed," suggested Siri. "Papa and Uncle Zoram are strong enough."

"No!" said Mama, her eyes still closed. "Do not move me at all."

We looked at each other in silence. "Wait!" suggested Zoram excitedly. "What about our tents? We have enough and to spare to cover her here!"

Nephi looked relieved and nodded. It took him a moment to find our tent packed away in our storage room, but they had it mostly set up by the time I had gathered some bedding and pillows to make

Mama comfortable. Mary found some herbs for Mama to chew to take away some of the pain and allow her to go to sleep.

"Now we watch and wait," sighed Mary as we stood at the door of the little tent looking at her.

"I wish there was something more we could do," I commented

"Pray," said Mary. "And gather the family."

I stared at her. "Gather the family? You make it sound as though Mama's going to die!"

Mary looked at me sadly. "Didi, Mama can't move or feel her legs. She is bleeding inside from her injuries. Unless there is a miracle..."

I sank down to the ground and sobbed. "Mama! My only Mama."

Jacob and Joseph again carried the sad news around to all the families. Knowing the sensitive nature of our family relationships, Nephi and I stayed indoors while Mori and Gid came with their families. Riddah and Bekka came later with their families, but their husbands never came. After they left, I kept vigil at Mama's side with Mary and Naola. Shortly after midnight, she breathed her last.

It was the end of an era, our parents' generation. We were now the eldest generation, the patriarchs and matriarchs. And what a fractured and divided lot we were.

In the morning, my sisters and I prepared Mama's body for burial. I was relieved to see that everyone attended the burial ceremony held that evening. Afterward Naola and Sam took Jacob and Joseph home to live with them so that they would not be alone.

Early before dawn after Mama's burial, I suddenly woke up. I listened. No, no children crying. Then I heard it again, a tap-tap-tap at the window. I put on my robe and went over to the shutter, opening it quietly.

"Psst!" said a voice just below the window. I looked down and saw Bekka huddled there. She gestured toward our front door.

I nodded, closed the shutter, and met her at the door. She bekkoned me outside, and I closed the door after me. She looked around nervously and then pointed to some bushes growing against the house. I followed her to them, and we sat down in their shadows.

"Didi," she whispered. "At risk of my own life, I am here. But I have to warn you. You have been so kind to us despite all." She took a deep breath and grasped my arm. "Laman and Lemuel are plotting to hurt . . . to take Nephi's life, and . . . and anyone else who stands in their way." She breathed again. "There, I've said it." A sob escaped her throat.

I leaned my head back against the house wall. My heart beat rapidly. I knew deep inside that this was coming with all the events of late, but to hear it said out loud made it suddenly frightening and very real. I looked at Bekka in the darkness. She was trembling. I hugged her. "Thank you, Bekka," I whispered. "Your efforts are very much appreciated. Go home now, before you are in danger."

She nodded, stood, and was gone. I sat outside a few minutes longer, pondering her warning and what we should do about it. I had no solutions.

On returning to our bedroom, I found Nephi kneeling at his bedside. Wondering what he was doing there, I knelt beside him and put my arm around him. He looked up, tears streaming down his face.

"Didi," he said, and hugged me tightly for a long time. When he was finished, we sat on the bed, arms still about each other. "Didi, you know how I have long prayed that my brothers' hatred would be softened, that we could find peace in our family? I have wondered when the Lord would answer this prayer and what was taking him so long. Then I realized he will not make people do things against their agency. I finally prayed that God's will would be done, and asked that he would tell me what I should do now."

He drew a deep breath. "This night I had a dream, a vision. It is a warning. My brothers even now are plotting to kill me. They will stop at nothing until I am dead. Perhaps others will lose their lives as well." He grasped my shoulders. "Didi, I have been commanded to take you and the girls, Zoram, Eli, Sam, and their families, and Jacob and Joseph far away from here, where Laman and Lemuel will not be able to hurt us anymore. That is the answer God gave me."

My shoulders slumped. This felt like we were running away from our problems, something that I had tried to teach our girls was not the best way. It would be giving up on our siblings; it would divide our family permanently. What was the use now of my promise to God that I would work to heal family relationships and bind us together?

On the other hand, when I thought about it, the idea of leaving was also a relief, the release of a calling that I could not fulfill, despite my past and present efforts. It also relieved me of the fear for my daughters' and husband's safety.

I looked up at Nephi. "Nephi," I told him, "I have followed you across deserts and across an ocean, and we have nearly starved together. I have tried to love and befriend those in our family who would rather hate us. If you were to say 'stay and defend,' I would do so. If you say 'go and start our lives over again,' I will follow. I know neither way is easy, but with God's help we can do it."

We both smiled at my last affirmation. Nephi himself had said this many times, and now I was telling it to him.

"I'll tell Zoram, Eli, Sam, Jacob and Joseph later in the morning," decided Nephi as he climbed back into bed. "I feel that we need to be gone by morning three days from now."

Three days. That left very little time to prepare and gather everything. Then I laughed to myself. On our desert journey, we could be packed in three hours and usually less! As my mind organized the packing and food preparation, I suddenly thought of others in my extended family. Matthew, who loved to study the scriptures, would have little spiritual nourishment once we were gone. Kora would be left to her husband's temper, with perhaps only Hagadah to defend her. Abisha, who had once or twice expressed a wish to live on a higher spiritual level, would also be left alone. And Bekka, dear Bekka, risking her life to warn us, would she be safe once we were discovered missing?

I turned over in bed. "Nephi," I whispered.

"What?" he answered. He too had been unable to return to sleep.

"Are we allowed to bring anyone else with us?" I asked. "I mean, believers like Matthew, Mori's son."

"Matthew." Nephi sighed. "What of Matthew?" He stared at the ceiling awhile. "It is imperative our brothers do not find out about our plan to leave. If you can accomplish that, and if he is willing to live the laws of God and not rebel against my leadership, then he may come."

I watched Nephi a moment more. "And if there are any others in danger as we are, may they come too?" I asked.

Nephi rolled over onto his side and looked at me. "Who else did you have in mind?"

"Kora. And Bekka." I didn't dare mentions any others.

Nephi thought again. "They must still follow the terms of my condition," he stated and then turned his back to me and closed his eyes.

I couldn't sleep any more. I got up and went to the storage room with a candle and started pulling out travel containers and equipment that we might need. The tents I would leave for Nephi to lift. I found a chest of my worn, old desert robes, and sat down to sort through them. These might be useful, but did I want them again? I much preferred the fabric Abisha and Mirimi had woven for me, and Siri's, though hers was not yet quite as fine. On the other hand, my younger children would want to see those robes, as part of the heritage that brought them here. The baby clothes in here would be needed though. I would definitely take some of Bekka and Jagadesh's baskets and bowls; I hoped Zenna had taken enough lessons from her Aunt Bekka to make more for us later. Elizabeth at least knew how to make good pottery. I still had some of the traveling food spices and recipes from Yadeesh. I found the little flute from Kora, the stone necklace Nephi had gotten for me from Riddah, and the collection of ointments and herbs from Hagadah. Yes, these must come too; I needed something from each of my sisters to remember them by. And what about something from my brothers? Well, Nephi was wearing the tooled leather belt and arm guards I had gotten for him from Gid. And Nephi had studied building rules from Mori and would carry those ideas into our new homes.

My mind drifted to my siblings and their families. Who should we in reality invite to come with us? Matthew was a definite must, not only for him, but for Siri. I knew the meaning of her glances at him and her sighs. In fact, she would be an excellent one to make contact with him, if she could gather her courage to approach him. Mary could contact Kora, under guise of checking her arm, and Mary would know for sure if we should extend that invitation to her. Now Bekka. I could go myself with Siri, as though we were visiting Shanna during her recuperation. I felt this would work. Was there anyone else? I couldn't think of anyone.

Dawn began lighting the sky, and I could hear the birds singing. I blew out the candle and went to make some breakfast. Nephi had fallen back to sleep, and for that I was grateful. He would need his energy. As a matter of fact, I would need mine too, but I didn't feel the fatigue yet. I began packing a lunch and gift basket of food for our trip to Bekka's.

When the girls awoke and had eaten, I sent Zenna and Leesha to play at Aunt Naola's house. Nephi had awakened and left to talk to Sam, Eli, and Zoram. I sat Siri down and explained to her what our plan was, with strict instructions to talk about it with no one, even with those who were going with us, unless specifically told to do so. Siri nodded gravely.

"I'm not even sure I'm going to invite Bekka with us," I confessed. "I'm going to feel out first whether she is in danger and whether she might be receptive to this. Then I will let God guide me."

Siri nodded again. We picked up our food baskets and left the house. On our way, we stopped at Naola's house to borrow a horse, as ours weren't ready yet to ride.

Sam helped us up onto the horse. "Nephi and I are going to try to train his horses this week for carrying packs. Do you think we'll accomplish it?" He winked.

"It'll take a miracle," I said, gathering the reins and starting the horse off.

"I think you'll do it, Uncle Sam!" Siri called over her shoulder to him. "They've already calmed down a lot. Some will even let us children pet and lead them!"

My mind was filled with how I'd approach Bekka. I had no plan by the time we reached her place.

Siri slid off the horse before me and ran up to knock on the door. I could hear her talking as I tied up the horse.

"Hi, Aunt Bekka! We came to see how Shanna is doing. Oh, yes, this is for you!" she smiled and handed Bekka her gift basket. I was proud of her for sounding so natural and being so calm. My own palms were sweating.

"Hello, Bekka," I said, giving her a hug, as was my usual with her of late. It had been a statement of trying to connect with each other around our husbands' emotional walls, and now my heart was already beginning to say a silent goodbye.

"Come in; visit with me for a little," Bekka swept her arm out to usher me into the front room.

I looked around, half expecting Lemuel to appear.

"Siri and Shanna are talking in the girls' room," said Bekka in answer to my visual searching. "Shanna's legs are healing nicely. Mirimi and the other children are at Riddah's, except my baby, and Lemuel is on a hunting trip with Laman."

I nodded and we fell silent. "Thank you," we both said at the same time.

"For the gift," finished Bekka.

"For everything," I said, trying to express with my eyes that the thanks included the big personal risk she had taken in warning us.

"Oh, that's all right," she said, looking down at her lap and picking at her fingernails.

"Is everything all right with you and your husband?" I ventured, trying to accent for double meaning.

Bekka waved her hand. "Pshaw. Lemuel is sometimes so busy, he hardly knows when I come and go."

Bekka had caught my meaning. Despite her casualness, I had heard a little tremor in her voice. She might not be as confident as she tried to appear. I looked around to make sure the girls weren't listening and then leaned forward toward her. This was my moment, I felt.

"Bekka, about your warning us about the plot against—"

"Hush, Didi," Bekka put her finger to her lips. "We are sisters, remember? I don't want any harm to come to any of you, especially to you who have the courage to serve the Lord out in the open. Oh, Didi! I wish Lemuel weren't so stubborn as to turn his back on God! I wish I were brave enough to live God's commandments, to praise and to obey him."

I stared at her. "Bekka! I never realized you felt this way about God! I thought that you, like Lemuel—" I paused and bowed my head. "Will you please forgive me for misjudging you?"

"Didi, don't berate yourself for it. I didn't always feel this way, only recently since almost losing Shanna. I suddenly realized that I was responsible for what my children learned, and that someday it might be too late to teach them about the really important things in life. And now I realize how important God is to me in my life. No, Didi, you have no reason to ask my forgiveness; I was rebellious like the others."

"Bekka," I said, catching one of her hands in my own. "I was debating telling you something very secret for your warning to us. I wanted to tell you of our planned escape to a place far from here so that you would know of our safety if you never heard from us again. But now that I know of your desire to serve the Lord, I tell you this instead. You and your children are welcome to come with us. We want you to be able to serve God freely and openly, without cause for fear. Will you come?"

Bekka looked down at the ground for a very long time until I began to think I had offended her. Then she raised her head and tears spilled down her cheeks. "No, Didi, I can't come. You don't know how much I want to go, to be with you, and live as you do. But I can't leave Lemuel. I may not like the way he acts toward God, but I love him, he is my husband, though at the beginning he would rather have married Riddah. And I feel all right now about his marrying Mirimi. Besides, my children need their father. I don't think I can raise them alone." Bekka paused and brought up her free hand to clasp mine in both of hers. "No, I will stay with Lemuel, live what I can of God's commandments, teach my children about God and his ways, and pray that Lemuel's heart may be softened, that we may turn as a family unto God. And if that fails and he never changes, I'll at least have tried my best. Perhaps my children will learn from our mistakes and follow the Lord. This is where my calling lies, Didi, and this is the path that I must take."

I was only getting to really know my sister, just as we were about to part. "Bekka, Bekka!" I was crying now too. "You are no coward. This choice that you are making is one of the most difficult to face. And instead of taking the easy way out for you by coming with us, you choose the more difficult, lonely path to follow. That takes more courage than I think I could ever find." I paused and then went on. "Nephi tries to describe to me how lonely it is to know more of God than one is allowed to tell and only because others are not prepared to hear. I will be praying for you that God will support you in what you are doing. And Bekka," I brought my free hand to join in our clasping, "I love you."

Her voice was as choked as mine. "I love you too, Didi." We gazed into each other's eyes for a moment and then embraced, very meaningfully this time. "I'll miss you," she whispered.

Siri was ready for us at the door. I knew I'd never be able to leave if I didn't go quickly. Turning back once as I climbed on the horse behind Siri, Bekka and I exchanged final waves. Then we were off.

"We are going by Uncle Laman's house," Siri announced as she turned the horse in that direction.

"No, Siri! I don't think we should," I protested. "I didn't bring anything to give them, we don't have a reason to visit, I don't want to raise suspicions or put us in danger—"

Siri laughed as she shrugged off my attempts to get the reins. "Don't worry, Mama. I know what I'm doing."

When we arrived, Siri slipped off the horse. "Stay there, Mama", she said and skipped toward the door with our lunch basket.

"No, Siri, I need that food—"

Siri turned toward me, took a wrapped bundle out of her apron pocket that looked suspiciously like our lunch, waved it at me, and hid it away again. When Riddah opened the door, Siri handed her the basket.

"Happy Birthday, Aunt Riddah. This is from Shanna and me," Siri curtsied and smiled. "We just wanted you to know we love you."

My mouth probably fell open. I hadn't thought about Riddah's birthday in a couple of years. Trust Siri to come up with that one. Riddah was waving at me as Siri ran back to the horse, and I waved back.

"See you all later!" Siri called. Then she climbed back onto the horse and directed us homeward. As we rode, Siri pulled out our lunches and we ate.

"If we're eating what was in that basket," I asked between bites, "what did you give Aunt Riddah?"

"Oh, lots of little things," Siri shrugged. "Some of the extra biscuits we took to Aunt Bekka's, some wildflowers, a poem Shanna had written for her, a couple of pieces of jewelry we had made. You know. I just thought you might want one last chance to see all your sisters again."

Siri was right. It was nice to have a last mental picture of Riddah, slender again after her recent baby, standing next to Jagadesh smiling and waving. What attentive and mature instincts Siri had.

"Oh, by the way, Mama," Siri was saying, "Shanna is coming over to spend the night with us in two days. She's probably talking to her mother about it right now."

"Oh, all right," I began. Then I stopped. She couldn't come that night nor ever again. "Siri, that's impossible, that's the night—"

"Relax, Mama, I know." Siri turned around to look at me, her eyes very serious now. "She knows."

I stared at Siri, my mouth agape. "You were to say nothing to her, Siri daughter of Nephi—"

"Mama, Mama," Siri soothed. "I didn't tell her. Well, not exactly. She just sort of announced that she was planning to go with us in three days, and she said she was nearly packed and ready to go."

I was still staring at Siri, visions of an ambush as we were all set to leave. If Shanna knew, who else did?

"Mama," Siri said. "I tried to pretend I didn't know what she was talking about. She told me she had a dream last night, about what her father was planning to do, and that God told Papa and all the believers to leave and live far from here. Mama, she wants to live with those who believe in God. She will follow the leader and laws of our community. You told me to follow the Spirit of God, and I did. So did Shanna. She has heard this from no one and has told no one. She is coming."

I thought of Nephi's words to me. Under the circumstances, she was a candidate. "Siri, does she realize that she will probably never see her parents again?" Siri nodded gravely. "Then who am I to counter God? She may come as far as I am concerned." I thought further. "What about your cousin Anna? You have been close to her. Is she supposed to come too, do you think?"

Siri lowered her head and was silent, thinking. "No," she said at last. "We haven't been as close lately. I don't sense that she is ready for this kind of commitment. She makes light of religious things, and I don't feel comfortable—"

"Never mind," I said, giving her a hug as we rode. "I was just asking."

"Mama, I will ask Matthew, though." Siri seemed to brighten. "He would want to come." She blushed. "I mean, he loves so much to discuss the scriptures with Papa—"

"I understand," I smiled. "I'll drop you off at the river boat so you can ask him."

When I got back home, Mary had just arrived.

"Didi!" she cried as she greeted me. "I did it! I actually asked her—"

"Shhh!" I said, trying not to look around. "Tell me when we get inside." She followed me into my storeroom, now turned workroom, and helped me fill bags as we talked.

"Well," Mary began again. "First I checked Kora's hand, which is healing nicely. Then I found myself expressing concern for her well-being and safety. She somewhat responded to that, confirming that there may be a concern there as we thought. I asked her, in a hypothetical situation, that if there were someplace she could go to be safe, away from her husband, would she do it?"

Mary paused in her talking and bag filling, and then turned to me. There was a tear on her cheek. "Didi," she said softly, "she said she would probably consider it very seriously. But there is a problem. She is sure her husband would not let her take the children, unless it was the baby, without pursuing her relentlessly until she and they were found. She doesn't know if she could leave her children, even in Hagadah's capable hands, especially knowing they would be at the mercy of his temper, but without her to defend them." Mary was quiet a moment, then she went on. "She would probably not leave unless there was a safe place to go far away and with other people."

I watched Mary as she slowly put items in the bag she carried. "So then what?" I prodded.

"Well, then we talked about a few other things, and I tried to get a sense of her religious commitment," said Mary. "I think she'd go along with Nephi's leadership. Then she suddenly got this funny look on her face, and she asked me if we were going to be leaving somewhere. I asked her where she got that idea, and she told me she dreamed about it last night." Mary laughed nervously. "Imagine that!"

Yes, imagine that, I thought. What a coincidence. Maybe Kora was supposed to come with us after all. "Then what happened?" I asked.

Mary laughed sheepishly. "I must have looked shocked or something, confirming to Kora what we were doing. She told me she would think seriously about it and let us know." Mary spread out the hand that was not holding her bag. "I didn't know if I'd get another innocent opportunity to speak with her. So we arranged to meet at the big hill behind your place before dawn the day we leave, if she decides to come. If she's not there, we're to go without her."

I had been watching Mary during the last part of her story. As she finished, I dropped my bag, went over to her and gave her a hug. "You did well, my dear," I told her. "It is Kora's choice now."

Mary returned to her home, and I took Zenna and Leesha out to our garden to see if we had anything grown enough yet to harvest. There were a few small potatoes, so we began to dig these up and bag them. Then Siri arrived, a big smile lighting her face.

"Guess what, Mama?" she began.

"Success?" I ventured, sitting back on my heels as I squatted.

She giggled. "Yes. I took some flowers to Aunt Abisha and Aunt Yadeesh, saving one big one for Matthew. Then he came running in from the field and invited me to go on a walk with him." She threw her arms out and laughed. "He is the nicest boy—"

Leesha was covering her mouth and giggling. Zenna was trying to imitate her big sister, dramatically throwing out her arms as Siri had.

"Stop it!" cried Siri. "That's not funny."

"Keep digging girls," I directed and then pulled Siri out of their hearing range. "Did you ask him about . . . you know."

Siri nodded. "He didn't have a dream like Shanna. But he knew we were leaving all the same. He will meet us here before dawn that day."

I sighed in relief. First task accomplished. Now if we could keep it all a secret, and finish our packing in the remaining day.

Mori came walking up the hill toward us. The girls and I stopped what we were doing and watched him. He stopped at the edge of our garden and looked down.

"Pretty small potatoes," he said. "I'd leave them in a bit longer if I were you, Sis."

My heart skipped a beat. Could he know?

"See, Mama?" Siri came to my rescue. "I told you we should wait a little longer. We can keep eating meat till they grow bigger."

I played along and scratched my ear. "Well, your father did say that too. But I wanted to get started on planting my maize crop—"

Mori leaned his head back and laughed. "You always had a mind of your own, Sis." Then his face grew serious. "I just came to remind you," his glance rested a little longer on Siri, "that our grounds are off limits to you. Though my wives do appreciate the flowers." He dropped a bag of what looked like Yadeesh's honey cakes. "Yadeesh sent these." He sighed. "We just don't want you and your kids spreading funny ideas about God and religion to me and mine. Understand me?" He looked at me steadily.

I swallowed and nodded. "I understand you, Mori," I answered.

Mori turned on his heel and walked back down the hill. Siri and I let out sighs simultaneously. "I thought he had discovered us," Siri stated.

I looked at her proudly. Her mind and tongue were quicker than mine these days. "I think not, thanks to you, my daughter."

We continued packing into the night, trying to do as much as possible inside and in the dark. During the next day, Siri helped her father with the horses. The mares were becoming more docile, allowing packs to be placed on their backs. The stallion however wanted nothing to do with the training.

"If only I had more time," muttered Nephi. "I sure would like to ride him someday, at the least I need him to keep the herd producing. But I don't know how we're going to take him with us. He won't even let me lead him."

"Let me try, Papa," Siri offered. She pulled some vegetable greens from the garden to feed him. Soon the stallion let her pet him and then put a rope around his neck. By that evening, he let Siri lead him around outside the corral. However, he would not let anything touch his back.

Nephi watched and shook his head. "You work wonders, my daughter. Do you think he'll let you lead him tomorrow?"

Siri nodded her head. When Shanna arrived after supper, they were back out with the horses, leading the stallion alongside first one mare then two. As it grew dark, Siri continued working with him, gently talking, feeding him more greens, walking him through trees and around the hill. Finally Nephi made the girls go to bed with slumbering Zenna and Leesha, while Nephi and I filled the last of our packs. He made a trip to the synagogue to obtain the brass plates, and packed them carefully with Lehi's plates, the sword of Laban, and the Liahona.

"I think that's everything," I sighed, straightening and stretching my aching back.

"I see you've even got the large wash bucket turned into a useful load," commented Nephi. "You know I can make you another one, Didi."

"I know," I said, hugging him. "But this is the first waterproof one you made, and I'm feeling very nostalgic about things right now."

He laughed. "You're usually very practical, Didi. But the way you packed all these things, if I didn't know better, I'd say you were pregnant!"

I smacked my forehead with the palm of my hand. "I never told you, did I, Nephi? I *am* expecting again!"

Nephi stared at me and then laughed again. "With all the other excitement . . ." He shook his head. "And here I've been letting you carry and lift all these things." He disengaged the broom from my hand despite my protests. "I don't think sweeping now will make any difference. It will get a lot dustier before anyone is ready to move in and use this place."

I looked around at my lovely home. "Others are going to use our house, our furniture."

"Why not?" Nephi countered. "Our nieces and nephews will be marrying and having families someday, and they'll need their own places." Nephi bit his lip as he touched a wall he had built and we had whitewashed together. "It's not the best workmanship, but it is dry and sturdy. And we can't take it with us."

He turned me around to face him, his hands on my arms. "When I married you, Didi, I made a promise to myself that one day I would build you a fine large house, better than this one even, where you could stay and never have to move. This now is my chance to do this, my love."

I embraced and kissed him. "I follow you to the ends of the earth, my husband."

He laughed. "Yes, you are doing that, aren't you? Well, let's get a little rest before we leave."

I pulled back. "There is something I must do first, Nephi," I said. "I'll be with you shortly."

I went over to the kitchen table where I had placed my cedar treasure box, containing some leather parchment pieces, paint, and a writing reed. I felt I wanted to leave something to those we left behind, and had decided on a note to each family, good memories we had had together, and telling them that I cherished our relationships. I picked up the reed and began to draw letters and characters onto the parchment. I was slow at first, trying to remember the shapes of the letters, and having to reteach my hand to make the movements. Then I got the rhythm and I wrote much more quickly, my hand almost keeping up with my thoughts.

As I wrote, I thought of the start of our journey, our hopes high that we would find a paradise, and in some ways, we had. I laughed to myself at my girlhood exuberance to follow my hero through adventures, striving against all odds and winning. It turned out to be a journey of battles, sometimes winning and sometimes losing, as I walked beside my very human husband. He, too, struggled to make the right choices in our daily battles. Sometimes the consequences of our choices brought joy, and sometimes they brought sorrow. Still, I would make many of them the same way again. I could wish some of my siblings' choices had been different.

Now here we were, at another crossroads of decision. Neither way felt like a winning choice, but leaving here felt like we were giving up on our siblings. God would never give up on us, and I hated not returning the favor on my family. Yet staying here was like committing suicide. If we left, would there be another chance to influence our siblings for good? Probably not. We certainly had no chance if we were dead.

"Your siblings have made their choices in another direction, away from me," spoke a voice, which I felt more than heard.

I looked around, expecting Nephi to be standing behind me. There was no one.

"As long as you don't give up, yours is a winning choice," said the voice again. "Your children and your children's children will have opportunities to influence your siblings' children for good. Be at peace."

I knew no one was in the room with me. The only light was the candle flickering on the table. But as I lifted my eyes heavenward, my whole soul felt light and bright and peaceful. I dropped to my knees and bowed my head.

"Thank you, Heavenly Father," I prayed. "Take care of my brothers, my sisters, and their families." I felt tears sliding down my cheeks. "I will follow thee always." I ended my prayer, dried my cheeks, and sat back on my chair at the table. I finished writing the letters and rolled them up. Hesitating for a moment, I looked through the treasures inside my cedar box, the white stone from Jerusalem, the string from Nephi's steel bow, Naola's pomegranate rind, the seashell from Bountiful. I placed everything but the bowstring back inside, thinking Nephi might want it someday, and placed the parchment letters on top. I wrote Bekka's name on the box and placed it in a wall niche near the front door. Then I joined Nephi on our bare bed.

He rolled over. "Is it time yet, Didi?" he mumbled.

I sighed. "I hope not. I could use a couple of hours of sleep."

He nodded. "You go ahead. I think I'm going to get up and start packing the animals."

A couple of hours later he woke me with a kiss. "Didi, it's time to get up. Sam, Eli, and Zoram are here with their families."

I yawned and stretched and sat up. For a moment, I wished I could keep sleeping. Then excitement for the journey ahead struck me, and I jumped up. As I pulled on my travel dress and combed my hair back, I thought about what adventures and new lands awaited us. What kind of home and community could we make this time? The possibilities would be fun to dream about.

I went and woke the girls. The two younger ones rubbed their eyes as I told them we were going on a trip today. Meanwhile, Siri and Shanna were rolling up the sleeping blankets and straightening their hair.

"Where are we going, Mama?" Zenna asked.

"I don't know exactly," I answered. "Wherever the Lord leads us."

As we packed the last of our bundles and ate some breakfast biscuits, Matthew arrived with his pack.

"I apologize for not bringing an animal," he told Nephi. "I didn't feel I had the right to take one belonging to my father. I will gladly carry my pack myself."

Nephi laid his hand on Matthew's shoulder and smiled. "You are most welcome to be with us, mount of your own or not. Thanks to circumstances, we have more horses than we otherwise would have. We have plenty of room for your pack on one of them."

Dawn began lighting the sky. I held Naola's twins as she climbed on one of their horses and then handed chunky little Mary to her. Nephi had insisted that I would ride one of Sam's other horses with Leah, the other twin, and I agreed, if he would first let me walk off the hill on which our home stood. Zenna with Leesha would ride one of Zoram's horses. Mary would lead the two horses carrying her young children sitting atop packs. The chickens were gathered into wooden coops and tied to pack horses. Jonah, Benjamin, Seth, and Shanna would lead the newly broken packhorses, roped together head to tail camel style, Siri leading the stallion in among them. Jacob, Joseph, Matthew, Sam, Eli, and Zoram riding other horses would herd the cattle, sheep and goats behind the new horses. Nephi, on another of Sam's horses and carrying the Liahona, would lead the whole group.

"Where is Mary?" Naola asked. "She's late. Doesn't she know we have to leave soon?"

I raised my head to respond and saw Mary and Kora coming up the back side of the hill. They were carrying her two youngest children, the next older girl walking beside Kora and clinging to her skirt. Their clothes were wet and tears were streaming down Kora's face.

I ran over to them and gave Kora a hug.

"I didn't dare take a boat or bring anything extra with us," Kora sobbed, rubbing her partially healed broken hand. "I wasn't even sure if we could make it across the river; we walked upstream half the night to get to a shallow enough place to cross. My little ones are so cold."

"Come," I told her. "We will get them into some dry things." While I pulled out of my pack one of my dresses and shawls for Kora, Siri found some of Leesha's and Zenna's dresses for Kora's older daughter and baby, and Naola found an outfit for her son.

"Thank you so much," said Kora, after everyone had been changed into dry things. She looked around at the group and then sat down on the ground, her arms going around her children. "I . . . I don't know if I'm doing the right thing by leaving," she said and started crying again. "It is so hard to leave my older children, and I still love my husband, except"—she swallowed and stopped crying—"they are their father's children now, and Hagadah will watch over them." She stood and turned to face Nephi. "Where do you want us to walk?"

Nephi smiled at her. "We have extra horses for you to ride. You must be exhausted anyway, and should rest for at least a few hours before walking." He embraced her. "We are very happy to have you come with us, sister."

Nephi unwrapped the Liahona from where it rested in a small bag tied to his horse's pack, and walked to the center of our group. Everyone hushed their talking.

Nephi bowed his head and offered a prayer for safe travel, bounty of nourishment along the way, and freedom from trouble from our siblings. Then he raised his head and looked at each of us. "Let us go, family," he said.

He mounted his horse, gazed at the Liahona in his hand, and then beckoned us to move forward down the back side of the hill. The children and pack animals followed first and then came the men with the herd animals. It would be slow traveling, and I prayed that we would not be followed.

As I led my horse down the hill, carrying little Leah in my arm, I looked back through the slight light of dawn at the house that had for a short while been my home. In my mind's eye, I pictured Bekka as I had left her in front of her house, standing tall and nobly despite the tears streaming down her face, her hand raised in farewell. I raised my hand toward the river valley, giving a silent last farewell to all the family we were leaving behind. If Bekka could so courageously do what must be done, so could I.

I turned my face forward toward our new destination, a land where we could worship God in peace, resolved wholeheartedly to the choice I had begun to make long ago when I left Jerusalem.

BIBLIOGRAPHY OF REFERENCES USED

***Nephi's Wife* by Madelyn S. Palmer**

The Book of Mormon

Clark, E. Douglas, and Robert S. *Fathers and Sons in the Book of Mormon*. Salt Lake City: Deseret Book, 1991

Hilton, Lynn M., and Hope. *In Search of Lehi's Trail.* Salt Lake City: Deseret Book, 1976

The Holy Bible; King James Version

Jadallah, Ahmed. Oral interview, Stewart Ranch. Woodland, Utah: 19 July 1998

Journey of Faith, DVD, The Neal A. Maxwell Institute for Religious Scholarship, Brigham Young University. 2006

Ludlow, Daniel H. *A Companion to Your Study of the Book of Mormon*. Salt Lake City: Deseret Book 1976

Nibley, Hugh. *Lehi in the Desert and the World of the Jaredites*. Salt Lake City: Bookcraft, 1952

Priddis, Venice. *The Book and the Map*. Salt Lake City: Bookcraft, Inc. 1976

Welch, John W., David Rolph Seely, and Jo Ann H. Seely, ed. *Glimpses of Lehi's Jerusalem*. Foundation for Ancient Research and Mormon Studies. BYU: 2004

Welch, John W., ed. *Reexploring the Book of Mormon*. Salt Lake City: Deseret Book, 1992

Disclaimer: This book is a work of historical fiction. I attempted to remain as true as possible to the original story, and to the culture of the time. However, some characters and names have been added. Additional explanations and suppositions remain the responsibility of the author.

Please read the original story in the Book of Mormon, 1 and 2 Nephi, and come to your own conclusions.

Printed in the United States
by Baker & Taylor Publisher Services